DELIVER THEM FROM EVIL

DELIVER THEM FROM EVIL

AMANDA DuBOIS

A CAMILLE DELANEY MYSTERY

GIRL FRIDAY BOOKS

 **GIRL FRIDAY BOOKS**

Published by Girl Friday Books™, Seattle
www.girlfridaybooks.com

Produced by Girl Friday Productions

Cover design: Emily Weigel
Project management: Sara Spees Addicott

Image credits: cover © Wikimedia Commons, Shutterstock
IMG ID# 110134574

ISBN (paperback): 978-1-954854-69-7
ISBN (e-book): 978-1-954854-70-3

Library of Congress Control Number: 2022905927

First edition

CHAPTER ONE

Jessica Kensington tensed as the rickety plane shimmied up off the iridescent Caribbean. She squeezed her eyes shut as a hand slid along her thigh. His doughy fingers made her skin crawl. She forced herself to put her hand tentatively over his, staring at the tiny island disappearing over the horizon.

Jessica dreaded reentering the chaos that was her life. *You've got to do what you've got to do,* she told herself firmly and piled her thick auburn hair up on top of her head. She stiffened as she felt his lips on her moist neck.

The dirty hustle of the Miami airport was as far from the sandy beaches of Grand Cayman island as Jessica could imagine. Her connecting flight was scheduled to depart in twenty minutes. He guided her quickly and efficiently through the crowded terminal, his soft arm tight around her waist. She was trapped, but then again, the situation was entirely of her own making.

"I'll see you soon," he whispered.

She extricated herself from his grasp and entered the Jetway. Alone.

—

Dr. Jessica Kensington flattened herself against the wall, dodging the gurney carrying a moaning woman toward the OB surgery room of Seattle's busy Puget Sound Hospital. She felt grateful to be back in the predictable world of obstetrics and gynecology—especially after the events of the past week. Her anxiety melted away as she relaxed into the comfortable scene.

"Welcome back!" A nurse pulled her mask over her face, hit the automatic door opener, and disappeared, pushing the gurney into the antiseptic-smelling C-section room with the help of a bevy of nurses in blue.

"Thanks," Jessica answered as the doors closed behind the entourage. Nothing had changed.

The charge nurse came over to greet Jessica. "How was Hawaii?" She held her arm up next to the doctor's. "Man, you sure tan well for a redhead. My parents were on Kauai last week and it rained the whole time. What island were you on?"

Jessica paused. "Maui," she lied. "And it's not a tan. It's wall-to-wall freckles." Jessica smiled as she reviewed the familiar grease board where the patients' names were listed. Her eyes locked on the third name from the top. Room 313. Jessica's heart pounded in her throat. "No one told me Helene Anderson was in labor." *Oh God. Not tonight. Not so soon.* She reflexively backed away from the board.

The nurse looked at Jessica.

Why did Anderson have to go into labor tonight? Jessica tried to steady herself. *Can't I just have twenty-four hours to unwind?*

"Anderson just came in. She's still in early labor. Only four centimeters." The nurse dumped two packets of sugar into her coffee. "So, how's your mom doing?"

Jessica tried to focus on the nurse, resisting the urge to turn and run. "Fine . . . thanks," she answered absentmindedly, pausing briefly to compose herself. "I'd like to augment Mrs. Anderson." Jessica nearly tripped over her words. "See if we can kick-start her labor." She stepped backward directly into the path of a patient pushing an IV pole, slamming the woman into the wall.

"I'm . . . I'm sorry." Jessica steadied herself on the patient's arm. She looked at the nurse as she released the woman from her grip. "We have to induce Mrs. Anderson. Tonight." She felt her chest tightening.

"Shit, Jessica, I don't have enough nurses to induce anyone tonight. This place is a zoo. Can't it wait till morning?"

2

The doctor struggled for breath, trying to calm herself. "I can sit with her myself." She stared intently at the name "Helene Anderson."

"You don't need to do that." The nurse ran her finger down the schedule posted on the bulletin board. "Let's wait till morning. The day shift has plenty of staff to do it for you." She drained her short Styrofoam coffee cup and put it on the counter. "Why don't you go get some sleep? I promise we'll wake you up if anything exciting happens."

A prickly feeling spread through Jessica's body. "I've, uh, I've got a full day tomorrow," she stuttered. "First day back after vacation. You know how it is." *I said that too quickly.* "I'd like to get Mrs. Anderson delivered tonight." The clock read 1:00 a.m. "I can do it myself." *I have to. It's up to me.*

The nurse shook her head. "Whatever suits you. I'll have someone mix up a bag of Pitocin for you."

Jessica turned toward the medication room. "I'll do it. It's no problem." She avoided direct eye contact with the nurse. "Really." Jessica unclenched her jaw and forced a phony smile. "You go take care of business. I'll call you if I need you."

"Can we clone you? I don't know a doctor in the world that would sit with a patient in labor all night," the charge nurse whined jokingly as she headed off to answer a call bell.

Jessica grabbed a bulging bag of lactated Ringer's solution from the shelf and steadied her hands as she drew up six amps of Pitocin. Slowly, she injected it into the IV solution, then leaned against the wall, closed her eyes, and took a couple of deep breaths. It wasn't too late to back out.

A nurse rushed in and slipped her key into the narcotics cabinet. She stopped. "You okay, Dr. Kensington?"

Jessica dropped the IV bag to the floor. "Yes . . . yes, I'm fine." She reached down and picked up the fluid-filled bag. "Just a little jet lag, I guess." Gathering her wits, she pushed the squeaky IV pump out into the hallway.

The nurse followed her. "What are you doing? I'll call a nurse to do that."

"No, you guys are too busy. I'm gonna 'Pit' Mrs. Anderson myself."

"You're what?" The nurse looked at Jessica in disbelief.

"Don't worry—if I need any help, I'll call one of you." Jessica winked. "But I'm pretty sure I can handle this on my own."

The nurse shrugged. "Okay, good luck, then."

It'll take more than luck. Jessica stopped for a moment outside room 313. *This goes far beyond the two people behind this door. Sometimes you have to sacrifice the few to protect the many.* She reached into her pocket and grabbed one of her little white pills, popping it into her mouth just as she forced herself into the room.

"Dr. Kensington! I thought you were on vacation." The blond patient was so tall that her feet hung slightly off the end of the narrow bed. "I was hoping you'd get back in time to deliver us. No offense to your partner, of course." She pushed an escaped strand of stringy hair up into a plastic barrette.

Jessica refused to look directly at either Helene or her husband, Tim. They were merely innocent pawns in this nightmarish scene. "Let's check and see how you're doing." Jessica climbed up onto the stiff bed so she could sit on the edge to reach the patient. She pulled on a glove and did a quick exam. "Yup, it looks to me like you're going to have a baby all right." She tried to sound lighthearted as she pointed at the IV bag hanging above the tangle of wires and tubing that snaked menacingly from the beeping pump. "I'm going to give you some Pitocin to get your labor going." Jessica didn't wait for an answer. She turned and readied the machine.

"Great!" Tim grinned. "Isn't it, honey?" He gently caressed his wife's muscular arm.

Helene looked worried. "They told us in our prenatal class that Pitocin gives you stronger contractions."

"It's no problem," Jessica said, trying to reassure herself as much as her patient. "We can give you an epidural if it gets too bad." She stuck the end of the tubing between her teeth and pulled off the cap. Glancing at the doorway, she plugged the medication into the IV. Jessica flinched as the machine let out a loud beep, indicating that it was infusing medication into Helene's vein.

"We're going natural." Tim rubbed his wife's shoulders. "Aren't we, honey?"

"I hope so." Helene looked down at her protruding abdomen that was encircled by the elastic straps of the external fetal monitor.

"Don't we need internal monitors if we're having Pitocin?" Helene asked.

"Uh . . . not necessarily." Jessica silently cursed the overzealous prenatal instructors as she tried to distract Helene by pointing to the computerized printout. "There. See that squiggly line? That's the baby's heartbeat. And this line here is your contractions. Oops, do you feel that one?"

Helene grimaced.

"Breathe, honey."

"Oooh." Helene exhaled loudly.

Over the next hour Helene's contractions increased both in frequency and intensity, to the point that they were literally stacked up, one after the other. Tim rummaged around in his duffel bag, pulling out various props they'd been instructed to bring along. One by one, Helene shot them down. She refused to stare at the picture of the waterfall; the fuzzy towel felt like fire on her skin; the supposedly peaceful music grated on her nerves; and she threatened her husband with immediate divorce if he ever rolled another tennis ball around on her lower back ever again. Her moans echoed down the hall.

As the contractions reached a nonstop crescendo, one of the nurses came rushing into the room. "What's going on in here?" the nurse questioned Jessica.

"Nothing." Jessica caught herself before she lost her cool. "I've got everything under control."

The patient grabbed the nurse's arm. "Help me!" she screamed, her eyes rolling back in her head. "Something's wrong. You've got to do something!"

The nurse unclenched the patient's grip. "You're on Pitocin; it always makes the contractions stronger." She looked at Jessica. "But those contractions are a bit close together, don't you think?"

"I'm watching her," Jessica snapped, then quickly composed herself. "Thanks, Deanne." Jessica pushed the patient's sweat-soaked hair off her forehead. "She's fine—just a few stacked contractions. I was just about to turn down the Pit." As soon as the nurse left, Jessica squatted down to look at Helene face to face. "Perhaps we should order you an epidural now?"

Helene's moan escalated into an ear-piercing scream as the next contraction reached its pitch and stayed there for over two minutes. Jessica shut the door. "How 'bout that epidural?"

"No," Tim announced. "No epidural. We're doing fine. Aren't we, honey?"

Helene tried, unsuccessfully, to lift her head up off the bed. She looked at Jessica with wild eyes. "Give me something," she panted. "Something's wrong!"

"Everything's going according to plan, isn't it, Doctor?" Tim asked.

"Absolutely." *In a manner of speaking.*

"I need an epidural," the patient stated authoritatively.

"Not yet, darling. You're doing such a good job."

He's a sweet man. That's good; she's going to need someone like him to get her through all of this.

Another contraction pounded the patient without warning. She grabbed her husband by the hair and pulled him down toward her. "Get me a fucking epidural." She pulled him closer. "Get it *now.*"

The husband turned his head awkwardly so that he could see Jessica while he tried to extricate his hair from his wife's death grip. "I . . . uh, think we'll go with that epidural now."

The doctor hit the call button. "We need anesthesia in room 313." She removed the fetal monitor. "Let's get you on your side so you'll be ready when anesthesia gets here."

The room suddenly became quiet as the constant thumping of the baby's heartbeat ceased.

"Is the baby okay?" Tim asked anxiously.

"It's fine; we just have to leave the monitor off so that the anesthesiologist can place the epidural," Jessica explained.

Helene stiffened as another contraction racked her exhausted body. "Turn that shit off!" She tried to catch her breath. "Please," she pleaded.

Jessica turned the infusion pump away from the patient's view and tripled the dose. "There you go, I turned it down. We can get back to business after you're more comfortable."

Helene was writhing around on the hard bed, groaning, when the anesthesiologist pushed her cart into the room. "How's it going, Jess?" she asked as she draped the patient. "You look like you've been on vacation."

"Hawaii." She wondered if her nose would begin to grow.

"Hold still, ma'am," the anesthesiologist directed the patient as she shrieked hysterically.

Jessica subtly turned up the Pitocin again. At this rate, it would all be over soon.

The patient dug her nails into her husband's hand and let out one guttural scream after another as the anesthesiologist tried to get her to hold still.

Jessica's eyes darted toward the blank monitor strip and up at the clock: 3:35. It had been twenty minutes since she'd removed the monitor. She turned the Pitocin down, knowing the contractions would quickly subside.

"Just a sec," the patient whimpered. "They're easing off now. Please try again." Her husband wiped her face with a cool washcloth. "Get that away from me!" she cried.

"Okay." The anesthesiologist repositioned the patient and felt the bones in her spine. "Hold still." She grabbed a long epidural needle, deftly placed it in the patient's back, threaded a thin plastic catheter through the needle, and injected the anesthetic. "Okay, kiddo, you're good to go." She tore off an extra-wide piece of adhesive tape and plastered it over her handiwork, then looked at the digital pager vibrating on her belt. "Gotta run." She hurried out the door.

Jessica took a deep breath and slowly placed the fetal monitor back on the woman's abdomen, dreading the hell that was about to break loose. An alarm sounded as soon as the baby's excruciatingly slow heartbeat filled the room.

Jessica jumped up as the charge nurse flew into the room. She gathered all her courage and took charge of the situation.

"What's going on?" asked the nurse as she glanced sideways at the doctor with a look of suspicion.

Jessica grabbed an oxygen mask and slapped it over the patient's face. "Fetal distress! Take her to the OR!" Jessica yelled as she pulled on a glove and quickly examined the patient. "She's completely dilated!"

Deanne, the nurse, hit the red emergency bell on the wall above the bed. "Set up the C-section room *stat*! We're gonna do the delivery in there in case we need to section her," she yelled as a cadre of nurses descended on the room.

The team waited for Jessica to hop off the bed before whisking the stunned patient out into the hall and through the heavy double doors to the OB surgery suite.

"You gotta push, hon!" Deanne lifted the patient's shoulders up off the bed.

"One . . . two . . . three . . . four . . . five . . . six . . . seven . . . eight . . . nine . . . ten." The nurse put the patient's head back down.

Jessica watched the pandemonium swirl around her as the nurses dropped the bottom of the bed and attached the big stainless-steel stirrups while another group tore open sterile packs, throwing surgical instruments out onto the long table at the end of the bed. Jessica slid her shaking hands into the gloves being held by the scrub tech. "Give me the forceps!"

The tech complied.

A nurse stared at Jessica.

"Let's do it." Jessica pursed her lips and exhaled as her pulse pounded in her ears. She slowly placed the forceps around the baby's head and pulled. If she could stall long enough, it would all be over.

The patient screamed.

"Seven . . . eight . . . nine . . . ten." The nurse shot the doctor a worried look as the baby's heartbeat bottomed out.

Jessica stopped pulling.

"What's going on?" asked the anesthesiologist as she hooked the patient up to the automatic blood pressure machine.

"Fetal distress," Jessica answered curtly.

"Shall we set up for a C-section?" asked one of the nurses.

"Not yet! Here's another contraction!" Jessica shouted, "Push! Push! Push!" She braced her foot up on the delivery table and pulled on the forceps with all her might. The nurses looked helplessly at one another as the baby's head protruded from the patient's perineum. "Got it!" Jessica grabbed a suction bulb off the table and sucked some soupy-looking greenish-brown fluid from the baby's mouth. "We've got thick meconium!" Jessica shouted to the nurse. She turned to the patient. "Okay, give me another push."

Nothing.

"Push!" the nurse yelled.

Nothing.

"I can't!" the patient sobbed. "Help me! Please help me!" She twisted her torso on the bed.

"Hold still!" Jessica demanded.

"I can't," the patient choked.

"You have to," the nurse ordered. "Now push hard." She leaned behind the patient to get her shoulders up and yelled, "Push . . . push . . . push!"

"Shit. Let's do a McRoberts!" Jessica said. Instantly two nurses pulled the patient's knees high over her abdomen and pushed hard just above her pubic bone in an effort to dislodge the baby. At the same time, Jessica put her entire hand in behind the baby's shoulders and tried to fold them together to allow them to fit through the narrow birth canal.

"Again!" shouted Jessica as she tried in vain to corkscrew the baby out. *God, please let this be over.* "It's not gonna come!" she yelled while she reached in and tried to free up the shoulder. "Set up for a C-section!" She turned to the anesthesiologist. "Put her out."

The anesthesiologist looked at Jessica. "What are you gonna do?" Her voice was taut.

"Just put her out!"

"Okay, okay." She turned back to her equipment and began getting ready to administer a general anesthetic.

"I'm gonna do a C-section."

The anesthesiologist furrowed her brow. "You're the boss."

The echoing screams became muffled as the anesthesiologist placed a heavy black mask over the patient's nose and mouth. She turned to one of the nurses and dropped her voice. "Get the husband out of here."

"I need to do a Zavanelli maneuver!" Jessica ignored the tension in the room. "Now!"

"Holy shit," the nurse said under her breath and pulled a red cord hanging next to the door, which caused an earsplitting siren to blast throughout the entire department. In seconds the room was filled with blue-clad women pulling more sterile packs from cabinets and setting up instrument trays. The smell of iodine wafted through the room as one of the nurses poured a basin of Betadine over the patient's prominent abdomen.

"Get NICU in here! Stat!" Jessica yelled as she re-gloved herself and took her position to the left of the patient. She looked at the anesthesiologist. "Is she out?"

"She is." She glanced curiously at Jessica, who immediately looked away.

"NICU's on the way!" shouted one of the nurses.

Jessica grabbed a scalpel off the instrument tray without waiting for the scrub tech. "Where's the resident?"

"Right here," said the skinny young man rushing into the room.

Jessica raised her voice. "Get under the drapes and shove the baby's head back up inside."

"What?" the resident asked as he fumbled to tie on his mask.

"We're doing a Zavanelli maneuver."

"I . . . I've never done that." He swore as one of the strings ripped off his mask.

"Just do what I tell you!"

"Okay," he responded hesitantly.

"Get under there and push the head back up so I can pull it out from above."

The young doctor looked at Jessica, holding his mask over his face in disbelief.

"Do it!"

He dropped to the floor. "Okay, I got it." His voice was muffled. "I'm pushing the head back up now."

"Well?" Jessica almost yelled at the resident.

"It's stuck." The resident was clearly panicking. "Oh my God, it's totally stuck."

"Push harder, and maybe twist it a bit," Jessica demanded.

"I'm trying!"

"Try harder!"

The room was silent as the resident rustled under the drapes.

"Shit, it's slippery," he whined.

"Hand him a towel!" Jessica ordered the nurse. "Stat."

"Okay. Hold on. I think I got it." The relief in the resident's voice was palpable. "It should be up in the uterus now."

"Good." Jessica closed her eyes for a split second as the resident backed out on his knees from under the OR table, poised on his haunches, his hands on his thighs. He took several deep breaths.

Jessica clutched the scalpel and sliced a huge incision up the patient's bulging abdomen. The clicking of surgical clamps and the buzzing of the cautery filled the eerily quiet room.

The neonatal team waited.

Within minutes, a misshapen head appeared. Jessica grabbed the baby, one hand under the back of its neck, and one hand around its slippery feet. She handed the nearly lifeless blue form, smeared with greenish-brown meconium, off to the neonatologist and turned her attention back to the patient.

"One-minute Apgar: zero," announced the neonatologist.

No heartbeat, no breathing, no muscle tone. Jessica nodded. She tried to swallow, but her mouth was too dry. She fought back the tears and deliberately sutured the patient. *It's over.*

"Five-minute Apgar: one. He's got a faint heartbeat."

Jessica bit her lip. She stopped for a second and said a quick prayer, asking for forgiveness as the NICU team whisked the baby off to the neonatal unit.

CHAPTER TWO

Camille Delaney glared at the insurance defense lawyer sitting across the conference table. It had been a long time since she'd dealt with a two-bit car accident lawyer like Winston Clark. But after leaving her prestigious practice at one of Seattle's top law firms to open her own solo practice, she had to pay the bills somehow. She wondered to herself how Clark justified harassing and intimidating innocent plaintiffs day in and day out. There had to be more to lawyering than money.

Winston Clark pulled his head back into his shoulders, causing his double chin to protrude over his mock turtleneck as he continued to question Camille's client. "So, tell me how this so-called li'l hit-and-run accident happened." He used the tip of his gold penknife to push the skin back on his cuticles. "I understand you believe this phantom vehicle was a silver Jaguar." He looked up. "What makes you think that?"

Gina Cipriotti stared at the lawyer for a moment. "Danny's friend Josh saw the whole thing."

Clark looked at his thick gold watch. "And how old is this Josh?"

Gina set her jaw. "Seven."

"Uh-huh." Clark nodded sarcastically. "So tell me what this seven-year-old supposedly saw."

Camille followed Clark's gaze to the downtown Seattle high-rises glimmering at the far end of the lake in the late-afternoon sunshine.

For a nanosecond she missed her old view from her office in the prestigious Two Union Square.

Gina appeared to be waiting for Clark to pay attention to her.

"Go ahead," he prompted, still staring out the window, "I'm listening."

Camille wondered if Winston Clark ever looked anyone in the eye.

"Josh saw a silver Jaguar come screeching around the corner," Gina said hesitantly. "It was heading straight for my Danny, who was in the crosswalk."

Clark's upper lip curled under. "How'd he know it was a Jag?"

"He's a seven-year-old kid with a huge toy car collection."

Clark snorted. "Did he get the license plate number?"

"There was no license plate on the car."

"Was it new or something?"

"Objection, argumentative." Camille threw down her pen.

Clark sat back and draped his hands over the arms of the chair, ignoring Camille. "What other evidence do you have that this mystery Jag had no license plate?"

"Objection!"

"This is a discovery deposition, counsel, I have every right to inquire into the circumstances surrounding the incident." Clark rolled his eyes toward the ceiling. "You're claiming the kid got some kind of brain damage after getting a little bump on the head. I'm entitled to question his mother about the facts of the accident."

Camille got up and paced along the edge of the tiny conference room. "It was hardly a bump on the head." She envisioned herself leaping across the table and choking the smug bastard. How dare he try to devalue such a serious head injury? "Danny was on the neuro floor of Children's Hospital for five days." She stared down at Winston Clark, using every bit of her five feet ten inches to gain advantage over her opponent. "My client has gone over the facts of the accident for the past half hour. Let's move along."

Clark stood. "I'll decide when we move along," he said shrilly as his eyes darted back and forth. He picked at his overly moussed hair and asked the court reporter to repeat the question about whether the Jag did or didn't have a license plate.

"I only know that Josh said there was no license plate."

"Very well." Clark skimmed his notes. "Now, let's go over the circumstances of little Danny's birth."

"What?" Camille snapped.

"Is that an objection, counsel?"

"This is a car accident case. Not a birth injury."

"With a head injury."

"So?"

"So, the neurological status of the kid is relevant."

Camille flopped back in her chair.

The client took a tissue from the box in the middle of the table and blew her nose loudly. Without waiting for Clark to even ask a question, she began to testify. "We tried for years to get pregnant, then through the miracle of modern technology, poof! It happened. Of course, not until we'd undergone a number of attempts at fertilization. I'll never forget the day we conceived our Danny. It was a Sunday, after church." Gina looked upward. "See, he really was the answer to our prayers . . ."

Camille held her hand out. "Hold on, Gina. Wait until there's a question posed."

"I'll need to order your medical records. Who provided your OB care?"

"Davenport Women's Health."

"I object to this line of questioning. We are not going to be providing any birth records on this case. Consider this to be an ongoing objection to any subpoenas issued for any of Mrs. Cipriotti's medical records."

"We'll take this up with the judge at a later date, then," Clark announced.

The defense lawyer flipped to a new page of notes just as Amy Hutchins, Camille's paralegal, poked her head in.

"Camille? You have a call." She raised her eyebrows expectantly. "It's urgent."

Camille stared at Clark. "We'll take a fifteen-minute break."

In order to get out of the cramped conference room, Camille had to wait for Clark to get up from his chair. He did so, slowly, smirking at her and shaking his head.

Gina trailed behind Camille and said loudly, "We're killing him in there. I wouldn't want to be on the receiving end of those steely dark brown eyes of yours for anything."

What planet is this woman on? Clark was just getting started.

Amy stepped between Camille and her client and whispered into her ear. "Is the dep almost over? I can't handle this kid anymore." She nodded her head in the direction of Gina's son, the hit-and-run victim.

"Danny! Stop it!" Gina charged across Camille's office, adroitly prying Camille's letter opener from her son's grasp to prevent him from stabbing it into the purple leather couch.

Camille watched as the slender woman frantically tried to restrain her son, wondering where little Danny had gotten his fiery red hair and freckles.

"Why's that lawyer so mean?" Gina asked Camille as she handed Danny a pack of pens and a coloring book, which he promptly opened and began to shred to pieces.

"I hate coloring!" he screamed. "You can't make me color!" He threw the pens down, scattering them across the floor.

Camille watched, horrified, as Danny climbed up on his mother and bit her on the arm.

"Stop that, Danny." Gina stood, grasped her son by the shoulders, and sat him down in Camille's easy chair. "We're at the lawyer's office. You have to behave." She rubbed her arm, which was beginning to turn red where Danny had bitten her.

"I hate it here," the boy sneered.

"Ms. Delaney is trying to help us."

Danny stood and stuck his tongue out at Camille. "Bitch."

Camille stepped back.

Gina shook her finger at her son. "Danny! You apologize this instant!"

The boy crossed his arms, narrowed his eyes, and glared defiantly at his mother. "Try and make me." He jutted his chin out.

"Camille, your call's on line one," Amy interrupted. "Why don't you take it at my desk?" She stuck a hot-pink Post-it on the lapel of Camille's gabardine jacket.

Camille pulled Amy aside and whispered, "Watch that kid." She snatched the Post-it and read *Possible malpractice case, line one.*

Camille sat at Amy's cluttered desk and picked up the phone. Maybe this would be the "big one."

"Hello? This is Camille Delaney," she said hopefully.

"Hi, Ms. Delaney, my name is Helene Anderson, and I'm looking for a lawyer to handle a malpractice case."

The big one? Who was she kidding? She could hardly afford to process a run-of-the-mill fender bender at this point in her not-so-illustrious career. Camille's stomach turned as she shuffled through the stacks of unpaid bills on Amy's desk. Realistically, there was no way she could finance a malpractice case. But she couldn't exactly hang up on the woman. "What type of case is it?"

"It's against my obstetrician. She pretty much killed my baby."

Camille paused. It wasn't the first time a client overinterpreted what had happened to her. But then again, Camille knew firsthand from her own childhood that there was nothing worse for a mother than losing a child. "What happened?" she asked softly.

"I don't know. I went to the delivery room and the doctor pulled the baby's head out. But it got stuck, so she shoved it back up and did a C-section."

Camille made a face. "What?"

"It was devastating." The woman's voice was barely a whisper. "My baby died a few days later in the NICU."

If this were true, the case had to be a slam-dunk winner. Camille searched her memory for anything she'd learned during her first career as a nurse about shoving a baby's head back in and doing a C-section. "It sounds outrageous."

"It was. Then, not long after it happened, I got a call from a lawyer named Harvey Lowe. He begged me for the case."

It didn't surprise Camille that her ex-partner would break every known ethical prohibition against the solicitation of a client. But it did surprise her that he went to such lengths to get a case with such limited damages. She shook her head curiously. It had finally come to this; she was getting Lowe's castoffs. Great.

"He kept trying to tell us that cases where the baby dies aren't worth that much—but that he could get us a bundle."

"Well, in a way, he's right. When a baby dies, there usually aren't enough ongoing medical expenses to support a big verdict." Camille swiveled in Amy's chair so that the pile of bills didn't distract her. "For some reason, juries rarely award significant pain and suffering damages to parents who've lost their babies." She thought back to the devastation her own family had gone through when her youngest sister had died from meningitis just before her first birthday. The tragedy had ultimately sent Camille's mother hurtling across the country to immerse herself into any cause that would replace the pain in her heart, while her father lost himself in his music. Some of the New York critics credited his success to the angst he suffered after the loss of his youngest daughter.

Camille tried to stay focused. "Juries always seem to buy into the defense lawyer's 'they can always have another' argument." Camille knew full well that a baby could never be replaced, but she also knew the facts of life in the legal system. "I know it's hard to accept, but there just isn't typically much chance of a big verdict in cases involving pain and suffering if there are no substantial medical bills." In one way, it made sense. There was no amount of money that could have put her family back together again after they'd lost baby Valerie. She knew the woman on the other end of the phone would likely never be the same either.

"Except Lowe said this case was different. He was relentless until we finally signed up with him."

Camille perked up. Why had Lowe wanted the case so badly? Maybe this one was worth something after all. Maybe she could find a way to afford to take it. "So, why are you looking for a new lawyer?" She really was curious.

"I fired him," the woman said matter-of-factly.

Things were looking up. "Why?"

"He's pompous and rude. And I got tired of his attitude."

The woman certainly had good judgment. Camille liked her better every second. "Why'd you hire him in the first place?"

"He told us he'd handled several cases against this doctor before, and he had the inside scoop on her. He told us no one else in town could get us a bigger settlement than he could." She paused. "Especially since it was 'just a dead baby case,' as he called it." The woman's voice cracked.

"Jeez, I'm so sorry." Here she was apologizing for her former partner once again. "Listen, not all lawyers are as heartless as Harvey Lowe."

A deep breath. "Do you know him?"

"Oh, yes, very well."

Camille had been Lowe's rising star until he unilaterally decided that she was stepping into his spotlight. As soon as he determined that she was competing with him for fame and fortune, he had her packed up and out of there in nothing flat. Camille's career with Harvey Lowe hadn't ended happily, but she had landed at a prestigious divorce firm where she had risen like a superstar before launching off to start her own practice the year before.

"Is Lowe any good?"

"Well . . . he's very . . . successful." She pictured Lowe climbing into his Learjet, with the flamboyant gold scales of justice painted on its side.

"If you ask me, he's a jerk. And I'm changing lawyers. I've heard that you're one of the best."

Camille smiled. It had been a long time since she'd heard those words in reference to a malpractice suit.

"So? You want the case?"

"I'd be honored." The words slipped out before she could stop them. Maybe this would be her opportunity to show a jury how to compensate a family that had been destroyed by the loss of a child. "When can you come in?"

"I picked up my medical records from Lowe's office yesterday. I'll drop them by today and we can meet next Tuesday if that's okay with you."

"Sure, that'd be great."

"I can't thank you enough, Ms. Delaney. You're the only other lawyer who has demonstrated any interest in my case." She hung up.

Camille looked at the receiver in her hand. So no one else would take the case. *What a chump you are.* She rubbed her temples as she pondered the pile of unpaid office bills. There was no way this dead baby case would be the answer to her financial woes.

CHAPTER THREE

Camille returned to find Amy torn between comforting the weeping Gina and trying to protect Camille's office from complete destruction at the hands of the redheaded hellion.

"You're back." Amy looked at Camille and widened her eyes.

The client pulled a mirror out of her purse and carefully wiped the mascara from her cheeks. "I was just telling Amy how long it took us to get pregnant with our little wild man here." Gina looked at Danny, who was spinning out of control in Camille's cream-colored leather desk chair. "I'm going to give you to the count of three to get down from there. One . . . two . . . three."

"You're on your own," Amy whispered as she unceremoniously handed Camille the tissue box and ran to answer the phone.

How had it come to this? Mixing it up with the likes of Winston Clark on behalf of an out-of-control kid who may or may not have been hit by a mysterious silver Jag. It was a lousy way to make a living.

"Danny, get down," Gina pleaded. "I'm sure you must think we've spoiled him rotten." She winced and shrugged playfully. "I've tried everything I can think of to get him under control."

Camille caught her chair just as Danny tipped it over backward on a particularly violent bounce.

"His therapist said he'd calm down once he got into the structure of a school setting, but it seems like he gets worse every year."

"Therapist?" Camille felt her face flush as she put her hand firmly on Danny's shoulder to keep him from tipping the chair over again.

"Didn't I tell you? Danny's been in therapy since he was four years old. I gave the records to Amy when I came in."

Camille looked at her watch. *Clark's gonna love this—now he can blame the kid's behavior on something besides the head injury.* It was an insurance lawyer's favorite tactic. It was going to be a very long afternoon. She got up and held the door for her client. "Shall we?" As she passed Amy's desk, she cocked her head in the direction of the boy and said under her breath. "This is definitely above and beyond the call of duty."

Amy placed her hand lightly on Camille's arm. "Well, I'm sure you can find some way to make it up to me."

———

After the deposition, Camille watched Clark squeal off in his bright yellow Porsche, leaving her dusty old Ford Explorer behind in the parking lot. Dejectedly, she noticed the blinking light on her phone and debated whether she should answer the fifteen voice mails that beckoned her. She shrugged; six o'clock was too late to return calls. An imposing pile of interrogatories stood on her desk. They could wait too.

One of the best parts about having her office in a marina was being able to get outside when she needed to clear her head. Houseboats of every shape and size, as well as huge gritty fishing boats, surrounded the busy urban lake. The parade of boats outside her window soothed her during the chaotic days in the feisty arena of litigation, while the reassuring buzz of floatplanes served as a constant reminder that the peaceful San Juan Islands were just a forty-five-minute flight away.

She grabbed her jacket and headed out to see if she could spot her husband, Sam, in the lineup of sailboats circling for the start of the "Duck Dodge." Every Tuesday since she could remember, Sam and their three daughters joined in the "just for fun" race on the lake. Even seventeen-year-old Angela wouldn't dream of missing a Duck Dodge. The girls adored their father as much as Camille did. She felt a rush of warmth as she located her family amid the boats, whose sails luffed in the still air. She smiled, hiked up her skirt, kicked off her high heels, and sat down on the end of the dock. With this wind, or lack thereof, her crew wouldn't be home until late.

Camille looked at her kayak, turned upside down a few feet away. It was a perfect evening to paddle home across the lake to their houseboat.

Amy appeared, a large manila envelope in one hand and two Mirror Pond Pale Ales in the other.

The icy cold of the beer bottle sent a chill up Camille's arm. "Thanks. You read my mind."

"I figured after a day with Win Clark, it was the least I could do. And by the way, you completely failed to notify the fashion police about the spiky new hairdo he's sporting." Amy rolled her eyes. "The big blowhard."

Camille glanced around and shimmied out of her black tights so she could put her feet into the invigoratingly cold water. "I guess I was so intimidated by his searing questions I forgot to file a report."

The starting gun for the sailboat race pierced the peaceful evening as Amy handed Camille the envelope. "That woman you spoke to on the phone dropped these by while you were in the dep."

Camille hugged the records to her chest, dreading having to confess to Amy that she had agreed to look at a malpractice case with such limited financial damages.

Amy raised her eyebrows. "Well?"

"Dead baby."

Amy's face fell. "Oh no, you don't."

"Hang on, hear me out."

Amy wagged her finger at Camille and mimicked Gina admonishing her son. "I'm going to give you to the count of ten to convince me. One . . . two . . . three . . ."

"Lowe had the case, but the client fired him," Camille said in a staccato fashion.

"Or he dumped her because he didn't want to deal with a malpractice case with no damages."

Camille watched as the sailboats nudged up against one another, vying for position. "Not necessarily."

"Look, Camille, I know what you're up to." Amy sat down next to her boss and dangled her legs over the end of the dock. "You're still trying to prove something to that asshole for firing you. It's been over ten years now. Time to get over it, my dear." Amy struggled to open her beer without breaking a nail.

"Here." Camille grabbed the beer, opened it, and handed it back to Amy.

"Be practical." Amy looked Camille squarely in the eye. "We can't afford to dump our limited resources into something like this now. Don't let your feelings about Lowe cloud your judgment."

"I'm not." Camille leaned over the edge of the dock and looked at her reflection in the smooth water. Amy had her pegged. There was nothing she'd rather do than steal a case from Harvey Lowe. And turn it into a huge winner. "This is not about Harvey Lowe."

"No, no, of course not." Amy shook her head. "It didn't bother you at all last year when he had his face on the front page of the *Trial News* with that little girl he got the ten-million-dollar settlement for."

Camille's shoulders tightened. "He probably falsified the records or something. You know, honesty is hardly his middle name."

"Well, he's obviously doing something right. You saw his new house on TV last spring when he had that campaign fundraiser for the vice president."

"And you know as well as I do that Harvey Lowe didn't get that showplace in the Highlands by doing anything right by most people's definition. Besides, just because he has a big fancy house, that doesn't mean he's happy," Camille offered half-heartedly.

"Yeah, you're right." Amy nodded sarcastically. "I'm sure he's miserable flying around in his Learjet with the sappy scales of justice plastered all over the side."

"He'll be miserable when I have my picture on the front of the *Trial News*. Let's take this case and turn it into something really big. We'll burn his sorry ass."

"Camille, it's a dead baby case. There are no financial damages. This is not the case to bring Harvey Lowe to his knees. You'll just look like a fool. Give it up."

Despite having the distinct feeling that Amy was right, Camille felt the stirring of a challenge bubbling up inside her. There must be a way she could convince a jury about what really happened to a family when they lost a child. "Actually, the case sounds like a piece of cake." She held up her hands as if to surrender. "You're right, it may not be worth much, but it's better than these shitty little car accident cases."

"Camille . . ."

"Just hear me out," Camille interrupted. "The doc pulled the baby's head out with forceps and it got stuck, so she shoved it back up and did a C-section."

Amy wrinkled her nose. "You're kidding."

"Lowe wouldn't have filed it if it wasn't worth something. I know him too well. There's money here, I can smell it." She knew Amy needed a raise as badly as she needed to prove the value of this baby.

"It's already filed? When's the trial date?"

"I'm not sure." Camille pulled her jacket around her as the wind suddenly whipped up out on the lake. Odd weather—dead calm one minute, small-craft warnings the next. She got up and walked gingerly over to her kayak, careful to avoid slivers. "I gotta get home and fix dinner."

"Are you leaving your car here?"

"Yeah, I'll get it tomorrow. I could use some fresh air."

Amy helped Camille lift the kayak into the water.

"I'm going to run these by my neighbor Cathy Swain. She's an obstetrician. See what she says."

After all their years together, Amy obviously knew when to back off. She changed the subject. "I think I'll call *Professional Woman's Magazine* and suggest that they do a spread about the 'kayaking lawyer.' You've got the bone structure and the creamy olive complexion to give you a pretty good shot at getting yourself on the cover."

"Flattery will get you everywhere." Camille laughed and stuffed the records into her backpack, which she jammed into the cargo hold of her kayak. She held the boat against the dock as it rocked in the increasingly rough water. "And while you're at it, see if they can recommend someplace that makes decent-looking Gore-Tex business outerwear." She pushed away from the dock.

The sailboats cut in front of her in the stiff breeze as orange and pink clouds chased each other over the skyscrapers at the south end of the lake. Heading out onto the choppy water, Camille reflected on the years she'd spent in the cosmopolitan glass-and-steel city: four years as a malpractice lawyer with Harvey Lowe, then ten as a high-end divorce gladiator for the Seattle elite.

She could hardly believe it was just over a year ago that she'd abandoned the big-city glamour to do her own thing in Fremont, Seattle's answer to Silicon Valley on the lake. Strangely, Fremont was beginning to feel like home.

A huge cabin cruiser chugged slowly past her, its skipper holding up his cocktail glass in a five o'clock salute.

Cheers.

She dug in her paddle and reminded herself why she'd made the big move. She'd wanted to be able to make a difference, representing regular people who had the misfortune of finding themselves battling the unconscionable insurance industry.

She should be delighted. She'd finally escaped from a testosterone-driven hierarchical law firm where the lawyers represented people using their children as a commodity in negotiating some far-fetched settlement—and now here she was, having to determine the value of a child's life. It occurred to her that the two ends of the legal profession weren't really all that different. The child was definitely still a commodity. "I guess that's what lawyers do," she said aloud. "Try and put values on things that are priceless." She turned to head into the wake of a huge tour boat. Her kayak bounced over the waves easily. The wind threw a cold spray across her face.

Still, the challenge of convincing a jury of the value of a baby's life intrigued her. But how on earth could she afford to proceed with this kind of case when she found herself scrambling just to make ends meet? Her houseboat dock was just yards away. Camille smiled with relief to see Cathy Swain on her deck, watering her plants.

Camille shouted, "Hey! Are you going to be around for a while?"

Cathy's deck looked like a florist's warehouse. She peered over the foliage and looked down on Camille. "Sure! C'mon over for a glass of wine!"

"Great. I have some records I want you to take a look at for me."

CHAPTER FOUR

Camille arrived home to find a piece of blue construction paper, cut in the shape of a sailboat, tacked to the front door of her houseboat. Her seven-year-old foster daughter's handwriting announced that the family intended to win the race tonight. Camille smiled at Gracie's artistic promise and unlocked the door, relieved that Cathy was home so early.

She whistled for the family greyhound, Jake, but there was no response. Wow, Sam really had taken the whole gang. Camille quickly pulled on a pair of loose-fitting gray jersey sweats and hurried upstairs to grab a bottle of chardonnay. She ran her fingers through her short dark hair and headed down the wide cement dock lined with large box-like floating homes. There were green ones and blue ones and yellow ones, but lately too many of them had been painted taupe—in case Seattle wasn't monochromatic enough already.

"Hello!" Camille shouted up the stairwell of her neighbor's recently remodeled houseboat.

Cathy peeked her head over the balcony at the top of the stairs. Most of the houseboats on Camille's dock had reverse floor plans, with the living areas upstairs so the residents could enjoy their views. "C'mon up!"

Camille ascended into the brand-new gourmet kitchen. Her stomach fluttered with envy as she took in the granite countertops with threads of lapis glistening in the early evening sunset. "God, this place is gorgeous." She stopped and looked at her friend, who sported a new two-inch-long haircut. "You cut your hair!"

Cathy tousled what was left of her strawberry blonde locks. "Do you like it?"

"It looks great. Did David do it for you?"

"Yup, and I hope you don't mind; I told him I wanted your exact haircut." Cathy laughed.

"Actually, if my hair wasn't black, we could pass for sisters. Too tall, too thin . . . but not rich enough . . ." Camille winked. "Yet."

Seeing the bottle of wine in Camille's hand, Cathy took a couple of handblown wineglasses from the shelf. "What's up?"

Camille opened a drawer and grabbed a corkscrew. "I got a new case today."

"Uh-huh."

The cork made a sucking noise as Camille pulled it easily out of the bottle. "It's an OB case. I thought you might be able to take a look at it for me."

"Jeez. It's been a long time since you had an OB malpractice case. I was beginning to like just being friends, no strings attached."

Camille poured two generous glasses of wine and followed Cathy out onto the deck, where each of them reclined on heavily padded wrought iron chaises. Cathy's deck faced west over the lake where the sun slipped quietly behind Queen Anne Hill.

Cathy held her glass up to the late-afternoon sunshine. "Nice." She took a sip. "So, tell me about your case."

"Have you ever heard of an OB doing a forceps delivery and then shoving the head back up and doing a C-section?"

"It's called the Zavanelli maneuver. I've read about it, but it isn't a procedure that's given much credibility. There's really no reason to get yourself into a situation where you'd have to resort to anything that risky." Cathy looked suspiciously at her friend. "Where did this happen?"

"Here in town, at Sound."

"You're kidding. How'd the tracing look?"

Camille pulled a roll of long graph-like paper out of her backpack and unwound it. "See for yourself."

Cathy sat up and hunched over the monitor strip. "Holy shit."

"What?"

"Well, the contractions are nonstop, and . . . let's see . . ." She studied the strip. "Huh, they kept turning down the Pitocin, which is certainly appropriate. And it's hard to tell exactly how hard the contractions were: they used external monitors." She looked up at Camille. "What happened to the kid?"

"He died a few days later in the NICU. Probably a blessing; he was almost brain dead when he was born."

"Jesus." Cathy had her nose buried in the patient's chart. She shook her head.

"What?"

"Did you know that your client was a gestational diabetic?"

"No . . ." Camille searched her memory from her training as a nurse. "Diabetics have big babies, right?"

"Exactly. I wonder if the patient had an ultrasound." She licked her thumb and paged through the chart. "Gee, I don't see one."

"Seems like the doc should have done one."

"Well, I always do. It's the one way you can confirm the size of the baby before labor, so you don't get into a situation like this."

"So, the doc shouldn't have been inducing her at all because the baby was too big?"

"No, it's okay to do a trial induction, but you don't want to get too aggressive with the forceps when you know you've got a big kid. And look here." Cathy pointed to the nurse's note. "The kid had thick meconium. That's when the baby moves its bowels in response to severe distress."

Camille nodded—her short stint on the labor and delivery floor in nursing school was coming back to her.

Cathy dropped the chart on the deck. "If you ask me, your doctor as much as killed the kid."

Camille froze. "'Killed' it? That's a pretty strong word."

"That's what it looks like to me."

Camille cringed at the familiar rush she felt whenever she evaluated a good malpractice case. It was what she hated most about being a lawyer: horrific tragedy, fabulous lawsuit. "So, you think I can prove malpractice?"

"Are you kidding? In my opinion, they might as well get out their checkbook. You used to be a nurse; I bet even this many years later, you can figure out what a mess this delivery was."

Camille leaned back and clutched the thick roll to her chest. "Well, I certainly don't ever remember seeing any doctor pulling out a baby's head and shoving it back up to do a C-section." She shook her head and almost smiled. "I knew this would be a good case."

"What are you so smug about?"

"Remember that jerk I used to work with?"

"That arrogant fat prick, what was his name?"

"Harvey Lowe." Camille made a face. "He solicited this client, and then she dumped him because he was such a creep."

"So, it's payback time?" Cathy winked.

"You got it. This may be the breakthrough case I've been waiting for."

"Well, congratulations." Cathy held up her glass in a toast. "Here's to the easy money you contingent fee lawyers always get."

Camille felt a prickle slide up her neck. "You know, people forget. Lawsuits are about someone's life. This family's baby died." Camille turned and looked wistfully out over the lake behind Cathy's houseboat thinking about baby Valerie.

"I know. And that, in a nutshell, is what I find so deplorable about the legal system." Cathy dropped her voice to mimic a deep-throated male lawyer. "I have great news for you, ma'am, your baby is brain damaged. You have a fabulous lawsuit."

"I hear you loud and clear." Camille had never gotten used to the idea that the worse someone's life was devastated, the more their lawsuit was worth, and the more money their lawyer made. It sucked.

"By the way." Cathy studied the label on the wine bottle. "What loser are you going to sue?"

"Her name's Kensington, Jessica Kensington. Ever heard of her?"

Cathy bolted up in her chair, nearly knocking her wine over. "Jessica Kensington did this? Are you sure?"

Camille shot her friend a worried glance. "Yeah, why?"

"Shit, Camille, Jessica's the president of the Seattle GYN Society. You'll never find anyone to testify against her. Everyone loves her."

"You're kidding."

"No, but I've got to tell you that even though she's universally loved by the docs and staff at the hospital, this isn't the first time she's gotten into trouble."

"So it shouldn't be too hard to find someone to testify, then."

"Au contraire, the docs have circled their wagons around her; no one around here's gonna help you on this one."

"I'll get someone from Eastern Washington, then."

"Oh no, you won't. She's way too well known across the state after being president of the GYN society. And besides, every year she has this dynamite Halloween party at her downtown penthouse. By the way"—Cathy swept her arm in an arc—"if you think this place is nice, you should see her condo. You feel like you're on some kind of movie set. It's Manhattan all the way."

"So she has a Halloween party—what does that have to do with my not getting an expert from Eastern Washington?"

"She invites docs from all across the state and gives awards for the best costumes." Cathy shook her head and smiled. "And now that the competitive spirit of the docs has gotten ignited, the costumes have become extraordinary, and the key is not to be recognized. I'm not kidding, there have been years where I had no idea who I was talking to until I saw them in surgery the next day. It's the medical social event of the year. No one's gonna risk getting taken off that invitation list. I'm telling you, everyone loves Kensington."

Camille struggled to hide her disappointment. "She can't be all that perfect . . ."

Cathy interrupted her. "And she was written up in the *Times* last year for her commitment to the public school literacy program. Dr. Perfect volunteers as a reading tutor at Chief Sealth Elementary School for kids with behavior problems. And of course, she works once a month at the free OB clinic for teens."

Camille sighed.

Cathy flipped through the records and let out a low whistle. "Jesus Christ. I can't believe this. Maybe she was having some kind of personal crisis or something."

"To the point that she kills a kid? Aren't doctors expected to leave their personal lives at home when they're dealing with life-or-death stuff?"

"In a perfect world, yes. But there has to be some explanation. You know when Kensington and I were in training, she had a shitload of personal problems; in fact, I think she took some medical leaves of absence for some kind of stress-related condition."

"What do you mean?"

"No one ever really talked about it, but she was off intermittently for a month or so at a time if I remember right. All the other residents had to pull together and cover for her."

"Is she unstable? Does she have a mental health history?"

"No . . . of course not, but you could call her high-strung, I guess. And maybe a little volatile." Cathy paused. "But that hasn't kept her from becoming the darling of the state OB association. She can really turn on the charm."

Camille watched the line of sailboats motoring in from the race, their sails flapping in the stiff breeze as the crews lashed them to the boom. Harvey Lowe wouldn't balk at the fact that the doctor he was evaluating was some kind of local celebrity.

She took a deep breath. "Look, I don't care who the hell Jessica Kensington is. She killed this kid, and I'm going to go after her. Period."

"Well, keep me out of this; I don't want to be deep-sixed from her party list." Cathy scrunched her shoulders as if she were expecting to have her ears boxed. "No offense," she added quickly.

"I'm sure I can find an out-of-state expert who isn't afraid of this local diva." Camille looked across the lake at her family beginning to drop the sails. "And if I can't find someone myself, I can ask Sam if he knows anyone, like from medical school or something."

"I wonder how many medical malpractice lawyers have doctor husbands who can get them expert witnesses at the drop of a hat?"

"And doctor girlfriends who refuse to testify for them?"

"You're persistent. You'll find someone."

"It's not always that easy. Most of you docs aren't all that enthusiastic about crossing over to the 'dark side.'" Camille raised an eyebrow. "Know what I mean, Dr. Deep Throat?"

"Okay, okay, I hear ya. But I'm sure you'll dig up someone. If anyone can, it'd be you."

Camille poured herself another glass of wine. "Then it's decided. I'm gonna sue Dr. Kensington's ass to kingdom come." She sat back and watched her family motoring the sailboat down the Venice-like canal. Camille laughed at her middle daughter, Libby, who nearly fell off the sailboat while she was waving to her mother. "Watch what you're doing!" Camille yelled.

"We came in second, Mom!" Grace shrieked from her perch on the bow. "We woulda come in first, but the other boat cheated, didn't they, Daddy?" Gracie held Sam's arm as he stood next to Libby, who was managing the tiller all by herself.

The canal was so narrow that Camille could almost touch her family as the classic twenty-six-foot Thunderbird glided by en route to its moorage next to their houseboat.

Angela hung from the boom as she tried to tie down the mainsail. "Our team was one guy and all girls! And we almost won!"

"Just you guys?" Camille shouted.

"Yup!" yelled Libby. "And Dad let me be the skipper!" Libby tousled her father's wavy salt-and-pepper hair, then squealed as he pulled her Mariners cap down over her eyes. "Da-ad!"

Camille's stomach did a gentle flip-flop as she watched her handsome husband calmly coaching his daughter to dock the boat easily into their slip. She couldn't wait to get home and feel his strong arms around her. Camille often wondered what she had done in a previous life to deserve a man like Sam.

She turned to Cathy. "I'd better get home and start dinner. Anything else you think I should know about the good Dr. Kensington?"

"Just that you're not only taking on the president of the local GYN society, but the daughter of Seattle's own godfather of gynecology."

"What do you mean?"

"You know Kip Davenport?"

Camille froze. "Of course. I've known Kip for years. He was one of my biggest referral sources when I was in the divorce biz. And we serve on the board of the Women's Law Center together. In fact, I've invited him to sit at my table for my mom's fundraiser on Friday."

"Well then, you probably shouldn't tell him you're suing his daughter until after he writes his charity check."

There was no way she could file suit against Kip Davenport's daughter. No matter how bad she had screwed up. Camille flopped back. Suddenly the comfy chaise lounge didn't feel so soft. "Shit."

CHAPTER FIVE

Camille watched with a twinge of envy as her mother, Pella Rallis, gracefully made her way up to the podium in the Grand Ballroom of the Four Seasons Hotel. Camille couldn't remember a time when her mother had shunned a spotlight. It was easy to hide in the center of a whirlwind.

Pella beamed as she looked over the room full of people attending the annual breakfast fundraiser for her refugee asylum program on her home island of Lesvos, in Greece. Camille had invited nine of her friends most likely to give generously to her mother's cause, and as usual, Kip Davenport was at the top of her list. She knew that the pictures of children in torn clothes living in the horror of the Moria refugee camp would tug at his heartstrings. Camille awkwardly took a seat across from Kip, her guilt mingled with confusion.

A hush fell over the crowd as Pella Rallis's melodious Greek accent filled the room. "After making the treacherous journey in an overloaded small boat from Turkey to Lesvos, the refugees find themselves in a camp built for about three thousand refugees. There are currently about twenty thousand people living in squalor in this camp. There is violence and infectious disease running rampant. Women and children wear diapers at night because it is too dangerous to walk to the toilets in the pitch-dark camp . . ." Camille's mother truly had a flair for the dramatic. As always, she had the room captivated from the minute she stepped onto the stage.

Pella had begun championing the causes of various underdogs shortly after Valerie had died of meningitis a month before her first birthday. Valerie's death had led to her parents' bittersweet divorce, and while still grieving her daughter's death, Pella had become a kind of activist-celebrity whose causes took center stage in her life. Pella had turned to her friend Bridget for comfort, and the two had ended up as a couple, jointly raising their two daughters. Both women taught at the local law school and were well-known community activists. Throughout their childhood, Camille and her stepsister, Eve, had had more than their share of cold cereal for dinner while their mothers organized marches or sit-ins. At the time, Camille figured that her mother considered her causes to be more important than her own daughter. But after having a family of her own, Camille realized that her mother had simply chosen to avoid facing the loss of her youngest daughter by taking on other people's pain.

Camille recognized the familiar feeling of jealousy mixed with pride as her mother's presence filled the huge hotel ballroom. There was no stopping this woman. Over the past several years, Pella had committed her life to the families who had become stranded near her hometown of Mytilini on Lesvos. It was as far from the reality of every-day life as she could get.

Camille briefly reflected on the irony of this powerhouse of a woman deeply committed to children on the other side of the world, while never quite making it to so much as one of her own grandchildren's swim meets or choir concerts.

The room filled with the sounds of sniffling as men and women alike dabbed away tears during the short video featuring children lined up to see a doctor in a tent at a makeshift clinic in the midst of unspeakable poverty, their devastated parents holding their child's hand, a vacant look of dejection in their eyes. A thundering round of applause exploded as the video ended and Pella introduced a table of young volunteer lawyers who had dedicated themselves to representing this forgotten population as they one by one were granted asylum and the right to start a new life far away from the refugee camps.

Camille glanced around the room at the several hundred well-dressed professionals. Success was certainly relative: here in the US, it was measured primarily in dollars, while at the camp on Lesvos, it was considered a successful day if no children got attacked or raped on their way to use the toilet.

As everyone at her table pulled out their checkbooks, Camille tried to make eye contact with her mother. It was the only indication that the two were related—their deep brown eyes. Other than that, Camille was her father's daughter, tall, dark-haired, and gangly. Her mom was a tiny powerhouse with flowing wavy gray hair, usually tied up in a utilitarian knot, but today it was cascading perfectly over her shoulders.

As the program wound to a close, Kip leaned across the table and handed Camille a check. "Do you have time for a latte?" His voice reminded her of a radio announcer.

A faint surge of nervousness tingled through Camille's solar plexus. He couldn't possibly know. "I . . ." Camille looked at her watch, trying to fabricate an excuse to make a quick exit.

"It'll just take a minute." Kip smiled. "I promise."

"Jeez, I have a meeting at nine thirty."

"Then I'll order your espresso to go."

Camille drew a breath. "Okay, I just want to say goodbye to my mom."

"Great, I'll see you in the lobby, then." Kip turned and shook hands with the mayor of Seattle.

Camille mingled over toward the podium where she spotted her mother in the midst of a throng of admirers. Being tall had its advantages. Camille craned her neck to see over the crowd.

Pella looked ravishing in a flowing, multilayered cream linen dress, quite a contrast to the overweight society matron in the tight red St. John knit who was hanging on Pella's every word. As they chatted, Pella unselfconsciously shook her long gray locks, swept the stray tendrils back off her face, and clipped her hair into a large mother-of-pearl barrette. She was certainly no slave to fashion. Camille looked down at her own dark gray business suit and trendy stilettos, wondering when her mother had last worn high heels.

Unable to get through the crowd, Camille caught her mother's attention and blew her a gentle kiss from her fingertips. In response, Pella melodramatically puckered a kiss across the vast room. An empty pang filled Camille's heart as she watched Pella fawn on her potential donors. Camille wondered if and when she'd really get some one-on-one time with her mother while she was back in the States.

Camille descended the modern stairway from the Grand Ballroom and stood on the landing for a second to gather her wits while she watched the handsome gynecologist schmoozing the lobby like a pro. Davenport met her at the bottom of the stairs and greeted her with a peck on the cheek.

"I appreciate your inviting me. Your mother's one in a million." He winked. "It's not often that a fundraising pitch makes me pull out my handkerchief before my checkbook." He raised his eyebrows and adjusted his tie in a joking effort to look debonair. "I'd like to have dinner with her sometime."

Me too.

"I'll give you her number." She elected not to try to explain the bicontinental relationship between her mom and her wife, a PBS news broadcaster, who generally saw each other every few months—if they could squeeze in the time. "Is that what you wanted to talk to me about?"

Kip led the way across the thick carpet to a couple of Eames knockoff chairs. "No, I'd like to ask you for a favor . . . It's personal."

Personal. Camille felt a brief flood of relief. This had nothing to do with his daughter. She admonished herself for her momentary paranoia.

Kip handed Camille a latte in a paper cup and sat down with his own in an oversized china cup and saucer. Camille briefly envisioned her mother and Kip Davenport together. They'd definitely make a handsome duo: a couple of silver foxes. But her mother's earthiness would definitely clash with his smooth sophistication, and besides, her mom had long ago switched teams.

Kip leaned forward. "I'd like to talk to you. In confidence."

Camille's relief was replaced with a wave of guilt. Here she was chatting up the unsuspecting father of a potential defendant. Maybe she should just grab the latte and make her getaway after all.

"It's my daughter."

Uh-oh.

"I don't know if you've ever met Jessica. She's an obstetrician. We practice together."

Camille had known that Davenport's partner was a woman, but he'd never mentioned that she was his daughter. Why would he keep that a secret?

"We try not to make a big deal of our personal relationship. Jessica's keen on privacy, and as you know, I'm hardly a shrinking violet." He patted his chest. "I've honored her wishes and kept our professional partnership entirely separate from our private lives. It's best that way."

Camille's heart pounded in her ears. Seattle could be such a small town. Well, she was in it this far. Her lawyer instincts took over. Maybe she could drum up some info on Kensington.

"So, what can I do for you?" she said, trying to reassure herself that this was just part of her job and not necessarily duplicitously taking advantage of a friend.

"Jessica's been out of sorts lately." Kip's voice softened like a concerned father. "Something's not quite right with her."

"Is she ill?" That would explain a lot.

"No, no, no." Kip shook his head. "It's nothing physical. It's more psychological. She's just not herself."

What's he driving at? Camille was no psychologist. Why was he telling her this? She looked at him expectantly, not sure exactly what to say.

Kip took a sip of his latte and put the cup down carefully. "You're probably wondering what in the world this has to do with you."

There's no way he could know about the case. Camille wondered why he had chosen this particular morning to expose his relationship with Kensington. "It seems Jessica has gotten herself in some legal hot water."

Oh shit.

Kip picked up a spoon and swirled the cinnamon around in the foam on top of his latte. "I don't know what's come over her the past couple of years," he said without looking up.

"Has something in particular happened?" Camille remembered Cathy Swain wondering if Kensington had been distracted the night the Anderson baby was born. Maybe Kip would shed some light on what the hell was going on with his daughter. There had to be some explanation.

"Jessica has been involved in a troublesome relationship with a man."

Well, this wasn't exactly the pearl she'd been looking for. Camille looked at Kip in confusion. "I'm not sure I follow you."

"She's made some serious errors in judgment." Kip drained his cup, then paused.

Ah-ha. She's gotten into some kind of trouble with this guy and needs a lawyer to extricate her. Camille began to relax as the stinging across her shoulder blades gradually eased.

"Jessica has always been somewhat emotionally unstable." He explained, "This relationship has gotten her completely tied up in knots and affected her judgment."

Maybe they bought a house together and she wants out. "Has she made some kind of bad legal decision?"

"What?" Kip almost snapped.

Camille was slightly taken aback by Kip's quick change in demeanor.

"Look, Camille," he said with a note of hostility in his voice. "Rumor has it that one of Jessica's patients contacted you about a possible case against her."

Camille drew a sharp breath. *How did he know?*

"I'm sure professional ethics prevent you from confirming my suspicions, but I'd like you to assume I'm in possession of certain knowledge about a specific patient."

Every fiber in Camille's body went on alert. "Where are we going with this, Kip?"

Kip's menacing stare frightened Camille for a moment.

"My daughter is the most important thing in my life and I won't have her destroyed by these ugly lawsuits."

"I beg your pardon?"

"Stay away from my daughter," he said slowly, his face contorting into an almost unrecognizable visage, his eyes narrowing into slivers.

Camille almost choked on her latte, suddenly afraid of her friend. She covered her mouth to regain her composure. "As you know, I can't really discuss my clients, or potential clients, with you," she stammered.

Kip looked at Camille, seething as he appeared to weigh his options. Finally, he spoke. "Jessica's been sued before, and it almost killed her."

This was like being in *The Twilight Zone*. Here she was being verbally attacked by someone she had always called a friend as he tried to convince her that his daughter was too fragile to withstand a lawsuit. The irony was not lost on Camille that his daughter, the doctor, had set up a baby to die in intensive care. She searched for something to say. "I'm sure it was very stressful for her. It always is."

"It was worse than stressful," Kip snapped forcefully. "The plaintiff's lawyer chewed her up, spit her out, and left her on the side of the road bleeding."

Welcome to the world of litigation. She tried to nod sympathetically.

"The lawyer was a smarmy little fellow by the name of Harvey Lowe," Kip said with a fatherly possessiveness. "I will not have Jessica exposed to those tactics ever again." His anger was palpable. "And it's happened to her more than once. She cannot tolerate it again." He sat up straight. "I won't allow it."

Camille had never seen this side of her friend before, but in addition to scaring her with his anger, he'd definitely piqued her curiosity. She wondered just how many times the diva had been sued.

"The insurance company hired a completely incompetent idiot to defend her." Kip's voice had taken on that unfamiliar edge again.

Camille shivered at the sinister tone.

"He never coached Jessica before her deposition." Kip's eyes narrowed. "She had no chance against that fat little asshole, Lowe." He shook his head. "All of the cases ended in huge settlements. I don't have to tell you that the astronomical medical expenses for the brain-damaged babies scared the shit out of the insurance company. They refused to take the cases to trial, on the heels of Jessica's poor performance in her deps."

It figured. Lowe got the huge damage cases with the doc nearly rolling over in her dep, and Camille got stuck with the nuisance dead baby case that would cost her a fortune to process, with little or no chance of a big verdict. But it was the right thing to do.

Camille locked eyes with the man whom she'd always called a friend. Slowly, she spoke. "Do you know anything about the facts of this case, Kip?"

"Why do you ask?"

He had to know it was a slam dunk. "What makes you think that if I don't take the case, Jessica will be off the hook? Surely, someone's going to take it."

"What are you driving at?"

"Well, if you're worried about how your daughter is going to be treated by the plaintiff's lawyer, why not have it be someone you know will do a straightforward, ethical job?"

Camille paused, surprised at herself. It might actually work.

Kip toyed with the silver spoon in his cup for what seemed like forever. "Huh." He nodded, eyes half-closed. Finally, he cocked his head at Camille. "You're proposing that you take the case, then go easy on her?"

Camille shook her head. "That's not exactly what I said." She paused. "I said I'd do an ethical job. I can't promise it will be easy for her."

Kip pulled his chair up, obviously engaged in the possibility. "But you'd have to agree with me that this case will likely settle after a formal demand is submitted to the insurance company. There's no way they'll want to take this case to trial."

"It's certainly possible."

Kip was clearly warming up to the idea. "You'll draft a forceful demand letter with declarations from respected experts?"

"Look, Kip, I'm sure you understand that I can't discuss strategy with you."

"Oh, oh, of course not."

Kip's rapid switch from adversary to team player made Camille suspicious of his intentions. Still, it seemed to be a reasonable way to proceed.

He continued to press. "I can get you any expert you need."

"Really, Kip, I'll take care of it. It's my job." She said it with more authority than she felt.

"Okay, but you'll let me know if you need anything. Anything at all."

"I think it'd be best if we just keep our relationship a social one. Let's not complicate things."

Kip held out his hand. "It's a deal then, counselor. You have my blessing to go forward with the suit against Jessica."

Blessing? Camille pulled back just as Davenport's iron grip enveloped her thin hand.

CHAPTER SIX

On the Tuesday after Labor Day, Camille whisked into her office carrying the Anderson records, which Amy promptly removed from her grasp.

"I'm impressed. You managed not to lose these over the holiday weekend. Hard to believe," Amy chided her boss.

It had been over six years since Amy had responded to Camille's ad for a paralegal. At the time, Camille had been a partner at Whitfield, Bahr, and Moses and was searching for a paralegal to help her get, and stay, organized. She'd be dead meat without Amy. Even in tough times like these, Amy had stayed at her side. Camille knew full well that Amy could name her own salary at any downtown firm but stuck with Camille out of loyalty. Over the years they'd become a team. It was like a marriage. And it worked both ways. Not many other law firms would accommodate a single mother's need to be totally available to her sons.

Amy pulled out a color-coded file and extracted a two-page document—despite all efforts to go paperless, Camille still liked an actual client file. "I know you spoke with Gina this weekend about Clark's offer."

Thank God the case would finally settle. The fee would bring in enough to give Amy the bonus she needed to get her son Nathan started at the orthodontist. Camille exhaled slowly through pursed lips. One down.

It was time to get going on the Anderson case. Camille dialed her friend and private investigator, Trish Seaholm. Hopefully, Trish could dig up some dirt on Kensington's errant love life. It was her only lead, and Camille knew she'd have to start somewhere. Maybe the affair had actually played some part in Kensington's behavior that night. Doubtful, but possible.

As Camille waited for Trish to answer, Amy appeared in her doorway holding a letter between her thumb and forefinger, as if it were contaminated with some rare virus. "You're not gonna like this."

Camille grabbed a pair of plastic drugstore reading glasses and snatched up the letter. Winston Clark was revoking his settlement offer based on some new information he'd dug up in the kid's therapy records. "Shit." Camille threw down the letter.

Amy slumped on the purple leather couch. "Now what?"

They both knew that the rent was overdue and their line of credit was maxed out.

"I'll think of something."

"How about you find some nice rich people to divorce? They're easy to work with, and you love helping people put their lives back together," Amy suggested.

"Remember that most of our divorce clients were doctors, and now that we've joined the dark side and are suing their pals, I've kinda lost my status on the A-list of divorce lawyers."

"I told you that you should think this whole thing through before you walked out on the fancy divorce practice . . ." Amy looked at Camille despondently.

Camille nudged the pile of Anderson records at her feet. "Way back when I was at Lowe's firm, I used an OB doc in Portland as an expert on baby cases. Can you find his name for me?"

Amy stood and held her hand out in a stopping motion. "You are not taking this loser of a case."

"There's more to this thing than you realize, Ame." Camille poured them each a cup of coffee and recited the events of the Friday-morning fundraiser.

"You really don't want to get locked into expensive litigation on something like this, with such limited value." Amy dumped the remnants of sugar from the empty box and looked inside. "We're out of sugar." She slammed the box onto the counter.

"There's Equal in the cupboard."

Amy looked at Camille as if she had suddenly turned into an alien. "Equal?"

Camille ignored the brewing culinary crisis. "I need an expert declaration to attach to my demand letter. I'm positive this thing will settle quickly. The Andersons need to put this behind them. Let's settle it and move on." Camille tried to convince herself as much as Amy. "Now, can you find me that number, please?"

Amy took a sip of coffee and grimaced as she picked up the phone. "I assume you want Helene Anderson to come in and sign a retainer agreement?"

Camille paused. This was it. If the insurance company refused to settle, their life would be hell until the trial in November.

"Camille? You want me to call Helene?"

The baby died. She had to help. "Yep, get her in here." Camille felt the familiar rush of energy that always accompanied a new case, especially when she knew she could make a difference in the lives of this devastated couple. "And then can you search the *Trial News* archives to see if you can find any articles about Lowe's settlements against Kensington? I'd like to see if any of his arguments might apply here."

Amy shook her head. "I hope I'm not telling you 'I told you so' a few months down the road." Amy's boys' smiling faces appeared on her computer as she logged in.

"Helene Anderson can come in at eleven!" Amy hollered a few minutes later as she rolled her chair back to her desk and hung up the phone. "I can't believe we're doing this." She came into Camille's office with a Post-it stuck on her left finger and a red folder under her arm, shoving a huge chocolate-covered doughnut in her mouth with her free hand.

"How's the diet coming along?" Camille asked.

Amy methodically licked her fingers. "A diet at a time like this would lead to certain death." She pointed a chocolate-laden finger at Camille. "You know this is the only thing that keeps me from completely losing it." The doughnut muffled her voice.

Camille plucked the Post-it off the clean finger and caught the folder before it landed on the floor. Before opening her own office a year earlier, it had been around ten years since she'd had a malpractice case; now this would be her second one in the last year. The first case she had handled in her new office had settled the past spring when she had learned that the doctor she was suing had basically been killing patients. The litigation had ended abruptly when the malpractice case turned into a criminal case of murder. There was no way this baby case would end so dramatically. But, still, she could feel her pulse racing as she dialed the Oregon Health Sciences OB department.

No luck. The expert she'd used the last time she'd handled a baby case had retired years ago. Maybe it had been too long. She flipped through her Rolodex and dialed one of her old malpractice buddies.

"Andrienne Scott, please. It's Camille Delaney." Camille watched a huge fishing boat glide past her office, blasting its horn to wake up the drawbridge attendant.

"Camille?"

"Hi, Andrienne." The bells and flashing lights caused the nonstop Seattle traffic to come to a standstill on the bridge. Camille closed the window to keep out the racket.

"Long time."

Camille sat back down. "Yeah."

The drawbridge rose and the big boat chugged through.

"So, what are you doing now? Rumor has it you're back in the malpractice biz. I hear you kicked Lincoln's butt last spring."

Camille scanned the piles of papers cluttering her desk. There was no way she was going to admit to Andrienne that she had stooped to taking auto cases to pay her overhead. Image was everything. Better change the subject. "I was wondering if you can give me the name of an OB who can sign a declaration for me in a dead baby case." Camille turned to a clean sheet on her lavender legal pad.

"Dead baby? It wouldn't happen to be against Jessica Kensington, would it?"

Camille dropped her pen. "Why do you ask?"

"That family's been making the rounds trying to find a lawyer for weeks, but Harvey Lowe filed an attorney's fee lien. He's really on a rampage."

Camille rubbed her eyes, wondering if she was up to this. "Did you turn her down?"

"Are you kidding? There's not enough money in a dead baby case to justify going head-to-head with Harvey Lowe over fees. I wouldn't waste my time."

Camille reminded herself it wasn't too late to call Kip and back out. "I appreciate the heads-up, but go ahead and give me a few names in case I do decide to get involved."

"Think it through carefully, Camille—you don't want to sink a pile of money into something like this. Especially if you end up in a big brouhaha with Lowe if and when the insurance company decides to fork over the dough. Hold out for a big one."

Easy for Andrienne Scott to say from her office on the twenty-fourth floor of the 1201 Third Avenue building. "I'll be careful. I promise."

———

On the third try, Camille finally got the nod from an OB expert. Now all she had to do was figure out a way to come up with the eight hundred dollars an hour to pay the guy. Unbelievably, the doc just happened to have a patient in labor with twins, so he offered to look at the records while he waited in the call room. Camille hypothesized that the good doctor must have his kids' tuition due this week, just like she did. Things were off to a roaring start.

Amy faxed the records while Camille got busy drafting her demand letter with an initial offer of five hundred thousand, hoping to get at least one fifty. With any luck, Amy would get her bonus in time to Christmas shop for her boys.

Just as Camille was polishing off her letter to the insurance company, the expert called back and explained that while there were limited occasions in which it was appropriate to do a Zavanelli maneuver, this wasn't one of them. Camille felt the edge of tension beginning to drain from her shoulders. Thank God someone would testify for her. He went on to explain that the fetal monitor tracing showed severe fetal distress and, given the fact that the patient had gestational diabetes, and therefore an increased chance of having a big baby, the patient should clearly have been sectioned much sooner. The expert commented that it was hard for him to believe that a doctor could stand by and watch a baby sink deeper and deeper into distress without intervening. He agreed to fax back a declaration laying out his opinion.

Once he received a retainer of five thousand dollars. Venmo would work nicely, he advised her.

———

Camille rounded the corner to the tiny waiting room just as a large blond woman who appeared to be of Norwegian descent came up to the reception desk.

"I'm Helene Anderson. I have an appointment with Ms. Delaney."

Camille smiled. "I'm Camille, come on back."

"My husband and I can't thank you enough for agreeing to look at our records." Helene's gray eyes pierced right through Camille, giving her a slight chill. There was something unsettling about the woman.

"Please, have a seat." Camille ushered Helene into her waterfront office and gestured to the sleek purple leather couch.

Amy came to the doorway with the fee agreement. "Would you like a glass of water or a cup of coffee?" she asked.

"No thanks." Helene's tight smile vanished as she turned to Camille. "I've read all about how juries don't place any value on the loss of a baby in this jurisdiction, but I need to tell you that there is no amount of money that can compensate us for what that doctor did to our family." She set her jaw and breathed heavily through her nose. "The loss of this child has devastated us beyond words."

Well, the woman certainly got to the point. Camille followed the client's lead and skipped the pleasantries. "I understand your outrage, but there are certain realities of litigation that any potential client needs to understand before getting into this process." Camille leaned forward on her elbows. "These cases can be unbelievably difficult for even the strongest of families."

"We're prepared for that."

"They'll dig through your entire past. It can get pretty ugly if you have any skeletons in your closet."

"I have nothing to hide." Helene stood.

"The defense lawyer will pull out all stops to humiliate you and make you doubt your resolve to continue what you've started."

"Let him try."

Camille watched as Helene looked at the array of family photographs jammed in every available space on Camille's bookshelves.

Camille went on. "I've been practicing law for years and I still wonder what's more stressful: the original tragedy that brings one to a lawyer, or the way the client is treated by the insurance defense lawyers once litigation is commenced."

"I want to reassure you, Camille, I can handle it. I was a member of the Olympic rowing team in 2004. We struggled all the way to Athens, then we pulled together and won a silver medal. I learned a lot about determination during those years." She looked deeply into Camille's eyes. "I especially learned about the importance of teamwork in surmounting an obstacle of that magnitude. I expect you and I will struggle together over the next few months." Helene's muscular legs carried her closer to Camille's bookcase. "Now, perhaps as fellow team members, we should get to know each other a bit better." Helene fingered the rope clay pencil holder Libby had made in kindergarten that stood next to Gracie's recently crafted paperweights.

"You have children," Helene said strongly. "Korean?"

This was a first. A client inquiring so directly into her personal life. Still, Helene had a point. They would be working closely and getting to know each other fairly well if things proceeded beyond the demand letter. A small amount of personal disclosure seemed okay. "Two adopted daughters and one foster daughter."

Helene's full lips parted into the most beautiful smile. "How old?"

"Seventeen, fourteen, and seven."

"How'd you happen to take on a foster child, if you don't mind my asking?"

Camille began to feel oddly comfortable with this Nordic woman. She paused, trying to decide how much personal information it was appropriate to share.

Helene's demeanor softened, and she dropped her voice. "I'm sorry, I didn't mean to pry. It's just that you seem to be a devoted mother. You've surrounded yourself with so much of your kids' stuff."

"It's okay. A lot of people wonder why we took on a foster child." Camille cradled her chin in her hands. "A few years back, actually about ten years ago, I quit working with your previous lawyer, Harvey Lowe." Camille picked up Grace's picture and ran her hand across the smooth glass. "And after I settled into my new career as a divorce lawyer, I got this great idea to take on a foster child. My husband and I'd adopted our other two when they were seven and four, so I had no idea what I was getting into with this adorable toddler."

Camille remembered fondly the chaos of toys and gadgets that had filled the house; and Gracie's midnight terrors that seemed to go on forever. Sadly, there would be no similar discord in the Anderson house. "But by the time I realized the task I'd undertaken, it was too late—I was hooked." She held up Grace's picture. "Can you blame me?" Camille hoped her monologue about her beautiful foster daughter didn't rekindle the distress Helene must have experienced when she returned home from the hospital empty-handed.

Camille remembered, ruefully, her own mother wailing in the night after baby Valerie failed to return from Children's Hospital and wondered if this supremely confident woman standing in front of her ever found herself weeping in the lonely darkness of night.

Helene took Gracie's picture from Camille. "She's precious." Helene smiled through her tears.

"I'm sorry. This has to be pure hell for you." Camille handed Helene a tissue.

Helene let the tears run freely down her face. "The reason I asked is that I want a lawyer who'll be able to convince the insurance company that this case isn't going to go away for one of their nuisance settlements." She looked at Camille through puffy eyes. "And I believe you can do it."

"Well, thanks, but I'm not a miracle worker. There's definitely a limit to what they'll pay."

Helene stood. "This is not about the money, Camille." She raised her voice. "I don't want their stinking money!" Helene gently put down the picture of Grace. "But I do want that doctor and her insurance company to twist in the wind for how they treat people who've lost children."

Camille watched the poised yet angst-ridden woman, pondering how she would go on after all was said and done in this case. Everyone certainly dealt with the pain of loss in their own way, and on their own timetable. A feeling of understanding about her mother's vendetta for good surged over Camille, much to her surprise.

Helene Anderson was a survivor, just like Pella Rallis.

"How can they live with themselves? Telling bereaved parents they can just have another child? It disgusts me," Helene spat.

Camille suspected this woman would do just fine with the rigors of heavy-handed litigation.

Helene smoothed her floral skirt. "You'll have to forgive my outbursts. It's just that I find this whole system so despicable at times." She shook her head. "I'm sure you must have something for me to sign."

Camille pointed at the lengthy retainer agreement, feeling a mixture of admiration and dread at having to notify Helene when the insurance company presented its meager settlement offer. But then again, maybe she wouldn't have to. If it came down to a battle between Helene Anderson and Jessica Kensington, Camille had a hunch Helene would hold her own quite well. Camille felt a rush of exhilaration as Helene put her bold signature on the retainer. Getting justice for women like Helene was why she had left the comfort of her former life as a divorce lawyer for the rich and opened a practice where she could represent regular people.

"I . . . I know I told you on the phone that we could cover the initial expenses," Helene said clearly. "But I didn't realize how much we'd have to come up with to pay off the hospital for the deductible."

Camille felt like a balloon, slowly deflating.

"We just don't have any money right now." Helene handed Camille the retainer. "I'm hoping you can float the costs for a while until we get our finances caught up."

Float the costs? It sounded so benign. It would hardly be a "float." It would be more like jumping into the rapids.

"I'll see what I can do." Camille hesitated, then realized that this was what being a people's lawyer was really all about.

Helene ignored Camille's trepidation and gave her a warm hug. "I just know you'll kick the insurance company's butt for us," she said, holding Camille by the shoulders.

Camille felt the rapids beginning to swirl her under and carry her away.

CHAPTER SEVEN

It was good to be home. Camille dropped her briefcase on the floor in the front hallway, where Libby greeted her from her perch on the stairs, her EarPods seemingly permanently implanted. "Mo-om! Where have you been?"

"Work." She glanced at her watch; it was six thirty, not any later than she usually got home. "What's up?"

"I can't believe you forgot!"

Camille searched her memory.

"School starts tomorrow, and you promised to get home by five to take me shopping for something to wear!"

Camille stifled a groan. So much for a nice relaxing evening watching the Mariners try to make it to the postseason.

"Okay, let's go!" She motioned for Libby to follow her. "Where's Gracie? We'll have to bring her with." She turned and hollered, "Gracie! Libby and I are going shopping! C'mon with us."

Skinny little Grace came tearing around the corner from the bedroom she shared with Libby on the first floor of the large "floating home." She was unusually tall for her age, but wispy just the same, with a classic second-grade smile. Despite her seven-year-old awkwardness, Camille knew Grace was destined to be a beauty.

"Grab your jacket. We're going to run over to U Village and do some back-to-school shopping." As the three of them climbed into the car, Camille waved at Cathy Swain, who had just pulled in.

"Whatever happened with that malpractice case?" Cathy shouted from her shiny blue BMW.

Camille grimaced jokingly. "I took it." She ducked.

"You are a certified nut!" Cathy shook her head. "Don't say I didn't warn you." She wagged her finger at Camille and squealed into the parking lot.

Gracie leaned forward from the back seat and put one arm on each front seat. "Hey, Mom! Trish called me—she said you weren't answering your phone."

Camille grabbed her phone and noticed the battery had died. Again. She did a mental calculation to figure out how much a new phone would cost as she plugged it into her car. She cursed the phone as she threw it on the passenger's seat.

"Sit back and buckle your seat belt," Camille said sternly, relieved that her friend had finally returned her call. There was no way she could proceed on the Anderson case without Trish. There was too much strange background information coming to light already, and it would take someone with Trish's expertise to help her put the disparate pieces together. She needed her pal on this one. Badly.

"Did she say what she wanted?" Camille asked.

"Yes. She said she broke her leg!" Gracie said proudly.

"Oh my God!" Camille nearly swerved off the road.

"Trish broke her leg?" Libby screamed. "And you didn't tell anyone?"

Grace's lower lip quivered. "I just did."

Camille regrouped and looked at Libby. "There's no reason to yell at her." She turned to Grace. "Exactly what did she say?"

"Something about the hospital," Grace lisped.

"Hospital!" Libby shrieked.

"Shh!" Camille held her hand up in Libby's face. "Did she say what hospital?" This couldn't be happening.

Tears began to snake down Grace's light brown skin. "I don't remember."

"Mother! We have to find her!" Libby directed. "If Trish is in the hospital, how is she going to work? Private investigators have to be able to sneak around."

"We'll find her." Camille pulled the car over in front of where the original Red Robin used to be, just south of the University Bridge.

Camille Googled the phone numbers for the three major medical centers in Seattle. On the second try she found Trish at Puget Sound Hospital where the nurse on duty told her that Trish was sleeping comfortably.

"We have to go see her, Mom! Now!" Libby was frantic.

Before Libby finished her sentence, Camille pulled a U-turn to head south on Eastlake, en route to "Pill Hill." The girls knew when to be quiet, so nothing was said as Camille snaked her way up the back of Capitol Hill. As she passed the row of medical office high-rises on Madison, she wondered to herself how she was going to be able to handle the Anderson case without Trish. Goddamn it.

———

When Camille and her entourage blasted into Trish's room, they found Sam sitting next to her bed reading a medical journal while she slept.

Camille kissed her husband softly on the lips. "What are you doing here?" she whispered.

"I gave a talk on drug-resistant staph at grand rounds this morning and ran into John Dexter, who told me he operated on Trish yesterday. I figured I'd better stop by and see how she's doing."

"What happened?" demanded Libby.

"Shh!" Sam cautioned his middle daughter.

Trish opened her eyes and smiled weakly. "Li'l windsurfing accident; I'll be fine."

Camille straightened the ID badge that was hanging crookedly from Sam's white lab coat. She loved the way he looked in his doctor garb. His curly salt-and-pepper hair made him look more and more distinguished as the years passed.

"Is Trish going to be okay?"

Sam shrugged. "Do I look like an orthopedic surgeon?"

"No, you look like an epidemiologist." She smiled. "But I have a hunch you may know a bit more about what happened than you're letting on."

Sam nodded. "Dexter just rounded on her. She had an angulated femur. He had to put a rod in. Says she'll be off her feet for at least six weeks."

"Six weeks?" Trish articulated what Camille was thinking.

Sam pulled his chair up close to the bed. "You made quite a mess of your leg, missy."

Trish shook her head. "Crap."

Libby slipped in between her parents. "Trish, can you work from here?" she asked matter-of-factly.

Trish smiled. "Are you kidding? I can work anywhere."

"Mother! You have to find her something she can do from the hospital," Libby announced.

Good idea. Maybe she could get Trish started on her laptop from her bed. Certainly, Trish would be bored to death just lying here.

Grace stood at the end of the bed. "I told them you were in the hospital." Her toothless grin filled the room as she nodded eagerly.

"Thanks, Gracie." Trish blew her a kiss. "You did a good job."

Gracie folded her arms proudly.

"Actually, there is something you can do for me. Once you feel up to it," Camille said.

Sam piped up. "Hold on a minute. She's just one day post-op. Give her a break."

Libby interrupted them. "Can I take Grace down to the cafeteria and get a snack?" Being the daughters of a university doc, the Delaney-Taylor girls were all too familiar with late-afternoon snacks in hospital cafeterias.

Sam handed them a ten-dollar bill. "Come right back."

"We will!" Grace shouted as they pumped their arms and wiggled their butts, speed walking down the equipment-lined corridor.

Sam pulled up a chair for Camille as Trish dozed off. "Did you see the text from your sister?" he whispered to Camille. "She's going to be doing a book signing at Barnes and Noble on September fifteenth, and she wants to come by and have an early dinner. Apparently she's going to be on some local morning talk show the next day."

Camille looked at her phone—dead battery, again. She grabbed Trish's plug and skimmed her sister's text. Eve had authored a string of highly successful how-to psychology books and seemed to spend more time promoting the books than she ever spent writing them—or studying psychology for that matter.

"Great." *That's all I need right now,* Camille thought to herself. Eve going on about whether she should get a loft in SoHo or a place in Oyster Bay out on Long Island.

"She said to call"—his voice took on a haughty English accent—"her personahl ahssistant to schedule dinnah."

"Jesus," Camille said under her breath as she scrolled though her unread texts.

Trish opened her bleary eyes. "I'm not so sure I'll be all that useful to you from here. I don't feel all that swift."

Sam's pager went off. He unsnapped it from his belt and held it up to see the digital readout. "Shoot. It's my research fellow. I forgot all about our meeting." He put his hand on Camille's shoulder. "Will you two be okay if I take off? We have to finalize the results of our STI project in order to have the first draft to the publisher by the end of the month."

"Go ahead." When Camille stood, she was exactly as tall as her husband. She kissed him and patted his perfectly tight butt.

Sam winked at Camille and turned to Trish, squeezing her hand. "I'll give Dr. Dexter a call tomorrow and see how you're doing."

Trish smiled weakly. "Thanks for coming."

Camille waited until her husband closed the door behind him, then turned to Trish, hoping she could pique her interest. "I've got a case against an obstetrician. Some local OB prima donna," she said hopefully.

Trish's eyes began to clear up. "Huh, an OB case." She nodded with approval. "That should turn the ol' finances around." She smiled drunkenly.

C'mon, Trish, where's that undying enthusiasm? "It's a dead baby case, so it's not exactly the answer to my financial dreams, but I get to do the right thing for a really nice woman and her husband."

"Which is why you moved out of your fancy downtown office to the lake in Fremont and took on the people's causes . . ."

Before Trish could continue, Camille got up and rearranged her covers. "I hired an expert today who said he'd sign a declaration saying that the doc violated the standard of care. I can get these people a quick settlement with that and a good demand letter. They'll get some semblance of justice and hopefully move on with their lives." She rinsed out Trish's water pitcher and refilled it. Once a nurse, always a nurse.

As she flitted around the room, Camille could feel Trish's concern about her taking on this case. She stopped to straighten a stack of towels on the windowsill.

Trish looked at Camille questioningly. "Where are you going to get the money to pay the costs of a case like that?"

Camille filled a basin for Trish to wash up in.

"That expert is gonna charge you, what? Four, five hundred an hour?" Trish asked.

"Try eight." Camille winced as she squeezed the excess water out of a washcloth and handed it to Trish. "It's a good case," she added quickly.

"I'm sure it will be a very good case for someone with the resources to properly process it." Trish stopped wiping her face.

Camille emptied the basin. "I'm never going to change people's lives handling hit-and-runs and whiplashes." She paused. "Besides, let's not lose sight of the fact that a baby died here," she said sternly.

"And there's nothing you can do to bring the baby back." Trish shook her head. "There's no way you're going to make any money on this one. Maybe you should go back downtown to the high-end divorce work. That's where the money is."

"It wasn't about money then either. I loved most of my clients, and I learned tons about businesses and all kinds of financial entities, but you know as well as I do that it was time for a change."

"Well, then, what about being happy with things the way they are? You have a great life. Look at that hunk of a husband you have. He could almost make me switch teams." Trish pointed at the door where Sam had made his hasty exit moments ago. "And there is no more delightful troupe of girls than those Delaney-Taylor characters."

"Yeah, my family's great; it's just that I have a problem with the two-bit fender-bender lawyer part of the equation." Camille unwrapped a stiff hospital toothbrush and squeezed a line of toothpaste across the bristles.

"Camille, you've got to learn to define your own accomplishments. It's not necessary to be on national TV, or in the front of a room of fawning admirers like your sister, Eve, or your mom in order to be a successful person."

Camille shook the loaded toothbrush at Trish. "You have to admit, a big settlement for these lovely people would be nice, though."

Trish held her hand out for the toothbrush. "It depends at what cost. Life's going to pass you by while you wait for your chance to make a difference. You might as well buy a lottery ticket."

Camille sighed and handed a paper cup of water to Trish. This was sounding too familiar. She and Sam had been down this road a few thousand times since she left the prestigious divorce firm on the forty-second floor of Two Union Square. "I'm just tired of seeing pictures of Harvey Lowe in the paper, climbing into his Learjet. He couldn't care less about the people he represents. It's all ego for him."

Trish swished the water and toothpaste out of her mouth. "And you're tired of seeing your sister on TV and your mother at the front of a room of her followers. And don't forget about your dad. There's no one in the New York jazz scene who wouldn't pay a few hundred bucks to get a front row table to see Connie Delaney live and in person."

Trish was right. One of the reasons she'd left the comfort of the downtown scene was to have the ability to take meaningful cases in hopes of making a name for herself. And here she was scraping a living together representing hit-and-run victims. Camille turned away and rinsed and repackaged Trish's plastic hospital toiletry kit as she blinked back the tears.

She envied Trish's love for her work. Whether she was sitting in front of a computer or out in the field conducting an undercover investigation, Trish was content. Kind of like Sam, happily whiling away his days in the lab, teaching medical students the wonder of infectious diseases. Neither Trish nor Sam had any need at all to be a superstar; they were just happy, well-adjusted human beings.

Camille wondered what was wrong with her. Why was she always searching for something that seemed to be just out of her reach?

CHAPTER EIGHT

Camille lay back on the weightlifting bench, took a deep breath, and tried to psych herself up to do one more set of chest presses. Through the giant window, she watched as the UW rowing crew slid down the glassy ship canal in the early light of dawn. Camille had gotten to the gym early in order to stage a "chance meeting" with one of the OB nurses at the hospital where Kensington practiced. Camille lifted weights in time with the music emanating from the studio where Deanne Stillerman directed her Zumba class through a Madonna-like headset.

"Nice job, everyone!" Deanne's voice boomed over the sound system as she finished stretching and threw a towel around her neck.

Camille hastily returned her weights to the stand and sprinted over to intercept the fitness teacher.

"Hey! Deanne!"

The short nurse had the shoulders of a linebacker and the chest and waist of a Playboy Bunny. She turned to Camille and smiled. "I haven't seen you in months. Where've you been? I thought you quit the gym."

"Nah, my knees couldn't take any more pounding. I'm sticking with weights for a while." Camille flexed her well-defined bicep jokingly.

The sturdily built woman feigned disapproval. "And how do you get your heart rate up just doing weights?"

Camille laughed. "You don't want to know."

Deanne leaned over the drinking fountain next to the locker room.

"Do I remember right that you work in the OB department at Sound?" Camille asked.

Deanne splashed water on her face and turned to Camille. "Yep, ten years now." She shook the water off her face. "Jeez, can you believe how fast time flies?"

"Tell me about it." Camille followed Deanne into the locker room.

The nurse sat down, untied her shoes, and kicked them into her locker while Camille straddled the stool opposite her.

"You know a doc by the name of Kensington?" Camille asked.

"Of course." Deanne peeled her sweaty workout suit off and tried to stuff her huge breasts into a skimpy gym towel. "Why do you ask?"

"I . . . I, uh, have a friend who's pregnant and is thinking about going to her."

"Oy! I'd never let any friend of mine go to Jessica Kensington."

Camille raised her eyebrows. "Why not?"

"She's a lot sweeter than she is smart." Deanne grabbed her shampoo and conditioner. "If you get my drift."

"Sweet?"

"Oy vey. Let me tell you. Back when I was new at the hospital, she was a nice, conscientious doc, everyone loved her. Then in the past few years something happened and now she's all over the place. She's a regular sugar-pie when she wants to be. And then boom—with no warning she turns into a major bitch." Deanne stopped. "No idea what happened to her."

Ah-ha, at last. Someone who isn't a card-carrying member of the Jessica Kensington fan club. Camille was dying to know what the nurse meant by her comments, but she could hardly follow her into the shower.

Deanne stopped. "I'm not kidding. Everyone around there thinks Kensington walks on water, but the truth is, she's gone off the deep end." Deanne held her hand out facedown and flopped it so her fingers pointed straight down. "You take my word for it, darling."

Camille stood on the scale and fiddled with the sliding weights. "What do you mean?"

"She's sloppy. Like I said, she used to be good, cared about patients, and was easy to work with. But now, she makes bad decisions and tries to cover them up by being, like, miss cheerleader." Deanne stuck her pointer finger into her cheek and bobbled her head back and forth, Valley-girl style. "I can't stand her," Deanne said and pulled the shower curtain closed.

—

Amy parked in front of their well-worn wood-frame office building and pawed through her sons' helmets and shoulder pads scattered throughout her car, trying to find her briefcase. The football gear reminded her that she was going to have to come up with money for the sports fees this week or the boys wouldn't be able to play. She sighed and brushed the dried mud off her purse, then extracted a giant chocolate éclair from a grease-stained bag, which she crunched up and threw onto the floor in anger. Her ex-husband hadn't paid any child support in almost six months. The asshole. She stuck the pastry in her mouth and headed for the front door, rummaging for her keys. Swearing under her breath at the ringing phone, she quickly slipped her key into the lock.

"Herro?"

"Amy?"

"Hol' on." Amy placed the sloppy pastry on a clean pad of paper and dumped her bags on the floor next to a huge stack of medical records. She wiped her mouth with the back of her hand. "Hello?"

"Hi, it's Missy."

"Oh my God, I haven't seen you in ages!" Amy remembered fondly the days she and Missy Barron had spent in paralegal school trying to understand the intricacies of legal research. "How've you been?" Amy stretched the phone cord over to the sink and measured the water for coffee. "Where are you working these days?"

"Harvey Lowe's. He does mostly big med-mal cases."

Missy Barron is working for Harvey Lowe? The coffee grounds skittered across the counter as she spilled the french roast. "Shit, hang on." She dropped the phone and wiped up the mess. "Hello?"

"I'm here. How's it going out in the Center of the Universe?" Missy asked, referring to Fremont by its cheeky little moniker.

"It's okay." Amy glanced at the ever-growing pile of unpaid bills in her in-basket.

"And how are your boys?"

Amy felt kind of like she was cavorting with the enemy. "Reilly just got elected class president," she stammered.

The aroma of coffee filled the small office as the machine began to gurgle and drip.

"Class president? How old is he?"

"Eight. Second grade." Amy wondered how Missy could work for that greedy little creep.

"And how old is Nathan now?"

"Eleven." *What's she getting at?* Surely Missy wasn't calling after all these years to get a status check on the boys.

Amy looked up into a delicate Asian face framed by spiky blue hair hovering above the reception desk. Her tongue bar glistened as she smiled.

"Oops, can you hold again? There's a messenger here."

"Sure."

Amy stamped the documents "copy-received" and grabbed the phone. "Thanks, Lucia." She waved at the messenger, then turned her attention back to Missy. "Sorry. It's kind of a one-person show around here."

"You like it?"

"It's okay. I love Camille, but it's getting old having to do every-thing myself."

"I couldn't imagine it. I finally got my own secretary. I haven't had to type a transmittal letter or schedule a deposition in over a year."

"Huh." *Must be nice to have a boss with an unlimited budget even if he does have an ego the size of Texas.*

"Let's schedule a lunch. You're working too hard out there on the lake. I want to talk you into coming back downtown."

Ah-ha, so that was it. Missy might as well save her breath. Amy would never leave Camille. The bells on the doorknob jingled, announc-ing Helene Anderson's arrival.

"The money's terrific down here," Missy added quickly. "I never dreamed I'd make so much as a paralegal."

There's more to life than money.

"Let me call you back." Amy looked at Helene and pointed to a seat. "Camille should be here in a few minutes." She turned back to the phone. "I gotta go."

Amy hung up the phone and pulled a mirror from her desk drawer, pushed her shoulder-length frosted hair back from her face, and spritzed it with hair spray. She probably could make more money downtown. Maybe she could just have lunch with Missy in order to find out, then convince Camille to give her a raise when they had some financial breathing room. She watched Helene making a cup of tea over at the kitchenette and reminded herself that there wouldn't be any raise soon. Amy leaned closer to the mirror and meticulously separated her eyelashes to prevent clumping.

Helene walked up behind the light maple reception desk and admired the pictures of Amy's sons. "They're darling."

Amy held her lipstick in midair. "Thanks." She turned to face Helene and put down her makeup. "I'm not sure I've had an opportunity to tell you how very sorry I am about you losing your baby."

Helene sat in a secretarial chair, rolled up next to Amy, and put a hand on Amy's knee. "Thanks." She dipped her tea bag up and down, then swiveled around to drop it into a wastebasket. "I appreciate how much help you've been, getting Camille to review the records and everything."

Amy felt a pang of guilt for having done everything she could to try to dissuade Camille from taking the case.

Helene stared at Amy. "I know most lawyers don't want to mess around with a so-called dead baby case." She looked at Amy's family photos. "But I know you guys'll do a great job for us."

"Thanks, we'll do our best." Amy turned away, unable to look Helene directly in the eye. This thing had to settle quickly with as few costs as possible. They couldn't afford it any other way. Amy pulled a letter out of the Anderson file and handed it to Helene. "Here's your copy of the demand we sent to the insurance company last week."

Helene put the letter in her purse and wandered back to the tiny waiting room where she glanced at an old copy of the *Trial News* sitting on the end table next to her chair. Amy gasped as she realized that the front-page article was the one about one of Harvey Lowe's cases against Kensington. That case had involved a baby who died shortly after birth. The pregnancy had been the product of an aggressive fertility treatment program. Lowe had convinced the insurance company that the baby had more value than a baby that was naturally conceived since the family couldn't necessarily have another one. He'd settled the case for six million dollars.

Amy bolted over and tried to nonchalantly straighten up the stack of magazines. There was no way Camille could force that kind of settlement in the Anderson case, she thought to herself as she shuffled the Lowe article to the bottom of the pile.

"Wasn't that Harvey Lowe on the cover of that magazine?" Helene asked.

"I . . . I don't think so." Amy shook her head a bit too forcefully.

"Sure it is." Helene sorted through the stack. "Let me see."

"I don't see anything about Lowe here."

"It's the one on the bottom." Helene grabbed the old edition of the *Trial News.* "See, here? It's Harvey Lowe." Helene skimmed the article. "So he actually convinced the insurance company that this woman's case was worth more than mine because she'd been a fertility patient?"

"I guess so."

"That's despicable."

Amy had an idea. "You know, Camille could make the same argument on your behalf if you'd undergone fertility treatment in order to get pregnant."

Helene shook her head. "Sorry. This one will have to stand on its own merits." Her eyes focused like a laser on Amy. "I'm sure Camille will be able to extract an appropriate measure of blood from Kensington and her insurance company for us—regardless of the circumstances of Zachary's conception."

Amy grimaced. After reading that, she knew Camille would have a hell of a time convincing Helene to settle for the pittance typically offered in cases like these. Her boys stared at her from her computer. She kissed her fingers and lightly touched the screen.

CHAPTER NINE

Camille blasted through the doorway in a whirlwind, two lattes balanced in one hand and her bulging Tumi backpack in the other. She glanced at Helene and knew immediately that something was up.

"Am I late?" she asked as Amy grabbed the cups so that Camille could shake Helene's hand.

Helene stood. At five ten, it wasn't often that Camille found herself eye to eye with another woman.

"I believe I'm a bit early," Helene stated. "It's a habit of mine." She paused. "Being early."

Camille looked at Amy. "Now there's a habit we could use around here."

"We?" Amy joked.

"Very funny." Camille took off her long black trench coat. "Give me just a sec, okay, Helene?"

Helene remained standing, her arms crossed. She shivered slightly and scrunched up her shoulders. "Take your time."

Camille hurried into her office and picked up the thin pile of checks Amy had left on her chair for her to sign. They'd been through the bills the day before and pulled out the ones that absolutely had to be paid and sent out in the morning's mail. Camille slumped when she reached Amy's paycheck. She knew Amy was facing big expenses this year and would receive no help at all from the boys' deadbeat dad. Camille grabbed her phone and Venmoed Amy another two hundred dollars. It wasn't much, but at least it would cover the upcoming football fees. And as soon as the Anderson case settled, she could give Amy a big enough bonus to get Nathan started at the orthodontist. Camille signed the checks and stuck them back in the envelopes. Hopefully, the Anderson case would tide her over until a really big case appeared.

Camille led Helene in from the reception area and took a seat in the easy chair. She gestured for her client to sit on the couch. She hated the idea of a lawyer sitting behind some big imposing desk, like she was somehow better than her client.

But Helene remained standing, which made it necessary for Camille to crane her neck in order to look up at her. "What's up?" Camille asked lightly, trying to enliven her client's stoic demeanor. Helene definitely had something on her mind.

Helene held out the letter to the insurance company that she had approved after many long and tortuous conversations with Camille the previous week. "I'm really sorry. I just can't do this." Helene burst into tears. "I can't just let them off with some kind of nuisance settlement." She wiped her nose. "Not after what they did."

Camille was torn between comforting her client and figuring out how to explain that the letter had already been sent and wasn't exactly open for discussion. "I know how upsetting this whole situation must be for you and your family." She handed Helene a tissue. "First you lose your beautiful baby, then some lawyer tries to convince you that the legal system just doesn't place a very big value on your loss." Camille paused; she hated having to tell a client that their loved one had limited value in the eyes of the legal system. "It's a lot to take in."

Helene held the unused tissue in her fist as her tear-streaked face turned red and blotchy. "I appreciate your sympathy, but you really don't know what we've been through." She sniffed.

I know more about it than I ever wished I would.

"Of course I don't." Camille wondered how her own parents would have handled the fact that baby Valerie just wasn't "worth" all that much. Looking back on the angst that Valerie's death had wrought on her own family, she decided that there was no amount of money that could even begin to compensate them. Why even bother?

Helene raised her voice. "How on earth can you expect us to give in to some little bean counter who sits behind a computer at an insurance company?" She wadded up the settlement letter and held it tightly. "You've demanded five hundred thousand dollars and told us to expect to settle for around one fifty." Helene held up the ball of paper still in her clenched hand. "I can't do it. I won't."

Oh brother. What now?

"I want you to revoke this demand immediately." Helene's voice was infused with a deep sense of outrage.

"Maybe we should talk about this a bit," Camille coaxed.

"What's to talk about? I've heard your feeble explanation about how lawyers put dollar values on babies' lives. But I just don't buy it. I know a jury would give us more. Lots more."

Camille was aware that she'd been rather forceful in encouraging the Andersons to settle their case quickly and quietly. She wondered if her own need for getting caught up with her bills had clouded her judgment. But as a seasoned professional who'd been down this road more times than she'd care to admit, she knew the insurance companies were right. They had a phenomenal record of convincing juries that a grieving family "could always have another baby."

"I know we've been over this a number of times." Camille felt ashamed of the way the legal system revictimized plaintiffs just by the outlandishly adversarial nature of the process. "It's just that going through a trial is way more stressful than most people realize. And it's horribly disappointing when the end result is the same or less than the settlement offered by the insurance company early in the litigation."

Helene didn't budge. "I don't care."

It was hard to blame Helene for her vitriolic reaction to the facts of life in the world of litigation. "And remember, this is basically a financial decision for you." Camille tried to be as soothing as she could. "Let's say the insurance company offers you a hundred thousand dollars next week. That means you'll get . . ." She grabbed a calculator and did some quick math, figuring 60 percent less costs. "You'd walk away with sixty-three thousand dollars in your pocket."

Helene sat stone-faced.

"Now, if we go to trial and get that same hundred thousand dollars in a verdict, let's see what you'll net." Camille scratched a list as she spoke. She glanced at Helene, trying to engage her in the process as her fingers flew across the calculator. "You'd net roughly thirty-four thousand dollars. After you pay the costs of processing the case."

Helene flexed her jaw and breathed noisily through her nose.

It certainly wasn't the first time Camille's dismal discussion of the financial realities of litigation seemed to meet with more than a little resistance from a stubborn client.

Still no reaction from Helene.

Camille continued, "You need to compare the thirty-four thousand net from a hundred-thousand-dollar verdict to the sixty-three thousand you'd net if you took a hundred-thousand-dollar settlement now." She pointed to the original number. "And, if you take a settlement now of, say, seventy five, you'll avoid the trauma of a trial and come out with somewhere in the neighborhood of forty-five in your pocket, which is more than the thirty-four you'd net with a jury verdict of a hundred. Is this making any sense?"

"Are you finished?" Helene asked, her voice low and gravelly.

"It's up to you; I just want you to think about it. Logically, if you can."

Helene stared at Camille for a few long minutes and then said slowly, "Let me get this straight. You're suggesting that we try to convince an insurance company to pay us one hundred thousand dollars to compensate us for the fact that Jessica Kensington killed our child. And you told us before that the settlement would have to be confidential."

"We discussed this last week. Almost all malpractice settlements contain confidentiality clauses."

Helene held out the *Trial News*. "This one didn't." She waved the newspaper around in Camille's face. The paper snapped as Helene hit it sharply. "Here's that jerk, Harvey Lowe, with some other poor souls whose lives that doctor ruined." She spat the word "doctor" disdainfully. "And you want us to accept what amounts to hush money!" The pages of the paper scattered as she forcefully threw it to the ground.

Camille grimaced when she recognized the *Trial News* article about one of Lowe's cases against Kensington.

Camille gently reached down and picked up the pages of the *Trial News* off the floor. She waited for Helene to calm down, dreading the conversation she was about to initiate.

Helene took a shaky breath and rubbed her eyes with her fists. "I'm just not going to betray Zachary's memory like that. He deserves better."

Zachary. It was the first time Camille had heard the baby's name. Butterflies flitted around inside her stomach. This was about a real live baby, not just the subject of an insurance settlement. She ached to speak with her heart and not her head. But that wasn't what lawyers did. They had to explain the risks and benefits of litigation.

"I want to go to trial," Helene announced defiantly. "I want justice for my baby." She glared at Camille and said almost threateningly, "And I don't care how much it costs."

Camille's shoulders slumped. "I know," she said sympathetically. "It's just not that easy." She felt the quick and easy settlement slipping away.

"What do you mean?"

"Like I told you last week, the system isn't set up to bring about justice. It's simply who can prove what, and what it's worth."

"We can prove that she killed my baby."

Camille nodded. "Well, she didn't technically kill the baby, but her malpractice is clear. But you can never be sure how a jury will see your case. And this particular case is complicated by the fact that Kensington is apparently quite the charmer, and that is not a factor to be ignored here."

Helene shook her head slowly. "Her personality isn't going to be of much help once the jury hears what she did to my baby."

"But like I've explained, the statistics are that the doctors win about eighty-five percent of all trials in King County."

"What about all the runaway jury verdicts you read about?" Helene asked. "There's a litigation explosion going on."

"Propaganda drummed up by the insurance companies."

"What do you mean?"

"People want to believe their doctors are infallible. It scares them to think that someone in their own family could be the victim of a medical mistake. The reality is that the juries usually side with the doctors because that's what they want to believe."

"So you're saying that we wouldn't win at trial?" Helene asked.

"No," Camille tried to soften the impact by dropping her voice. "I'm saying that the odds are against it."

No response.

"And even if we did win," Camille continued, "the next question is how much a baby is worth to a jury."

Helene covered her mouth to catch her choking sob. "He was priceless."

"Of course he was. It's just like I told you, the insurance defense lawyer will argue to the jury that despite this tragedy, your baby was replaceable."

"Jesus Christ!" Helene methodically pulled apart the clump of tissue she had wadded up in her hand. "You keep saying that!" She wiped her eyes, then looked searchingly at Camille. "What's wrong with these people anyway?"

It was the same question Camille had asked herself every time she read about a big loss, or whenever she'd gambled and lost herself.

To date, she had failed to come up with an answer as to how a perfectly nice, seemingly caring and compassionate person could become so cold and unfeeling once they entered a jury box. She had no brilliant response.

Helene blew her nose into the shredded tissue, then silently gathered her purse.

Camille stood to usher her client to the waiting room. "Why don't you discuss this with your husband and call me back tomorrow." She sheepishly held up the settlement letter. "I'm sure the insurance company won't even have looked at this yet."

Helene stopped in the doorway and spoke very slowly and deliberately. "I will get justice for what they did to my son." She looked harshly at Camille. "With or without your help."

CHAPTER TEN

Camille stood in the middle of her office staring at the pictures of her three girls, wondering what she'd do if any one of them were taken from her. She tried to imagine how Helene Anderson, or for that matter her own mother, felt after losing a child—but it was too overwhelming for her to wrap her brain around.

Helene's question echoed inside her head. What was wrong with those people?

Maybe she should take a shot at convincing a jury of the value of a precious baby. But the tingle of enthusiasm for actually taking the case to trial sputtered and died when she looked at the pile of bills beckoning her. Trying the case could bring her to financial ruin. The costs would be in the tens of thousands of dollars. She gazed out the window toward the lake, where the wind was whipping up a late summer storm.

Amy's voice came over the speakerphone, "Your mom's on line two. And I'm taking off for lunch in a few minutes. You need anything?"

"No, go ahead." Camille picked up the phone. "Mom?"

"Hello, darling, I just wanted to give you a call and say goodbye. My plane leaves in fifteen minutes."

"Plane?" Her heart sank. "I thought you were sticking around until the beginning of October." *Sometimes you just need your mom.*

"I was, but I got a call from one of our advocates. There's been a terrible accident." Pella raised her voice in order to be heard above the background din of the busy airport. "A mom was trying to use some kind of camp stove and the line got clogged. Her tent blew up with her and her five children inside. I need to get back and put together a video about how to properly operate a camp stove—and I have to get it translated into eight languages so I can take it to all the tents in the camp. My team has started production, but I need to be there to supervise. We lost five children. The camp is like a village and the village needs to come together and mourn."

And when we lose a child in the US, we sit around and try and figure how much it's worth, Camille said to herself, then paused. What had her mother said? When the village loses a child . . . Huh . . .

"Be careful, Mother."

"I love you, dear. I'll be in touch."

Maybe she could convince a jury that they were the village and this was their child. Camille grabbed her jacket and headed out to the dock to think her idea through. Amy followed as far as the parking lot and paused as she opened her car door. "Is everything okay with your mother?"

"Everything is more okay with my mother than it is with me."

Amy climbed into her car. "Are you all right?"

"Yeah . . . Yeah, actually, I'm fine." Camille closed Amy's door gently.

Amy started her car, then rolled down the window. "I'm off to lunch with a friend. Want me to bring you anything?"

"No, I think I'll walk up to the poke place and get something to go." She waved as Amy drove away. When she turned around, Camille noticed Helene Anderson sitting in her minivan looking out at the water. She walked over and knocked lightly on the window. "Want to take a walk out onto the dock? It's a great place to watch a storm brewing."

Helene hesitated for a moment, then silently followed Camille toward the folksy little marina in front of her office.

When they reached the end of the pier, Camille put her hand on the large blond woman's arm. "Look, Helene . . ."

Helene still clutched the rapidly disintegrating tissue in her fist. "You don't have to try and convince me anymore."

Camille held up her hand. "No, let me finish." She pulled her jacket close to protect herself from the thin spray coming off the intermittent whitecaps on the lake. "I'm sick and tired of making excuses for the system." Camille paused. "You're completely right, there's no amount of money that can compensate you for what you've lost. And any insurance defense lawyer who tries to minimize Zachary's value in front of a jury should be ashamed of themself." Camille took a deep breath. "I'd like to take a shot at convincing a jury of the value of your baby's life."

It was hard to distinguish between the rain and the tears Helene brushed from her face. Camille locked her gaze onto Helene's clear gray eyes. "I'd like to take your case to trial."

—

The first elevator bank in the Columbia Tower deposited Amy on the fortieth floor. From there she rounded the corner of the "sky lobby," past the Starbucks, to the smaller elevators that took her to Harvey Lowe's office on the seventy-fourth floor. There, she approached a receptionist who could have been Cindy Crawford's younger sister.

"I'm here for Missy Barron."

The receptionist sized her up. Amy could tell from the snooty look that the receptionist had decided that Amy was neither an important lawyer nor a client. "Name?"

"Amy Hutchins." Was it her imagination or did they keep this place a bit on the chilly side?

"Hang on." The Cindy Crawford look-alike turned her attention to the ringing phone bank. "Law Offices of Harvey Lowe." She grabbed a pile of mail and gracefully began slitting it with her razor-like opener.

Amy hovered by the window, watching the dark clouds creep ominously across the sky from the south.

Several minutes passed and the receptionist beckoned her. "Who did you say you were here for again?"

Was the woman not listening or was she just stupid? "Missy. Missy Barron," Amy snapped.

"Oh, right." The woman scanned the huge console and hit a button. "Missy, there's someone here for you." She looked up at Amy. "Your name?"

Amy bristled. "Amy," she said with an edge in her voice. "Amy Hutchins."

"Says her name is Amy Hutchins." The receptionist resumed her mail-opening routine and said without looking up, "She'll be right out."

The scene at the Law Offices of Harvey Lowe was reminiscent of the firm that Amy and Camille had left just a little over a year earlier. Warm and fuzzy it wasn't.

The jangle of Missy's familiar armload of bracelets preceded her as she rounded the corner to the ostentatious lobby. Missy ushered Amy into the elevator and hit the "up" button. The only place that was higher than Lowe's office on the seventy-fourth floor was the exclusive Columbia Tower Club. Amy had fond memories of Camille taking her up there for lunch when they worked downtown. It seemed like a lifetime ago.

"Harvey gives us all individual memberships to the club on our fifth anniversary with him," Missy explained as she led the way across the dark marble floor to the ornate desk where the hostess greeted her by name and showed them to their table.

Amy took a seat facing north, looking down over Lake Union where she recognized their tiny wood-frame office building, about five miles north of downtown. From her vantage point, she could see the shadow of the storm making its way across the lake until it had completely enveloped their office.

Their lunch was perfectly prepared and the conversation friendly, but as soon as the waiter delivered their dessert, Missy got to the point. "I guess you're wondering why I called this little meeting."

Amy rotated the triple chocolate mousse in the tall parfait glass, appreciating it as if it were a true work of art. With all the restraint she could muster, given the huge chocolate trophy in front of her, she looked up at her friend. "I have to say I'm a bit curious. Not that it isn't nice of you to lavish me with this kind of masterpiece." She respectfully scooped a spoonful of the fragrant chocolate into her mouth and closed her eyes.

"We're going to have an opening for another paralegal."

Amy sat up, swallowing before she was able to completely savor the liquid heaven melting throughout her entire body. "I beg your pardon?"

"Harvey likes to personally choose his staff, and he says he's heard lots of good stuff about you." Missy smiled. "I told him we went to school together, so he asked me to scope you out and see if you'd be interested."

"Jeez. I'm flattered." It was all Amy could think of to say. "But . . . I really can't leave Camille," she added quickly.

Missy scooted her chair closer and pushed her stylish brown flip behind her ears. "I know you guys are close, but you've just spent the last hour telling me how tough it is for you, being a single mom and all." Missy looked around the room. "Look at this place, Amy. Who'd have ever thought I'd be hanging out in the most exclusive club down-town?" Missy giggled. "I'll admit, working for Harvey has its moments. But for the most part, it's un-fucking-believable up here."

Amy took in the surroundings. The difference between being here literally floating over the rumbling storm, and being down on the homey little dock in the funky Fremont neighborhood couldn't have been more distinct. It was impossible to qualitatively differentiate the two. But then again, she didn't intend to.

Finally, Amy spoke. "Camille and I have been through too much together for me to just up and leave her."

"I know you're loyal to Camille. But what about your boys?" Missy's bracelets tinkled as she folded and smoothed her napkin.

Suddenly the chocolate mousse didn't seem to be the center of the world anymore.

"I know you'd do anything for Camille. And she'd do anything for you," Missy said gently. "But it doesn't sound like she can bail you out this time. She simply can't afford you anymore."

Amy toyed with the long parfait spoon. "How much did you say the starting salary is?"

"Ninety thousand. Plus bonuses."

That was twenty thousand a year more than she was making now. "But how can you stand working for Harvey Lowe?"

"He's not what you think." Missy held up her hand. "I know. I know. He's an aggressive son of a bitch to other lawyers. But he treats his staff like royalty. Really." Missy hunched her narrow shoulders forward. "Last year I got a thirty-thousand-dollar bonus."

It would be the ultimate betrayal, her joining Camille's nemesis, Harvey Lowe. Amy hadn't been with Camille back then, but from everything Camille had told her, Lowe'd been a real shit to her and had as much as kicked her out of his firm. Amy wondered if Camille would have made the "temporary" ten-year switch to divorce law if she and Lowe hadn't come to such a parting of ways. Camille seemed much more suited to malpractice litigation. It was definitely where her heart was.

"I don't know, Missy. Camille and Harvey have quite a history. I'd feel like such a traitor."

Missy nodded knowingly through pursed lips. "Yeah, but aren't you kind of a traitor to your boys by staying at a place where you can't even afford the orthodontist?"

This was hitting too close to home. Amy looked at her watch and stood up abruptly. "I gotta get back." It wasn't until she was halfway across the dining room that she looked back at the barely-touched chocolate mousse silhouetted against the gathering storm.

—

Camille sorted through the stacks of pending soft-tissue-injury files that had been piling up on her office floor. They'd have to wait until she got a break in the Anderson case. She kicked off her high heels and climbed up on a chair to reach the heavy obstetric textbooks on the top shelf of her bookcase and blew the dust off each one as she dropped them to the floor with a noisy thud.

The place was actually looking like it had some semblance of order. Amy would be shocked. Camille pulled out a giant flip chart—the one with the sticky pages, so she could attach them to her office wall. She hopped up onto the arm of the slippery leather couch so she could tack the top edges of each piece as high as she could reach.

She uncapped a red marker pen with her teeth and wrote in block letters: *TO DO*. Under that she listed: *1. Background check—Kensington (Trish); 2. Call Deanne Stillerman (Camille); 3. Two more experts (Camille); 4. Organize med recs (Amy); 5. Notice of appearance (Amy); 6. Draft interrogatories (Amy).*

On the next piece, she wrote *WITNESSES*. That one would be left blank for a while.

Camille stepped back and admired her list before turning her attention to the desk, where she swept up all the extraneous papers and deposited them on Amy's counter. Turning her attention back to her office, she methodically organized her medical textbooks. She picked up a dog-eared book and flipped randomly through the musty-smelling pages, knowing she'd have the pertinent chapters nearly memorized within a few weeks.

Finally, with the thick text in hand, she sat back and swiveled around in her chair, energized at the feeling of being at the helm of her own "command central."

Enough lollygagging, she admonished herself. She dialed Trish, who was still stuck at home on bed rest, and announced that she was on her way downtown to bring her some groceries and find out how the preliminary investigation of Kensington was coming along.

But first things first. Camille dialed Deanne Stillerman, the nurse who moonlighted as an aerobics instructor. "Hi. It's Camille. From the gym?"

"I know who you are," Deanne said quickly.

Camille flipped to a clean piece of lavender paper. "If you have a minute, I'd like to ask you a few questions about Jessica Kensington."

"I knew it! You're gonna sue her, aren't you?"

Deanne worked for a potential defendant in the case. "I guess that'd be confidential."

"I hear ya." Deanne snapped her gum into the phone. "What do you want to know?"

"I was just wondering if you know anything at all about her personal life, anything going on with her that'd be disruptive." Camille was searching for something that would explain the doctor's complete lack of concern for the fetal distress on the monitor strip.

"Let's see," Deanne said. "She's the president of the gynecology society, which says more about her perky personality than her skill as a doctor."

"Hmm." Camille wondered why Deanne had such a thorn in her side about the popular doctor.

"And . . . she spends an awful lot of time in Hawaii. Apparently her mother is pretty sick or something. Her Highness was gone a lot last winter. And she takes off abruptly a couple of times a year, which screws up all the schedules of the OB staff. She's usually out for a month or so. It's totally rude of her, but to be honest, it suits me just fine, thank you very much."

Camille jotted a few quick notes. "Anything else?"

"Nothing that comes to mind."

Camille elected not to pressure Deanne this early in the investigation. "Well, thanks for your time."

"I know you can't tell me anything, but I hope you kick her butt. I'm sure you'll find out sooner or later that this isn't her first fuckup."

Ah-ha, here it comes.

"I cover in OB ultrasound every once in a while, and I can tell you from firsthand experience, the woman is a quack. And you wouldn't believe the delivery she botched a while back." The line beeped. "Oops, I got another call. I'll see you around the gym." The line went dead.

Camille held the phone in her hand, wondering what other kind of trouble Kensington had gotten herself into.

———

The bells on the front door jingled and Amy shouted, "I'm back!"

Camille ran out to greet her trusty paralegal. "You'd better sit down."

Amy hung her navy peacoat in the closet and sat.

"Are you feeling okay?" Camille asked.

Amy popped open her compact and put her full attention on lining her mouth with a deep burgundy pencil. "Fine," she said through stretched lips.

"I told Helene I want to take her case to trial," she said evenly.

"You what?" Amy looked at Camille, her lips lined but not yet filled in.

"I just can't sit around and let some insurance adjuster dictate how much a baby's life is worth."

Amy dropped her hand holding the lip liner into her lap. "You're not going to make any money on this, you know." She shook her head.

"You're probably right, but I want to see what we can do in front of a jury."

"Camille . . ."

"What is Reilly worth to you? Or Nathan?" Camille asked.

Amy stared at Camille for a full thirty seconds. "What?"

"You heard me. You'd do anything for either of those two kids. They're the world to you."

Echoes of the argument Missy had used when she tried to convince her to abandon Camille reverberated in Amy's head. "That's . . . that's not the point," she stammered. "Taking on a case like this has to be a business decision for you." Kind of like what her mother kept telling her about finding a better paying job downtown—*it's business*.

"That *is* the point. I'm sick of making business decisions about someone's life."

"But that's what lawyers do." *And so should paralegals with expensive kids.*

"Not this one."

Amy was silent.

CHAPTER ELEVEN

Camille dropped her canvas grocery bags on the stoop and pushed Trish's doorbell.

"C'mon up!" Trish's voice squawked from the tinny speaker.

Anxious to find out what Trish had uncovered, Camille reorganized her bags for the trek up the three flights to Trish's loft.

A pile of brightly colored pillows supported Trish's casted leg on the couch. "I feel so stranded up here."

Camille handed Trish a veggie burrito from the burrito window at the corner of First and Pike.

"My favorite." Trish smiled hungrily. "You're such a pal."

The sink and refrigerator stood side by side along one wall next to the open industrial shelving where Camille found a vase. She stuck in the bouquet of dahlias she'd bought from the Hmong farmers at the market.

"They're beautiful, thanks."

"So, did you find out anything about Kensington?" Camille asked eagerly.

"You're gonna love this." Trish stretched to reach her steno pad on the end table behind her. "On March twenty-first, 2020, she had one point two million dollars go in and out of her bank account."

Camille abruptly stopped arranging the flowers. "You're kidding." *Where the hell did an OB-GYN get one point two million dollars all at once?* She covered her ears. "And whatever you do, don't you ever tell me where you got this info!"

Trish winked and put her index finger up to her lips. "My little secret."

"One point two million? Where'd it come from?"

"Beats me. One point two mil, in and out in one day."

"Any idea where it went?"

"All I know is it was wired to an offshore account."

"That sounds ominous."

"Actually, it's not as unusual as you'd think. Lots of people have offshore trusts set up to minimize their taxes."

"Is that legal?"

"It depends on who you ask. The IRS likes to make people think it's not, but from what I understand, they have a lot of trouble convincing the tax courts of that."

"Why would Kensington go to such extremes to avoid taxes?"

"She probably has an aggressive tax accountant."

"Huh." Camille sat on the edge of a bright orange vinyl chair, circa 1955. Trish's loft looked like a kindergarten class had exploded inside of it. "Can you find out exactly where the money went?"

"I can only tell from the transaction number that it went out of the country. Every bank has an ID number, so if I had a number to check, I could tell you if it was that bank or not. But that's about all." Trish peeled the aluminum foil from her burrito. "So? Have you unearthed anything about the good doctor?"

"All I know is that Deanne Stillerman, that nurse who teaches aerobics at the gym, hates Kensington."

"Yeah, but doesn't she hate everybody?"

"I don't know her that well. Does she?"

"I think so." Trish dipped her burrito into the container of extra-hot sauce. "I remember when she was in some kind of snit over the Zumba schedule and she went around bad-mouthing the gym manager to everyone who would listen."

"Well, she told me that Kensington is a quack." Camille got up and grabbed a red-and-yellow polka-dot napkin from the kitchen. "But everyone else in the world thinks she walks on water."

"I'd take Stillerman's opinion with a huge grain of salt, then."

Camille handed Trish the soft cloth napkin. "She also said that Kensington's mother was in the hospital, or a nursing home, in Hawaii, and Kensington was spending a lot of time over there visiting her. And that she seems to disappear every once in a while, with no notice. Might be related to her mother. It's hard to have an ailing parent so far away."

Trish raised an eyebrow. "I wonder if the mom died and left an inheritance."

"Like around one point two million dollars?"

"Maybe." Trish nodded.

"It's possible."

"What else do you know about her?"

"Well, her dad's a friend of mine."

Trish shook her head. "I assume he doesn't know you're going to take his daughter to trial."

"Nope. As far as he knows, I'm going to turn a quick settlement and be done. I haven't figured out how I'm going to tell him about the change in plans."

"Hand me my laptop." Trish pointed across the room to where the built-in bed was hidden from view by a giant piece of vintage Peter Max fabric.

Camille complied and reached behind Trish to plug it in.

"I'm going to search the probate files to see if Kensington's mother comes up. That way we'll know if she died. That might explain the one point two million."

"First we need to find her name." Trish's fingers flew across the keyboard. "If she was divorced in King County, it'll be in the court record. We can go by decades. There were two hundred and forty-three Davenports divorced in King County from '90 to '99, but no Kips," she announced with a trace of disappointment in her voice.

"Well, obviously, Kip's a nickname. Can you pull up the medical licenses?" Camille offered.

Trish dove back into the virtual world inside the thin laptop. "He's a gynecologist, right?"

"Yep."

"How does Kimbrough sound? The address is 935 Madison."

"That's him. No wonder he goes by Kip."

"Here we go!" Trish announced proudly. "Kimbrough and Moyna-Lou Davenport, divorced in January 1990." Trish squinted at the screen. "Huh . . . that's weird."

"What?"

"The file's sealed," Trish said slowly.

Sealed? *Why on earth would Kip Davenport's divorce file be sealed?* "It doesn't matter." She'd figure that out later. "We just need the mother's name to check the probate database."

"Right," Trish agreed and logged on to the probate search engine. "I'm not getting any hits under Moyna-Lou Davenport."

"I wonder if she has a different last name."

"I'm searching just plain old Moyna-Lou and coming up empty."

"Well, it's an unusual enough name; if she had an estate in probate, we'd find it." Camille looked at her watch. "Shit, I gotta run. My sister is bringing some friend to dinner in an hour, and knowing her, it'll probably be some weirdo. I better go start cooking."

"You know, I'm pretty far behind in a bunch of my other cases, Camille. I'm not going to be able to spend as much time on this one as I usually do." Trish grimaced. "I hope that's okay."

"No problem; Amy can run most of the computer searches we need at this stage of the game."

"Be nice to her, she's an angel," Trish shouted as Camille gathered up her grocery bags.

—

Camille's sister, Eve McKane, arrived precisely at five thirty. It was hard to believe the attractive woman was merely five feet tall; her energy took up the entirety of any room she entered. She tilted her cheek up for Camille to kiss and sashayed past her in four-inch heels to allow a portly woman to enter behind her.

Eve waved her hand at her sister. "Camille Delaney. Dr. Laurabelle Flores." Eve wiggled up the stairs in her very tight and very expensive brown suit. "LB is a retired UW professor of psychology, very famous. She taught me everything I know," Eve added almost as an afterthought.

Camille had Eve's usual, a Manhattan, very dry, on the counter awaiting her arrival. And, as always, Eve seized it with her usual sense of entitlement. Camille wondered if Eve had ever uttered the phrase "thank you."

Camille listened as Eve explained that her seventy-two-year-old mentor was presently in the midst of earning a PhD in some kind of quantum metaphysics program.

Camille handed the woman a glass of zinfandel and asked her about the origin of the richly embroidered shawl she had wrapped around herself.

"It was my mother's. I grew up in a small mining town called Mapimí in Mexico. My dad was the chief engineer at a silver mine."

Camille opened her mouth to ask the professor about her interesting childhood but was interrupted by Eve, who wanted to be updated about the whereabouts of her colleagues from graduate school.

Camille listened with half an ear as the stately professor rambled off name after name in a deeply melodious voice. The Mexican accent was mesmerizing.

As she threw together the ingredients for the bouillabaisse, Camille decided that the professor's deeply creased face and coarse black hair reminded her of her mom's old friend Dolores Huerta, the Latina workers' rights organizer, who was one of her own personal heroes.

Laurabelle closed her eyes and breathed in the aroma of the saffron as the stock bubbled on the stove. "It smells marvelous." She smiled at Camille, then turned to Eve. "And when does your new book come out, my dear?"

"It's out." Eve clicked open her Bally briefcase and pulled out a copy of her newly released hardback, then uncapped her Montblanc and inscribed the front cover. "Here's your specially autographed edition." She handed the book to her professor.

Laurabelle smoothed her thickly veined hands over the front of the book. "Thank you, Dr. McKane." She shot a coffee-stained smile at Eve.

Camille thought she detected a slight tone of whimsy in the professor's response as she paged through the up-and-coming bestseller *Extricate*, on how to get out of a doomed relationship. "I'll certainly cherish it," Laurabelle almost smirked.

Camille's well-manicured sister spread three crackers with exactly the same amount of tapenade and arranged them geometrically on a cocktail napkin. She was clearly waiting for Laurabelle to interrogate her about the book, so she seemed more than a bit surprised when Laurabelle turned to Camille.

"And what do you do, Camille?" Laurabelle enunciated each word perfectly.

What a surprise, somehow Eve had completely forgotten to fill in her dinner guest on anyone's career but her own. "I'm a lawyer."

"My, I don't know how anyone can maintain any sense of moral equilibrium in that line of work." The professor pulled her colorful wrap tightly around her bulky frame.

Well, she doesn't mince words. How refreshing.

"Speaking of moral equilibrium," Eve interrupted, "I have a chapter in my book about the morality of using an affair as an excuse for ending a relationship. It's all about keeping firm boundaries."

As usual, Camille could make little sense out of her sister's simplistic pop psychology. "Boundaries" seemed to be the trend of the moment. Whatever that meant.

Laurabelle nodded thoughtfully. "An interesting proposition."

Camille loved the nuance with which her stepsister's mentor handled Eve's not-so-subtle narcissism.

"You know," Eve said authoritatively, "we each have our own sense of where we draw the line between truth, half-truth, and white lies. We all certainly have our own secrets, and we're completely within our moral boundaries to keep them to ourselves."

Laurabelle looked at Eve with what appeared to Camille to be blatant curiosity.

"What's your area of psychology, Laurabelle?" Camille asked.

Eve's jaw tightened noticeably. "She's an international expert in Stockholm syndrome, where victims become somehow unified with and identify with their abusers. I've devoted a full chapter to what makes some people choose abusive partners." She fondled her book.

"Wow, Stockholm syndrome. That must be fascinating," Camille said to Laurabelle with genuine admiration.

"Fascinating but also very discouraging." Laurabelle sighed. "It was tremendously fatiguing always to be dealing with abuser personalities."

"How did you manage?" Camille asked.

"What a coincidence! I'm working on a new book on how to look on the bright side in what appears to be a no-win situation." Eve sounded like an advertisement on a Christian TV station. "I've come up with ten affirmations to repeat five times a day, depending on the circumstances, that is."

Laurabelle smiled at Camille, then turned and spoke to Eve as if she were addressing a small child. "Well, that sounds like it will be a very helpful text." She looked back to Camille. "I struggled with it every day."

Eve pursed her lips. "Let's see, how can I simplify this?"

Camille and Laurabelle both stared as the tiny author took a leather-clad notebook from her briefcase and began to outline her quick and easy affirmations for cheering up any situation.

Camille ignored Eve. "Did you actually treat the abusers? Or did your work focus on the victims?" she asked Laurabelle.

"I worked with both."

Eve's face twisted into the pout she adopted whenever she wasn't the center of attention. Some things about a person never change. Camille noted that Eve's expression looked the same today as it had when she was five.

Camille turned back to the professor. "What causes someone to victimize another person like that?"

"Well, sometimes it runs in families. An abused child will on occasion grow up to be an abuser himself."

Camille was fascinated. "Is there a genetic component?"

"Some kinds of mental illness have been proved to be genetic, but there isn't any clear evidence at this point that this type of behavior is biological."

"What do you think?"

The professor smiled. "I've always thought it was more than a coincidence that some families seem to have more than their share of crazies."

Camille laughed. "Is that a scientific term?"

"Well." Laurabelle shrugged. "Sometimes you just have to call it like you see it."

CHAPTER TWELVE

Camille arrived at the swim meet just in time for the last few events of the evening. She settled herself in the middle of the bleachers and waved to Angela who, as the team captain, was leading a raucous cheer. But Angela was too caught up to see her mother sitting alone in the midst of the frenetic crowd.

As she looked around to locate Sam, Camille couldn't help but notice the familiar visage of Vern Bagley, the managing partner of the well-oiled insurance defense machine hired to defend Kensington. The guy was despicable. For the past few weeks, Camille and Amy had been working night and day putting out brush fires initiated by Bagley's team of eager young associates. And every day it seemed as though they were falling further and further behind.

The only good thing was that Camille had found an expert witness to review the case. He was from a small town called Ojai, in the mountains east of Santa Barbara, California. The guy had trained at USC, and he sounded like he could hold his own in a deposition. And that was what mattered.

Sam's familiar voice was a welcome relief. "Is this seat available?"

Camille raised her face to kiss her husband, who looked relieved to be finished with his turn timing the swimmers on the pool deck.

"We winning?" she asked.

"Kicking butt."

Sam stuck his index finger and thumb into his mouth and whistled loudly, distracting Angela long enough for her to forget where she was in her cheer. Angela frowned jokingly at him and returned her attention to her team. Camille loved the girls' devotion to Sam, but she was beginning to feel a bit left out of their lives lately.

"Hey, isn't that Harvey Lowe over there?" Sam shouted to be heard over the commotion.

"Where?" Camille craned her neck.

"Climbing up the bleachers, over there." He pointed as Harvey Lowe sat down immediately next to Vern Bagley, directly under the banner of the exclusive Lakeside School. It figured. The last time Camille checked, the tuition at Lakeside had topped forty thousand a year.

"I'm surprised to see Lowe here with his kids," Sam commented. "I've never seen him at a swim meet before."

Camille went cold when she saw Lowe and Bagley sitting together, laughing. "It must be his night for visitation. He got divorced a few years ago," she said absentmindedly.

"Mom!" Gracie shouted. "How come you didn't come home and pick us up?" She climbed onto Camille's lap.

"I'm sorry, honey. I had to work late."

"It's the regionals," Grace announced, like she knew exactly what a regional was.

"I know, darling." Camille hugged her foster daughter tightly, thinking about Helene Anderson. She'd never share a moment like this with Zachary. That in and of itself had to have value to a jury.

Another swim meet, another late night at the office, Camille thought as she and Sam walked hand in hand through the dark misty parking lot after the meet. She turned to her husband. "I've got to go back to the office for a few hours. I couldn't ask Amy to stay late again. I have to respond to another one of Bagley's ridiculous motions. It's due by noon tomorrow, and I've hardly started on it."

Sam held the door to his Audi SUV while the girls climbed in. Gracie opened her door back up just as he pulled out. "I'm gonna stay up till you get home, Mommy. It's past your turn to read to me."

"Gracie! Don't you ever open the door while the car's moving!" Camille shouted, then leaned in and kissed the tall, skinny girl. "I may be late. Maybe Daddy should read to you tonight."

Gracie returned a stern look. "It's your turn."

"I'll see what I can do." Camille gently closed the door, kissed her fingers, pressed them up against the window, and held them there for a moment. As she turned to get into her empty car, she bristled at the nasal voice of Vern Bagley behind her.

"I'm surprised you were able to get away with all the discovery I've got my associates sending your way." He chuckled condescendingly. "Those kids are going to kill themselves staying up all hours trying to think of ways to make you and your client's lives miserable over the next couple of months. I hope you're up to it."

Camille felt her face flush. *The arrogant bastard.*

"You know," Bagley said authoritatively, "Lowe's blowing a gasket about your stealing the case from him. He's already contacted the insurance company to be sure that they don't release any funds to you until he gets his attorney's fee lien satisfied." He pointed his remote at a large black Tesla. "Even if you win, which you won't with that pervert from Ojai as your expert, you won't see a dime for years."

Why would he call her expert a pervert?

He turned and got into his car and rolled down his darkened window as his two daughters got in the back seat. "Lowe's gonna make you twist in the wind over this one."

Camille shivered as the silent black car whisked off into the darkness.

———

Late at night, it always seemed as though the warm familiarity disappeared from her office. Camille put a cup of water into the microwave and chose a bag of caffeinated black tea. She put her face over the fragrant brew in an effort to wake herself up as she turned on her office light and booted up the computer.

In the eerie bluish glow of the screen, Camille grabbed the giant stack of paperwork she'd been avoiding all week. There was only so much one could expect from a devoted paralegal, and missing almost every one of her sons' football games for a whole month was too much. Camille clicked open her response to Bagley's latest motion that Amy had kindly started on before she left that afternoon.

Camille sighed and looked at the clock. Nine thirty—it was going to be a very, very long night. She rubbed her eyes and organized the plethora of research notes she'd taken earlier that day. Slowly, as her thoughts began to jell, she commenced typing.

———

The jangling of her phone awakened Camille from a sound sleep. She jerked her head up and rubbed her kinked neck. How long had she been sleeping slumped over at her desk?

"Hello?"

"Honey, are you all right?" Sam sounded concerned, to say the least.

"Yeah. Yeah, I'm fine. I guess I dozed off," she answered groggily. "What time is it?"

"I just woke up to go to the head and realized you weren't here. It's three thirty. Time to come home, sweetheart."

Camille looked blearily at her half-finished response and groaned. "I can't. I have to finish this. It's due by noon tomorrow." She tried to blink herself awake. "Thank God you called."

"This case is getting out of hand, Camille." Sam's voice was stern.

"Can we discuss this some other time?" Camille yawned. "I gotta get this thing finalized."

"Are you sure you're safe there all alone?"

Camille looked out over the still marina outside her window. "I'm in Fremont, remember? The most exciting thing that ever happens around here is when all the naked bicyclists take to the streets in the Solstice Parade every June."

"Do you have the security system turned on?"

No use telling Sam the system hadn't been usable since the building owner had rewired it himself while trying to install a new phone system for the insurance agent next door.

"Everything's okay. I'll be fine."

"Okay, when will you be home?"

"I'm not sure. Can you drive the carpools again?" she asked sheepishly.

"Of course. I love you, honey."

"I love you too." Camille got up to go splash water on her face.

Camille typed frantically through the night as the clock slowly crept forward. She couldn't remember the last time she had pulled an "all-nighter." Gradually, her response to the insipid motion began to take shape. At exactly 6:35 a.m., Camille hit the print icon and grabbed her gym bag to go freshen up. The exhaust fan in the decrepit bathroom rattled and died as Camille squeezed out the remnants of toothpaste and dropped the tube into the trash.

It seemed like eons ago that she'd stood out in the rain and pledged herself to Helene Anderson. At the time, she knew she was biting off a bit more than she could chew, but she had no idea it would be this bad. Well, thank God for Amy. Camille looked at her watch. Amy would show up in a couple of hours and properly e-file the motion with the court.

Camille charged back into her office and got her phone on the umpteenth ring.

"It's me." Amy sounded upset. "Nathan got a concussion at the game last night. I have to take him in for a CAT scan this morning."

"Is he okay?" Camille dropped into the chair behind the reception counter.

"I don't know. The doctor said he'd be fine. He just ordered the CAT scan as a precaution." Amy sounded uncharacteristically down. "I'm so freaked out. I have no idea how I'm gonna afford the uninsured part. Their dad certainly isn't going to be any help."

"We'll think of something. Just take care of Nathan. The money'll come." Where it'd come from wasn't abundantly clear at this point, but things were bound to turn around. They had to.

"I hope so." Amy had obviously been crying. "Listen, I have to stay home with him for a few days and keep an eye on him." She sniffed. "I'm really sorry I won't be able to come in."

"Don't worry about me. I'll be fine."

"Okay, call me if you need anything."

Camille hung up the phone and wondered where she could possibly come up with the money to help Amy pay her medical expenses.

Last month Reilly had broken a finger at football practice, and the emergency room bill co-pay was astronomical because Amy's deductible under her individual plan was so high.

Camille tried to remember the last name of the banker she'd met at field day at the girls' school last spring. She riffled through her box of business cards. There it was: Christina Davis. She dialed the number.

A twenty-minute call with the banker was all it took to secure a business loan for fifty thousand dollars. The banker had helped her transfer some of the stock from the girls' college funds as security. Not a problem. It was just a short-term loan, due in six months. She'd pay it back with the proceeds of the Anderson case, and no one would be the wiser, but there was no way she could let either Amy or Sam know what she'd done. They'd both flip out. It shouldn't be so hard to keep it from Sam for six months. The statements from the broker would come to her office email, so no one would be the wiser.

She'd need to give Amy some kind of explanation, though, for where she had gotten the money. Camille grabbed the stack of fender-bender files she'd shoved into the corner to make way for the Anderson case and stuck them into the back of the file cabinet where Amy wouldn't see them. It was simple, really. She'd just tell Amy a couple of cases had settled while she was home with Nathan. That way she could give Amy a thousand bucks to help with the co-pay for the CAT scan and get Nathan started at the orthodontist. By the time Amy figured it out, the Anderson case would be settled and the loan paid back.

—

From the breakfast nook of her tiny apartment, all Amy could see was a continuous drizzle leaking through the roof into the dark carport. The grill of her Toyota Corolla seemed to be begging for the tune-up she couldn't afford. A feeling of despondency crept over her as she waited for her ancient computer to come alive.

Amy busied herself formatting a motion to compel her ex-husband to come up with the back child support and uninsured medical expenses. She wondered why she even bothered. As an Alaska fisherman, her "ex" had mastered the art of getting paid under the table so there was nothing for the court to garnish. She sorted through the batch of bills she'd copied to attach to her motion. There were dental bills, after-school care invoices, uninsured medical expenses, sports fees, and Reilly's tutoring. The calculator on her computer screen showed the total to be $10,527.35. Amy shook her head. There wasn't a snowball's chance in hell she'd squeeze any money out of the creep.

"Mom!" Nathan hollered from the living room where he lay glued to *Gilligan's Island* on Netflix. Amy smiled at how Nathan and his friends had taken a liking to vintage TV shows. Mrs. Howell was fussing with her feather boa as Amy flew into the cluttered living room, nearly tripping over the wires attaching the various games to the flickering TV.

"You okay, honey?" Amy caught her breath and sank into the maroon crushed-velvet couch with virtually no springs left in it.

"I'm hungry." Nathan rubbed his eyes.

Amy put her hand on her son's forehead and caressed her way down his cheek. She bent over him and tried to see his pupils—not exactly sure what she was looking for, but it seemed like the thing to do when someone had a concussion.

"Let's get you some cereal."

"I want a Big Mac."

"Grandma's coming over to watch you in an hour so I can go to the grocery store. I can pick something up while I'm out."

Nathan turned his attention back to Gilligan, who was trying to convince the skipper to let him catapult himself to another part of the island in some contraption the professor had rigged up. Nathan leaned forward, his mouth hanging open as if he were trying to fall out of the shabby apartment and into the tropical island scene. The phone rang, and Nathan patted around the frayed quilt, trying to locate it without taking his eyes off the TV.

He answered it and handed it to his mom. "Here you go."

Not that it made any difference, but Amy opened the drapes. The front of the apartment faced north onto an austere cement courtyard littered with the neighbor's kids' scooters and pickle ball paraphernalia. Neither Amy's entryway nor her apartment ever really saw the light of day. The place was so shady that she had long ago given up the battle to keep the moss from overtaking the faded welcome mat.

Amy snatched the phone and sat in front of her laptop perched on top of an array of the boys' homework strewn across the kitchen table, where the legal caption on her divorce paperwork seemed to be mocking her from the screen.

"Is this Amy Hutchins?" The man's voice was vaguely familiar, but Amy couldn't quite place it.

"Yes," she answered tentatively.

"Hello, Amy. Harvey Lowe here."

Amy felt like the wind had just been knocked out of her.

"Hello? Are you there?" he asked.

"I . . . I'm here." What was she supposed to say? How had he gotten her cell number? Oh my God. She reflexively reached up and primped her hair as if he could see her in her baggy flannel pajamas.

The man at the other end of the phone laughed. "I can't say I blame you for being surprised to hear from me of all people."

"Well . . ."

"I hope I'm not imposing—calling you midmorning."

He actually didn't sound all that bad. "No, it's fine."

"If there's a better time, I'd be happy to call you back."

Better time for what? Amy wondered. "It's fine. I can talk." She paced back and forth across the tiny kitchen.

"Great." He got right to business. "Listen, Amy, I know you had lunch with Missy recently and she told you about the paralegal job we have available."

"She did." Amy tried to modulate her bounding pulse by taking slow breaths.

"Look, I'm sure you're aware that Camille and I had a rather unfortunate parting of ways a few years back, but I'm hoping you won't hold that against me here." He laughed softly. "I've asked around, and your name keeps coming up as one of the best in the business."

Who did he ask? Amy wondered.

"I've spoken with Lorrey Lincoln, Win Clark, and Vern Bagley, to name a few."

Amy felt like he was reading her mind.

"And they've all said they'd hire you away from Camille in a heartbeat if they thought you'd consider switching to the dark side." He chuckled again.

Well, they had that right; there was no way she'd ever work for an insurance defense firm. But, still, it was flattering that opposing counsel had spoken highly of her. Her pulse seemed to be coming back down out of the stratosphere.

Lowe continued. "Missy tells me you have a couple of sons."

Amy nodded. "I do." She kicked a green nerf ball with her fuzzy slippers.

"And you're a single mother."

It was creeping her out, Harvey Lowe knowing her life story.

"I don't mean to pry," he continued, "but I have a hunch that it hasn't been easy raising the boys on your own."

He really didn't seem to be as big a jerk as she'd been led to believe.

"At our office, we like to think of ourselves as a big family."

Actually, he seemed pretty nice. "Huh."

"Your boys like football?"

"Are you kidding? You've obviously done your homework, so you know I have two budding quarterbacks." Amy was feeling almost comfortable now.

"You're right. I knew that," he admitted almost bashfully. "I just wanted to find a way to let you know about our great perks. I have a luxury box for the Seahawks, and I try to make it available for the staff at least half the season."

"Wow." What was she supposed to say?

"Is there any way you'd consider making a change?" There was a note of pleading in his voice. "I have a bunch of extremely complex cases in the middle of litigation, and Stephanie's husband has been transferred to Austin with some biotech start-up thing. There just aren't that many paralegals who can jump right in and get up to speed."

"I . . . I don't know. I'd have to think about it."

"I'm prepared to give you a ten-thousand-dollar signing bonus and a starting salary of ninety thousand a year. Plus bonuses."

Jesus Christ. "Can I get back to you?"

"You bet. I'm pleased you'll even consider us." His voice was warm and friendly. "You'd love it here, Amy. We work hard, but we have fun together."

Even if she wanted to . . . There was no way. "I'll call you later this week."

"Great," he said and hung up.

Amy looked around at the dreary seventies apartment with the olive-green shag carpeting and closed her eyes, imagining how it would feel to be caught up with her bills. *You are not leaving Camille. How can you even think it?* She opened the refrigerator covered with the boys' artwork and football schedules. She took out a quart of Häagen-Dazs and tried to savor the first icy bite of Mocha Almond Fudge.

Then she began to cry.

CHAPTER THIRTEEN

Amy whistled as she sorted through the pile of paperwork on Camille's desk, searching for the last page of interrogatory answers Camille had asked her to finalize. Her mother had agreed to watch Nathan for a couple of hours so Amy could run into the office and get caught up. She had intentionally chosen to come in when she knew Camille would be in court. She didn't think she could face her after the strange phone call from Harvey Lowe.

What was this? She picked up a document containing the familiar boilerplate of a bank loan, then sat and read it slowly. Amy shook her head in confusion. It was completely out of character for Camille to do something like this without consulting her. Obviously, Camille had felt compelled to find a way to afford the Anderson case and to try to help her with her boys' upcoming expenses.

Amy read on. *Oh God.* Camille had pledged part of her girls' college funds as collateral for the loan. The initial pang of guilt escalated into a full-blown panic attack. There was no way she could ask Camille for a raise now. Not knowing this. Amy raked her hair away from her face. *I'll bet she didn't tell Sam about this either.*

Well, this pretty much ruled out any chance of being able to sign Nathan up for the select football team. He was so excited to have been chosen. She couldn't bear to tell him that she couldn't possibly come up with the money.

Maybe Camille couldn't afford her anymore and didn't have the heart to lay her off. Amy closed her eyes and tried to imagine her life without Camille. It could be that it would be best for everyone if she moved on. She looked around; there was no comparison between this homey little office and the mausoleum downtown. But she had to do what she had to do: for herself, for Camille, and mostly for her kids.

Amy took a deep breath and dialed Lowe's office.

—

"I hate that motions calendar!" Camille announced without saying hello. "I had to wait two and a half hours for the hearing because opposing counsel was late signing in."

Amy followed her boss into her office, threw herself on the couch, and started to cry.

"What's wrong?" Camille hurried to her side.

"Nathan made the select football team."

"Wow . . . ," Camille offered quizzically. "That's great." *So why the tears?*

"It's going to cost me a fortune." Amy closed her eyes tightly.

Camille mentally counted how much of the loan she could afford to part with and still have enough to pay the experts in the Anderson case.

Heavy mascara streaked down Amy's cheeks. She tried to rub it off but only succeeded in smearing it all over her face.

"It's okay, Amy, we'll think of something." Camille was frantic. Amy was her rock. She'd never seen her like this.

"No. We won't think of anything. There's only one answer. You can't afford to keep me anymore."

Camille's stomach hurled into her throat. It had never crossed her mind that Amy would leave her. "Don't say that, Amy." Tears welled up. "I'll come up with the money, I promise."

Amy's eyes were vacant as she shook her head despondently. "It's not fair to either of us anymore." She choked back a sob. "I can't afford to deny my boys life they deserve just so I can work in a place that makes me happy."

Camille closed her eyes. She couldn't argue with a mother who was willing to give up a job she loved so she could give her kids a better life. Camille felt a surge of guilt. She had been so selfish.

"I recently found out that I can make almost one and a half times my salary if I go downtown. And I just can't say no to that." Amy covered her face with her hands. "I'm so sorry, Camille. I am so sorry," she cried.

Camille rubbed Amy's back. "It's okay." She watched outside the window as a sailboat awkwardly tacked, its bright red spinnaker collapsing into the lake. The boat foundered as its crew frantically tried to rescue the spinnaker.

"The job I've been offered is at Harvey Lowe's office," Amy blurted out.

Camille felt like she'd been kicked in the stomach.

"I'm so sorry," Amy said over and over. "I'm so sorry."

Camille gathered her wits, trying to think of something to say. Anger began to replace sorrow and confusion. She tried to speak, but her mouth was too dry.

Amy stood. "I gotta go." She ran from the room and stormed out the front door.

CHAPTER FOURTEEN

Every few minutes the phone rang. Thank God for voice mail. Looking around the cluttered office, Camille picked up and tried to read the thick OB textbook she'd highlighted earlier that week but was completely unable to concentrate. She turned to review another one of Bagley's pointless motions.

Forget it.

Damn that Amy anyway. Who the hell did she think she was? And how could she justify mutinying in the middle of their biggest case ever? And for what? To go to Harvey Lowe's sweatshop. Camille panicked; there was no way she'd survive even a week without Amy.

"Enough! I'm going home," she said angrily to the empty office as she slammed the door behind her and hurried out to her car, where she barely heard the muffled sound of her cell phone ringing deep in her purse.

Camille reached for the volume and turned down the classic rock she'd hoped would blare away her troubles.

"It's Dr. Greg Fitzharris, from Ojai. I hope you don't mind me calling you on your cell phone. I've been trying your office, but I keep getting lost in voice mail."

"I'm sorry . . . I've had a little staff reorganization." That was an understatement.

"Listen, I won't take much of your time."

"Don't be silly, I appreciate all of your help."

"I don't know whether I mentioned to you when we spoke before that my son has some fairly serious medical problems."

Camille hesitated, curious but not wanting to pry. "No . . . no you didn't."

"He has osteosarcoma." He paused. "Bone cancer."

Camille froze. She'd often wondered where parents got the strength to survive the life-threatening illness of a child. "I am so sorry." She closed her eyes tightly, trying to squeeze away the image of one of her own being that sick. "That's awful." It was all she could think of to say.

"Thanks. Actually, what I wanted to tell you is that he's going to be having surgery shortly after Halloween."

"Oh my God."

"They have to amputate his leg, and he begged us to let him go trick-or-treating on two legs."

The doctor sounded so strong.

"Well, please don't worry about this case. You just focus on taking care of your son."

"Don't think I'm going to leave you hanging. It's just that my wife has been shouldering most of this over the past couple of months, and I feel like I really need to pitch in and help out."

"I understand completely."

"Listen, I'm going to have some time this weekend, so I can give you a call and go over some of my findings on Monday, then I'll be pretty much out of commission for a couple of months."

"Thanks so much, I'd really appreciate it," Camille said. "I just got served with a summary judgment motion, which means that I'll need a declaration from you to attach to my response. I hope it's not too much trouble."

"Not a problem; I'd like to get as many projects off my plate as I can before the surgery. It's one less thing for me to worry about."

What a nice guy.

"You have kids?"

"Two daughters and one foster daughter."

"Healthy?"

"Very."

"You're lucky, you know."

"I know."

—

Camille pulled up in front of the row of mailboxes at the top of their houseboat dock, where Cathy Swain stood sorting through a handful of envelopes.

"Hi." Cathy smiled.

"Hi," Camille answered glumly.

"You don't look so great. Is something the matter?"

"Nah, just a hard day at the office." It was unlikely Cathy really wanted to hear about the disaster that was her day. "I'll survive." Sure she would.

Cathy pulled out an oversized, obviously expensive-looking envelope. "Hey! Look at this." She tore it open and held up a hand-painted party invitation in shades of orange and black. "Remember Kensington's Halloween party that I was telling you about?"

Camille stepped closer to see the invitation. "Wow. It's beautiful."

Cathy's face fell. "And I'm on call this year." She dropped the invitation into the recycle with the rest of the junk mail. "Damn it."

Camille automatically plucked the invitation out of the dumpster. "You mind if I save this? Gracie's always looking for cards to paste onto some art project or other."

"Go ahead," Cathy said as she climbed back into her car.

—

Camille couldn't face going inside just yet. How could she explain to Sam that Amy had quit? If he thought she'd been working too hard before now, just wait till he got a load of what would happen around her office without Amy.

Camille wandered down to the narrow waterfront minipark just a block away and sat on the bench as a flock of ducks noisily flapped down onto the gray lake in front of her. She pulled out her phone and dialed Trish.

She swallowed hard. "Amy quit."

"What?" Trish hollered. "Are you kidding?"

"Nope." Camille didn't even try to stop the onslaught of tears. She spoke between sobs, telling Trish about Amy's lucrative job offer at Harvey Lowe's office. Not that she blamed Amy for wanting more money or anything. But the timing . . . And her choice of where to go . . .

"Jeez, Camille, I don't know what to say," Trish commiserated. "I wish I weren't laid up with this bum leg. I'd love to help. But then even if I could, I'm so far behind on my background checks for the nanny agencies and preschools, I wouldn't have much time."

"I know." Camille's heart sank even further. She'd secretly hoped Trish would offer to take up some slack for her while she figured out how to get some secretarial help. "I'll be fine," she said in an effort to convince herself as much as Trish. Camille turned her face up to the rapidly increasing drizzle, hoping it would wash away her tears before she schlepped home.

—

The houseboat smelled wonderful. What in the world? No one other than her ever cooked. Camille crept curiously up the stairs into the huge room with a kitchen at one end and a living area at the other, separated by a walnut slab dining table. She stopped. There stood Sam, surrounded by their three girls in front of the industrial stove that Sam had given her two Christmases ago.

Confusion swirled around inside Camille's head. On one hand, she was devastated beyond words at losing Amy, but on the other, she felt guilty for worrying so much about her own troubles when there were people with real problems, like Greg Fitzharris, who was grateful just to have his son alive.

Priorities, she reminded herself as she entered the cheerful family scene.

"What's going on?" She tried to sound perkier than she felt.

Gracie shrieked and ran over to bury her foster mother in hugs. "Daddy's taking cooking classes!" She grinned widely. "We're having chicken catch a . . . catch a . . . chicken catches something." She ran back and circled her long, skinny arms around Sam's waist. "Aren't we, Daddy?"

Sam? Cooking classes? Faint hints of jealousy—or was it sadness?—nudged at Camille. Somehow she always liked the fact that she was the family chef. But she could hardly blame Sam for wanting to be able to do something other than order takeout on those nights that she wasn't home, which had admittedly been more frequent of late.

"It smells wonderful." She tried to hide her misty eyes as she kissed each of the three girls, one by one, then stopped in front of her husband. "Really. Just wonderful." She suddenly felt like a stranger in her own kitchen, torn between wanting to chuck it all to stay home to be a wife and mother and wanting to kick Bagley's butt around the courtroom in the process of winning a multimillion-dollar verdict for the Andersons. But the prospects of that scenario ever coming to fruition seemed to diminish with each passing day—today in particular.

Camille stopped. This case wasn't just about money. It was about the loss of a child. Passionate feelings of love and warmth enveloped Camille as she watched her daughters dancing around the kitchen with their father. She wondered if she really could convince a jury to place a dollar value on this experience. Slowly, a feeling of resolve rose from the center of her being. Of course she could. At least she had to try.

"Hey, Mom," Angela hollered. "Our class is going on a trip to Washington, DC. Can I go?"

Camille caught Sam's worried gaze. He didn't have to say anything. She recognized The Look. The "what about the money" look. "We'll see," she answered.

Angela held up a paper. "Here's the thing I have to fill out to reserve a space." She reflexively handed her mother a pair of glasses as Camille kicked off her shoes and skimmed the application.

It reminded Camille of Amy, always anticipating her every need. She knew it'd take years to train someone else, if and when she could afford it.

"I was thinking. I can get an after-school job to help out with the money part," Angela said proudly. "What do you think?"

Camille smiled at her daughter. "It's an idea. What kind of job would you like to try?" She struggled to hide her fatigue.

"Kaitlin's working in her mother's lab." Angela raised her eyebrow in anticipation. "I was thinking . . . maybe I could help out at your office after school. You know I'm good on the phone."

"That's for sure," Camille laughed.

"I'll bet Amy'd like some help. You guys have been so busy lately."

Sam smiled from his station over the stove. "It sounds like a great idea to me, hon. You could use all the help you can get around there."

Camille nodded. It would be better than nothing; she was going to have to pay someone, and it might as well be Angela, at least in the short term. She couldn't imagine how she'd be able to keep on top of the paperwork being flung at her nonstop by Bagley's underlings. And, God knew, Helene deserved a lawyer who had time to do something other than file stuff and shuffle paper. There was a ton of investigating to be done.

"Actually, your timing is perfect." Camille paused before dropping the bombshell. "Amy's decided to go back downtown and work some-place where she can make more money."

Sam stopped with his mouth open, about to take a taste of the tomatoey chicken concoction bubbling on the stove. "What did you say?"

Camille looked at Sam, trying to draw support from his steady presence. "You heard me."

Sam dropped the wooden spoon into the pot and came around to hug his wife. "Are you okay?"

Camille shrugged, unable to speak.

"I can help too," fourteen-year-old Libby chimed in. "You know I can type really fast."

Camille reached out and held Libby's hand while Sam rubbed her shoulders.

"Get your mother a glass of wine," Sam instructed Angela, then turned to Camille. "Want to talk about it?"

Feelings of guilt overtook Camille as she selectively explained to Sam about the situation at work, telling him about everything. Except for the bank loan.

CHAPTER FIFTEEN

Trish thrashed around in her Pullman-style bed in the evening twilight. It was impossible to sleep through the night with the clunky appliance strapped to her "previously broken leg," as she'd euphemistically labeled it, so she had taken to napping in the late afternoon.

She looked blearily at her phone. *Five thirty! Oh shit.* She bolted up and shoved aside the mishmash of different sized pillows she'd learned to position in order to find even the slightest degree of comfort.

How many more days of this nonsense? She squinted to see her Children's Hospital calendar. One just like it was stuck to almost every refrigerator door in Seattle.

"Twenty-one days and counting!" Her cheer echoed throughout the high-ceilinged loft. Time to get back to work, she admonished herself for sleeping away the entire afternoon. She hobbled to the bathroom and splashed her face with cold water.

The slim laptop whirred to life as Trish transported piles of pillows from her bed to the couch and located her ever-present steno pad. She picked over the stack of files containing background requests from nanny agencies and preschools. The bread-and-butter work of a private investigator: boring, but regular. Trish chastised herself for being such a snob. Thank God she had something to do while she was laid up like this.

Think money, Trish instructed herself. But it was no use. Being closed in like this was more than she could stand. She took a moment to thank her lucky stars that she wasn't, and never had been, one of the drones who got sucked into the huge high-rises every morning and expelled forcefully at the end of each day. There was no way she'd ever spend countless hours snaking her way down the freeway into the city from the suburbs. She turned to look out the west-facing window and watched the giant superferry gliding across the black water carrying thousands of office workers who claimed to love the island lifestyle on Bainbridge Island, across Puget Sound from downtown Seattle. But Trish couldn't imagine being a slave to the ferry schedule either. The islanders paid too high a price for their supposed idyllic lifestyle. On their commute into the city every morning, the ferry's bathrooms were jammed with women jostling for a place in front of the mirror to put the finishing touches on their makeup, while others clamped curling irons to the tips of their trendy hairdos. And then, on the way home every evening, those same workers were glued to their laptops finishing up their workday; after waiting in the frigid ferry terminal, it took them about twenty-five minutes just to board the gigantic vessel. Nope, there was no way she'd ever join the ranks of the white-collar sisterhood.

Trish turned to her computer and shook her head. The reason she'd left her job at the Seattle Police Department was to get away from the stifling paperwork and anti-gay discrimination so she could get into something where she could be really creative. And now this. She sneered at her leg and popped another ibuprofen as she sorted through her files.

Over the course of her career as an investigator, the background work had become tolerable only because it could be squeezed in among real live investigations where she got to solve actual mysteries. Like what the hell was going on with Camille's weird doctor.

Poor Camille. What was she going to do without Amy? Trish glanced at the clock. If she managed her time right, she could run some computer checks on Kensington and discover the source of the one point two mil that had skipped in and out of her bank account last winter. Not that it necessarily had anything to do with Camille's case, but you never knew. Maybe Kensington's mother had died. And it had shaken the doctor up so that she couldn't concentrate; hence her lack of judgment the night of Helene's labor. It was a long shot, but the thing Trish loved best about her job was the feeling she got following a thread of one thing leading to another, never knowing exactly where it'd all end up.

Trish threw aside the stack of paperwork and grabbed a thin folder labeled "Kensington." One thing was for sure—finding Kensington's mother, the mysterious Moyna-Lou Davenport, would be a lot more exciting than scrolling through criminal files for Barb's Babysitters.

The only lead at this point had come from the snippy Zumba instructor, Deanne Stillerman, and Trish questioned the usefulness of anything from someone like Deanne. But it was all they had, and it was as good a place as any to start.

Stillerman had told Camille that Kensington spent a lot of time visiting her mother in Hawaii, Trish noted as she moved through the prompts into the state of Hawaii computer system. It shouldn't be too hard to locate someone with a name like Moyna-Lou Davenport.

Finally! After several dead ends, there she was! "Yes!" Trish pumped her fist.

"Why, Moyna-Lou, you li'l devil," she said aloud. "Alive and well in the land of aloha."

There goes the inheritance theory. But it did explain why Kensington spent so much time in Hawaii. Trish hooked the laptop up to the printer and guided out a sheet containing Moyna-Lou's address at a place called Kahana Care.

Probably some kind of retirement community, Trish decided. Moyna-Lou must be, what? In her seventies? Trish dialed Kahana Care in Hawaii and immediately recognized the accent of the operator as that of an island local. Trish had lived in Hawaii when her father was stationed at Hickam Air Force Base, and had quickly adopted the local pidgin that was a cross between English, Japanese, and the ancient language of the original Hawaiians. Her dad hated it.

"Hello, I'm calling for Moyna-Lou Davenport."

"Her confirmation number?"

"I beg your pardon?"

"I am sorry, ma'am, we cannot give out any patient information without a confirmation number." The woman's cadence was clipped.

"Well, can you tell me if she's even a patient there? I'd like to . . . send her flowers."

"I am very sorry, ma'am, I cannot. Kahana Care is a full-security facility. We are not allowed to give out any information whatsoever."

"Um, thanks anyway."

"My pleasure, alo . . ."

"Wait!" Trish interrupted. "Can you at least tell me what kind of facility Kahana Care is?"

"No, ma'am. I am sorry. I cannot."

The line went dead. What the hell? A full-security retirement community? Trish went back to her computer to search for any information available about the secretive Kahana Care.

Nothing.

Well, they must be interested in new business. Trish hit redial, prepared to disguise her voice in the unlikely event the operator might recognize her.

"Kahana Care, how may I assist you?" the woman with the familiar accent greeted Trish.

This was fun. "My mother is interested in your facility. I'd like to speak with someone about the amenities you offer," she said in her haughtiest voice. Trish loved pretending she was rich.

"Ah, I will transfer you to new patient admissions, ma'am. Please hold."

So it was a nursing home of some kind.

"Aloha. This is new patient admissions," a friendly man's voice answered.

Trish jumped into action. "Hello, my name is Therese Stafford." She always used pseudonyms with her own initials. For good luck. "My mother is interested in your facility, and I just wanted to check it out for her."

"Do you have a physician referral?"

"Yes . . . yes we do."

"All right. Let me get to my computer." There was a pause.

"My mother has heard such marvelous things about Kahana Care." A good brown-nosing never hurts when you're trying to get information out of someone.

"Why, thank you. It is a lovely place . . . Now, who is your mother's treating psychiatrist?"

Psychiatrist? Trish quickly Googled Seattle psychiatrists. "It's . . . it's . . . MacDonald. Dr. Livonia MacDonald." *Why had he asked specifically for a psychiatrist?*

Another pause.

"I'm sorry, ma'am. I don't see a Dr. Livonia MacDonald on our referral list."

"I don't understand." This was the most truthful thing she'd said to the guy so far.

"Kahana Care only serves patients from an extremely limited group of referring doctors. As you know, it's a very exclusive institution."

Exclusive? Then money would talk. "Oh, gosh. Mummy was going to take the Lear over to check out the facility next week. I don't know how I'm going to tell her you won't see her."

"Your mother is able to travel alone?"

Apparently not. "No, no, I would be coming with her of course."

"Well, maybe we can refer your mother to one of our own psychiatrists for an evaluation," he groveled. "That way we can facilitate a referral."

Atta way, Jeeves. "What a fabulous idea," she gushed.

"Okay. What is your mother's diagnosis?"

Trish searched her memory for the name of some kind of psychiatric illness that'd necessitate hospitalization, but wouldn't be so disruptive that she'd be considered an undesirable patient. "Depression . . . Chronic depression."

"Ah . . . Excellent. We may have a bed available for a patient with that diagnosis. Our more acute patients are housed on a different unit. And, unfortunately, there's a lengthy waiting list for those highly sought-after beds."

Visions of *One Flew Over the Cuckoo's Nest* drifted into Trish's awareness. This was the last thing she'd expected.

"I want to be sure Mummy doesn't feel out of place over there. Can you tell me a little bit about the other patients?"

"Of course. We are an exclusive inpatient hospital that houses only chronic psychiatrically disabled patients. Highly disabled."

Trish began to wonder what kind of condition Kensington's mother was in. And who on earth was subsidizing her lifestyle.

"Your mother, with depression, would be among our least affected. Most of our patients are here on a permanent basis."

She imagined Moyna-Lou with matted hair, sitting wild-eyed on the edge of her bed, incessantly rocking back and forth.

"Our patients live out their lives being pampered by our extremely attentive staff," the man bragged. "Our staff-to-patient ratio is two to one," he added proudly.

"It sounds perfect." Trish paused, wondering how she'd get the guy off the phone. Ah, here we go. "Oops. My mum's on the other line. She gets frantic if I don't answer my cell. Can I call you back?"

"Certainly, Ms. Stafford. I shall look forward to your call."

Trish hung up the phone triumphantly. So Kensington's mum was in a mental institution. Leave it to Camille to come up with a case like this. Now she was really curious. Who could afford to bankroll the gig? Kensington's one point two mil might come in handy. But more importantly, what the hell had happened to cause Kensington's old lady to end up in a psych ward?

Trish looked at the clock. Eight o'clock. She had time to do a quick search on the good Dr. Kensington herself before getting geared up for "Nanny Check." It was going to be a long night.

But first, she pulled up Grubhub to order a Red Mill cheeseburger and Babe's special onion rings—and a couple of sides of secret sauce.

After placing her order, Trish typed through another set of prompts to uncover whatever mysteries awaited to be discovered about Jessica Kensington, MD.

Here she is. First medical license: Dallas, Texas. Graduated from SMU med school in '06.

Where'd she get the name Kensington? Must be divorced. Trish smiled. Divorce files frequently contained a wealth of useful information. She input a family court search for Kensington in Texas and waited.

Here we go. The computer announced that the Kensington divorce file was available to download. What the hell went on in Kensington's divorce to have generated that number of documents?

"Damn wireless," Trish shouted up at the ceiling as the download icon crept slowly forward.

Trish limped to the door to get her dinner from the kid with greasy hair who took off before she could even thank him.

Returning to the couch, she scrolled through the preliminary pleadings with one hand and dipped an onion ring into the sauce. The first pleadings were just the standard forms and would likely yield no interesting tidbits for her investigation. As the documents hypnotically scrolled by, Trish caught her breath.

Wait a minute. What's this? Child custody and support orders? Since when did Kensington have kids? Trish double-clicked and searched for the declarations that always accompanied the smutty motions.

She shook some Tabasco on her burger as the husband's declaration filled the screen. Wow. Kensington had accused her husband of sexually abusing the kids. Not surprisingly, he had violently denied the charges and demanded a full investigation. What else was new?

Trish had investigated cases like these a thousand times. If the ex was some kind of deviant, where were the kids now? No one had ever mentioned Kensington having any kids. She took a slug of her cold latte from the morning and anxiously scanned the next document.

Apparently, Kensington had accused her husband of sexual improprieties with all three kids, including the little boy. Jesus Christ. Trish stopped for a second to wonder if Kensington really believed her accusations or was merely the victim of some overly aggressive lawyer whose clients always discovered sexual abuse shortly after retaining them. The whole situation made Trish's stomach turn, and for a moment, she felt a surge of sympathy for Kensington. Either she had been married to a real creep, or some unethical lawyer had taken her for a ride. Neither alternative painted a very nice picture.

Trish spent the next few hours lost in the never-ending juicy divorce pleadings. She skimmed the predictable motions in which one accused the other of violating various court orders, reading carefully to see if there was anything that would help her investigation. She was getting sleepy and frustrated that there was really nothing of interest, other than the fact that it looked like the legal fees had likely crept up into the hundreds of thousands of dollars.

Bored by the predictable goings-on in the hotly contested custody dispute, Trish perked up as she reached the end of the motions docket and got to the trial briefs. She fluffed her pillows and settled in to read the husband's trial brief.

Holy shit!

Trish grabbed her phone to call Camille and realized it was almost 1:30 a.m. This would have to wait until morning.

This time her inability to sleep wouldn't be because of the contraption on her leg. Her mind raced.

—

At 6:30 a.m. Camille rolled over in bed and answered the phone on the second ring.

"Get over here," Trish demanded. "You are not going to believe this. I've been up all night slogging through some ugly divorce pleadings." She paused. "And boy did it pay off!"

Camille knew better than to pump Trish for information when she used that tone of voice. She bolted up. "I'm on my way."

Sam came out of the bathroom, a towel wrapped around his trim waist.

Camille peeled off her oversized T-shirt and jumped into the shower. "Can you get the girls to school?" she shouted over the sound of the pounding water.

Sam pulled aside the shower curtain. "What'll you give me if I do?"

"You'll see . . . later." Camille shook her head and splashed water at her husband.

"How much later?" He refused to close the shower curtain.

"Sam! It's a school day."

"So?"

Gracie charged into the bathroom, pulled down her PJ bottoms and sat on the toilet. "Mom, please don't make me be late again."

"Daddy's taking you."

"And Mommy's so grateful that she's going to give Daddy a big treat when he gets home tonight." Sam winked at Camille and turned back to his fatherly duties.

—

Camille sat on the floor next to Trish. The woman looked perfect even in a ragged pair of sweats. Must be the all-American turned-up nose sprinkled with freckles and the straight blond bob.

"Listen to this!" Trish automatically handed Camille a freshly delivered bagel. "Kensington's ex-husband argued in their divorce case that Kensington was some kind of nutcase."

Camille dipped the bagel into the smoked salmon cream cheese and took a chewy bite. "What do you mean?"

"He said that Kensington had some psychiatric disorder that made her, quote, 'hypervigilant about issues involving sex abuse,' end quote."

"What the hell does that mean?"

"According to the husband's expert witnesses, who examined Kensington at length, Kensington had some kind of mental condition that made her think that she saw sex abuse everywhere, even when there was no proof. And the expert insisted there was absolutely no evidence of sex abuse in their case."

Before Camille could say anything, Trish clicked to the guardian ad litem's report. "That's not all." She was on a roll. "The court-appointed PhD psychologist agreed with the father."

This was wild.

Trish went on to explain that both the guardian ad litem and Child Protective Services had conducted exhaustive investigations and had concluded that there was no evidence of abuse. Further, they opined that Kensington was psychiatrically unable to care for her children because of the harm that came to children when one of their parents constantly asked them if the other was touching their privates.

Camille wrinkled her nose: *gross*. Kensington constantly asking her kids if their dad was touching them? What would that do to their little psyches? This was too much—even for a family law case.

"This has 'Nanny Check' beat all to hell." Trish laughed.

"What did the judge decide?" Camille asked.

Trish clicked open the court order and read authoritatively:

"The court, having heard evidence, hereby finds the following: That there is no credible evidence that Mr. Kensington sexually abused the children; and that there is convincing evidence that Dr. Jessica Kensington is mentally unstable and unable to effectively parent her children. Therefore, it is in the best interest of the children for them to only see their mother during supervised visitation until such time that she has obtained sufficient therapy to treat her psychological problems. The court orders that the father be given primary custody of the three children, with the mother having supervised visitation every Wednesday evening until further order of this court. This court expressly reserves jurisdiction to modify the mother's supervised visitation at such time that her treating psychologist and the guardian ad litem determine that it is safe for her to have unsupervised visitation." Trish shook her head. "Can you believe this shit?"

This was big. Really big.

"And I haven't even gotten to Mama Moyna-Lou." Trish paused dramatically before launching into a narrative of her conversation with her new pal at Kahana Care.

By ten o'clock, Camille's butt had fallen asleep. She stood to stretch. "I think I'll see if I can get a meeting with that psychology professor friend of my sister's, Laurabelle Flores." The tingling that had started at her tailbone spread down her legs as she tried to walk. "Maybe she can help us figure out how all this psychological gobbledygook fits together." Camille hobbled around the tiny apartment, trying to walk off her sleeping legs.

The professor answered the phone on the sixth ring and breathlessly explained to Camille that she was just on her way out the door to walk her dogs. Not a problem, Camille responded, she could use some exercise herself. They agreed to meet for a walk around Green Lake, the Seattle equivalent of Central Park, just a few miles north of downtown.

Thank God for retirement. It usually took weeks to get an appointment with an expert. Camille pulled on her Mariners baseball cap and hurried out into the hazy fall day.

CHAPTER SIXTEEN

No one would ever guess that the elderly woman in the black nylon jogging suit was a world-famous psychologist. Camille approached the professor, who stood and tried, unsuccessfully, to unwind her two English bulldogs' leashes from around her legs. Unable to extricate herself, the professor unclipped one of the dogs and held his collar while she attempted to untangle the mess.

"Here, let me help you with that." Camille squatted down and scratched one of the dogs under the chin while she straightened out the confusion at the professor's feet. Camille looked up. "Thanks for agreeing to meet with me on such short notice."

"It's my plea-sure."

Camille had forgotten how delightful Laurabelle's Mexican accent was.

The professor hit the button on the handle of the retractable leash and played around with it, startling herself as it zipped back into place. She was an absentminded professor if ever there was one.

Laurabelle turned her attention to the two frolicking dogs. "We always love to have company on our walks," she said in a baby talk kind of voice. "Don't we, boys?" The smaller dog clumsily sat up on his haunches and promptly fell over backward.

"They're darling," Camille laughed as she helped the dog right himself.

Laurabelle handed Camille one of the leashes and looked at her conspiratorially as they started off around the crowded lake. "So, tell me about this mysterious doctor of yours."

As they walked the lunging dogs, Camille recited her recent discoveries about Kensington's mental health, or lack thereof.

"Well, you're certainly right." Laurabelle stopped at the brick bathhouse and leaned over the ancient drinking fountain. She stood back up. "This is an unusual woman you're dealing with."

"So, what do you think?"

"First, let me preface this by explaining that this isn't exactly my area of expertise, although I have authored several papers and lectured extensively on sexual abuse as it relates to Stockholm syndrome."

"Explain what that is again," Camille prompted.

"It's where a victim identifies with their captor or abuser. Like what happened to Patty Hearst."

What a character: in the quarter mile from the wading pool to the old bathhouse she'd transformed from wacky dog lover to absent-minded professor to national psychology expert.

Camille looked out at the abandoned swimming raft while Laurabelle kneeled down and extended a cupped hand full of water to Thoreau, who haughtily turned up his nose. *The little guy certainly knows what he wants.* Camille admired his bullheadedness.

"He likes to get his own drink." Laurabelle pointed toward the shoreline. "I'm happy to share what I know that might be helpful to your case, but you have to understand, I'm operating with pretty limited information."

Camille followed Laurabelle to the water's edge, wishing she could get the professor to forget the dogs and focus on her case. "I understand."

The dog launched across the spongy grass to the water, where he leaned over to get a drink and promptly slid headfirst down the muddy bank. The dog thrashed around before pulling himself back up. He sputtered anxiously as Laurabelle cooed to him, "It's okay, sweetie. Come to Mama."

Frustrated, Camille attempted to redirect the conversation. "You were saying . . . about what might be going on with Dr. Kensington?"

"Ah, yes." Laurabelle vigorously rubbed the shivering dog. "Both the doctor and her mother have some kind of psychiatric problem."

We know that, Camille thought to herself.

"Now, this in and of itself isn't all that unusual. In fact, mental illness often runs in families."

Camille wished the professor would get to the point. "So, can you draw any scientific conclusions based on the stuff in her divorce file? Can I prove she's really crazy?"

Laurabelle looked up and shrugged. "Crazy?" She held her hands out, palms up. "Who knows? We're all a little crazy." She sat on the grass and put the towel over her knees, pointing at the bedraggled dog on her lap. She fed him a dog biscuit that had appeared from her pocket.

"What I'm really wondering is whether I have any chance of proving that Kensington's psychiatric difficulties might have affected her medical judgment."

"It's difficult to say."

Camille pulled the stocky professor to her feet so they could resume their walk among the virtual expressway of people of different sizes and shapes. She began to wonder if this meeting had been a complete waste of time.

"Your doctor certainly doesn't appear to be grossly affected." Laurabelle waited while the smaller dog neurotically circled several times before relieving himself. "You did say she's the president of the GYN society, didn't you?"

"Yeah, and from what I hear, she's quite charismatic."

"Well, obviously, I can't make any diagnosis without examining the patient." The professor stopped to scope out a group of retired men sitting on metal-frame lawn chairs on one of the public docks, their fishing lines nicely silhouetted against the glassy water. "Don't you think the guy in the red fleece is a hunk?" She winked at Camille. "I see him here all the time."

And from world-famous professor to overgrown teenage girl. The "hunk" couldn't have been a day under seventy.

"He's cute," Camille agreed. "Now, about the doctor?"

"I can come up with some possible diagnoses based on what you've told me about the psychological reports, the MMPI and WAIS testing, but I'd rather review the reports myself to see exactly what the experts said."

Now we're talking. "I understand you can't actually diagnose someone based on a bunch of legal pleadings," Camille coaxed. "I'm really just asking for your impression of her."

Laurabelle stopped and watched a bird up in a willow tree tussle with a wad of ribbon attached to a deflated helium balloon. "Okay." Laurabelle abruptly took on the demeanor of a professor. "My hypothesis would be that your doctor has some kind of personality disorder, which may have been exacerbated by a posttraumatic stress event."

Ah-ha, a personality disorder. "Can someone like that practice medicine?"

"Not all personality disorders are disabling," Laurabelle explained professorially.

Camille jerked her dog's leash to keep him from straining on it. "How so?"

"Like everything else, there are degrees of disorder. It's a very gray area."

"Can a personality disorder be controlled by medication?"

"Medication isn't always appropriate for these patients. But patients with personality disorders often have anxiety that is treatable with meds."

Camille dodged a double amputee flying by on a race-style wheelchair. "So, do you think Kensington may be on some kind of psych meds?" she asked hopefully.

"It's certainly possible."

Camille paused to think. "Is there any way to prove that, if Kensington has a personality disorder, it might have caused her to behave erratically, or have a significant lapse in clinical judgment?"

"You'd have to find out a great deal more about her history and current condition. It would be a major undertaking."

A flock of Canada geese landed on the path directly in front of them. Camille raised her voice to be heard above the barking dogs and hissing geese. "When I took this case, I thought it would be simple. I can't believe what it's turned into."

The dogs stubbornly stood their ground in the face of the taunting gaggle of geese. Camille liked their style. Nothing was too much for these two.

She waited for the geese to disperse. "I'm not sure I'll be able to prove that Kensington's mental condition had any bearing whatsoever on her ability to practice. Maybe I'm on a wild-goose chase." She smiled. "No pun intended."

Laurabelle stopped. "Didn't you tell me that this doctor as much as killed an innocent little baby?"

"It certainly looks that way."

"Well, what if you're right? What if the doctor's behavior was caused by some kind of psychiatric disorder? It could happen again."

Oh my God. It had never really occurred to her that the case was about much more than just baby Zachary.

"Camille, my dear, you have no choice. You must pursue this. You have a responsibility to find out if this doctor is somehow impaired and put a stop to her if she is. Isn't that why you do this work? To make a difference?"

For a moment, the chaos reverberating around the lake shifted into slow motion. The eccentric professor was right. Camille was transfixed by the deep brown eyes set in Laurabelle's wrinkled face.

Laurabelle nodded. "I thought so. You will do whatever is necessary to find out exactly what is wrong with this woman. And I will help. End of discussion."

CHAPTER SEVENTEEN

"Goddamn this fucking printer!" Camille banged the huge piece of equipment that was sporadically spitting out copies with black streaks running down the center. Bagley had objected to her motion to compel Kensington to undergo an independent psychiatric examination, and Camille's strict reply was due in court in less than two hours. She plopped down on the floor in front of the behemoth and put her head in her hands. Amy had only been gone for a week and the place had gone completely to hell.

"Anyone here?" Came a voice from the reception desk. "Hello? Messenger, anything to pick up?"

"Can you wait just a couple of minutes? I'm . . . having a little technical difficulty," Camille responded weakly. From her spot hunched over on the floor, Camille looked up into the face of a messenger with spiky blue hair and multiple pierced facial parts. She was clad from head to toe in black leather.

"Problem with the printer?" the messenger asked politely.

Camille glumly held up the streaked copy.

The messenger caught it as it fluttered to the floor, crumpled it up, and tossed it into the recycle box. "You're out of toner."

Camille propped her chin in her hand. "Can it be fixed? I was going to do a quick review of my motion before I have to e-file it."

"If you have an extra toner cartridge."

As the leather-clad messenger started opening cupboard doors, Camille could almost count the number of navel rings marking the center of her flat tummy.

Scratching her head, Camille considered getting up to help, then decided it would be too much trouble. She was exhausted; trying to practice law and be her own paralegal at the same time had proved to be too much. Something had to give.

"By the way, my name's Lucia."

Camille pointed to the gold lettering over the reception desk. "I'm Camille, Camille Delaney."

"I know." The messenger smiled. "Ha! Here it is!" She held up an odd-shaped black object and opened the ominously silent machine. "You'd better pay attention if you want to know how to fix this yourself next time."

Next time? If she didn't get some help soon, there wasn't going to be a next time.

The phone rang and the messenger grabbed it. Camille admired her boldness.

"Law offices of Camille Delaney." She shrugged quizzically at Camille, who nodded thankfully in return. "And who shall I say is calling?" She punched the hold button. "A Dr. Fitzharris. From California?"

Camille's heart fluttered. "Oh my God. I need to talk with him. Never mind, I don't have time to print and review that motion."

Lucia looked at her watch. "Go ahead, I can pop on this computer and e-file your docs with the court. The motion is due by noon, yes?" When she smiled, her tongue stud glistened behind perfect white teeth. "I promise."

"You are a lifesaver." Camille smiled; of course a messenger would know the court deadlines. "I'm not sure how to thank you."

She quickly scribbled her court e-service password on a sticky.

"Go." Lucia pointed to the blinking light on the phone. "Doctors don't like to be kept waiting, don't ya know?"

Fitzharris was full of good news. He had determined that the Anderson baby had been completely healthy when Helene's labor began. And the labor had appeared to be progressing quite nicely, then for some reason Kensington had administered Pitocin in dosages that shouldn't have produced the results they did. In fact, the contractions intensified as the Pitocin was decreased. It didn't make any sense. Fitzharris wondered whether the dosages of Pitocin charted were accurate.

Camille listened as she watched Lucia intently commandeering the reception desk computer. The doctor went on to explain that the Pitocin caused Helene's uterus to contract so violently that the blood vessels became constricted and cut off the oxygen supply to the baby.

Maybe I can talk Lucia into helping out part time, Camille thought to herself as the doctor summarized his findings—the sustained lack of oxygen had caused the baby to suffer irreversible brain damage.

She'd never considered the possibility that Kensington had lied about the dosages of Pitocin.

Lucia poked her head into Camille's office and fluttered her fingers in a waving motion. She pointed at the carrier pouch slung over her shoulder and gave Camille an A-okay sign: "I have the discovery responses you left at the desk. I'll get them over to Lowe this afternoon."

Camille wanted to at least get Lucia's phone number but couldn't exactly interrupt her most important witness. Grudgingly, she waved back and turned her attention to the doctor, who explained that, in his opinion, it was inconceivable that a patient could have so many tetanic, or unrelenting, contractions at the dosage of Pitocin that had been charted.

"I'm just not sure how you're going to prove that a board-certified obstetrician could have mismanaged a Pitocin induction to this degree," he pondered. "Not to mention that she should never have done such an aggressive forceps delivery on a gestational diabetic in light of the risk of fetal macrosomia."

Just like Cathy had said—only now she had it as sworn testimony.

"You mean she was likely to have a large baby due to her diabetes?"

"Exactly."

Back on with the lawyer hat. "Can you sign a declaration stating that the doctor violated the standard of care and that her violation was the proximate cause of the baby's injuries, and ultimately, his death?"

"Sure, no problem."

Camille felt the tension of the morning's debacle with the printer drain from her shoulders. "Great. That's just great."

"It's my pleasure. You want to draft a declaration for my signature?"

"Sure. I'll email it to you in the next couple of days."

Camille hung up and tried, unsuccessfully, to locate the format for a doctor declaration in the computer system. Nothing was easy anymore.

———

"Mom?" Angela's voice traveled in from the reception area. "I'm here!"

"In here, honey!" Camille felt guardedly optimistic about the plan to have Angela help out after school. Anything would be an improvement at this point.

"What do you want me to do?"

Camille pointed to a heap of paperwork spilling from her outbox. "You can start by organizing and filing this stuff. Then you need to scan it into the system. Let me show you."

Talk about being a fish out of water, Camille thought to herself as she tried to make heads or tails of Amy's color-coded filing system. Masses of red, purple, and blue folders had been crammed into the file cabinet in no recognizable order whatsoever. Oh well, Angela was plenty smart, she'd just have to figure it out as best she could. Camille returned to her desk.

"What do I do with this?" Angela wandered into Camille's office holding some kind of pleading.

Camille felt the top of her head for her glasses and swore. She opened three desk drawers before locating a pair. "Oh my God, where'd you find that?" It was a deposition notice for Dr. Fitzharris. The docketing system had been shot all to hell since Amy left. It was virtually impossible to keep track of and respond to all of Bagley's motions, not to mention schedule depositions. Camille knew she was sinking fast.

She skimmed the document. "Goddamn it!" The dep had been noted for the first week in November. There was no way Fitzharris would be available in the middle of his son's medical crisis. If the defense lawyer was anyone other than Bagley, she could just pick up the phone and reschedule the dep, but with him on the other side, she'd have to file a motion to quash the subpoena. Shit. She threw the dep notice on top of the rapidly growing stack of motions from Bagley's office.

Angela perked up when the phone rang. "I'll get it!" She lunged. "Camille Delaney's office . . . Sure, hang on." She held the phone out for her mother.

"Who is it?" Camille asked expectantly, relieved at not having to answer the phone for a change.

"I dunno. Some woman."

"You have to ask who's calling so that I can decide if I want to speak with them or call them back," Camille explained slowly.

Hands on her hips, Angela narrowed her gaze. "You mean you might want me to lie and tell someone you're not here?"

Camille cocked her head at her daughter and peered over her half-glasses, her fleeting optimism quickly disappearing. "'Not available' would be more accurate."

"So? Aren't you gonna pick up?"

"After you get back on the phone and see who it is," she snapped.

"Mother! I'm going to sound like a complete idiot! First I say you're here, then I ask who it is. They're gonna know I'm lying if I come back and make up some phony excuse that you're not available." Angela flailed her arm at the phone. "You gotta talk to them!"

Angela had been there less than a half a day, and already the office was saturated with teen angst. No point exacerbating the situation. "Fine." Camille picked up the phone. "Next time you ask who it is." She punched the blinking light so hard she broke a nail. "Camille Delaney." She winced and shook her hand in pain.

"This is Wanda Harper, from Mr. Bagley's office. I'm calling to confirm the currently pending motions in the Anderson case."

Camille pulled a legal pad out from under the pile of obstetric textbooks on her desk and began noting the litany of motions as the secretary officiously read them off. There was no way Camille could keep up at this pace. As she was hanging up the phone, she heard her mother's voice in her head: *Always hold out for a miracle. You never know what's around the next turn.*

Angela stormed into Camille's office and threw herself onto the couch. "When do I get a break? I have got to call Erica and find out what happened between her and Justin. And I have no idea where the party is after the swim meet Friday night."

This was likely not the miracle her mother had in mind. "How's the filing coming along?"

"It's easy."

"But are you making any progress?"

"Yep, I'm almost done. Can I go home soon?"

Camille looked at her watch. "You've only been here a couple of hours. I'm not exactly sure how you were able to do all that filing so quickly."

Angela pulled a long pink strand of gum from her mouth. "So, can I at least take a break?"

What on earth could have led her to believe that her seventeen-year-old daughter could possibly be the answer to her woes? "Five minutes." Camille returned to the chapter on uterine overstimulation and tried to ignore the craziness going on around her: just like Fitzharris had explained, too much Pitocin would cause the uterus to contract so intensely that it would cut off the oxygen supply to the baby, thereby causing brain damage. Camille was in the middle of taking lengthy notes on the sequelae of placental insufficiency caused by uterine hyperstimulation when the phone rang. She wrote on her note pad: *What happens when there are too many uterine contractions? The placental blood flow is impaired.* One of the biggest challenges in a medmal case was making the medical jargon understandable to jurors.

"Angela! Can you get it?"

"I'm on my cell!"

Camille felt like she was in the middle of a bad dream. She sighed. "Camille Delaney . . . Sure. Hold on." This was ridiculous. "Angela! It's for you!"

"Tell them I'll call back!"

"You tell them. I'm trying to get some work done here!"

Camille got up and slammed her door so that she could concentrate on the intricacies of uterine pathophysiology. She picked up the phone on the second ring, realizing that her crackerjack new receptionist obviously had better things to do.

"Camille Delaney . . . Hang on . . . Angela! Line three!"

Angela poked her head through the door. "How do you do a conference call around here?"

"Jesus Christ, Angela. This is a law office, not a teen crisis line."

"Just tell me how to do a conference call and I promise I'll leave you alone."

"I don't want you to just leave me alone. I want you to answer my phone," Camille pleaded. "And finish the filing!"

"Calm down, Mother." Angela blew a big pink bubble and popped it loudly. "I'll figure it out myself." She impatiently flipped her long black hair as she ran from the room.

"The instructions are on the little plastic thing that pulls out from the bottom of the phone!" Camille called after her.

On her way to make herself a cup of tea, Camille skidded on the stack of papers strewn across the floor of the reception area. "What are you doing?" She held her hands out in frustration. "I thought you said you finished this filing."

"Shh!" Angela held her hand over the receiver. "Erica's breaking up with Justin, and she conferenced me in so I could be a witness."

Camille got her tea and returned to her office, determined to master the complexities of fetal oxygenation. Office organization would have to wait.

"Mom! Someone's here!" Angela shouted from the reception desk.

Did the kid ever get up off her butt? Camille hoped whoever it was, they weren't too important. The place looked like it'd been hit by a typhoon.

Oh my God, how embarrassing. "Hi, Helene." *This is great. Just great. My most important client walks in on this chaos.* Camille reached down to gather up the papers blanketing the floor. "I'm . . . I'm sorry for the mess."

Helene's forced smile was unconvincing. Something was wrong. Helene looked around, obviously trying to look unaffected, but Camille could only imagine what she must be thinking. A surprise visit from Helene Anderson was the last thing she needed today.

"I'm sorry for stopping by without calling." Helene hesitated. "Is this a bad time?"

Bad time? Could there be a worse time?

"No, no, it's fine. Come on in." Camille set the disheveled pile of papers on the reception counter and glared at her daughter. She'd had it. "Get this place picked up," she hissed. "Now." She took the phone roughly out of Angela's hand and ceremoniously hung it up before following Helene into her office.

"Here." Camille gestured as she grabbed an armload of articles about gestational diabetes and fetal distress off the couch. "How are you doing?"

"Not so good." Helene sighed as she plopped down heavily.

That makes two of us.

"What's going on?" Camille sat on the ottoman, trying to look professional.

"I can't sleep at night, then I can't get out of bed all day. I have no appetite and absolutely no energy. I don't know what to do."

Camille nodded silently.

"Every time I close my eyes at night, I'm haunted by visions of Zachary's limp little body hooked up to all those machines. And nothing the doctors did could save him. I feel like it was my fault. I should've checked up on that Dr. Kensington. I should've known . . ." The tears started.

Jeez, here she was feeling sorry for herself because her office was a mess, and the woman in front of her was dealing with the death of a child.

"It's not your fault," Camille said gently. "And it's normal to be depressed after what you've been through." She leaned over and touched Helene's arm. "Have you spoken with your doctor?"

Helene looked flatly at Camille through her tears. "You really think I'd go to a doctor?"

Helene's anguish filled the tiny office.

"Look, Helene, just because you had a problem with Kensington doesn't mean you should never go to another doctor again."

"Maybe someday, but not now." Helene's gaze remained completely blank.

A moment of silence passed while Camille searched for something to say.

"Well . . . things on your case are coming along nicely."

"What about the summary judgment motion you told me about? What exactly is that anyway?"

"It's when the other side says, 'we want to see what you've got.' Basically they file a motion that says you can't proceed unless you can prove you have an expert who'll support your case." Camille tried to look confident. "Like I told you, we need to have an expert who will testify in court that Kensington violated the standard of care, and that that violation caused the baby's subsequent medical condition and ultimately his death."

"So, do we have one?"

"We do." Camille nodded. "He's a really nice guy and feels very badly about what happened to you. He's going to sign a declaration for us to attach to our response."

Helene smiled through her tears. "I didn't mean to come in here and act like an ungrateful brat." She dug into her purse and pulled out a small wooden box. "I brought you something."

Camille gently took the hand-painted artifact. "It's beautiful." She turned it around so she could admire it from all sides. "Did you paint this yourself?"

A slight nod and a sniffle. "It's a family tradition. We call them wish boxes." Helene's voice was hoarse from crying. "Whenever we really appreciate something that someone else does for us, we make them a wish box." Helene looked Camille directly in the eye. "And I appreciate that you've agreed to take my case to trial."

Camille noticed that the world "wish" was written in metallic silver script diagonally across the top of the orange-and-purple box.

"Open it up," Helene urged.

Camille complied. Inside was a little piece of decorative paper.

"The tradition is that if someone does something really special for you, and you wish for a particular outcome, you write what you're wishing for on a piece of paper and put it in the box." Helene reached over and removed the paper from the box. "See?" She unfolded it. "It says 'justice.'"

Camille bit her lip. It didn't seem to be an appropriate time for her get on her soapbox about the so-called justice system. "It's lovely."

"By giving you the wish box, it seals our joint intention to see that justice is done in this lawsuit." Helene put the paper back inside the box and placed it in Camille's hand, then gingerly bent Camille's fingers around the box and held Camille's fist in her hand. "There. It's as good as done."

Camille wished she shared her client's sense of hopefulness. "Thanks, I'll put it right here, on my desk. It'll remind me that we're in this together."

"I really want to keep you as my lawyer; I trust you, Camille." Helene took a tissue from her purse and blew her nose. "But I keep getting these calls from that Harvey Lowe."

"What?" A prickle went up Camille's spine. "Are you kidding me?"

"No, he keeps trying to get me to go back to him. Says your office is coming unglued." Another nose blow. "Something about Amy quitting."

That scum, Camille thought to herself. "Amy took a job downtown so she could spend more time with her sons. The hours around here got to be too much for her."

"Lowe says you couldn't pay her because you're broke." Helene picked at the wadded-up piece of tissue. "I really hope you can afford to keep our case, because I like you a lot." Helene smiled weakly. "Can you? I don't believe Harvey Lowe works for justice at all, only money. So, I'd really rather not have to deal with someone like him if I don't have to."

"You won't. I promise." There was no way Lowe was going to snatch this one from her. No fucking way. "I'm in the process of replacing Amy," Camille said in her most reassuring tone. "And for now, my daughter is helping out. Don't worry, everything around here is fine," she lied. "Just fine."

CHAPTER EIGHTEEN

The only thing that set Amy Hutchins's office apart from the other thousand cubicles floating high above the city of Seattle was the shrine to her two sons on the barren oak bookcase. The boys' smiling faces provided a constant reminder of why she was here instead of where her heart was: in Camille's cramped Fremont office.

Another overstuffed banker box. In the past three weeks she'd closed more files than she'd processed in her entire career with Camille. Why Lowe paid her such a huge salary to work as a file clerk was beyond her. Hopefully the job would get a bit more interesting eventually.

According to the small marble clock on the credenza, it was almost time for her afternoon sugar fix. Would it be the chocolate éclair or the chocolate bear claw today? Decisions, decisions. Maybe there was one redeeming feature of coming back downtown after all: the unsurpassed selection of chocolate at the various cafés.

Who are you kidding? Amy asked herself. *There's nothing redeeming about this place. Except the money.* The boys' pictures smiled in agreement.

The familiar ringtone of her mother pierced the barren cubicle. "Hi, Mom."

"Any luck finding an apartment?"

"There are a few possibilities, but I'm a little nervous about taking on a bigger rent payment." Amy wondered how she would explain to her mother that things just weren't working out as she'd hoped.

"We already discussed you using your signing bonus to pay your first, last, and deposit."

"I know." Amy stared at the five-foot-high stack of banker boxes that took up an entire wall in her office. "It's just . . ."

"Stop it, Amy. No job is perfect. You'll get used to it. Remember, you have more than yourself to think about here."

She knew better than to argue when her mother used that tone of voice. "I know." She slumped over her huge desk. "It's just that they don't give me anything to do. They're using me as a glorified file clerk."

"Poor thing. Working a lucrative stress-free job in a fancy downtown office," her mother said sarcastically. "Most people would kill for a job like that."

"Not me. I like to be busy."

"Then find something to do."

"Like what?" Her mother always brought out the petulant teenager in her.

"I'm sure there are plenty of things that need doing around a big office like that."

Amy closed her eyes. The thought of another day at this place made her nauseated.

"Well, dear, you'd better not take too many personal phone calls. You best get back to work now."

Typical. Complete denial that anything at all could possibly be wrong.

"I was just checking to see that you followed through on that apartment search," her mother added cheerfully.

"Bye, Mother." Amy dropped the phone onto her desk and began indexing the contents of the thousandth box.

Jeez, Lowe certainly managed to find experts in exotic places. Amy cataloged the travel file in front of her. Camille always seemed to get her experts from boring Midwestern towns, like Cleveland or something. Actually, the expert Camille had hired in the Anderson case was from Ojai, California. If she had to be this bored, she could at least daydream. Ojai would be an interesting place to visit—kind of a cross between Southern California and Wyoming. She imagined Camille dressed in Wranglers and designer cowboy boots heading into a dep. The mental image made her laugh out loud.

Amy wedged the file back into the box and wondered how the Anderson case was progressing. The Ojai doc had certainly seemed encouraging after he'd reviewed the records. For a moment, Amy considered picking up the phone and calling Camille. Nah, too soon. She knew it'd be a while before Camille would cool down.

One more file, then it's off to the bakery. Amy opened the last folder in the box.

Talk about a small world; Amy skimmed a bill from a private investigation firm in Santa Barbara, California. The invoice was for the "Ojai job." It must have been some big-ass investigation; the PI had charged Lowe twenty thousand dollars for two days' work. Amy turned to the next page in the file. Her heart leapt into her throat. Things were suddenly getting a bit more interesting.

———

Camille opened the heavy doors to the courtroom for her early morning motion, hoping she hadn't forgotten anything. It was the first time in her entire career she'd processed an entire motion herself, without the help of any support staff. Well, it hadn't been completely a solo performance. There was that messenger with the spiky blue hair who'd appeared out of nowhere. Camille cursed herself for not getting the girl's phone number.

As she entered the courtroom, Camille's face flushed at the sight of Vern Bagley, leaning over the bailiff's counter, joking with Judge McIntyre.

"So there I was . . ." Bagley laughed. "Standing on the eighteenth tee, and my five iron is nowhere to be found!" The judge's and attorney's guffaws stopped abruptly, and they turned to ogle Camille in her tightly fitted black suit.

Camille's mouth went dry as Kip Davenport shot her an icy stare. He gently took his daughter by the arm and ushered her to her seat. The intimate father-daughter interaction made Camille think of her relationship with her own parents. Her mother, literally halfway around the world in Greece, her stepmom investigating the latest international crisis, and her dad, probably just waking up somewhere in New York, in time to have his early afternoon "breakfast" right before his rehearsal for another performance in some smoky jazz club by 9:00 p.m. *I wonder if any of them would be there for me, like Kip is for his daughter,* Camille asked herself. But she already knew the answer.

What happened next caught Camille entirely by surprise. Jessica Kensington pulled away and rudely turned her back on her father.

What an ungrateful bitch. Doesn't she realize how lucky she is to have a father like Kip?

"Ms. Delaney." Bagley stood between his client and Camille. He shook Camille's hand, then looked over his shoulder at the judge. "Looks like we gotta get back to work, Your Honor." Bagley's laugh turned hollow. "We're ready for argument whenever you are."

This was bad news. The judge and Bagley were obviously friends. The bailiff stood as Camille tried to make some semblance of order out of the documents she pulled from her briefcase. In the mélange of papers, Camille discovered Gracie's spelling homework, which she tried to nonchalantly stuff back inside.

"The court will hear arguments on the plaintiff's motion to compel Dr. Jessica Kensington to undergo an independent psychiatric examination in the case of Anderson versus Kensington; King County cause number 1-22-3456-SEA," the bailiff announced loudly to the empty courtroom.

The judge looked bored already. "Counsel?" He wiggled his index finger at Camille, indicating that she was to step forward.

Camille approached the bench and spread out her materials on the ledge where Bagley and the judge had been laughing together only moments ago. "Thank you, Your Honor," Camille said in her clearest courtroom voice. "As you know, Civil Rule 35 (a) provides for the physical or mental examination of a party upon good cause shown." There was no need for Camille to look at her notes; she'd practiced this so often, she could argue it in her sleep. "And there is clearly good cause for the court to order a CR 35 exam in this case."

The judge turned to boot up his computer. It wasn't a good sign.

If she wanted to get his attention, it was now or never. Camille raised her voice. "This is a case involving the death of a baby, Your Honor."

She emphasized the word "baby" each time she said it. "If this baby died due to the mental illness of the attending doctor"—she pointed directly at Kensington—"evidence of the doctor's mental illness and its impact on the innocent baby would unquestioningly be admissible and highly germane to the plaintiff's allegations of negligence."

The judge looked up from his computer. Good.

Camille continued, "As set forth in Dr. Flores's declaration, which is attached to my motion as exhibit A, there is ample evidence that Dr. Kensington has a mental disorder. The jury in this case is entitled to know if that disorder had any impact on her ability to provide treatment to Helene Anderson."

"Let me get this straight," the judge growled. "You seriously want me to order a board-certified physician to undergo a mental evaluation based on the opinions of a couple of hired expert witnesses in a decades-old custody battle involving the defendant and her ex-husband?"

Things were definitely going from bad to worse. She doubted that any amount of brilliant arguing would turn this guy around.

In an effort to feign confidence, Camille threw her shoulders back and stood as tall and erect as possible. "Dr. Laurabelle Flores is a nationally recognized professor from the University of Washington and she's of the opinion that the disorder, as outlined by the experts who evaluated Dr. Kensington during her divorce, more probably than not impacted the doctor's clinical judgment." Camille held up Laurabelle's declaration.

"I read your materials, counsel," the judge said impatiently.

"Your Honor," Bagley interrupted, "if I might?"

"Go ahead, counsel."

Bagley pulled out a thin stack of papers from under his neatly typed notes. "I have here a copy of a chapter in a book on psychic phenomenon authored by Dr. Flores."

Camille bolted over to intercept the document. "I object!"

Bagley turned his shoulder to Camille and handed the papers to the bailiff.

"Your Honor! I object to defense counsel presenting additional evidence at this hearing. It's a clear violation of the court rules. If he wanted the court to consider any book chapters, they should have been included in his response. Anything offered at this late date must be ignored by this court."

The judge adjusted his glasses and scanned the papers.

"Your Honor!" pleaded Camille.

"Overruled," the judge said slowly as if he were speaking to a child.

"As you can see, Your Honor, this so-called expert upon whom Ms. Delaney relies is a proponent of psychic healing."

Flabbergasted, Camille nearly shouted, "Laurabelle Flores is an international expert. She's published papers worldwide on Stockholm syndrome." Camille felt completely out of the loop, not knowing what the judge and Bagley were looking at. "Your Honor, may I at least see a copy of the chapter?"

Both the judge and Bagley ignored her.

Bagley spoke up. "No responsible judge would rely on a declaration from this kind of quack."

Camille's blood was boiling. "Objection! I object to Mr. Bagley characterizing Dr. Flores as a quack."

"I've heard enough, counsel," the judge said forcefully. "The court has reviewed both parties' materials and has determined that there is no convincing evidence at this time that would indicate that this defendant's alleged psychological problems years ago had any bearing whatsoever on her ability to perform her duties as a physician now."

The judge looked through his half-glasses and shuffled the paperwork in front of him. He looked down on Camille and stated loudly, "This court specifically finds that the various declarations of these hired guns in some ancient Texas divorce case are not in any way relevant to this action. And I will not consider any more of these histrionic so-called expert declarations in this courtroom." He glared angrily at Camille, who couldn't decide if it was her overwhelming anger or bitter disappointment that had rendered her speechless. "And, Ms. Delaney," he added, "don't you be bringing this court any more baseless declarations from retired university professors. If you wish me to even consider finding in your favor in the future, I strongly suggest that you find yourself a credible expert, not some character from the psychic network." The judge smirked at Bagley. "Motion denied." He banged his gavel.

A chair screeched across the courtroom floor as Kip Davenport vaulted from his chair to follow his visibly shaken daughter out into the hallway.

Camille gritted her teeth in abject humiliation. It was bad enough to lose the motion, but to be reamed out in front of Kip was more than she could bear. Especially since she'd completely obliterated their friendship over this case. Exiting the courtroom, it was all she could do to keep from breaking into a full run. Instead, she walked officiously toward the elevator bank, as if losing this type of motion happened every day.

Nearing the elevators, she noticed Kip and Jessica engaged in a heated discussion at the end of the hallway. Jessica glared at her father and gesticulated wildly, her seething anger palpable even at a distance. Kip tried to calm his daughter by patting her on the shoulder, but Jessica twisted away and snapped loudly enough for Camille to hear, "You get the hell away from me!"

Kip didn't try to hide his pain as Jessica raced to the stairwell and slammed through the door, leaving her dejected father alone in the faded marble hallway.

Disgusted, Camille hit the elevator button. While she waited, she reflexively reached into her pocket for her cell phone to call Amy. She always reported the outcome of her motions—good or bad. Suddenly, she stopped. What was she doing? A mental picture of her empty office wafted into her consciousness. Feelings of loneliness and abandonment swept over her and she clenched her jaw to blink back the tears. She couldn't break down here. Not now.

———

Finally! Free at last. She had made it! Trish carefully climbed out of bed and grabbed her crutches. Just yesterday, the orthopedist had given her a clean bill of health. She could actually go out and enjoy the sunshine. She wished Gigi were home. They'd been together only a year, but they hadn't ever spent so much time apart—only eight more weeks until Gigi's visiting pathology professorship in Europe ended. Trish knew what an honor it was for Gigi to have been chosen to go to Oxford for a semester, but she couldn't help wishing she'd hurry home.

Wistfully, she picked up one of the many romantic cards Gigi had sent from London. Trish teared up as she read the steamy inscription on the back of an old-school postcard picturing a bank of fog floating over Buckingham Palace. She briefly wondered if the folks at the post office ever stopped to read stuff like this. A momentary wave of embarrassment washed over her as she gently kissed the card. She'd never missed anyone like this in her entire life. Trish took the card into the bathroom with her and taped it to the mirror next to the picture of a breathtakingly beautiful Black woman. Gigi was standing on the bow of the ferry, beaming her signature toothy grin with the Seattle skyline awash in the pink glow of sunset over her shoulder.

She briefly considered making herself a latte with the machine Gigi had sent her but decided it would be much more satisfying to go to her favorite espresso place, the Cherry Street Coffee House in Belltown. Trish stopped to check her email before heading out into the glorious day.

Her heart sank. Nothing from Gigi yet this morning. She skimmed down the short list of emails, mostly from clients. *What's this? Confidential re: Gregory Fitzharris MD . . .* Huh, wasn't that Camille's expert in the Anderson case? Trish clicked on the subject line and curiously began to read the text.

What the hell? Who was this from? She read the email address at the top of the screen. Anonymous. Great. Trish sat on the edge of the couch and lost herself in the virtual world of email distribution. The best she could determine was that the email had originated in an internet café somewhere in downtown Seattle.

I guess more important than who this is from is whether it's true, Trish thought to herself as she typed her way into the California medical disciplinary board web page and followed the directions to find out how to check up on actions pending against a doctor.

"Oh my God!" she said out loud. "Camille is gonna freak."

CHAPTER NINETEEN

The rooftop deck of her houseboat served as Camille's own private hideaway where she went to be alone. Over the years, she'd spent many an hour surveying the busy lake from this vantage point, and today it was certainly as good a place as any to try to get over her humiliating defeat in court. The fresh air would surely clear her head.

Snuggling up in her fleece jacket, she picked up the *Trial News* article on one of Harvey Lowe's big settlements against Kensington. How the hell had he gotten so many cases against this one doctor? She'd found three so far—all for brain-damaged babies who had died shortly after birth.

Who gets multimillion-dollar settlements in "dead baby" cases? Camille read the article for the umpteenth time. Lowe had based his argument to the insurance company on the fact that this wasn't "your average dead baby case." According to Lowe, the parents had been treated for infertility for years, so he took the position that this was actually a "premium" baby, and they couldn't just "have another one" as the defense always tried to convince the jury.

What an offensive thing to have to argue. Like one baby had more value than another. Too bad Helene Anderson hadn't been an infertility patient.

Camille watched the succession of floatplanes gliding down onto the lake, carefully avoiding the cadre of pleasure boats out enjoying the chilly fall day as she reread for the third time the chapter that

Laurabelle had authored on spiritual mind healing. It wasn't that big a deal—people had been studying this stuff for centuries. She knew Laurabelle had taken up metaphysics after retiring from the U, but she didn't know she'd authored papers on the subject. The judge had obviously just been looking for some reason to deny her motion.

Camille sighed; it was too late to affidavit the judge and request reassignment. This case was becoming a full-blown nightmare.

From down at water level, Trish's familiar voice yelled, "Anybody home?"

"Up here!" Camille stood and looked over the railing to see her friend paddling up in her kayak. "What are you doing out of bed?"

Trish pushed her straight blond hair back from her face as she turned to look skyward. "The doctor says I can kayak if I don't put any weight on my leg. I rigged up the rudder so I can control it with my left foot."

"Very clever!"

"C'mon down and go paddling with me for a little bit," Trish coaxed. "It may be our last chance this season. There's supposed to be a windstorm tonight, and that always brings nasty weather."

"I'm kind of working up here." Camille pointed back at the deck.

"Well, work as you paddle. We can talk about your case." Trish gestured, nearly losing her balance as she craned her neck to see Camille. "Besides, I have some new information you're gonna want to know about."

Camille glanced at the stack of paperwork she'd stuck under the leg of the weathered Adirondack chair to keep it from blowing away.

"So, come on down." Trish clutched the edge of the deck outside Camille's bedroom in an effort to steady herself.

"I guess this stuff can wait. I'll be right there." Camille gathered up her things, climbed down the ladder, through the kitchen, then downstairs and out onto the deck off her bedroom that was littered with the family's water toys.

Trish pointed to the parking lot, where Cathy Swain was loading a dock cart with a week's worth of groceries. "Who's the woman with the blue BMW?"

"She's an OB-GYN who lives on our dock. And she's straight, and you're in love. Remember that gorgeous pathologist who's coming home in a mere eight weeks?" Camille said as she picked up her kayak and slid it gently into the water.

Trish ignored the not-so-subtle jab. "Do people ever tell you that you two look alike?" she asked as she held the kayak next to the dock so Camille could climb in. "Except your legs are longer."

"Yeah, especially since she went to my hairstylist and told him that she wanted a cut just like mine."

"Wow. All she has to do is dye her hair black and you two could pass for twins." Trish leaned forward to watch Cathy pushing her dock cart across the parking lot. "She's quite the babe." Trish nodded approvingly, then added, "Hey! If she's an OB-GYN, she must know your wacky defendant."

"She does, and don't use the term 'wacky' so lightly," Camille joked as she led the way down the middle of the canal behind the row of houseboats, waving at a neighbor who was watering his newly potted plants. The pansies and winter cabbage reminded Camille that fall was upon them.

Continuing to paddle, Camille recounted her crushing defeat in court. It felt good to finally have someone to unload on. She knew she'd missed Amy's camaraderie, but she didn't realize how much until she began to let loose with Trish.

"And my office is coming apart at the seams," she added as they headed out onto the lake, where they stopped long enough for a tall Bayliner to streak past them. "Whatever happened to the seven-knot speed limit out here?" Camille asked rhetorically as the slender kayaks rolled in the boat's wake.

Trish splashed toward the transom of the retreating cruiser. "There. Does that make you feel better?"

"A bit." Camille laughed.

"Back to the office issue: You've got to get some help. You're going to get sued for missing a deadline or something, Camille."

"I have Angela coming in after school." *Like that's any help at all.*

Trish rolled her eyes. "Oh, that'll do it. I'm sure that between personal phone calls, she'll keep you out of trouble and on track."

"How'd you guess?"

"I was seventeen about a lifetime ago."

"Me too," Camille answered wistfully.

"Seriously, how's it going?"

"Seriously?" Camille recognized the familiar pit in her stomach. "I have no support staff. I just got my butt kicked in court in my most important motion. My now ex-friend Kip Davenport hates my guts. And I took out a bank loan behind Sam's back in order to process a case I probably have no business pursuing. Other than that, things are going swimmingly."

Trish paddled up next to Camille. "You took out a bank loan?"

"Yes, and if you tell Sam, I'll kill you."

"Jesus, Camille, he's going to find out, you know."

"No, he won't. I used the girls' college fund as collateral, and I'll have the loan paid and the accounts back to normal before anyone knows."

"You know, maybe you can't afford to process this case."

"I have to. No one else in town will take it. And besides, it's too late to turn back now."

"Why can't you refer it out?"

"You know the damages in these types of cases are typically small. No one wants to take that kind of risk with such a limited upside reward."

"So, why should you?"

Camille pointed to the north shore with her paddle. "Let's go over to Gas Works Park and talk." She looked up at the succession of floatplanes, ferrying weekenders up to the San Juan Islands for a fall getaway. "It's too hard to talk with all this racket."

As reflected by its name, Gas Works Park was designed around an ancient tangle of machinery that had once been a working gas factory. Years ago, the city had painted the twisted giant a deep charcoal gray, and it stood proudly at the north shore of Lake Union where it faced the cosmopolitan city at the opposite end of the lake. From where Camille and Trish kayaked, the contrast between the old and the new couldn't have been more striking.

Trish reached the shore first and waited for Camille to come help her out of her kayak. "I'm stiffer than I thought," Trish admitted as she leaned on her friend's arm and limped gingerly up to the grass at the top of the steps. "I've been on that couch too damn long."

"Easy," Camille urged as she helped Trish get comfortable on the grassy bank.

Trish looked at Camille. "Okay, the way I see it, we have to figure out a way to make something out of the fact that both the doc and her mother have some kind of mental illness. The psychologist said Kensington's behavior might have been incited by some kind of post-traumatic type of reaction."

"But the judge won't let me prove it. And he humiliated me in front of that dickhead Vern Bagley."

"Stop whining. Your proof's going to go to a jury, not the judge and his cronies."

Camille smiled appreciatively. *Sometimes you just need a friend to knock some sense into you.*

Trish plucked a wide piece of grass, placed it between her thumbs, and blew. The weak whistle defused the tension and made them both laugh. "Okay. What *exactly* do you have to prove?"

"I need to prove that Kensington violated the standard of care in her treatment of Helene. But since juries tend to give the doctors the benefit of the doubt, it would be awesome if we could give them an excuse to explain her complete mismanagement of the labor and delivery—so if we could show that the doc's psychiatric condition made her unable to exercise appropriate judgment when she was caring for Helene and her baby, that would be cool."

"Okay. Got it. Any other way you can prove that she's impaired, other than a court-ordered examination?" Trish flicked the blade of grass.

Camille thought for a moment. "Only if I could get ahold of her psychiatric records or something."

Trish perked up. "What if you could show that she's still taking some kind of psychiatric medication?"

"That'd be helpful, but no judge is going to let me see her medical records." Camille reached for the Frisbee skidding to a stop at her feet and tossed it to the border collie waiting anxiously at the water's edge.

"What if we could search her house and find some kind of medication?" Trish asked.

"How could I do that?"

"Once my leg is healed up, I can find a way to get into her place and go through her stuff to see what kind of medication she's on."

"Great idea, but it'd take too long. You won't be fully back on your feet by our trial, which is in about a month." Camille flopped back and watched the clouds skip across the clear sky. "Nice try, though."

"Maybe I can hack into her pharmacy records, then."

"You'd have to search every pharmacy in Seattle." Frustrated, Camille jammed her hands into the pockets of the jacket she hadn't worn in a few weeks, where she felt a thick piece of cardboard. She pulled out the fancy party invitation and stared at it for a moment. Then she smiled.

"What's that?" Trish asked.

"My entrée into Kensington's palace," Camille announced.

"What?"

Camille held the card up like a Wimbledon trophy. "It's an invitation to Kensington's legendary Halloween party." It might just work.

"Kensington invited you to a party?"

"No, she invited my twin sister, the OB-GYN with the blue beamer."

"What are you talking about?"

"Every year Kensington has this huge blowout costume party. She invites a bunch of OB-GYNs from all across the state. And Cathy Swain is on the list."

"So you're gonna go with Cathy?"

"No." Camille smiled. "I'm gonna go as Cathy."

"Oh no, you don't!" Trish wagged her index finger in front of Camille's nose.

Camille grabbed the finger. "Why not?"

"You leave the undercover stuff to me."

"I did okay checking out Willcox in Arizona last spring," Camille bragged.

"As I remember it, you got yourself locked inside the bad guys' lab and I had to rescue your sorry ass."

"That was my training mission. I can handle this one on my own."

"Sure you can." Trish shook her head. "But I do like the idea of getting inside the doc's house. Let's figure out a way for me to do it for you."

"First of all, it's not a house; it's a penthouse in a full-security building downtown. And second, there's no way you're going to break in there with a bum leg."

The border collie scampered in front of them and bounded into the lake after his beloved Frisbee.

"Building security is no problem. Most of the systems they put in those condos are a piece of cake to get past," Trish said.

"Not that one. I've been to fundraisers up there in one of the other penthouses. Those people have beaucoup original artwork hanging all over the place. Believe me, no one would live somewhere with all that priceless stuff on the walls if there wasn't one mother of a security system in place."

They ducked as the dog emerged proudly from the water, Frisbee between his teeth. As expected, he shook himself just a couple of feet in front of them.

Trish ran her hand over her face to get the thin film of mud off. "So, what do you propose?"

"I'll get into some outrageous costume and pose as Cathy for the evening. According to Cathy, the whole idea of the party is not to be recognized. It's the perfect plan."

Trish looked skeptically at Camille.

"What?" Camille whined. "You said Cathy and I could pass for sisters."

"Who's going to save your butt if you get caught?"

"I'm not going to get caught. I have a friend who's a master at disguises." Camille pointed directly at Trish. "I believe I recall a certain long red wig and Broncos jacket that served you pretty well in Arizona."

"I don't know about this." Trish grimaced.

"You said you'd help me with the case. Here's your chance."

Trish turned to her side to push herself up. "Oh my God, I almost forgot the reason I dragged you out here in the first place." She eased herself back down.

"You mean other than to encourage me to go on an undercover mission into Kensington's place?"

Trish smirked. "Actually, I wanted to give you a heads-up on your OB expert from California."

"What do you mean?"

"The strangest thing happened. I got this anonymous email. And I really mean anonymous. I traced it every way I know how, and I have no inkling who sent it." Trish paused. "All I know is that it came from one of those internet cafés where they have a line of computers for public use. It's from downtown Seattle."

"What'd it say?"

"Here, see for yourself." Trish handed Camille a crumpled piece of paper.

Camille read. "Confidential re: Dr. Gregory Fitzharris." She looked curiously at Trish. "Gregory Fitzharris: Plaintiff's expert OB-GYN in Kensington v. Anderson. Doctor under investigation by the California medical disciplinary board for inappropriate sexual relationship with two female patients. Licensure action pending."

She looked at Trish, wild-eyed. "You have to find out where this came from."

"I'm trying, but whoever sent it knew exactly what they were doing and they didn't want to be discovered."

"So, is it true?" Camille held the paper out as if she were afraid of it.

"I checked with the California medical disciplinary board and it is true that there's an investigation underway. But the doc is vehemently denying the charges," Trish added quickly.

Suddenly, Camille felt dizzy. "Greg Fitzharris couldn't possibly have gotten tangled up in some weird relationship with a patient. He's been dealing with his son's terminal illness for God's sake."

"You know," Trish lectured, "you cannot show up in court with this guy, even if he's not a pervert. Bagley'll eat him alive."

Camille drew a sharp breath at the mention of the word "pervert."

"What's wrong?" Trish asked.

"Bagley called Fitzharris a pervert when we were talking that night after a swim meet."

"Sounds to me like your expert is dead meat, girlfriend."

"Goddamn it!" Camille wadded up the paper and threw it forcefully toward the collie, who gleefully ate it in one bite.

CHAPTER TWENTY

Ah, peace and quiet at last. Having Angela help out had seemed like a good idea at the time, but in actuality she had become a bit of a hindrance around the office. Camille forced herself to disregard the disturbing information she had learned the previous day about the goings-on at the California medical disciplinary board, and tried to concentrate on the obstetric textbook in front of her. There was no way Greg Fitzharris could have gotten himself into the kind of trouble he'd been accused of. It just didn't fit.

She flipped open the thick book. She was old school—always best to hold a book rather than reading some dense scientific journal online. She put on her glasses and scanned the table of contents for the chapter on gestational diabetes. No matter who she used as a testifying expert, she'd still have to learn the complexities of this disease.

How could this happen? The one expert who would help her gets in trouble with the disciplinary board, just when she needs him the most. *Stop it*, she scolded herself and focused on the text.

Why hadn't Kensington elected to do a C-section when it became obvious that Helene had CPD, cephalopelvic disproportion, which was the technical description for the fact that the baby's head didn't fit? There had to be some reason Kensington disregarded every single sign of trouble in Helene's case. Especially since she had gestational diabetes. Camille pushed away the complicated book and opened the file on Kensington's mental health history. The answer had to be in there somewhere.

Her heart fluttered with nervousness as she fingered the Halloween invitation. Could she really get away with crashing Kensington's party? What made her think she wouldn't get caught? It was October 30, and the party was the next day. What was she going to wear? Not to worry, she and Trish were scheduled to meet the next day to come up with something that would work.

Camille looked up from her desk to see the messenger with the blue spiky hair standing in her doorway.

"Ms. Delaney?"

"I don't have anything for you today, Lucia, thanks." Camille smiled.

Lucia stepped closer to Camille. "Actually, I was wondering if you have a minute."

Even the leather and studs couldn't hide the scared little girl behind the pseudo-harsh eyes.

"Of course. Have a seat. What's up?"

The girl was obviously trying to muster up her courage to speak. "I, uh, I have this problem I was hoping you could help me with." She self-consciously twirled her nose ring.

"I'd be happy to." Camille's maternal instincts made her want to reach out and hug the tiny being. "What kind of help do you need?"

"I think I need some kind of restraining order or something." Lucia's voice was barely a whisper.

Restraining order? *The poor thing, what kind of trouble could she have gotten herself into?* "Is someone bothering you?"

"My boyfriend. He tried to strangle me last night."

Camille got up from her desk and motioned for Lucia to join her on the couch.

Lucia fought back the tears.

"What happened?" Camille asked.

"We're in this band together, and he gets really jealous if any guys flirt with me. He always tells me it's my fault." She chipped the blue fingernail polish off her short nails as she spoke. "I didn't do anything. This guy just stood in front of the stage and stared at me." She bit off a hangnail. "And Rocky just flipped out when we got backstage." The tears started. "He slapped me across the face, then grabbed me by the neck." She reached up with both hands and massaged the area around her Adam's apple. "I was too scared to go home, so I spent the night in my car."

Camille imagined how she'd feel if this was one of her own daughters. She put her arm around Lucia and held her. "You did the right thing." She rubbed Lucia's shoulder. "You did exactly the right thing."

"But I don't know what to do now. All my stuff's at his place."

"The most important thing is that you're safe. We'll find a way to get your stuff back." Camille dabbed away the tears. "Do you have anyone you can stay with?"

"Yeah, I can stay with my friend Shayla."

"Good." Camille smiled. "Now, we need to get started on a protection order, so you'll be safe."

"I . . . I don't have any money to pay you."

"Don't worry about it."

"I was thinking. You look like you could use some help around here." Lucia smiled and sniffed. "Ever since Amy left, the place has kinda fallen apart."

Camille laughed. "You noticed."

"I could get you caught up on your filing," Lucia said hopefully, "and answer the phones. I used to be a secretary."

One prayer answered.

Lucia continued. "I'd do it in trade, for your help with the restraining order."

"That's not necessary. I'd be happy to pay you for working. You're going to need something to replace your lost income if you're not singing with your band anymore."

"Well, you're right about that." Lucia perked up. "How about I work here in the mornings, then I can still do my messenger runs in the afternoon?"

"Will that work for the messenger company?"

"Oh yeah, they're really flexible. They'll schedule me whenever I tell them I'm available."

Camille nodded. "Okay, we can give it a try." She returned to her desk. "Now, let's get started on that protection order." She sat at her computer and began to type.

"Ms. Delaney?"

Camille looked up at the scared young woman.

"There's something you should probably know about me before you agree to help with this."

Camille raised her eyebrows and cocked her head to the side.

"Will it matter to the judge if they find out that I did time in prison for drugs?" Lucia hurriedly added, "And I totally understand if you don't want to help me now that you know."

Camille paused, wondering what had transpired in this young woman's life that had led her down this path. "The court has the responsibility to protect any citizen regardless of their background. So, no, it makes no difference at all."

Lucia grabbed a tissue from the box on Camille's desk and blew her nose. "I figured I should tell you, you know." She shrugged. "The conviction follows me everywhere. I can't get an apartment, and it's rough getting a job. I'm not sure where I'll live if I have to move out of Rocky's place."

"Well, let's get this restraining order filed, and I'll make some calls to see if I can help with at least a temporary place for you."

"Thanks, I don't want to be a burden. My parents might help, but I try really hard to live my life independently. They were so disappointed in me for getting involved in drugs and everything."

"I'm a mom, and although I can't imagine what I'd do if one of my kids got caught up in drugs, I'd like to think I'd be there for them when they need me."

Lucia smiled. "Ever read that book—*Tiger Mom*? That's my mom. I'll spend the rest of my life making up for what I did."

"Your mom should be proud of you. You have a good job. And I'll help you find a place."

Lucia sat up straight and threw her shoulders back just a bit. "I've been clean for two years, three months, and twelve days."

Camille's maternal instincts took over. She stood up and walked over to the waif-like young woman and put her arm around her. "I am absolutely positive that your mom is super proud of you." She hugged her. "That's a huge accomplishment."

It didn't take long to get the pleadings together, and Lucia was on her way to court to present her declaration to the commissioner in less than half an hour.

"Thank you so much. I'll be here tomorrow morning at eight, okay?" Camille handed Lucia a key to the office. "See you then!"

She stood in the middle of her office and rolled her head around on her shoulders, trying to work the kinks out of her upper back. She looked at her watch. Time for a quick trip to the gym before heading out to the bar association judicial appreciation dinner. She turned the phones to voice mail and hit the light switch.

———

Brandi Carlile serenaded Camille through her headphones as she huffed and puffed through the last five minutes on the StairMaster. She squeezed her eyes closed and cheered herself on silently. "You're almost there. You can do it."

She opened her eyes in response to a gentle tap on her shoulder. "Psst!"

It was Deanne Stillerman.

"Hi," Camille said breathlessly.

"You almost done?"

Camille looked at the digital timer. "Two minutes." She squeezed a stream of Talking Rain spring water into her mouth.

"We need to talk," Deanne whispered conspiratorially.

What difference did two minutes really make? Camille ground the ridiculous-looking machine to a halt and grabbed the towel hanging from the handlebars. She wiped her face. "What's going on?"

Deanne looked from side to side. "It's Kensington," she whispered loudly.

Camille motioned to the juice bar in the lobby. "Can I get you something?"

"Cranberry juice and a poppy seed muffin would be great, thanks."

The two women sat down at a table against a huge Plexiglas wall enclosing the racquetball court. Inside, two sweat-drenched men dove for the ball.

"So?" Camille asked, trying to hide her feelings of anticipation.

"I got to thinking about the discussion we had a while back about that bitch Jessica Kensington."

Camille startled as a ball careened off the clear wall next to her. She scooted her chair away.

Deanne continued, "I thought about you the other day when Kensington had another mishap in the ultrasound department. I figured it might be helpful to your case."

This ought to be interesting. "Thanks, I appreciate it."

Deanne took a sip of her juice and looked around the lobby slowly. "So, here's the scoop." She leaned forward. "Kensington's down in ultrasound doing a chorionic villus sampling on some woman who'd been an infertility patient."

Camille grimaced. "A what?"

"Chorionic villus sampling. It's where the doctor takes a tiny tissue sample of a placenta in an eight- to ten-week fetus, to test it for genetic defects." Deanne looked through the Plexiglas as one of the men threw himself against the wall.

"Ah." Camille's nurse training was coming back. "I vaguely remember that term."

"Well, Kensington digs around in this woman's uterus so much that she might as well have been doing a pregnancy termination. I couldn't believe it." Deanne made a Yiddish-sounding guttural rasp. "Ugh! So what am I supposed to do? Who am I but some schlocky nurse watching as the doctor's performing some kind of roto-rooter on this screaming woman."

Camille stiffened. "Oh my God, so what happened?"

"Well, I take the patient to the recovery area, where she promptly has a full-blown miscarriage."

What the hell? Camille wondered to herself.

"Then Kensington shows up all solicitous and everything and sits with the patient and cries with her." Deanne rolled her eyes.

"Jeez."

"So, I get to thinking." Deanne slammed down her juice bottle. "This is around the third time that I can remember seeing Kensington screw up one of these procedures on an infertility patient. It's like she has some kind of personal vendetta against these women."

Camille was speechless.

"Don't you think it's weird, her messing with infertility patients like that?"

"Yeah," Camille said slowly, wondering if this had anything at all to do with her case. "It's weird all right."

"Do you think this will help you in your lawsuit?" Deanne looked on as the men exited the Plexiglas cubicle. She cleaned her teeth with her tongue. "Do I have any poppy seeds in my teeth?" She pinched her cheeks.

"You're fine." Camille winked.

"Hey, Deanne!" The taller man sauntered up to the table. "Wanna shoot some hoops?"

As Deanne got up, Camille felt for a moment like the girl left behind at a junior high school dance.

"You ready to get your butt kicked?" Deanne laughed flirtatiously as she took the stance of a well-schooled point guard.

"Not if you spend the whole time worrying about breaking a nail, like you did last time," he teased.

Deanne turned to Camille. "I gotta run. See you around?"

"Sure, go ahead."

Deanne shot Camille an enthusiastic smile of success.

Camille nodded approvingly. "Have fun!"

Deanne ran back and whispered into Camille's ear, "I hope you nail that bitch."

—

The judicial appreciation dinner was in full swing when Camille located her place at a table of women lawyers with whom she'd volunteered at the Women's Law Center, a nonprofit organization that offered pro bono help to marginalized people. Camille had recently coauthored a brief on the importance of specifically defining domestic violence as a tort, which would allow women who were victimized to obtain damages in civil suits against their abusers.

She silently took her seat and automatically scanned the room in an effort to locate Harvey Lowe. Even after all these years, she still dreaded running into him, so at every event she attended, she apprised herself of his whereabouts to prevent an unexpected meeting.

No luck. She started on her salad as the president of the King County Bar driveled on with her opening remarks. Then came the predictable introductions of the various judges in attendance, along with their campaign chairs. Camille had leaned over to visit with the woman who had coauthored the domestic violence brief with her when she heard Judge McIntyre being announced. She whispered that she had a case in front of the chauvinist jerk, and then stopped cold when his campaign cochairs were announced. There, standing on either side of the judge, were Vern Bagley and Harvey Lowe.

Camille dropped her fork. Suddenly, her appetite had vanished.

CHAPTER TWENTY-ONE

The next day, Lucia greeted Camille by holding up a book that had arrived in the morning mail. "Is Eve McKane really your sister?" She opened the book. "It's autographed! This book is on the *New York Times* bestseller list, you know."

Lucia hadn't struck Camille as one who would be familiar with the contents of the *New York Times* anything.

"She is."

"Wow!" Lucia nodded enthusiastically. "You think she'd autograph a book for my grandma?"

Camille leafed through the mail. "I'm sure she'd be delighted." She surveyed what had looked like the scene of Hurricane Katrina just the day before. But this morning the desktops were clear and the piles of paper had been sorted and stacked neatly. Camille felt like crying with gratitude. "Jeez, this place looks great!"

"I decided to come in and get an early start." Lucia grinned. "We need to spend some time going through these stacks so you can tell me what you want done with all this clutter." She gestured.

"It'd be my pleasure." Maybe things were about to turn around after all, but Camille had to admit, she'd hardly expected her guardian angel to be a formerly incarcerated woman sporting blue hair and a tongue stud. "Did you have any trouble with the restraining order yesterday?"

"Nope, the commissioner signed it without even asking me any questions. I stayed at my girlfriend's last night."

"Good for you."

Lucia followed Camille into her office. "Now, I just have to find a permanent place."

"I'll help you. No worries."

"Actually, it does worry me. It's not easy for someone with a criminal record to rent a place, but I appreciate any connections you might have." Lucia picked up an old cup of tea from Camille's desk and wiped the coaster off with her sleeve.

Camille flipped through her sister's book. How was it that Eve could afford three houses and a New York loft just by writing this kind of brainless self-help nonsense? She plopped into her cream-colored leather desk chair.

"I skimmed the first few chapters," Lucia admitted sheepishly.

Camille looked up. "What'd you think?"

"Well . . ." Lucia hesitated.

"Really," Camille prompted, "I want to know."

Lucia sat on the edge of the purple couch. "I just don't think relationships are simple enough to lend themselves to a one-size-fits-all type of treatment."

This little dynamo hadn't ceased to surprise her ever since she'd rescued Camille from the wayward printer. "How so?"

"I don't know." Lucia shrugged. "I guess I'd have to say that everyone is a product of both their biological predisposition as well as their environment, so I don't know how it would be possible to address all kinds of relationships in just one book." She held up the thin volume. "Especially one little book like this."

"I have to admit, I agree with you." Camille smiled.

Lucia popped up to answer the call bell at the reception desk. When she returned, she had a pleading in hand. "It's a . . ." She read the heading, "Witness Disclosure List, from Bagley's office." Wrinkling her nose, she handed the document to Camille. "You know, you can tell a lot about a law firm by how their receptionist treats the messengers."

"So how do the Bagley receptionists treat messengers?"

"Like scum."

"Somehow that doesn't surprise me." Camille nodded as she turned to the extensive list of witnesses, which could have just been e-filed with the court and served on her by email, but Bagley was all about show, so he always had hard copies hand delivered. Jesus Christ, who hadn't they hired to defend Kensington? The thing read like a "who's who" of the University of Washington OB department. Bagley's cover letter stated that they'd be happy to schedule any depositions she'd like to take as soon as they received a prepay of eight hundred dollars an hour. She bounced back in her chair. What in the world was she doing trying to handle a case of this magnitude with the assistance of her seventeen-year-old daughter and a blue-haired punk rock singer recently released from prison?

"You ready?" Trish blasted through the doorway. "Seaholm costume design at your service!"

Camille hugged her friend. "You really think I can pull this off?"

"Hey, this was your idea, not mine." Trish held Camille's chin in her hand and turned it one way, then the other. "I can disguise you any way you want. What you do once I'm finished is up to you."

Lucia stood in the doorway. "You going to a costume party?"

Camille smiled as Trish turned to Lucia. "Hi, I'm Trish." She looked questioningly at Camille.

"I'm Lucia."

"Lucia's going to work for me part time in the mornings."

Lucia's smile was perfect. "Nice to meet you." She shook Trish's hand. "You a costumer?"

"Private investigator," Trish responded.

Lucia raised her eyebrows, then turned to Camille. "You know, if you're looking for a cool costume, I'd be happy to help. My mom is one of the lead singers in the San Francisco Opera, and when I was a kid, I was in lots of operas myself. I have a bunch of her old costumes in my storage locker. They're way too big for me."

Camille's jaw dropped. "Opera?" She checked her internal biases as she stopped to wonder how the daughter of an opera singer ended up in prison on a drug charge. This girl was a mystery.

"My parents made me take classical voice starting in first grade. Like I said, my mom's an opera singer, and my dad's in the orchestra. It was obvious from early on that I had a pretty good voice, so they had me in lessons forever. I actually love opera." She cocked her head. "Maybe someday I'll go back to it."

If she'd been given a hundred guesses as to the avocation of the woman standing in front of her, Camille would never have guessed opera.

"Hard to see me as a mini diva, yeah?"

"That'd be an understatement." Camille winked.

"Anyway. I'd be happy to lend you one of my mother's costumes. It'd probably fit you. She's really tall for being Japanese."

"She'd love it," Trish answered.

"What did you have in mind?" Lucia asked.

"We need something that no one will recognize her in."

Camille was beginning to feel invisible, being talked about as if she weren't even there.

"How 'bout Madame Butterfly?" Lucia suggested.

"Perfect!" Trish shouted. "It's perfect, we can do Japanese makeup. No one will ever recognize you. This'll be great."

—

Camille sat as still as a statue in the passenger seat of Trish's Mini Cooper. The giant wig made her head feel oddly out of balance. And the beautiful red kimono was more than a little difficult to walk in. But, on balance, she had to admit, she really looked quite spectacular. Trish glanced over, and Camille demurely averted her eyes and fluttered the hand-painted silk fan in front of her face.

"That Lucia is certainly a find," Trish said as she pulled into the loading zone down the street from Kensington's building. "You look outrageous. No one will ever recognize you in that getup."

"Yeah, and it's perfect because I don't have to talk, just look shy and fan myself whenever someone talks to me."

Trish looked at her inquisitively.

"Remember, the whole point of the party is not to be recognized." Camille pulled down the visor and primped in the mirror. "No one's allowed to ask who anyone else is."

"Great." Trish opened her backpack and handed Camille a super tiny cell phone. "Here, stick this in your belt. And don't be afraid to use it if you get into trouble." She held up an identical phone. "My number is on auto-dial. Just press one."

"And you'll hobble up and save the day?"

"I'll think of something." Trish turned to Camille. "You ready?"

"As ready as I'll ever be. Let's do it." Camille turned to face forward as Trish darted out into traffic and got in line for the valet. In front of them, a line of Mercedes and Volvos deposited festively attired partygoers. Camille and Trish waited and watched as the array of well-disguised doctors made their way into the art deco lobby of the elegant condominium.

"Remember, you're just there to get a look around for any sign of psychiatric medication," Trish lectured. "You take pics of whatever you find and run. Got it?"

"I'm off." Camille hiked up her kimono and waited as the solicitous valet opened her car door and offered his hand to help her out of the trendy little Mini Cooper.

"Believe me, I'll hurry back. I promise." Camille blew Trish a kiss as she cursed the funny socks Lucia had fitted to go with the Japanese slippers as she jumped to avoid a puddle between herself and the sidewalk.

The elevator was jammed. Next to Camille stood a knight in full armor and a lady-in-waiting. Directly in front of her was some kind of ice princess accompanied by a Greek god. There was a Roy Rogers cowboy-type couple and a pretty good Elvis imitation, who had the accent down cold. One of the creatures from Star Wars offered to push the elevator button.

"I assume you're all going to the thirtieth floor," he joked.

"Hold the elevator!" hollered an overweight man dressed as Captain Hook.

Camille caught his eye and quickly looked away. She'd handled Captain Hook's divorce a couple of years ago at Whitfield, Bahr, and Moses. She covered her face with the handy-dandy fan and carefully studied the shoes of everyone in the tiny cubicle.

Please let me get out of here without getting myself disbarred.

Jessica Kensington, dressed to the nines in a stunning Cruella de Vil costume, gushed over her guests as they noisily disembarked from the elevator. It was *101 Dalmatians* to the max. Kensington held a long silver leash with a live Dalmatian, and a basket of real black-and-white-spotted puppies sat by the elevator door.

The place was everything Cathy had described. The dramatic foyer led to a glass-enclosed room floating high over the city. It was like a giant greenhouse; even the roof was glass. And the only word for the furniture was decadent. Metallic silver throw pillows of all shapes and sizes were scattered across the floor and on the various black couches and club chairs. And the art. The one wall that wasn't pure glass held a gigantic twenty-foot-tall abstract piece Camille knew she recognized from a local Seattle art collector's magazine. Wow.

A waiter dressed as a court jester dodged a couple of Dalmatians as he held out a tray of glasses filled with champagne. It was tempting, but she was working. She shook her head and smiled behind her fan.

Oh shit, here comes Kip Davenport. Camille ducked behind a fragrant tree that smelled divine. She looked up to see several plump oranges hanging from the branches. *Who grows oranges in Seattle?*

Kip glad-handed his way through the crowd as if each guest was a long-lost cousin. Camille briefly wondered if he'd ever considered a career in politics.

She backed away from Davenport and nearly bumped into the tuxedoed string quartet. Standing up against the wall, Camille tried to discern the layout of the unusual condo. On the north wall a spiral staircase led to some kind of balcony overlooking the huge greenhouse. She glanced at her tight skirt and odd slippers and wondered how easily she could navigate the steps. It was possible, but it wouldn't be a pretty sight.

She wandered off to the left, where the catering staff had overtaken the rather small kitchen. Obviously, this place wasn't designed for a gourmet cook, although it was cool. Black lacquered cabinets hung over black marble countertops, and the sinister black appliances looked as if they'd never been used.

Camille snaked her way through the crowd to the other end of the narrow kitchen, where she found a bedroom overlooking an infinity lap pool that appeared to be magically suspended over the Pike Place Market thirty stories below.

Outside, a festive group surrounded a dramatically positioned fire-pit, whose flames cast playful shadows on the wisteria that covered the opposite wall.

Camille crossed the monochromatic gray bedroom to where a door led to a dressing room, and beyond that, an all-marble bathroom suite. She shuffled into the bathroom and locked herself in. Before she could turn around, an especially huge Dalmatian shot up from his nap and launched into a tirade of barking. Camille stifled a scream in her throat, then turned to the frenzied dog.

"Shh!" Camille held her hand to calm the growling animal. "Here, baby," she cooed as he bared his teeth at her.

Another round of canine hysteria.

Camille hiked up her kimono and held the doorway to the water closet open—she threw in a loofa sponge that had been sitting next to the sink. "There you go, boy."

The dog lunged, then skidded to a halt as Camille slammed the door behind him. She could hear him growling and chomping on the bristly sponge.

Camille quickly turned to the vanity. Ha! She rifled through the drawers and then the medicine cabinet. Pay dirt. Risperidone and Xanax. That afternoon, she'd called Laurabelle to get a list of the names of the various psychiatric drugs that Kensington might be on. But anyone who read *Cosmopolitan* knew these two drugs. She pulled out the tiny phone Trish had given her and was taking a picture of the bottles when another large unlabeled bottle caught her eye. It was filled with white pills that were scored down the middle. She poured a few out on the counter and snapped pictures of the front and back of the pills for later identification.

As was common, the bathroom had a door that probably went back to the front hallway. Time to make a hasty retreat. She opened the door and found herself in a black-paneled study. Not surprisingly, it was spectacular. The bookshelves went up the sides of the room about twenty feet, and there was another balcony at the top of a metal ladder that looked more like a work of art than anything utilitarian. Camille felt like she was on a movie set. As she hurried across the room to the door, the name of one of the books on a shelf caught her attention.

She gasped as she realized that almost all of the books directly over the computer referenced psychopathic behavior, and most were about psychopathic killers. There was a shelf full of books on sexual deviancy, three on the genetic predisposition to psychopathic behavior, a few on sexual torture, and several on sexual psychopaths. Camille held her breath as her gaze gradually swept the room. The whole scene struck her as particularly weird in light of the strange allegations in Kensington's divorce file.

Strewn across the desk were a number of scholarly articles on sexual abuse and the genetic predisposition to sexual psychopathy. Camille stood frozen in place. There was definitely something creepy about an obstetrician having a library like this. She couldn't stop herself from plucking one of the books from the shelf and leafing through it. Her heart raced as she noticed that most of the pages contained highlighting, as if Kensington were studying the genetic predisposition to sexual psychopathic behavior. *Eech!*

After replacing the book, Camille began snapping some pictures of the books. As she got closer to the computer, she noticed that Kensington had left it on. She clicked on the mouse and watched as a QuickBooks program filled the screen. Camille glanced at the door and hurriedly scanned backward through the electronic check register. There were monthly payments to Kahana Care, the psychiatric hospital where her mother was a patient, and monthly deposits to an account called "Marblemount."

Hmm, there's a little town on the west slope of the Cascade Mountains called Marblemount. But it seemed highly unlikely that the glamorous doctor would have a place in a dying little logging town like that.

Camille shuffled through the papers in the mail basket and found something addressed to an Eric Davenport in Marblemount. Must be her brother or something. Opening the envelope, she saw a check with both Kensington's name and Eric Davenport's name on it. The check was written to him and signed by Kensington.

This woman's supporting her entire family, Camille thought to herself as she stuck the envelope into her belt. *No use pushing your luck. Better get out of here.*

She turned away from the computer and noticed a set of keys on the ledge. Enough. She slipped the keys up her sleeve and headed to the doorway that she figured would lead her to the foyer and back out. Locked. No surprise there. Why would Kensington want anyone to discover her lurid interest in this psychopathic shit? Camille turned back to the bathroom door where she had entered.

"Oh, excuse me," she said reflexively as she walked out of the part of the bathroom where the toilet was into the main area where Kensington herself stood, leaning over the sink applying her lipstick in front of the mirror.

"Cathy, is that you?" Kensington asked anxiously. "I know it's you. It has to be," she giggled.

Camille froze. Flutter. Flutter. The fan was going a mile a minute. *Better play along.*

"Where in the world did you ever find that costume? It's utterly spectacular!"

Camille tensed as Jessica reached out and ran her hand along the smooth silk kimono. She girlishly held the fan over her face.

"You are the perfect Madame Butterfly," Jessica announced. "My father took me to see it in San Francisco for my birthday a few years back. The lead singer was an amazing Japanese opera diva. You look exactly like her."

Camille nervously fingered the keys that had slid out of her sleeve into her hand and held her breath as Jessica shifted her gaze to Camille's fist. Time for a little diversion. She dropped the fan with a clatter. When she bent down to pick it up, the top-heavy wig slid off to the side.

"Ha! I knew it was you," Jessica announced triumphantly. "I recognize the haircut. What'd you do, darken it for the party?" Jessica nodded. "Actually, it's a good idea, a few blond hairs escaping from under that wig would have surely given you away." Jessica blotted her lips and opened the door to the water closet. Camille dodged out of the gigantic bathroom just as the huge black-and-white dog lunged out of the tiny enclosure, front teeth bared for a fight.

Camille pushed the tall wig back in place as she flew out of the bathroom seconds ahead of Jessica Kensington's scream.

CHAPTER TWENTY-TWO

Never had Camille suffered such a long elevator ride. She clutched Trish's cell phone and tried to relax. How the hell could Trish stand doing this for a living? The whole time she'd been in Kensington's condo, she felt like there was a giant neon light flashing over her head screaming *IMPOSTOR! IMPOSTOR!*

The swirling night air caught Camille's kimono, causing it to fly up around her thighs. She shoved it down with one hand and grabbed her wig with the other, then waved frantically at Trish, who was reading Seattle's alternative newspaper, *The Stranger*, behind the steering wheel of her car.

Camille startled as she felt a hand gently gripping her upper arm.

Turning, she found herself face to face with Kip Davenport. Her mind went blank.

"I'd love to take you for a drink if you don't have any other plans tonight," he said flirtatiously.

Where was that little silk fan when she needed it?

"By the way, my name's Kip, Kip Davenport." He flashed Camille his best politician's smile.

Camille coughed and drew a shaky breath, clueless as to what to do next. If she said a word, she'd definitely be busted.

As if on cue, Davenport's cell phone rang. He listened and turned to Camille. "I'm sorry, it looks as if I'm needed at the hospital." He motioned to the valet to get his car. "It seems I interrupted you in the middle of hailing a cab." He stepped off the curb and flagged a yellow cab as it streaked by. Opening the door, he bowed. "Your carriage, Madame Butterfly."

Camille smiled at Kip as he closed the door behind her. She leaned over the seat. "I'm just going up a few blocks," she said to the driver through her rapidly tightening throat. "To the Inn at the Market."

Camille turned around and thankfully saw Trish blinking her brights as she squealed out behind the cab. She shot her a text to follow her.

As soon as the cab turned the corner onto Stewart heading down into Pike Place Market, Camille turned to see that Trish was, in fact, right behind her. She leaned forward and said to the driver, "This is great, I'll get out here." She handed him a ten-dollar bill for a three-block ride and hopped out, waving at Trish.

"Calm down, no one's following you." Trish laughed as Camille collapsed into the tiny car. "This is not a TV spy show."

"Mission accomplished," Camille announced breathlessly. "Did you see Davenport talking to me out there?"

Trish winked. "I'll bet he was in a pretty big hurry to get to the hospital, huh?"

"How'd you know?"

Trish held up her steno pad with Davenport's cell phone number written inside the front cover. "Rule number one: always bring along a list of vital information on any undercover operation."

Camille exhaled loudly. Now that she was safely ensconced in Trish's Mini Cooper, she felt a rush of pride. "It actually wasn't that bad. Kind of like how people describe giving birth, pure hell while you're in the midst of it, but all rosy when you look back on it after the fact."

"Let's go get a drink. I want to hear all about the party," Trish answered. "See how my prize student held up."

"Where do you expect me to go looking like this?" Camille pointed at her face.

"I've been sitting here watching lots of people dressed up. It's Halloween night and everybody's partying. Besides, we're at the Market, for God's sake. You'll fit in perfectly."

"Okay, let's go to the Pink Door, then. Gwendolyn won't laugh at me." Gwendolyn was Camille's old pal, the owner of the ultimate Seattle restaurant known mostly to locals, since it wasn't exactly easy to locate behind the unmarked simple pink door on Post Alley.

Just like Trish said, Camille was hardly the only one in the restaurant's candlelit bar sporting an extravagant Halloween costume. Many patrons were clearly celebrating the holiday, while others had on get-ups that may or may not have been intended as costumes. It was an eclectic crowd to say the least.

Gwendolyn waved from across the bar and soon appeared with two light pink cocktails in delicate martini-type glasses.

"They're on the house." She smiled and looked curiously at Camille.

"It's me," Camille stated loudly.

"Thank God, I knew you couldn't be Gigi. It'd be impossible to cover her skin tone with that makeup. And I could only hope that Trish wasn't out fooling around while Gigi's away."

"I can't believe you said that!" Trish interjected. "I am literally counting the days."

"I know you are." Gwendolyn turned to Camille. "You definitely win for most luscious costume of the evening." She fingered the long kimono sleeve. "This is fabu!" she gushed.

"Why thank you."

"You two hungry?"

For the first time that evening, Camille realized she was famished. She nodded.

"I'll have the chef make you your favorite chicken with a thousand herbs if you'd like." Gwendolyn cocked her head. "It's not on the menu, but we can whip it up especially for you."

"Yum! Thanks," Camille answered quickly, wondering how easy it would be to eat in the elaborate costume.

"Make it two," Trish added, then waited for Gwendolyn to take her leave. "So?"

Camille fumbled around in her obi and pulled out Trish's little phone to show Trish the pictures of the two pill bottles, the scattering of unidentified pills, the envelope addressed to Eric Davenport, and the set of keys. She felt like a little kid emptying out her trick-or-treat basket.

Trish read the names of the meds on the two pill bottles. "I get the psych meds, but what in hell is she doing with oxy? That's serious shit."

"Oxy?" Camille asked. "You mean oxycodone?"

"Yeah. What's a doctor doing downing opioids?"

"How do you know these are oxycodone?"

Trish looked at Camille, her eyebrows raised. "What kind of PI would I be if I couldn't identify the most commonly abused opioid?"

Camille shook her head, once again amazed at the breadth of her friend's random knowledge. "I have no idea what Kensington is doing with a huge unlabeled bottle of oxycodone. Wow. This case keeps getting weirder."

"Well, excellent detective work!" Trish held up her drink in a toast. "To Madame Butterfly." She took a sip and looked skeptically at her glass. "What is this shit anyway? It's not bad."

"It's champagne and raspberry liquor. Gwendolyn calls it 'Angelica's Kiss.'"

"Okay, back to work," Trish instructed.

Camille began to relax as she recounted the contents of the doctor's enigmatic library. "So, what do you think?"

Trish was obviously stupefied. "I have absolutely no idea."

"Me either." Camille paused. "The psychologists who evaluated Kensington in the divorce said she had some kind of problem with hypervigilance about issues involving sex abuse."

"That she saw it everywhere, even where there was no evidence that anything was wrong," Trish completed Camille's thought.

"I guess she's been reading up, then," Camille hypothesized.

"How many books would you say there were?"

"Twenty. Thirty," Camille estimated.

"Jeez."

Camille picked up the envelope lying on the table in front of her. "So, who do you think Eric Davenport is?"

"Brother?"

Camille nodded. "That's what I was thinking. Maybe you can do a background check on him, then I'll go pay him a visit."

"What for?"

"See what I can find out about Kensington's past that might lead us to something interesting." Camille leaned forward and propped her chin on her hands. "I have a brilliant investigator friend who taught me that if you follow up on every lead, you're sure to dig up something marvelous."

"Well, at least you listen." Trish drained her glass. "Now can I have a real glass of wine?"

A waitress in a red-and-white-striped spandex tube top appeared with two heavily seasoned pasta dishes topped with grilled chicken.

"Can we please have a bottle of chianti?" Camille asked as the woman grated a brick of fresh parmesan over their plates. "God that smells good."

"One bottle of chianti coming up," the waitress said as she wiggled away in her skintight turquoise jeans.

Spinning her pasta around her fork, Trish continued, "So, let's assume he is her brother; what makes you think he'd be willing to talk to you?"

Camille stuck a well-loaded fork into her mouth. "I'll think of something, give me a minute."

"Here we are." Gwendolyn placed a bottle of chianti on the table and took a corkscrew out of her pocket. "Who's going to taste?"

Camille pointed at Trish, who swirled the wine around in her glass and gave it a try. "It's great, thanks." She smiled.

As soon as Gwendolyn left, Camille changed the subject. "Have you had any luck trying to find out who sent you that email about Fitzharris?"

"No, but I did find out some more about the charges." Trish's voice drifted off as a troupe of belly dancers marched out from behind the small stage and began gyrating through the jam-packed bar to the sound of pulsating Middle Eastern music, finger cymbals setting the beat. The gold-embroidered costumes that hung on their prominent hips seemed to be moving separately from the rest of their bodies. Trish watched, mesmerized.

Camille waved her hand in front of Trish's face. "Earth to Trish," she laughed. "You were saying . . . about the complaints against Fitzharris?"

Trish raised her voice to be heard over the exotic music. "Oh, yeah." She watched the dancers out of the corner of her eye. "Apparently, two different patients came forward and accused the doc of fondling them during GYN exams."

"Two?"

"That's what the charging documents say," Trish said as the performers snaked their way back up onto the stage and continued their engaging dance.

"I can't believe Fitzharris would be diddling patients while his kid is in the middle of being diagnosed with cancer." Camille took a long sip of wine. "It doesn't make any sense."

Trish gazed intently at the entertainment for a minute, then refocused on the issue at hand. "Well, people do deal with stress differently, but I'm with you. It doesn't seem very likely that someone would get involved in a sex scandal when their kid is so sick."

"Can you do some more research and see what you can find out about the guy?" Camille asked.

"Sure, but I don't think anything I find out will have much bearing on your ability to use him at trial."

Camille and Trish clapped as the dancers finished up one number and started another.

"Until this thing's resolved, your doctor is poison as a witness," Trish stated authoritatively.

"I know." Camille soaked up some sauce in the bottom of her bowl with a chunk of french bread. "Especially after the judge reamed me out about the declaration I got from Laurabelle."

"All the more reason for you to be extra careful about your witnesses' credentials," Trish agreed.

Camille poured them each another glass of chianti and proceeded to recite the details of her visit with Deanne Stillerman at the gym the day before. "I don't know what Kensington's propensities about mucking up the pregnancies of infertility patients is all about, but I have a hunch that there may be a relationship between her misadventures in the ultrasound department and Helene's case."

"How so?" Trish asked.

"I don't know, it's just that the issue of infertility keeps popping up. You know those cases Harvey Lowe handled against Kensington?"

"Yeah."

"One of the articles featured in the *Trial News* involved an infertility patient."

"You're kidding!"

"Nope, apparently it was the foundation for his theory of the case."

"What do you mean?"

"He argued that the baby who died was the result of an infertility program so he had more value than your 'run of the mill' baby, since he was so difficult to conceive."

"Jesus. He actually convinced a jury that one baby has more value than another?"

"He didn't have to. The insurance company settled out of court. Even they didn't want to try and convince a jury that this little kid was replaceable after what the family had to go through to get pregnant."

Trish shook her head in disbelief. "I can't believe you do this for a living. Having to try and put a value on the life of a person. Baby or not."

"You don't have to tell me how weird it is," Camille agreed as she fingered the envelope addressed to Eric Davenport. "I've got it! I'll tell him I'm doing an article on Kensington for the local GYN newsletter and I'm interviewing her friends and family," Camille announced proudly. "What do you think?"

"I think whoever taught you how to investigate these things did a helluva job." Trish paused. "Do you even know where Marblemount is?"

CHAPTER TWENTY-THREE

Angela's voice came over the speakerphone. "Bagley's office on line one."

She was learning, Camille smiled to herself as she picked up the phone. "Camille Delaney."

"Ms. Delaney, this is Wanda Harper, from Mr. Bagley's office." The woman sounded about as emotional as a frog. "I'm calling about your request to take Dr. Kensington's deposition."

Camille riffled around on her cluttered desk. Where was that damned pad with her witness scheduling notes? She dropped the phone that she had cradled against her shoulder and cursed under her breath as she retrieved it from the floor. "Hello?"

"The doctor is not available this week or next."

"Not available?" Camille narrowed her eyes and shook her head. That asshole Bagley. "Until the week before trial?"

"Yes, ma'am."

Camille snapped. "The doctor has to make herself available before then."

"I'm sorry, ma'am, I'm just repeating what I've been told. You cannot depose Dr. Kensington until November seventeenth. Shall I book that date for you?"

Why was every single thing with Bagley a fucking federal deal? "No, you cannot book that date for me. I would like you to book me a date next week, like I said in my letter."

"All I am authorized to do is schedule a deposition on November seventeenth. If you want another deposition date, you'll have to take it up with Mr. Bagley himself."

"No, if I want another date, I'll serve Mr. Bagley with a subpoena and he can go to court to quash it if he wants." Camille slammed down the phone. Surely Bagley could find better things for his team of hungry associates to do than argue motions about scheduling depositions.

Angela stood in Camille's doorway. "Jeez, Mother! You didn't have to be so rude to that woman."

"It's part of the game." Camille rolled her eyes. "The lawyers on the other side make money by the hour, so they get paid to refuse to agree to anything."

"Isn't that just a waste of money, though?"

"Of course. But it's the insurance company's money, so the lawyers don't really care. Besides, they're just trying to wear us down."

"Well, don't you make money by going to court too?"

"No, I'm getting paid a percentage of whatever I make, so there's no incentive to spend more hours on a case. And it's better for the plaintiff to get their case settled quickly, so they can go on with their lives," Camille explained. "Then there are the insurance companies, who want to drag everything out so they can keep the money they know they'll have to pay out sooner or later. That way they can make interest on it. They never want to pay any claims until the last possible minute."

Angela nodded. "I get it. They want to make you work harder in hopes that you'll give in sooner so they don't have to pay as much."

Camille smiled; if her seventeen-year-old daughter could figure this out so easily, why did the judges always let the insurance lawyers get away with running the regular people's lawyers around in circles? Could it possibly be that they needed them to finance their judicial campaigns?

"We need to send Dr. Kensington a subpoena for a deposition." Camille was relieved that Angela had actually begun to learn Amy's computer organization. "Do you think you can find one in the system?"

Angela shrugged. "I guess so."

"Just pick a day next week and put in the subpoena. We're going to end up in court over this anyway."

Why couldn't Bagley just do one thing cooperatively, without dragging her tired butt into court for every single damn thing? Camille could almost hear the cash register going off down at Bagley's office. Cha-ching. Cha-ching.

She looked out her window as the rainy weather gave way to a crisp Northwest day. The air always seemed to have a crystalline quality after a heavy rain. She paused. This would be the perfect day to check out Eric Davenport of Marblemount. Angela's school was having parent-teacher conferences this week, so she'd be at the office all day to answer the phone. Camille grabbed her car keys and headed out.

——

Camille exited I-5 in Mount Vernon and headed east toward the slope of the Cascade Mountains. *Life is certainly different up here,* she mused as the blankets of farmland led her toward heavily wooded foothills. Being a city girl at heart, Camille figured the purpose of a drive in the country was simply an opportunity to get caught up. With nothing but time on her hands, she decided to check in with Trish.

"I'm on my way to have a visit with Eric Davenport. Any luck finding out anything about him?"

"Nothing. Not a goddamn thing."

"What do you mean, nothing?"

"I mean that I can't even find a birth certificate on the guy. As far as the federal government is concerned, he doesn't exist."

"You're kidding. What do you make of that?" Camille turned off the highway and stopped at an intersection at the one and only stop sign in the tiny hamlet of Concrete, about twenty miles west of Marblemount.

"Maybe there is no Eric Davenport," Trish suggested.

"I'll find out soon enough." As Camille waited for a huge logging truck to go through the intersection, she looked through the front window of an ancient diner where a table of sixty-somethings sat smoking their way through lunch. "You ever been up around Marblemount?"

"You mean the land that time forgot? In my estimation, it's a bit strange up there. No place for a big-city gal like you."

"Hey, I walked up a paved path to the tourist information center at Mount Rainier once."

"I rest my case."

Camille continued up the two-lane mountain highway framed by towering evergreen trees. "You think I'll find the guy up here?"

"Who knows? Just be careful. And call me when you're on your way back home so I know you're okay."

The pitch of the highway increased as it wound farther into the rugged mountains. If she'd blinked, she would have missed Rockport, the last town before Marblemount. As she got farther and farther from civilization, she thought about one of her mom's favorite old Stones albums, *Through the Past, Darkly*. Dilapidated little houses spewed spirals of smoke from dirty brick chimneys, their windows covered with plastic for added protection from the wicked winter weather. Sprinkled between them were single- and double-wide mobile homes, all with at least one old pickup truck on their property in some state of disrepair.

Camille looked at her watch, acutely aware that darkness fell in November at around four thirty. She had only a couple of hours to find the supposedly nonexistent Eric Davenport. Rounding a bend, she found herself smack in the middle of Marblemount. *At least parking won't be a problem,* she said to herself as she pulled over on the deserted main street.

"Table for one?" The waitress behind the cash register of the antiquated diner had the husky voice of someone who'd spent a fair amount of her meager income on Lucky Strikes.

"No, no thanks. I'm looking for an old friend." Camille smiled in response to the woman's suspicious look. "His name's Eric Davenport."

The woman picked up a rag and ran it over the already spotless counter. "Can't help ya."

Camille searched for a response and realized she had no identifying information about Kensington's alleged brother.

"Sorry." The woman appeared to be intentionally avoiding Camille's gaze.

"Thanks anyway."

The bells hanging on the doorknob jingled as Camille closed it behind her. Across the narrow street stood what appeared to be an old-fashioned general store.

"Can I help you, miss?" asked the portly middle-aged man in a crisp pharmacy jacket.

Best to try a different tack. It probably wasn't all that often a stranger came in search of one of the townsfolk. Camille took a seat at the soda fountain. "Do you make a good root beer float?"

The man grinned widely. "Are you kidding?" He shouted to the back of the store, "Bernice, there's a pretty young lady out here who's looking for a root beer float." He turned back to Camille. "The wife makes the best floats in the county."

The wife and the waitress across the street obviously went to the same beauty parlor for their matching bouffant dos. They reminded Camille of a joke her mother told when she channel-surfed past the Christian TV stations: "The bigger the hair, the closer to God." Camille smiled. Judging from the height of their hair, these women could actually be saints.

"One root beer float, coming up." Saint Bernice winked.

Small towns like this must keep the tobacco companies in business, Camille thought as Bernice stuck a cigarette between her deep pink lips.

"You don't mind if I smoke."

It was more of a statement than a question.

"Of course not, go right ahead," Camille said as the woman retreated to the back of the store to grab a bottle of root beer from the cooler.

The floor creaked as the pharmacist walked up behind the counter and leaned forward over his protruding belly. He propped himself on his elbows. "I hope you're not expecting to get over the pass. The highway just closed for the winter last week."

Bernice slid Camille's root beer float down the counter, where it stopped exactly in front of her. The woman smiled from the midst of a cloud of smoke, looking like she'd just made the winning basket in the local high school tournament.

Camille sucked the cool liquid through the old-fashioned metal straw. Not bad.

"Actually, I'm a reporter doing a story on a doctor down in Seattle. I'm trying to locate her brother to interview him."

Bernice hurried over and stood next to her husband. "Reporter." She nodded approvingly.

"I'll bet you're looking for Davenport." The man smiled proudly.

Jackpot.

"His sister's a big-time doctor," added Bernice. "So's his dad."

"Don't know what happened to him." The pharmacist shook his head. "Must've been in the wrong line when the good Lord was handing out brains."

"How so?" Camille asked.

"The guy's more than a little bit nuts."

Bernice circled her index finger around her ear, making a "crazy" signal.

Wow. Seems to run in the family.

The man leaned closer. "Takes a list of medication as long as your arm."

Bernice interrupted, "All prescribed by his sister, the doctor." She raised her eyebrows and nodded.

Camille paused. "Huh." It had to be more than a coincidence that the Davenport family was single-handedly supporting the psychiatric branch of the pharmaceutical industry.

"Guy comes to town once a month," the man started to explain.

"On the fifth," Bernice added.

"Picks up an envelope, cashes his check at the bank, then comes back and pays cash for everything." The man cocked his head in the direction of the post office window at the front of the store.

Bernice chimed in, "Always pays cash. For everything."

Camille wondered about the significance of the cash, certain that it was somehow related to the "Marblemount" entries in Kensington's QuickBooks program.

"Always," the husband echoed, "cash."

These two were sweet, always finishing each other's sentences.

"Do you know where I'd find him?" Camille asked.

Bernice lit a cigarette from a butt smoldering in the ashtray next to the cash register. "Sure do, but I'm not sure you should go out there alone." She waved her hand in front of her face in a futile effort to keep the smoke away from Camille.

Camille blinked the blue smoke out of her eyes. "I'm sure I'll be fine. I shouldn't be out there too long."

"What d'ya think, Bernie?" the woman asked her husband.

Bernie and Bernice? Too cute.

The husband stroked his chin. "I wouldn't let my daughter go out there into those woods alone."

The woman shook her head back and forth violently. "Nope. Absolutely not." She held her hands out in front of herself.

"Not safe," agreed Bernie, mimicking his wife's head shaking.

Camille held up her cell phone. "I'll be fine; if anything happens, I can call for help."

"It's pretty far out there in the middle of nowhere," Bernice stated. "But be careful—the cell coverage in these parts is sketchy at best."

"Too isolated for a girl to go by herself," Bernie agreed.

"I'll just be there a little while. Really. I'll be okay."

Bernice looked at her husband. "We'll watch for her to come back off the mountain. Someone needs to know she's out there."

"Okay." He looked at Camille. "If we give you directions, you promise to stop by on your way back? Just to let us know you're safe."

"And you take our number." Bernice pointed to a pad on the counter. "Write down our number, Bernie," she said bossily. "And give her the directions to Davenport's place."

Bernie busied himself searching for a pen in an overflowing junk drawer.

Camille pulled a piece of paper out of her purse and wrote the directions as Bernice and Bernie dictated them in unison.

"You be careful," Bernice shouted through a plume of cigarette smoke.

"I promise."

"We'll watch to make sure you get off the mountain okay."

"No problem." Camille waved from the doorway. "Thanks!"

Camille noted that the shadows were beginning to lengthen and the air had taken on a definite chill since she'd gotten to town. It always got dark early in the mountains. She looked up at the jagged peaks, behind which the sun had already set.

Better get a move on.

CHAPTER TWENTY-FOUR

The dry branches of the winter foliage screeched against the windows of Camille's Explorer as it bumped and ground its way up the steep drive to Davenport's place. Camille braced herself as another deep pothole appeared out of nowhere. The car pitched to the point that Camille was sure she'd topple over into the thicket. No wonder Davenport only came to town once a month.

The SUV's wheels spun up over the last rise and across a quickly flowing creek. Camille pulled up in front of a weathered old cabin. *This better be the place.* She exhaled to calm her nerves. A mountain woman she wasn't.

The door to the cabin opened abruptly, and a wild-looking mountain man with matted red hair appeared on the porch. Before Camille could catch her breath, the man took a stance and pointed a long-barreled rifle directly at her. She froze.

The man narrowed his gaze and swaggered over to her car.

Camille's mouth went dry. She glanced to her right, then to her left, trying to decide if she could turn the Explorer around on the mud flat. No way.

The man cocked the rifle and blew out her left front tire. The vibration felt like the tire had exploded inside her chest.

Camille watched in horror as the man advanced, smashed out the driver's-side window, and put the gun up against her temple.

"What the fuck are you doing on my property?"

Camille closed her eyes and held her breath, praying for him not to pull the trigger.

"I asked you a question." He jabbed the gun at her head.

"I . . ." The reporter story she'd been practicing on the way up the mountain quickly became a naive memory.

"Never mind. I don't give a shit what you think you came here for." He opened the door to the SUV. "I know what you're gonna do now."

Camille clutched the steering wheel in a death grip.

The man stepped back, his rifle aimed at Camille's head. "Get out."

Camille could feel the bile creeping up the back of her throat as she struggled to gain her footing on the soggy ground. Her legs wobbled, and a feeling of light-headedness came over her.

The man smiled a haunting, violent smile. "I haven't had a lady friend out here in a very, very long time."

Camille blinked away the tears that burned in her eyes and tried to assess her situation. The man moved so close to her that she could see their breath mingling in the cold air.

"I sure hope you can cook, bitch." His laugh sounded more like a wheeze as he pointed his gun, indicating for Camille to walk ahead of him.

As she stumbled toward the small cabin, she noticed the absolute stillness of the woods. She knew that it would be a bad idea to go inside the cabin.

"Move it!" He shoved her toward the porch steps.

Camille slipped in the deep mud and nearly fell.

"I like a woman with long legs."

Something inside Camille told her to try to secure the psychological advantage. She regained her footing and turned to face her captor.

The guy grinned.

Something odd about his smile.

"So . . . can you cook?" he leered.

The teeth. They didn't go with the wild eyes and matted hair. They were perfect.

Camille braced herself against the railing. She wasn't going in there willingly.

"I'm getting cold, and I'm getting hungry," the man announced. "Now, get inside." His hand encircled her upper arm as he pulled her to the front door and jiggled the lock.

"I got a freezer full of steaks. We can have us a nice romantic dinner, then we're gonna have us some real fun," he said without letting go of her arm.

The man's wheezy laugh turned to a cough as Camille tried unsuccessfully to wrench her arm from his grasp. *Stay strong.*

"You're not going anywhere, little lady."

She pulled away and tried to estimate how far it was back to the main road. It was at least three miles; and the terrain definitely favored someone who was familiar with the area. Suddenly, she remembered the couple at the general store. She'd have to find a way to call and alert them to her rapidly deteriorating situation.

The man lurched inside and threw Camille onto the floor, slamming the door behind them.

Camille's hip banged against something hard in her pocket. The cell phone. She bit her lip to try to stop the pain.

The man locked the deadbolt with his key and shoved it into the front pocket of his jeans.

Locked inside a remote mountain cabin with a lunatic. Now what? Find all potential exits. Camille turned to survey the room and stopped cold. Every wall was lined with hardback books from floor to ceiling. The place looked like it had been put together by a professional decorator. Not exactly what you'd expect for a filthy mountain man in the middle of nowhere.

The guy sat on an expensive-looking leather chair without lowering his gun. "Get up."

Camille complied, slowly, making sure that her cell phone stayed deep within the pocket of her jacket. Her pulse seemed to be moderating as she sized up the calamity in which she found herself. Panic wasn't going to get her anywhere.

"Got me a real nice kitchen for you to cook me some dinner in."

He had that right. The centerpiece of the kitchen was a huge commercial stove.

"Steaks're in the freezer, and wine's on the rack next to the fridge." Another point of the gun.

Camille hobbled over to the kitchen, looking for a way out. Oddly, there was not one window in the place. And the only door was directly behind the man.

Camille's pulse quickened again as the man ogled her. No point in pissing him off any more than he already was. She tentatively opened the freezer and found it jammed with neatly labeled packages of meat.

"Get me some wine," he sneered.

Go along until you can figure out how the hell to get away from him long enough to call Bernie and Bernice, Camille instructed herself. She pulled out a bottle of wine and glanced at the label: Sterling Vineyards 1994? This bottle must've cost a hundred bucks. The corkscrew slid easily into the smooth cork. Maybe she could get the guy drunk enough to pass out.

"Glasses are to the right of the sink."

Her hand shook as she poured a generous glass of wine. Gathering her wits, she walked assertively over to hand it to him, determined not to let him sense her fear. "Good year for cabs, 1994." She hoped her voice was as clear as she intended it to be.

Returning to the kitchen, Camille surveyed the bookshelves and noted several books on astrophysics and biochemistry. This was too weird. Closer to the kitchen, there was a computer station built into the wall. As she reviewed the books above the computer, her stomach did a flip. Shelves full of books on psychopathic killers. Déjà vu. *What the hell's going on?*

"I want smoked salmon spread and crackers with my wine."

This guy is nuts. Camille opened the huge refrigerator and located a container of smoked salmon spread, recognizing the label as being from a gourmet mail-order house. As she rummaged through the cupboards, searching for crackers to keep the guy happy, she tried to calm herself by imagining she was talking the situation through with Trish.

So, we have a mother who's in a psychiatric institution, a daughter on antipsychotic meds, and a brother who's a prime candidate for an extended stay at Western State Hospital. She concentrated on keeping her breath slow and steady. *Obviously, these people have some kind of hereditary psychiatric disorder.* A deep breath. Her thoughts turned briefly to the charismatic Kip Davenport. *Poor guy, he clearly married into some kind of psychotic gene pool. No wonder he's so protective of Kensington.*

Suddenly, an escape plan popped into her mind. *There has to be a month's supply of medication around here somewhere.* Camille began opening drawers.

Nothing.

Must be in the bathroom. She bolstered herself and walked confidently toward the only door leading from the small room.

"And where do you think you're going?"

"To the bathroom," Camille snapped. "You mind?" She was getting pissed.

"There aren't any windows in there either." He laughed.

Camille slammed the bathroom door behind her and quickly opened the medicine cabinet. Ah-ha. Like sister, like brother. She closed her eyes in gratitude, then shoved a handful of little white pills into her pocket. Quickly, she pulled out her cell phone. Rule number one: always bring vital information along with you when you've been kidnapped and held hostage. Trish would be proud; Camille uncrumpled the piece of paper in her pocket and dialed Bernie and Bernice. She bounced up and down anxiously. Please answer.

Silence.

She looked at the phone. No signal. Shit.

On to plan B, whatever that is . . .

She flushed the toilet before heading back into the kitchen.

"Don't forget my hors d'oeuvres."

Camille glared at Davenport and began opening cabinets until she found a dish. She surreptitiously emptied her pocket, crushed the stack of pills, and hastily mixed the white powder into the spread. That should knock him for a loop.

As she set the crackers and spread in front of Davenport, she wondered how long she could drag out the meal preparation while the medication took hold.

Davenport shoved a handful of fully loaded crackers into his mouth and banged his wineglass on the table, demanding more.

He was becoming increasingly belligerent as she placed the wine bottle next to him.

"Make mashed potatoes."

Perfect. It'd take a while to peel the potatoes, and hopefully, Davenport would be getting sleepy by then. Camille slowly washed the pile of potatoes. How the hell had she gotten herself into this mess anyway?

Davenport sauntered across the room and stood so close behind Camille that she could smell the combination of smoked salmon and wine on his breath. He roughly grabbed her butt.

Camille stiffened and blinked back the tears as she slowly peeled the potatoes. Her fingers tingled with numbness from being under the frigid water for so long.

Davenport roughly spun her around to face him and pulled her belt until she was up against his hard chest. Another wheezy laugh sprayed spit all over her face. She tried to turn away, her chutzpah beginning to fade.

"Scared?" He ran a heavily calloused finger across her face where a lone tear snaked its way down her cheek.

She glared at him.

He grabbed her breast.

Camille gathered her courage. "You want mashed potatoes or not?"

He threw her toward the stove. "Get busy!"

The potatoes made a loud plopping sound as Camille dropped them into the boiling water with shaking hands. Briefly she considered trying to figure out a way to dump the pot onto Davenport, then dismissed the idea as basically impossible.

As Davenport returned to his chair, he stumbled slightly. Camille watched, praying that the medication would soon take hold.

"Get me some of that cheese in the bottom drawer of the fridge."

Slowly, Camille unwrapped the strong-smelling block of yellow cheese. Oddly, she was unable to locate any knives.

A loud snort emanated from across the room. Camille held her breath and cautiously turned to look at Davenport, who had just jolted himself awake. He leered at her sleepily.

She put the cheese on a plate and walked slowly toward him, her arm fully outstretched. After the incident in the kitchen, she was determined to keep her distance.

"Hurry up!" He squinted as though he were having trouble focusing.

She placed the plate on the table and slowly backed away, not taking her eyes off him, hoping that he would fall into some kind of stupor.

"What the fuck are you staring at?" he slurred.

Camille stopped in her tracks.

Davenport stood and reached for the back of his chair to steady himself. Suddenly, he lunged at Camille, who jerked away and ran across the room. A lamp crashed to the floor.

Davenport followed, unsteady on his feet. "Goddamn it! Get over here!"

She moved toward the kitchen, all her concentration on the group of knives she finally located, hanging high above the stove.

Davenport followed her gaze and threw himself between her and the stove. "Oh no, you don't." He faltered and clutched the butcher-block counter with one hand and reached for Camille with the other. He had her blue-jean jacket in his grasp and was pulling her toward him. In one movement, she slid out of the jacket.

By now, Davenport was weaving around the room, crunching across the shards of broken lamp. Camille avoided his violent lunges, parrying away as he threw his weight clumsily in her direction. How much longer could this go on?

The potatoes boiled over, splattering water across the stove and creating a plume of steam.

Davenport stopped for a moment, then turned and charged at Camille, tackling her to the floor.

Panicked, she reached for one of the wrought iron barstools and yanked on it until it crashed down on top of her attacker, barely missing her own shoulder.

Davenport let out a moan that sounded like that of an injured elephant and lurched to his feet, his hands clapped to either side of his head. He fell against his easy chair in a daze.

Thank you, God. Camille sat up and scooted on her rear end away from the lumbering giant, barely noticing the glass that she'd ground into the heel of her hand. Defeated, and fighting complete exhaustion, she braced herself to prepare for whatever he'd do next.

Thankfully, Davenport lay on the floor, slumped up against the chair with his head hanging straight back and a thick strand of drool dangling from the corner of his open mouth. He heaved a sleepy snort.

Camille waited a moment, then warily approached Davenport and kneeled in front of him. She took a breath, gently reached her hand into his pocket to extract his keys.

His eyes rolled back into his head and he let out an angry growl. He clenched her hand in his hairy fist.

Camille tried to pull away.

His fingernails drew blood from her wrist.

She winced and tried to pry his fingers off her.

He jerked her toward him and grabbed her short hair. As he attempted to stand, his legs buckled under him, leaving him groveling on the floor at Camille's feet.

Her fingers shook as she hurriedly unlocked the front door. As an afterthought, she grabbed the rifle, not that she had any idea how to work the thing. Rule number two: learn how to shoot a gun. She took off down the steep drive.

It was pitch black under the moonless night. Camille ignored her useless Explorer sitting lopsidedly on three wheels. Her foot sank to the bottom of a water-filled pothole. She extracted it forcefully and skidded farther into the woods.

At the bottom of the bluff in front of the cabin, Camille stopped long enough to gather her wits. The tears came fast and furious. She wiped her face with her sleeve and willed herself to buck up. As she stumbled down the treacherous road, a searing sensation tore across her cheek. She swore and shoved a brittle branch away from her face, feeling a sticky liquid running down her neck. *Goddamn it, get me out of here.*

Camille managed to make it what seemed like several hundred feet in the blackness when she heard a howl come from the bushes immediately to her right. She stopped in her tracks, wishing she knew something about wilderness survival. Rule number three.

Was it a coyote? Or a wolf? Would he be afraid of her, or did coyotes attack people? She vowed to quit teasing Sam for his addiction to the Discovery Channel.

A thin animal charged out of the ditch. Terrified, Camille jumped back. Her ankle buckled under her and she hit the ground hard. The animal moved slowly toward her in a stalking crouch.

"Get away!" She screamed. "Go on!" She struggled to get up but slipped in the mud. It was some kind of giant catlike thing. A cougar?

The animal was less than a yard from her now. She picked up a rock and threw it at the animal, missing him by several feet. He continued his approach.

The sound of a gunshot reverberated through the woods and the large catlike animal fell into a heap. Was it a cougar or a bobcat? Camille couldn't be sure, but she was glad she didn't have to find out.

She began to exhale the breath she didn't know she'd been holding, then stopped as she realized Davenport must have somehow woken up and followed her. She closed her eyes and cowered. He'd won.

Camille felt as though she was drifting out of her body. The sound of a car door slamming seemed to be echoing down a metallic tunnel. No one ever told her that gun smoke smelled like cigarettes.

"I told you, Bernie!"

It was Bernice's raspy voice.

Camille bolted up, slamming herself back to consciousness, ecstatic to see the matronly figure of the pharmacist's wife hurrying over to rescue her.

"I told you we shouldn't have let her come out here all alone!"

Camille watched as the glow of Bernice's ever-present cigarette seemed to float next to her as she knelt down next to Camille.

"Oh my lands! Look at her, Bernie! She's a mess. I knew that Davenport was trouble on wheels. I knew it from the first time I laid eyes on him." She pushed Camille's hair back from her face.

Bernie hitched up his pants as he exited the truck, a long rifle in one hand.

"What did he do to you, honey?" Bernice turned to her husband. "I told you we should have followed her up here." She took a long drag on her cigarette. "Anyone who takes that many drugs, prescribed or not, is a calamity just waitin' to happen."

Bernie walked with the stiffness of an old-time cowboy; the expression on his face made it clear that this wasn't the first time Bernice had engaged the "I told you so" routine. "Where's your car, miss?"

Camille's mouth was so dry, it took her a minute to find her voice. "I . . . I had a little car trouble up the road a way."

Bernie leaned down to help Camille up.

"Not so fast, Bernie, she's got a broken ankle." Bernice shoved Camille's pant leg up and shook her head at the swelling that was visible through Camille's sock.

"I'm fine." Camille pushed herself up, anxious to get back to civilization.

"She's okay," Bernie announced. "Hop in, we can go up and give you a tow."

"No!" Camille shouted. All she needed was for Bernie and Bernice to find Davenport drooling in his chair. "I can call a tow truck in the morning. Really." She wanted out of these fucking mountains. Now.

"You sure?" Bernie wasn't able to completely hide the concern in his eyes.

Camille pointed to her foot. "I'd like to get some ice and an Ace wrap around this. I can deal with my car later." Nothing was going to keep her in these mountains a nanosecond longer than absolutely necessary.

"You heard her, Bernie!" Bernice stuck the smoldering butt in her mouth and awkwardly grabbed Camille under her arms. "Let's get this girl home so she can get cleaned up."

———

Bernie and Bernice's house was exactly what Camille would have expected. Crocheted afghans and throw cushions in every imaginable shade of baby blue and pink covered the matching floral couch and chair.

Camille used an old princess phone to call Trish to come and pick her up while Bernice opened a can of cream of mushroom soup and dumped it over some leftover chicken. She sprinkled a can of fried onion rings over the top and slid the casserole into the vintage sixties oven.

"This'll just take about twenty minutes. I'm sure you're starving."

After getting cleaned up, Camille sat at the dinette table with her foot perched on a chair, an ice pack slowly melting through her sock. There was something comforting about watching Bernice cut up the head of iceberg lettuce and grate a carrot on it. It struck Camille as odd that the homey scene could feel so much like a vague childhood memory, especially since she was unable to muster up any vision of her mother actually cooking while she was growing up. Camille had heard stories about mushroom soup casseroles but had yet to experience this all-American dish.

Bernice put the Tupperware bowl on the table in front of her guest. Camille wasn't exactly sure if she'd ever actually eaten the bright orange french dressing Bernice had poured generously over the salad, but at this point Camille would consider beanie weenies a delicacy. And surprisingly, the fried onions on top of the bubbling concoction smelled better than she expected.

A flash of headlights panned across the steamy little kitchen as Bernice dished up three generous helpings.

Trish.

—

After the Midwestern extravaganza, including some type of Jell-O dessert, the two women hit the road. Camille never really relaxed until she saw the lights of Seattle on the horizon when they were about five miles north of the city.

"So, we have a crazy doc with a crazier brother," Trish summarized Camille's recitation of her first, last, and only trip to Marblemount.

Camille nodded. "Yup. And apparently a crazy mother too."

Trish wound her way through the gridlock of Friday night traffic heading downtown. "Are you sure all this mental illness stuff has something to do with what happened to Helene Anderson?"

"I don't know, but the more I read in the obstetric literature, the more it seems to me that the only reasonable explanation for what happened is that Kensington had an episode that caused some kind of psychotic break. There's no other way to explain her complete disregard for the safety of Helene and her baby."

Trish took the Roanoke exit off the freeway and turned down the hill to the houseboat neighborhood on Lake Union. "What do you mean?"

"There's just no way that a doctor could not know that Helene needed a C-section. All of the signs were screaming at her."

"So, either she's psychotic"—Trish pulled into Camille's parking lot—"or she's a completely incompetent idiot"—Trish turned off her headlights and killed the engine—"or she killed the baby on purpose."

The two friends looked at each other.

"You think she killed that baby, don't you?" Camille whispered.

Trish shrugged. "What do you think?"

Camille tried desperately to block out the voice inside her head screaming "murder!" She wasn't prepared to come right out and say it.

"We have to come up with some kind of evidence to prove that she intentionally killed that kid." Trish's voice was low and emphatic.

Camille slumped in her seat. "Actually, we just need to show that she was negligent in her care of Helene, but it would be nice if we had some explanation for why she provided such crappy care. And that's super hard to prove. At this point, all we have are a few pictures of some psych prescription bottles and a picture of some oxycodone scattered on her bathroom vanity and a shaky theory about possible psychosis."

Trish looked directly at Camille. "We need a witness who can testify about Kensington's mental health."

"But before we get a witness, we need some evidence for them to rely on." Camille searched her brain, trying to come up with a plan. There had to be someone, besides Kensington's brother, who could shed some light on the cause of her mental instability. "Who can tell us what might have caused her to lose it?"

She sat up quickly and faced Trish.

"The mother," they said in unison.

CHAPTER TWENTY-FIVE

Camille arrived home to find Sam sitting under the lone light in the living room of the cozy houseboat. He startled awake. "Where've you been?"

She collapsed into the huge armchair and snuggled up against her husband's warm body, relieved to be safe once again. A half-finished glass of red wine glimmered on the coffee table. She reached out and finished it off. "Nice to be home."

Sam ran his finger down her cheek. He stopped abruptly and sat up to look more closely at her face. "What happened?"

"Nothing." She reached up and traced the pathway of her husband's finger along her cheek, feeling the sticky remnants of blood. If Sam even thought for one minute that she was in physical danger, he'd pressure her to dump the case for sure. And as gentle as he was, when he put his mind to something—he always got his way.

Sam looked at his wife. "Camille?"

She playfully pulled his hand from the deep scratch etched on her face. "Let's go to bed."

"It's after midnight. Where've you been?"

"Working. C'mon, come to bed." She stood up and tried to tug him to his feet. "I miss you."

"That's my point." Sam reluctantly allowed himself to be teased. "You're never home."

Camille wrapped her arms around Sam and kissed him long and hard on the mouth. "Can we just not talk about the Anderson case? Just for an hour or so?"

Sam pulled away. "Look, this isn't working. You're gone almost every night. And what the hell happened to your face?"

There was no way she could tell Sam about her tête-à-tête with Kensington's mentally ill brother. Then again, he'd surely see the bruises Davenport had inflicted on her. "I went out to Granite Falls to interview Kensington's brother and I had a little accident." It was partly true, she tried to convince herself. "It's no big deal. I'm fine."

Sam stood back and looked Camille up and down. "What kind of accident?"

No need to get him overly concerned. "I kinda skidded off a muddy mountain driveway on the way up to Davenport's cabin. I'm fine. Really."

Sam's face was expressionless. "How'd you get home?"

"Trish came and got me." Camille couldn't tell if Sam's silence was a sign of anger or hurt or worry, or all three. She hated it when he gave her that look.

"You're in over your head, Camille."

"It's okay. I'm really making progress."

"It's not about the case." He paused. "It's about us."

"It'll all be over soon." Camille tried to keep the panic out of her voice. "I really need to do a good job for these people."

"What about us? What about the empty chair at the dinner table every night? This case is too much for a one-person office."

"I can handle it. I promise."

Sam took her hand in his. "But I can't. I need you home. With me."

The man was gorgeous. And sweet. What had she done to deserve a husband like this? He looked like he was going to break into tears.

"You have to slow down," he pleaded.

An idea popped into Camille's head. "How about a weekend in Hawaii? Just the two of us?"

Sam perked up.

"Maui," she added. "We haven't been to Maui in years. We can go next week and be back in time for Thanksgiving."

His face fell. "I can't. I have to get that article submitted to the *Journal of Pathology* by December first."

Looks like I'll be traveling alone to go see Moyna-Lou.

"But it was a nice idea." Sam leaned over and kissed Camille, then led her gently downstairs to their dark espresso-brown sanctuary where he slowly undressed her.

—

Sam was right. The family needed her. Camille waited as the girls piled into the rental car, all three talking at the same time. She'd nearly forgotten how frenzied the morning carpool could get. How had she let this lawsuit overshadow her commitment to being there for her kids?

Not to worry. The trial was coming up in two weeks, and it would all be over by Thanksgiving, one way or another. But first, there was a minor matter of how she'd get to Hawaii and back without Sam finding out she was gone. He was really getting fed up with her being away from home so much lately. Well, so was she, but it wasn't going to last forever. She waved goodbye to Gracie, who skipped up the walkway to the towering old brick school.

It took all day for Camille to find another OB-GYN to review the Kensington case. She coaxed the copier to life and shoved in the stack of medical records. Not being able to afford an "ivory tower" expert from a university setting, Camille finally had to settle for a more affordable guy from Whitefish Bay, a suburb of Milwaukee. The doc wasn't willing to testify that the Zavanelli maneuver was malpractice in and of itself, but he was clearly on board about Kensington knowing that a patient with gestational diabetes wasn't a candidate for an aggressive forceps delivery. He agreed to testify that Helene Anderson should have been scheduled for an elective C-section rather than having been allowed to go into labor.

Standing in front of the whirring machine, she reviewed the defense list of expert witnesses, wondering how her Whitefish Bay expert would hold up against Bagley's onslaught of university all-stars. Camille calmed herself. The medicine wasn't all that complicated. Her doc should do just fine.

But she'd never come up with eight hundred dollars an hour for each of Bagley's five experts. It was going to cost ten thousand bucks just to depose them. Shit, there was no way her bank account would hold up for the duration of this case, not to mention her upcoming Hawaiian adventure.

Camille eased herself into her desk chair, leaning to the left in an unsuccessful effort to keep from putting unnecessary pressure on her aching right hip.

Turning to the accumulation of car accident files stacked behind her desk, she tried to zero in on which one would settle most quickly. It was her only hope of raising the badly needed funds to continue her march to justice.

Ah-ha! Cipriotti. By now, Winston Clark had surely been able to bill an adequate number of hours reviewing the boy's counseling records. He should be ready to move on to the next part of the gravy train. She briefly reviewed the file. Yep. Definitely time for her to take the money and run.

Camille picked up the phone and shivered as she remembered the little brat trying to butcher her furniture. That case would never see the inside of a courtroom.

"Winston Clark, please."

"I'm sorry, Mr. Clark is on vacation for the next three weeks."

Camille closed her eyes. Now what?

She turned to her computer and redrafted the Cipriotti settlement letter, certain that she could squeeze around fifty grand from the supercilious Winston Clark. The letter would be waiting for him when he got back from vacation, and she'd probably have her check by the end of the month.

Camille flipped aimlessly through her notes on the Anderson case, not sure what, if anything, she hoped to find. Even a teensy tiny inspiration would be welcome at this point. Why had she agreed to take the case to trial? If she hadn't, she could probably get it into a settlement posture and get the Andersons something for what they'd been through, get herself out of debt, and most importantly get herself back to her family where she belonged.

It was time to change course.

She had to convince Helene to get this whole thing behind her. Agreeing to take this case to trial must have been some kind of pipe dream. As she dialed the phone, Camille shuffled the pages of the file and came upon the old copy of the *Trial News* with Harvey Lowe's face laughing at her from the cover.

As she waited for Helene to come on the line, Camille skimmed the article about Lowe's brilliant "premium baby" theory. What a pile of bullshit: an infertility baby being worth more than any other kid.

Helene's husband answered and told Camille that Helene was out in the garden, so it would take a few minutes for him to get the phone out to her. Camille said she'd hold.

Infertility. What had Deanne said about Kensington and the infertility patients? Something about her having a personal vendetta against them. Why on earth?

"Hello?"

No words came from Camille's mouth. How could she convince Helene to abandon her crusade?

"Hello?" Helene raised her voice. "Camille?"

An idea popped into Camille's head. "I was . . . I was just calling to ask if you'd been treated for infertility before you got pregnant with Zachary."

"Amy already asked me that, and I told her no!" Helene sounded offended. "You're not going to be able to make that deplorable argument that this pregnancy was more unique than any other."

Shoot, so much for that brainstorm. "Well, I just thought I remembered your saying that you'd been trying to get pregnant for a long time before you conceived Zachary." If she had evidence that Helene had been an infertility patient, she could steal Lowe's argument. She had to admit, the "premium baby" theory certainly seemed to scare the insurance company into coming up with the big bucks. "I just wondered if you'd been an infertility patient, that's all."

"I said no!"

Why did she sound so edgy?

"If you haven't, it's no big deal. I was just exploring possible theories of the case."

"Well," Helene hesitated. "Actually, we did have Tim's sperm count measured, but it came out perfect. No problem." She stumbled over her words. "Absolutely no problem with his count whatsoever. Everything came out great. Just great."

Camille could hear the sound of some kind of power gardening equipment in the background.

"We've been pruning Zachary's rose garden." Helene's voice softened. "We planted it in his honor this summer. I like to come out here and talk to him when the whole thing gets to be too much. We've become good friends, Zachary and I. Anything new on the case?"

Camille couldn't do it. She couldn't even suggest that they consider changing their plans to go to trial. Her family could tough it out for a few more weeks. They had to. "Everything is coming along quite nicely."

"You're amazing, Camille." This was certainly an abrupt change in demeanor. "I can't tell you how much we appreciate you taking on the insurance company for us." The edge had completely disappeared from Helene's voice. "No one else would even consider it."

Of course no one else would have considered it. Camille felt like the Lone Ranger. And she really missed Tonto.

As she hung up the phone, Camille's eye caught the colorful wish box that Helene had painted for her. She opened it slowly and unfolded the distinctive piece of paper inside: justice.

What justice?

The longer she stayed in this wacky business, the more foreign the concept became. She crossed her arms on her desk, laid her head on them, and had a good cry.

CHAPTER TWENTY-SIX

This was ridiculous—telling Sam she was going down to California for a quick meeting with her expert, then hopping a plane and heading halfway across the Pacific. Camille jostled into her seat next to the huge man with his aloha shirt straining at the buttons. Out of Seattle at 6:00 a.m. and back from Maui on the red-eye tonight. Aloha yourself.

A wave of exhaustion overcame her as she realized that she had five uninterrupted hours spread out ahead of her. She stuck the flimsy earphones in her ears and fell asleep before the end of the opening credits of the "lighthearted romantic comedy."

As she fastened her seat belt on the approach to the island of Maui, Camille looked at her watch and thought about her girls. Right about now, they'd be just finishing up their lunch break at school. Who was she to criticize her own mother for being halfway around the world? At least her mom was honest about what she was up to.

Camille's cab lurched to a stop under the pagoda-like archway of Kahana Care. The place looked more like a five-star resort than a psychiatric institution.

An eager administrator greeted Camille in the airy lobby and held out her hand. "How may I assist you, ma'am?"

"I'm here to see my aunt. Moyna-Lou Davenport?" Camille answered tentatively.

"Do you have an appointment?"

Trish had prepared Camille for the possibility that it might not be easy to slide past the front desk. *Here goes nothing:*

"No, I'm just here on vacation and I thought I'd stop in for a quick visit."

"Right this way, ma'am. I'll need to check the computer."

Camille followed the Asian woman in the fitted red crepe suit over to an open office with a sizable glass desk. The room looked out over foliage thick with flashy blossoms. As the woman opened a file on her computer screen, she asked Camille her name.

Camille crossed her fingers under the wide bamboo chair. "Serena, Serena Davenport."

The administrator scanned the screen with her scarlet fingernail. "Ah, yes, here you are," she beamed. "Please, come with me. I'm sure your aunt will be thrilled to see you."

That was it? Camille marveled at what Trish could do on the internet. How she'd found the name of Jessica's cousin, the nurse, was a mystery to Camille. Until this very moment, she hadn't been entirely convinced that she'd actually gain admission to the highly secretive institute.

"My name's Mrs. Higa," the woman offered as she held a key card up in front of a well-concealed infrared sensor on the wall next to the large door that had obviously been designed by an accomplished metal sculptor.

The sound of the heavy door clanging shut behind them seemed distinctly out of place in this Garden of Eden. Camille's eyes darted around the huge tropical courtyard as she hurried to keep up with her hostess, who clicked across the flagstone terrace in patent-leather high heels.

Another imposing metal sculpture doing double duty as a door. It creaked on its hinges as Mrs. Higa held it for Camille.

In the smaller courtyard behind the second door were several adults sitting in pairs. To the left sat a man and woman staring into a bubbling fountain. Camille noticed that the man's knuckles were white from the way he held on to the bench. He was rocking ever so slightly and looked as though he was convinced that he'd fall off the end of the earth if he eased up on his death grip. The woman whispered into his ear, and he stiffened even more.

"As you know, our patient-staff ratio is two to one, twenty-four hours a day here at Kahana Care."

Camille tried to figure out how much it must cost to keep someone in a place like this. "Now I know why my aunt Moyna-Lou loves it here so much." Who wouldn't? The thought of whiling away her days in paradise briefly wafted across Camille's consciousness to the tune of the old Stones song about Valium: "Mother's Little Helper."

A couple of men, one rather young and one much older, stood doing some kind of calisthenics in front of a bougainvillea bush. In a moment, seemingly out of the blue, the older man burst into tears and hugged his companion, clinging to him as he cried.

Camille and Mrs. Higa stopped as a woman pushing a wheelchair passed in front of them. The passenger spoke nonstop to no one in particular, and her escort responded gently. Suddenly, a fiery bird swooped down and landed in front of them. The patient didn't flinch; she just continued her animated one-way conversation with the breeze floating in over the ocean. The place reminded Camille of her psychiatric nursing rotation at Western State Hospital. She'd never forgotten the feeling: creepy and fascinating at the same time.

Another courtyard. This one with rooms opening directly onto the conservatory. On closer inspection, Camille noticed that there were thready metallic screens separating the rooms from the fragrant vegetation.

Mrs. Higa stepped up to the last patio on the left and said softly, "Hello? Mrs. Davenport's niece Serena is here."

A wide-bodied Pacific Islander hurried over to let Camille through the loosely woven artistic screen that doubled as a security gate.

"This is Mrs. Davenport's nurse, Rose," Mrs. Higa said.

Rose smiled broadly as she closed the screen behind Camille. The clanging sound was higher pitched than that of the heavier doors. Nevertheless, no one was leaving this room without a key.

"My land." Rose's large hands settled on her hips. "Miss Moyna-Lou, sweetheart, you have yourself a visitor." Rose led Camille across the high-ceilinged room to where her patient sat gazing out over the melodious surf.

Camille stopped. Moyna-Lou Davenport looked like an aging movie star. She was spectacular. Her cheekbones created the framework for an utterly perfect face. And her pouty lips were frozen into a vacant smile.

Moyna-Lou didn't look up as Camille took her hand and said, "It's me, Serena."

The hand was limp.

"Auntie?"

Rose put her arm around Camille and whispered into her ear, "I just dispensed her afternoon meds."

Camille felt the heat of Rose's body.

The nurse pulled a chair up so Camille could sit next to "her aunt," whose green eyes looked out past the horizon, unfocused. Moyna-Lou reminded Camille of someone who'd been smoking way too much pot.

"Tea?" Rose asked.

"Please," Camille answered absentmindedly, wondering how she could possibly get any information about Kensington's mental health out of the obviously stoned woman.

The tart smell of Japanese green tea preceded the nurse. "I couldn't believe my ears when they said Miss Moyna-Lou had a visitor." She handed Camille the cup. "The only time she ever gets a visitor is on her birthday and then again on April first."

That was odd; it was common knowledge that Kensington visited her mother almost monthly.

Camille looked at Rose. "Hasn't Jessica been here lately?"

"Nope." Rose scooted up a large wicker chair for herself and plopped her mammoth frame into it comfortably. She patted Moyna-Lou on the shoulder. "Her birthday and April first. Only time Jessica ever comes to see her mom." Rose rearranged her patient's loose white hair across her shoulders.

"Why April first?"

"April fools!" squawked Moyna-Lou, sending a jolt up Camille's spine. "April fools!" Moyna-Lou threw her head back and shot forth a laugh that cackled in a crescendo.

Rose jumped from her chair and kneeled at her patient's feet, surprising Camille with her agility. The nurse smiled up at Moyna-Lou, took one of her feet in her muscular hands, and initiated a tempered foot massage. "It's the only thing that calms her."

Moyna-Lou grinned sleepily at Camille and giggled. "April fools," she whispered as she slumped back in her chair.

Camille wondered what could possibly cause someone to cycle from a vacant stupor to a frenzied outburst and back to never-never land in a matter of minutes. She leaned toward Rose as Moyna-Lou drifted off. "What kind of medicine is she on?"

"You name it. Her daughter the doctor insists that we keep her one breath short of a coma."

It was certainly working.

Rose continued with the foot massage as Moyna-Lou sat back up and tried to focus on Camille.

"Serena?"

"Yes, Auntie?" Camille hoped the trepidation she felt wasn't apparent in her voice. The outburst was definitely freaky. "I'm right here."

Moyna-Lou winked. "Sure you are." As she rolled her eyes, a half smile spread across her well-sculpted face.

Was she more alert than she let on? Did she know Camille wasn't her niece from Dallas?

"What is it about April Fools' Day?" Camille asked the nurse, who was working diligently on the other foot. "Do you know?"

Rose grabbed the arm of Moyna-Lou's chair and grunted as she pulled herself up.

Moyna-Lou interrupted. "That baby came," she said softly, "April fools." Her narrow shoulders began to shake.

Baby? What baby?

Rose waddled over and wetted a washcloth, then gently caressed her patient's face with it.

"I'll tell you what, it was the beginning of the end for Moyna-Lou, that April first." Rose returned to the sink. "How she goes on . . ."

Camille walked over and stood next to the billowing nurse. "What happened?" she asked quietly, wondering if there was any possibility that any of this was remotely related to her inquiry.

A bony talon grabbed Camille's shoulder from behind, causing her heart to skip a beat. Moyna-Lou looked at Camille with wild eyes and dug her fingernails through Camille's jersey dress. "That baby screamed and cried, and screamed and cried, and screamed and cried, and screamed . . ." Camille could smell the old woman's sweet breath on her neck. She froze as Rose removed Moyna-Lou's hand from Camille's shoulder and guided her patient back to the chair.

"Remember when Jessica had her baby? Your uncle delivered the baby at home, on April first. Jessica was just fourteen years old." Rose looked at the elderly patient and lowered her voice. "It didn't set well with Miss Moyna-Lou."

"And the baby screamed and screamed . . ." Moyna-Lou looked at Camille. "He screamed and screamed and screamed . . ." Her expression escalated along with her voice until her entire body was vibrating.

Was that what had sent Jessica over the edge? Having a baby at such a young age? Camille imagined her fourteen-year-old daughter, Libby, laboring at home and giving birth. It was incomprehensible. Why had they delivered the baby at home?

"I hate that baby." Moyna-Lou smiled when she said it. "Hate it, hate it, hate it." She clenched her thin fists.

Of course Jessica's having delivered a baby at home hardly explained her mother's psychiatric difficulties, nor her brother's. Still, Camille felt a pang of sympathy for young Jessica Kensington having to go through the torture of a home birth at fourteen years of age.

"That must have been very difficult for Jessica," Camille said.

A look of recognition came over Moyna-Lou. "Ah. You want to know about Jessica." It was more of a statement than a question.

Camille nodded in response.

Moyna-Lou snickered.

Camille waited.

At first Camille hardly noticed the slight tremor in Moyna-Lou's hand, but by the time the shaking started working its way up her arm to her shoulder, Camille became concerned. She looked around for the nurse, who was straightening the bed.

"Rose, does she always shake like this?"

Rose glanced at her watch. "My lands, you need your next dose already, girlfriend?"

The shaking continued.

"I'll be right back." The nurse dropped a pile of pillows on the floor and hurried to the bathroom, where Camille could hear her unlocking a cabinet.

As soon as Rose was out of earshot, Moyna-Lou stopped shaking, leaned forward, and whispered, "You're not Serena."

Camille held her breath.

"You're here about Jessica, aren't you?"

Camille's eyes darted toward the bathroom door and back to the aged beauty queen.

"We all fell apart when that baby showed up."

Amazingly, for the moment, the old woman appeared entirely oriented.

Moyna-Lou stared at Camille for a moment. "Jessica hurt someone else, didn't she?"

Someone else? Camille hesitated. "Why do you ask?"

The old woman smiled. "You want to know what happened to Jessica."

Camille nodded.

"Don't let her fool you." Moyna-Lou shook her head. "Jessica's every bit as crazy as that little boy was. Or her father." Moyna-Lou winked. "Actually, she's crazier than the whole bunch of 'em." She laughed a shrill, screeching laugh. "Bad blood. Bad, bad blood."

Camille was dumbfounded.

Rose appeared with a small silver cup about the size of a shot glass and dumped a colorful pile of pills into Moyna-Lou's palm.

Once again, the woman appeared to be returning from the edge of psychopathy to full coherence.

"You know, Serena, I just might want you to be my pen pal. No one else in the family gives a damn about me over here." Moyna gulped down the handful of medication.

Okay, this was getting a bit surreal. The old lady knew Camille was an impostor. But here she was offering herself up as a newfound pen pal. *There must be some reason she wants to stay in touch.*

"Isn't that nice?" Rose commented, not the least bit surprised about her patient's abrupt change in demeanor. Apparently she wasn't being paid to second-guess any diagnoses. Just fawn solicitously and don't ask questions. "Why don't you write down your address for Moyna-Lou? It would be so lovely for her to have a pen pal."

Camille hesitated, wondering if she should give the woman her real address. If she did, she certainly stood a chance of being found out. She held the pen over the pad engraved with the Kahana Care logo.

Moyna-Lou inclined her head slightly. "I can keep a secret, you know." She scrunched her shoulders like a naughty little girl.

"Go ahead, dear," Rose coaxed. "I know your family's not exactly close. I promise we'll keep this just between the three of us. Moyna-Lou gets so lonely at times."

So what if Kensington found out she'd been here? What could she do about it anyway? There was no way Camille was going to get any information if she didn't find a way to stay in touch. She wrote Serena Davenport, then inscribed her office address and phone number.

Camille handed the notepad to Rose. "Thanks. I'd appreciate it if you'd keep this confidential. You're right about our family; I'd just as soon they not know exactly where I live."

The pad disappeared into the pocket of Rose's muumuu.

Moyna-Lou's arm felt papery to Camille's moist fingertips. "So, whatever happened to Jessica's baby?" she almost whispered.

Moyna-Lou's eyes lost focus again.

"Was the baby okay?"

A look of serenity came over Moyna-Lou.

Camille searched the patient's face, looking for some sign of the cogent woman who seemed to come and go with the wind.

Very slowly a smile grew from somewhere within the beautiful Moyna-Lou. "We'll never tell." She spoke in a singsong manner as though she were reciting a nursery rhyme. "Never, ever tell about the baby." She pretended to zip her lips shut and throw away an invisible key.

CHAPTER TWENTY-SEVEN

Camille sat on a cold wrought iron chair watching the professor get her garden ready for winter.

"I'm telling you, she's loony tunes," Trish announced. "That's a scientific term," she said to Laurabelle, whose upper torso disappeared under an enormous rhododendron bush.

The wizened woman backed out butt first and sat on her haunches. "Well, we already know that there's some degree of looney tunes in the family." She winked at Trish. "It seems to me that the bigger question is whether we can prove that Kensington's actions as a doctor are due to some kind of mental illness."

One of the bulldogs snorted over to Camille and rolled around on his back at her feet. "I can't imagine why she'd try to cause miscarriages in women who've gotten pregnant after infertility treatment." She reached down and rubbed the dog's belly. "Maybe it has something to do with her teen pregnancy, but for the life of me I don't see the connection."

"It might." Laurabelle pushed a strand of hair out of her face with the back of a muddy gloved hand. "But for the moment we need to figure out why your doctor treated Helene Anderson with the same cavalier attitude that she treated those infertility patients."

"Can we tie together the family's mental illness with Kensington's actions?" Camille asked.

"If you ask me, they're all nuts." Trish threw a stick for the smaller dog to chase. "The mother and Kensington and her brother." The dog returned with the stick and Trish repeated the drill. "I can't believe the judge won't let you prove it."

"I can prove it if I can make it relevant to my case. That's the challenge. Making it relevant." Camille's frustration was beginning to get the best of her.

"There's something about those infertility patients," Laurabelle mused aloud. "And there may well be a connection to the teen pregnancy."

"What do you think it is?" Camille asked.

Laurabelle stood stiffly and grabbed the shovel that was leaning against the rusty wheelbarrow.

"Here, let me do that," Camille offered as she removed the implement from the professor's grasp. The mahogany-colored loam released an organic fragrance as Camille spread it over the raised vegetable bed that had been put to rest for the winter. Both dogs bolted over and snapped at the dirt as it fell from the shovel.

"Okay," Laurabelle thought out loud. "There has to be something that sets off some kind of PTSD reaction in Kensington when she does procedures on those infertility patients."

"You think she's resentful of people who are trying to get pregnant?" Camille asked.

Laurabelle shook her head. "I'm not sure. We need to find out the common thread that links those patients."

"Well, even if there is one, how does Helene Anderson fit into the picture?" Trish asked.

"We won't know until we find out more about the other patients." Laurabelle dropped to her knees and patted down the topsoil as quickly as the dogs loosened it with their paws. "Do you know if Helene was treated for infertility?"

"She wasn't," Camille said flatly. "I already asked."

"Well, how can you find out about those other patients?"

Camille put her chin on the handle of the shovel. "Beats me." She looked at Trish. "Any ideas?"

"I'm thinking."

"Is there any way we could find out what those patients look like?" Laurabelle asked.

"I don't think there's any way to find out anything at all about them. Everything is protected by the confidentiality statutes," Camille said.

"I wonder if all the patients are blond like Helene or something," the professor wondered.

Trish shook her sun-bleached hair. "Don't look at me. I'm not about to lay my body down for Kensington to do her roto-rooter thing on my privates."

"I wasn't suggesting it would be something that simplistic. But my money says the more you can find out about those infertility patients, and compare them to Helene Anderson, the more likely you are to find out why Kensington's doing what she is." Laurabelle gathered her garden tools and hollered for her dogs.

Camille looked at her watch. "I'd better get back to the office. Thanks for your help." She hugged the stocky professor. "It sounds like we have our marching orders."

Trish limped up beside Camille. "We'll think of something." She held Camille's arm as they walked together out to the car.

"Don't tell me you really think Kensington's mom had any idea what you were doing over there," Trish said as Camille pulled out of the driveway of Laurabelle's well-worn craftsman house in the Wallingford neighborhood.

Camille shook her head. "I don't know." She stopped and faced Trish. "I could have sworn she knew exactly why I was there one minute, then"—she snapped her fingers—"she was lost in the ozone the next."

"Camille, she's probably hopped up on those drugs she's being prescribed. She has no fucking idea what's going on."

The car behind them honked gently to remind Camille the light had changed.

Camille turned her attention to the road. "You weren't there to see her. It was incredible, first she's fixated on a point just beyond the horizon, then she pierced right through me with these shocking green eyes as if she wanted to tell me something." Camille looked to her left and admired the Seattle skyline in the distance. "So I gave her my address."

"You what?" Trish shouted. "Jesus, Camille, you don't honestly think you're going to hear from her, do you?"

"I might." Camille sped up to merge onto Highway 99 and over the Aurora Bridge, from which she could see her office building on the waterfront hundreds of feet below.

—

Amy stared out the window of her spartan office. Never having allowed herself to fully embrace the fact that she was now an employee of "The Law Offices of Harvey Lowe," she hadn't made any effort to make the cubicle her own.

Time ground along aimlessly day after day, and she'd yet to be assigned to a single case. In fact, she hadn't been asked to do a god-damned thing since she'd finished indexing the stack of closed files two weeks earlier. Yesterday a secretary had asked her to help her copy the exhibits for a motion. But that'd been it. Nothing more. Nada.

This was absurd. She finished off the double chocolate fudge brownie that had nearly jumped out of the pastry case at her favorite new café, Coco Loco. After licking the gooey mess from her fingers, she dialed Camille's office. It was time to make up.

"Camille Delaney's office."

It was an unfamiliar voice.

"Hello? Anyone there?"

Amy's heart pattered in her chest, and it wasn't from the chocolate rush. "Uh, is Camille in?"

"She's out meeting with an expert. Can I take a message?"

Expert? Amy wondered which case Camille was working on. It had to be Anderson. Good. Camille had found a new expert. That doc from Ojai had trouble written all over him.

"Hello? Would you like me to take a message?"

She'd been replaced. Just like that.

"No. No, thanks. I'll call back."

Maybe it had been a bad idea, calling so soon. She really wasn't ready to face Camille. The guilt had done nothing but escalate since she'd left. Her mother, the diehard Catholic, would be so proud.

Well, if Harvey Lowe didn't have anything for her to do, maybe she could go back to working on the Anderson case. It was the least she could do after abandoning Camille. Amy headed down the hall to the jam-packed file room. Locating the *A* section, she slid out the expando containing the Anderson file. Obviously Lowe hadn't had a chance to do much work on the case before Helene had fired him. Amy smiled at the thought of Lowe's pudgy little face when he realized Helene had chosen Camille over him.

Amy scanned the pages of attorney notes, then turned to correspondence.

Huh. A draft demand letter.

She took a moment to peruse it. Another "premium baby" argument. Strange: she hadn't realized Helene had been an infertility patient.

"Amy?"

It was Lowe.

She shoved the file back into the archives. It didn't matter where.

"Yes?" Her voice cracked.

"Here"—he handed her a foot-high bunch of papers—"do something with this." His Shortness turned and walked away. Amy wondered what had happened to the friendly man that had convinced her to mutiny and join his majestic ship. She felt like a complete schmuck.

Amy watched Lowe blast off toward his office, and she surreptitiously turned back to Anderson. She emptied a file containing Helene's medical records, setting aside a manila envelope labeled in Missy's distinctive back-slanted script: *Records given to patient.* Amy was already quite familiar with the contents of the records Helene took from Lowe's office and gave to Camille. She continued to leaf through the file. There didn't appear to be anything particularly interesting.

She picked up the proposed demand letter again. Why had Lowe drafted a settlement letter about Helene as an infertility patient?

Amy restacked the records and opened another file folder. Then another. Finally she located a file labeled "Damages." She skimmed through several pages of Missy's notes and shook her head.

Nothing.

What was this? She carefully opened a sealed envelope.

Oh my God. In her hand she held a medical transcription of an artificial insemination procedure performed on Helene Anderson by Kip Davenport.

—

Trish entered another internet café and looked around. After being on her feet all day, the ache in her leg had become more than a little distracting, but she wasn't going to let that stop her from figuring out who had sent the mysterious email about Camille's expert, Greg Fitzharris. To date, all she'd been able to figure out was that the email had come from a public internet source, and she had narrowed it down to either an internet café or the library. She opened the door to the tiny establishment with pulsating grunge music thumping its beat out to the sidewalk. Trish wasn't entirely sure what she was looking for but hoped something would jump out at her.

Nothing particularly notable here. She exited out onto Second Avenue, in the hip downtown neighborhood of Belltown, and wearily pulled herself up onto the first bus that stopped, disembarking several blocks later in the heart of the financial district.

As soon as she hit the pavement, her cell phone rang. It was Camille. "Yeah?"

"That asshole Bagley is still refusing to make Kensington available for a deposition."

Trish walked into the last café on her list and got in line for a latte. "He has to let you depose her; what's he trying to do?"

"Make me go to court again."

The thick aroma of chocolate filled the snug little establishment. "What reason do they give you that she's supposedly unavailable?"

"What do you think?"

"Another trip to see poor sick mama?"

"You got it."

The woman at the table by the fogged-up window logged onto a computer and took a spoonful of sinfully dark ice cream.

"You think she's really even going anywhere?" Trish asked.

"You tell me."

Trish watched as the young man behind the counter flirted with a middle-aged gentleman dressed in a pair of obviously expensive gray pants and a cashmere turtleneck. The clerk held a chocolate éclair in the palm of one hand and an oversized brownie in the other as though he were the scales of justice. The customer couldn't make up his mind.

"Go with the brownie," Trish whispered over the man's shoulder.

He did.

"Triple tall nonfat latte to go," she said to the barista, then resumed her conversation with Camille. "Look, why don't I follow Kensington for a while? It's the only way we can find out where the hell she's really going . . . if anywhere."

"Do you have time?"

"Sure, I'm not exactly making any progress trying to figure out where that email came from."

A woman walked by with the biggest banana split Trish had ever seen.

"Actually, Bagley tells me Kensington's going to be out of town with her mother, which we know isn't true. If we find out Bagley's lying, I'll make a motion and get sanctions against him. That way I can afford to pay you for your stakeout."

"Thanks," Trish said to the clerk and headed for the door. "I'm going to call it a day, I'm not having any luck." She clicked her phone closed.

Stopping on the street, Trish took a sip of the latte. Wow: perfect. She'd have to remember this place. She turned to check out the name of the tiny store snuggled in between two towering high-rises.

Huh, Coco Loco. Cute.

CHAPTER TWENTY-EIGHT

Looking at her calendar, Camille realized that today was the day she'd requested to depose Kensington. If what Bagley told her was true, the doc should be on her way to visit her mother in Hawaii. And just as they'd planned, Trish was sitting in front of Kensington's condo waiting.

"Look, Mommy!"

Gracie crashed into Camille's office from the conference room where she'd been assiduously working on her science project. Trailing behind her like an odd-shaped flag was a full-sized cutout of her body. The assignment had been to glue red strings of yarn stretching from the red crayoned heart along the limbs as though the strings were veins.

"See?"

There was something comforting about the smell of Elmer's glue. It took Camille back to her childhood when she and Eve watched cartoons while they worked on art projects together at the kitchen table. On those days Camille would almost forget about baby Valerie. And that her dad's grief had caused him to pretty much abandon the family. Yep, Elmer's glue felt safe.

"Wow! Great job!" Camille could see beyond Grace into the conference room, where the long antique table had been transformed into an operating room table, with red yarn hanging like blood into pools on the floor.

Camille fingered the soggy butcher paper. "How'd you do that?"

"Easy," Grace bragged. "I just lied down and Libby cut around me to make the body . . ."

"Mom, this just came in." Angela handed her mother a letter from Bagley's office.

Camille scanned it. "Of course."

"What?" demanded Libby.

"I've been trying to schedule a doctor's deposition for over a month, but they kept putting me off, only scheduling it for next week." Which was one week before trial, Camille noted to herself as she put the letter on top of the pile of correspondence covering her desk. Bagley had her running in circles and she couldn't seem to stop it.

"Mom! Line three!" Libby yelled. The office had definitely become a family affair. "It's Trish!"

Camille grabbed the phone.

"She's heading for the airport!" Trish announced breathlessly.

"You're kidding."

"Yeah, I'm right behind her barreling down I-5 in her fancy-ass car."

Gracie dropped her artwork on the floor, climbed up onto her mother's lap, grabbed a fuchsia magic marker that smelled like strawberries, and scribbled on a legal pad. A pang of guilt washed over Camille as she watched her foster daughter. Not much of a three-day weekend. She'd have to make it up to all of them after the trial.

"Do you think she's really going to see her mom?" Camille asked.

"Beats me. I'm gonna follow her into the airport."

"Okay, keep me posted."

Gracie finished off the last sheet of paper and slid to the floor behind Camille, where she continued her coloring.

It was impossible to keep track of the number of motions she'd filed and responded to so far in the Anderson case. Camille pulled up the most recent one: Motion to Compel Defendant to Make Her Experts Available for Depositions. She knew her bank account was dwindling rapidly, and she barely had enough to pay one of them, never mind all three.

"Oh my God, I forgot to call Win Clark back to see if he'll settle Cipriotti," Camille said aloud to no one in particular. If she could just settle that case for the little redheaded kid, she might be able to afford some really nice trial exhibits.

She knew that insurance companies liked to clear their books at the end of the year, so they frequently settled cases during November and December. Besides, it was the only one she had that was ripe for settlement. And she was desperate for money.

"Mommy, hand me the orange marker, please." Gracie held her hand out like a surgeon.

Camille booted up her computer and searched for the email where Clark had given her his number in case she needed to reach him during his vacation. She grabbed her phone and dialed, then absentmindedly handed Gracie the marker as she waited for Clark to answer.

"Win Clark here."

"It's Camille Delaney."

"Hello, Camille," his voice dripped with sarcasm. "I've been expecting your call."

"I hadn't heard back from you since I sent you the last demand on Cipriotti."

The other end of the line was silent.

"So, I thought I'd call and give you an opportunity to get it off your case list before the Thanksgiving holiday."

"How do you propose we do that?"

"Well, you could send me a check . . ."

"Jesus. Under the circumstances, I'm not sure I can do that."

The magic marker squeaked as Grace colored furiously at Camille's feet.

"Why not?"

"Well, for starters, who do you suggest is going to endorse it?"

"I had Gina Cipriotti appointed as guardian ad litem." Clark's circuitous gamesmanship was wearing thin.

"That's my point."

"What's your point?" There was nothing Win Clark liked better than to jerk a plaintiff's lawyers around.

"Oh my God." He actually sounded genuine.

"What?" she asked.

"You haven't been reading the paper or watching the news?"

Camille surveyed the anarchy that had once been a fairly normal law office as Gracie handed her the old *Trial News* with the picture of Lowe and his young client. Shit. Gracie had colored in the face of the little girl in the wheelchair. As she took the article from Gracie's grasp, Camille noted that the kid in the picture looked vaguely like Danny Cipriotti.

"Have you?" Clark repeated.

"Have I what?"

"Have you seen last week's paper?"

"Actually I can't remember the last time I even saw a newspaper, why?"

Camille could hear Win Clark exhale. "Jeez, Camille, I hate to be the one to break the news to you, but your little redhead was all over the news last week. He even made the cover of *Newsweek*."

This couldn't possibly be leading anywhere good. "What happened?"

"It seems little Danny Cipriotti has the dubious distinction of being the youngest child ever to be charged with murder one."

"What?" She threw the *Trial News* to the floor.

Clark lowered his voice. "They found him in his parents' room, with their gun. He was covered in blood."

The room began to spin. "Oh my God."

"He killed them in their sleep, Camille."

———

Trish stuck her hair up into a baseball cap as she ran across the airport parking lot. Just as she reached the elevator lobby, she put on a pair of red plastic-rimmed glasses and her Broncos jacket, then threw her backpack over her shoulder. She dodged an elderly couple in order to make it into the elevator with Kensington, whose wheeled Tumi suitcase had inadvertently stopped the door from closing.

The airport was a zoo. Trish panicked, praying that there'd be an extra seat for her on whatever flight Kensington boarded. She got in line directly behind Kensington and smiled at her.

"Off to the sunshine, or just to visit family?" Trish asked Kensington.

"The Cayman Islands." Kensington avoided eye contact.

Shit, what was the likelihood that she'd be able to get on a plane to the Caribbean at this time of year?

Trish rummaged in her backpack for her passport. It was easy to find; the pack was nearly empty. Not to worry, there'd be plenty of time to pick up whatever she needed if and when she got to their destination. And in the meantime, she did have her favorite disguises and vital documents. She glanced at the list of departing flights. The doctor must be going through Miami.

How the hell was Camille going to be able to afford a same-day ticket to Grand Cayman island anyway?

"Next?" The agent spoke loudly from the end of the long counter.

"Any chance I can get on the flight to Miami?"

The middle-aged man grimaced as he hammered on the keyboard. "Gonna cost ya."

"That's not the half of it. I'd like to get from Miami to Grand Cayman on the next available connection."

"Returning?"

"Open return."

The man shook his head. "It's your lucky day."

Trish braced herself. "How much?"

"Three thousand four hundred twenty-eight fifty-two."

"Ouch." Trish winced. "I'll be right back." She headed across the lobby and called Camille.

———

Camille hit the speakerphone button on the first ring.

"Any chance you can come up with"—Trish paused—"three thousand four hundred twenty-eight dollars and fifty-two cents?"

"Are you kidding?" Camille rolled her eyes at Lucia, who was organizing the articles on gestational diabetes into a trial notebook. "You know I'm broke," Camille spoke loudly to be heard on the speakerphone.

"Well, Kensington's on her way to the Caymans, and I thought I'd follow along to see what the hell she's doing there."

"The Cayman Islands?"

"Yup."

"Any idea why?"

"Nope. Unless she's going to check on her offshore bank account." Trish laughed.

Camille tried to stop the tears that were beginning to sting. "I don't think I can do this anymore."

"Camille! Snap out of it! What's wrong with you?"

"This is too much. I can't afford to send you to the Cayman Islands."

"Don't you have a credit card?"

"It's maxed out."

"Well, how much cash do you have left?"

"I don't know," Camille whined. "A little less than two thousand."

"Surely you can come up with around fifteen hundred more."

"I can't." Camille closed her eyes tightly. "I need the money to pay the defense experts for their deps. And as it is, I can only afford to depose one of them for a few hours."

"Take 'em on the fly."

"You mean not depose them before trial?"

"You know what they're going to say anyway. You've memorized every fucking article that's ever been written on gestational diabetes and the famous Zavanelli maneuver."

Camille paused, touched by Trish's undying confidence in her legal abilities. It wasn't often that a lawyer skipped taking an expert's deposition, only to take them on for the first time at trial.

"You can do it."

Camille could detect the urgency in Trish's voice even over the speakerphone.

Trish continued, "I think we need to get our priorities straight. Let's use our resources to find out what the hell's going on with Kensington."

Lucia waved her hands from her perch on the floor.

Camille held up a finger as if to say, "Just a sec."

"Even if I do decide to take the experts on the fly at trial, I still can't afford the ticket to the Caymans." Camille slouched. "I'm fifteen hundred short."

The tiny blue-haired woman interrupted softly, "Camille?"

Camille mouthed, "In a minute," to Lucia.

"There's some reason why Kensington's lying about where she's going. I really want to follow her," Trish urged. "We've gotta find the money for this ticket somewhere."

Must be the royal "we."

Lucia ran to her purse and returned with a Visa card and plopped it down on Camille's desk. "Here."

Camille fingered the card and looked at Lucia. "Don't be silly, I'm not using your credit card." She handed it back. "But thanks anyway."

"What?" Trish asked.

"Lucia wants to finance your trip with her own personal Visa card."

"Why not?" Lucia demanded. "We need to get to the bottom of this, and it sounds like we have no choice but for Trish to get on that plane."

"But I'm not taking your money."

"Go ahead, I trust you. I know you're good for it."

"Make up your mind. That flight leaves in twenty minutes!" Trish shouted.

"Please. My parents gave me the card to use in emergencies, and the way I see it, this qualifies as an emergency."

"This is your parents' card?"

Lucia smiled. "They're rich; they probably won't even notice."

"They won't notice a three-thousand-dollar ticket to the Caymans?"

"Let's just say it won't be the first time I've made a spontaneous purchase to travel somewhere exotic," Lucia said sheepishly.

"C'mon, Camille, we can pay her folks back later. I gotta get on that plane!"

Camille shrugged. "Okay, let's do it." She was in it this far, what was a few thousand more dollars at this point? Trish was right. She could take the experts on the fly at trial if she had to. And it was beginning to look like there was no other choice.

CHAPTER TWENTY-NINE

Camille's shoulders stung as she pounded out pages and pages of the notes she'd ultimately incorporate into a detailed outline that she'd use to prepare for Kensington's dep, then trial. She was just beginning to hum along when she realized it was almost six o'clock. Out of the corner of her eye, she noticed a new email beckoning her from the computer screen. *Mom?* She clicked it open.

My darling Camille:

Just thought I'd drop you a line and let you know I'm thinking about you with Thanksgiving right around the corner. We just won a huge ruling from the European Ombudsman—they found that there was grave misconduct on the part of the experts who have been interviewing our asylum seekers. Unfortunately, the clients had already been deported, but the Ombudsman put protections in place in the event this continues. Needless to say, we're thrilled that an official body has confirmed what we've been saying for years and has made an actual finding of maladministration! The people here continue to amaze and inspire me. They are always looking forward, never back. Always looking to what the

future will bring. I'm very lucky to be in their presence.
The work over here is deep and rewarding.

I miss you, Sam, and the girls with all my heart,
and can't wait to see you when I come home for a visit
sometime in the spring.

Love, Mom

In the spring? Camille had hoped she'd see her mom before that.

Her mother was so lucky to have found work that made such a huge difference in people's lives. What must it be like to be involved in work that was all about looking ahead? The legal system was strictly about looking through the rearview mirror and trying to right a wrong by extracting a measure of blood from the wrongdoer in an effort to make the victim whole once again. It was never really about moving forward. Never about trying to prevent another wrong—not about really making a difference. Camille absentmindedly picked up the key ring she'd grabbed from Kensington's condo on Halloween night and jingled the keys. She was sick of spending her career looking backward. Turning to sort through the keys, she wondered what they might unlock.

Maybe she could do something that would make a difference. Maybe she could try to stop Kensington from destroying another patient's pregnancy. That would give her some measure of satisfaction. Maybe she could figure out what was behind Kensington's inexplicable need to cause miscarriages in these poor women. She might even be able to help Kensington in some way.

Camille held up each key, one by one. *One of these has to unlock Kensington's office. And the explanation for the doc's inexplicable behavior has to be in there somewhere.* Camille threw up the key ring and caught it.

———

It wasn't often someone got to go on a business trip like this. Trish looked down on the string of tropical islands spreading out below her. As they neared the largest chunk of land, the captain's British accent came over the tinny speaker in the cabin of the vibrating little plane.

Five minutes and they'd be on the ground. Trish checked to see that her seat belt was tight, then watched as Jessica Kensington put down the book she'd been reading. Looking closer, Trish recognized the cover of *Extricate*—Camille's sister's latest bestseller. Something about getting out of a crappy relationship. It seemed unlikely that the psychobabble of Camille's sister could help this woman.

Kensington rummaged in her purse and took a mirror out and methodically applied the perfect amount of makeup.

Must be meeting someone here. And whoever it was, the doc was definitely anxious. Kensington tried three times to get her mass of auburn locks up into the right style. Finally, she cocked her head and carefully pulled several wavy strands out of her updo so that they softly framed her face. Another go-round with the lipstick.

Trish sat forward, curious who Kensington was getting all dolled up for.

It wasn't the smoothest landing ever. The tiny plane jolted and rattled as it hit the runway.

As soon as they stopped taxiing, Trish stood, hunched over, waiting for the door to be opened. She didn't want to miss seeing Kensington's arrival in the terminal—and in particular she didn't want to miss seeing who might be waiting to meet her.

Trish had only been half kidding when she'd hypothesized that Kensington was en route to some mysterious offshore bank account. It had to be more than a coincidence that Kensington had chosen Grand Cayman island, of all places. Especially in light of the one point two mil that had whisked quickly in and out of the doc's local account.

Not seeing Kensington exactly bolting out of her seat, Trish slowly sat back down and pretended to look for some lost item under her seat.

Oddly, after all the primping, Kensington was the last passenger seated on the rapidly warming plane. Trish watched as Kensington took a series of deep breaths while she subtly shook her freckled arms and alternately opened and closed her eyes. Was she having some kind of seizure or anxiety attack?

The thickly accented flight attendant looked at Kensington questioningly. "Can I help you, ma'am?"

Kensington ignored the woman and closed her eyes, apparently focusing on her breathing.

The petite woman was obviously anxious for the last of her passengers to disembark so she could get home. She looked at Trish. "Did you lose something?"

Trish emptied the seat pocket in front of her. "I can't find my sunglasses." She feigned an exasperated frown. "I must have left them in Miami."

The attendant smiled. "I'm sure you won't have any trouble replacing them here on the island."

The accent made it sound like the woman was half singing.

"There's a place on Front Street that has a terrific selection." She ushered Trish to the front of the plane, past Kensington, who was just beginning to gather her purse.

Once off the plane, Trish waited in the thick humidity.

Finally. There she is.

Trish followed Kensington through customs, then faded into the periphery of the crowd so she could see who might be waiting to greet the nervous doctor. She sighed as Kensington looked at her watch, then headed down the short concourse before abruptly melting into the anonymous throng.

Shit.

Trish schlepped along behind Kensington toward the baggage claim, alert to Kensington's every move.

It was obvious from Kensington's assertive stride that she knew exactly where she was going. She must've repinned her hair into place fifty times by the time they got to the open-air lobby. Out came the compact and lipstick again. The woman was certainly jumpy. Kensington stopped and held out the small mirror, critically checking her entire face before slipping into a festive cocktail lounge a couple hundred feet from baggage claim. Without hesitating, the doctor moved quickly to the back of the establishment and took the last stool at the far end of the bar as though she'd done it a number of times before.

Trish grabbed a seat by the doorway and watched Kensington with genuine curiosity.

When Kensington was on her third gigantic tropical drink, a nondescript-looking man carrying a huge bouquet entered the nearly empty bar and almost ran to the back. He looked like he was going to explode with delight as he enveloped Kensington in his arms and buried his face in her neck.

Oh no. Trish closed her eyes. How was she going to explain to Camille that she'd convinced her to spend her last few dollars to finance a trip across the continent so that Trish could spy on the defendant having an affair with some short, fat guy. On closer observation, Trish could see the man's expensive brand-new sandals and crisp linen shorts. Okay, so he was a short, fat, rich guy. But the huge sapphire pinky ring was a bit much. She wondered for a moment if this was why Kensington was reading Eve McKane's book on dumping your boyfriend. This might be interesting, but certainly not what she was hoping for on this surveillance.

Well, as long as she was here, she might as well follow along and see where they went. A good detective always takes at least a hundred pictures. Trish looked at the empty bottle of Heineken in front of her and wished she'd tried a couple of those fancy drinks Kensington had been pounding down. It might make it easier to report this debacle to Camille.

Trish watched as the man directed his tall girlfriend through the lobby, then into a limousine with the name of a resort written in curvy script on its side. Trish took out a pen and inscribed the name on the palm of her hand before hailing a cab to take her into town, where she hoped to find a cheap, but clean, room.

—

Amy caught Missy Barron just as she was packing her briefcase to leave for the day. Her familiar armload of bracelets jangled as she motioned Amy to the wingback chair across from her heavy walnut desk.

Amy stuck her hand deep into the box of Oreos she had brought down the hall with her. "Do you remember a case called Anderson?"

"You bet, why do you ask?" Missy organized a tall stack of pink message slips and held them up. "Can you believe this? These are all new client calls from just this week."

So Lowe had his pick of cases. No big surprise there.

Amy offered Missy the half-full box. "I was just closing the file and I noticed a sealed envelope with some kind of medical record in it."

Missy cocked her head.

"I just wondered if I should file it in with the medical records, or if there was some reason it was kept separately." It seemed like a plausible question.

Missy took the bait.

"That woman was so weird. It's the first time I ever remember Harvey actually firing a client." Missy gently took one cookie out and carefully twisted it apart.

"What do you mean he fired her?" That definitely wasn't the story Helene had told Camille.

Missy inched forward in her chair and handed back the box of Oreos.

Amy declined.

Missy put the box on the corner of her desk. "This woman comes to us with a perfect premium dead baby case."

Amy looked quizzically at her friend. "Premium dead baby case?" She tried to sound curious, but she had a sinking feeling she knew where this was going.

"Harvey kinda coined an argument to make in cases where a client loses a baby either by miscarriage or by being stillborn when the pregnancy was the result of some kind of fertility treatment."

Amy couldn't believe it. "You mean this Anderson woman lost the baby she'd conceived during fertility treatment?"

Missy methodically licked one half of the Oreo clean. "Yeah, but she refused to let us make the argument."

"Why?"

"It turns out that she never told her husband that she'd had herself artificially inseminated."

Uh-oh.

Missy leaned forward. "If she'd have let us make the argument, it would have been a slam dunk of a case."

"How so?"

"The doc who messed up the delivery is this witch we've sued at least three times I can think of. The woman's a real quack. I wish the disciplinary board would shut her down."

"So you think Harvey could have gotten Anderson a pile of money based on the fact that she'd been an infertility patient?"

"That and the fact that the doctor would probably screw up in her dep like she did the other times we sued her. Which, of course, made the value of those cases skyrocket."

"What'd she do?"

"Beats me—it seems like the doc has some kind of guilt attack and all but admits she screwed up." Missy nibbled on the remaining half cookie. "Then she goes after the nurses."

"What do you mean?"

"In one of the cases we had, Kensington let this baby linger along in fetal distress for hours before she sectioned the mother."

"And then she blamed the nurses?"

Missy nodded. "Said the nurses didn't call her soon enough. Then they didn't get set up fast enough." She paused. "Then she started in on the anesthesiologist." She rolled her eyes. "It was a plaintiff's dream case. The doc only had five million in coverage, but by the time she finished with her dep, we were able to name just about every conceivable defendant. Harvey settled it for twelve million."

It figured. Lowe got the easy money and Camille had to limp along with the shitty damage case. "How much did Harvey think he could get on Anderson?"

"If she woulda let him make the premium baby argument, she'd have gotten at least a couple of million."

"Jesus."

"I told you the guy's a genius."

Amy ignored the comment. "Why'd he fire her?"

"Case wasn't worth enough to pursue without the big damage argument. He got so pissed at her, he told her to go find another lawyer." Missy stood and grabbed her briefcase. "He completely flipped out—said he'd make sure she never saw a dime out of that case. It was completely out of character for him to behave like that."

It didn't come as much of a surprise to Amy. Camille had told her the kind of grudge Harvey Lowe had carried after she left his office a decade ago with several of her own cases. According to Camille, he was just waiting for a chance to ruin her.

Missy stopped in the doorway. "I pity whoever takes her case. This woman is one huge pain in the butt." She paused. "You gotta wonder about a woman who'd lie to her husband about something like being inseminated."

So Helene Anderson had been lying all along. Amy had to find a way to alert Camille. And quickly.

———

It had never entirely cooled down in the tiny attic room of the hostel where Trish had finally found a vacancy sometime after midnight. She reluctantly donned the long red wig she always kept in her backpack and lathered on as much lipstick as she could stand. A pair of oversized sunglasses, and she was good to go. Not that she'd expect Kensington to recognize her, but you couldn't be too careful.

Before heading out, Trish shot Camille a short text. She was hesitant to transmit her feelings of frustration about the distinct possibility that she was on a giant wild-goose chase, so she just sent the sketchiest of messages and told Camille that she'd call back soon with more details. At least they'd proved that Kensington had lied about being in Hawaii, for whatever that was worth.

Trish stopped to admire herself in the strappy sundress she'd purchased in the gift shop of the Miami airport during their layover. "You look positively hetero," she said aloud to her reflection before closing the creaky door.

As she took a seat at the poolside bar where the lovebirds were staying, Trish tried to ignore the sweat that was rapidly building under the heavy wig. She ordered a large orange juice, with a side of ice. Thankfully, there was a basket of flatbread on each table and several along the bar. Trish grabbed a few and quickly stuffed them into her purse, then slid down a couple of seats and ate an entire basket before her juice arrived.

Life on a budget.

Once she'd satisfied her appetite, she scanned the patio and located Kensington and her boyfriend. The guy was fawning all over the good doctor.

What's up with this woman?

Rather than reciprocating her man's devotion, Kensington stiffly toyed with the bamboo napkin holder, staring at the lavish fruit plate in front of her. The doctor looked distinctly out of place among the happy vacationers laughing easily at tables scattered around the pool. Trish decided that the doctor looked more like she was waiting for a root canal than having a leisurely breakfast with her lover in utopia.

Well, it was probably part of her mental condition. Hadn't Laurabelle told them that people with backgrounds like Kensington's were likely to have problems with interpersonal relationships?

And Mr. Wonderful seemed completely oblivious to Kensington's rigidity. What a surprise. A guy who's so busy focusing on himself that he's missing the fact that his girlfriend appears to be lost in the ozone. The guy's heavily jeweled Rolex reflected a momentary blast of sunshine in Trish's eyes as he ordered another round of mimosas with a flourish.

Maybe he's the one with the offshore bank account.

Trish watched as the man instructed Kensington to close her eyes, then clasped a substantial strand of diamonds around her neck. *Wow.*

When Kensington opened her eyes, the boyfriend was holding a small mirror. But when Kensington saw her reflection, she blanched, then slowly reached for the necklace, stopping before she actually touched it, as if it were some kind of poison.

Jesus Christ—here she was with this rich guy panting all over her and literally showering her with diamonds, and she looked like someone just told her that her puppy died.

Maybe Laurabelle was right. Maybe there is something to this psychobabble shit after all. Trish wandered behind an oversized flowering bush and, out of habit, snapped a few pictures of the happy couple.

CHAPTER THIRTY

It seemed to take forever for Sunday to roll around. Camille entered the elevator in the high-rise medical building where Kensington and Davenport had their office. She pushed the button for the eleventh floor and fingered the key ring that was nearly burning a hole in her pocket. She'd waited until the weekend, knowing that no one in the medical biz had office hours on a Sunday. And she was right; the place was dark and deserted. She read the directory outside the elevator and headed down to the end of the hall where she found a doorway made of heavily etched glass: "Davenport Women's Health."

This was it.

Camille withdrew the keys and quickly tried the first one.

No good.

Next.

Nope.

Two more to try. Camille hadn't even considered the fact that none of the keys would fit.

You're in.

Camille slipped into the classy waiting room and gently closed the door. Stopping for a second to gather her wits, she surveyed the spacious office. A quick walk around led her to the computerized medical records station. Much to her surprise, the last computer in the bank against the wall had been left on.

Might as well give it a try.

With shaking fingers, she typed in a billing search for chorionic villus sampling and amniocentesis. A list of hundreds flashed across the screen. Camille held her breath—this was almost too easy. She quickly cross-referenced the list with miscarriages. As the list pared itself down to eleven patients' names, Camille hit the print icon, then hurried over to grab the list. According to Deanne Stillerman, some of them had suffered miscarriages during or shortly after the actual procedure.

It didn't take long for Camille to find and print the relevant chart notes on chorionic villus sampling procedures. Ah-ha! Just like Deanne said, Kensington did a CVS on the patient to determine whether the pregnancy had any genetic problems, and during the procedure, the patient suffered a miscarriage. Camille's stomach turned. Sure enough, the patient had been a longtime infertility patient.

Slowly, a stack of chart notes began spitting out of the huge printer as Camille made her way down the list. She glanced at her watch and resisted the urge to study the charts more closely. She'd be out of here in twenty minutes. Then she'd have all the time in the world to review the data in hopes of finding a common thread that Laurabelle could evaluate.

Slam!

A high-pitched woman's voice pierced the silence. "This is so nice of you to see us on a Sunday, Dr. Davenport."

"No trouble at all."

Kip Davenport's voice was like foil on a filling to Camille.

"Just part of the job. I need to be available to my patients whenever they're ovulating. And those eggs don't always wait for Monday morning." He laughed.

A wave of nausea overcame Camille as she whisked the pile of charts off the printer and flattened herself against the wall in the cramped medical records room. Gathering her wits, she began to look for a place to hide as her heart pounded in her throat.

What the hell was she doing here anyway? This was Trish's bailiwick. Why hadn't she waited for Trish to return from her foray to the Caribbean?

She winced as Kip opened the door to the examining room. There was the familiar crinkling of the paper drape as he handed it to the patient while the doctor, his patient, and her husband made small talk.

"I'll be right down the hall, in the lab, getting the specimen ready to inject into your uterus."

"Take care of that test tube, doc!" the woman called down the hallway. "Ethan wouldn't want to have to spend another ten minutes in that little room looking at girlie magazines again unless it's absolutely necessary."

"Shh!" the husband admonished his wife.

"I'm kidding!" she said as she shut the exam room door.

From where she stood plastered to the wall, Camille could see Davenport pull something out of the fridge under the lab bench—probably some kind of stabilizing compound—she craned her neck to see the doctor extracting fluid from a test tube into a long thin tube attached to a plastic hypodermic syringe. Not a particularly romantic way to get pregnant.

Camille held her breath as Davenport held the instrument up to the light to check that the fluid was at the tip of the catheter. If he looked thirty degrees to his left, she'd be busted.

"We're ready!" the woman's voice called.

"Coming!" Davenport flipped off the light in the lab. Camille exhaled and imagined the patient and her husband anxiously waiting to start their family. For a moment Camille felt a pang of sorrow for having alienated this nice doctor from her life forever. He was certainly committed to his patients, coming in on a Sunday and all. And he had such a nice, relaxed bedside manner.

Uh-oh. Camille caught her breath as she realized that Davenport would have to write a note in the patient's medical record after the procedure. She glanced around the room and decided that it would be imminently stupid to stay here where he'd likely see her from his perch at the computer bench. Camille gathered her copies and tiptoed across the hall.

Closing the door behind her, she quickly realized she was in Davenport's fancy office. *Shit.*

She spied a door across the room and tried the knob. It led to a small hallway with an exit sign indicating a back entrance. Another door was ajar. Kensington's office! Best to hide in there in case Davenport decided to stick around and catch up on his desk work. Just as she was getting ready to exit Davenport's office, she spied a familiar-looking small decorated box on his windowsill. Camille picked it up and felt her face flush as she noticed Helene Anderson's curly script. Helene wasn't even a patient of Kip's. Why on earth had she given him one of her wish boxes? Camille knew the answer would be written in loopy script on a piece of paper inside the box. According to Helene, the custom required the person giving the box to write their wish on a piece of paper, then put the paper into the box in order to seal the deal.

What had Helene wished for when she had given Kip Davenport a wish box?

Camille leaned toward the hallway and confirmed the muffled sounds of the patient and doctor still in the exam room. She quickly opened the box and unfolded the pink piece of foiled paper.

A perfect insemination and a perfect baby.

Camille froze. A perfect insemination?

She'd asked Helene if she'd undergone treatment for infertility, and Helene had clearly told her no. According to Helene, Tim had passed his sperm test with flying colors and that had been the end of that.

Camille ran through all the possibilities about why Helene had lied to her as she snuck out the back door of Davenport's clinic, the pile of chart notes tucked in her cross-body bag. Rather than a chance run-in with Kip in the elevator lobby, she entered the cold staircase and began running down the stairs.

—

It'd do, Trish thought to herself as she spread the musty blanket she'd taken from her attic hideaway. She watched as Kensington and her pasty-white pal frolicked in the surf. *I hope he has plenty of sunscreen on.* She'd been tailing the twosome for a couple of days now, and so far, they'd done nothing except spend an ungodly amount of money shopping and wining and dining. Trish subtly snapped another batch of pics as the couple ran from the water and across the pristine beach.

She pulled out a handful of crackers she'd taken from the restaurant that morning and stuffed them into her mouth. Who'd have thought that those days traveling around Europe on a shoestring would have prepared her so well for her life as a private investigator? She washed the crackers down with a warm pop.

Huh. Kensington seems to finally be relaxing in the blinding Caribbean sunshine. Trish watched as the boyfriend poured the doctor a fruity drink from the picnic that had been packed for them at the hotel. Trish sighed and crumpled her pop can. *Must be nice to be rich.*

She had almost dozed off when she realized that her targets were gathering their stuff to leave. Trish reached up to her neck and retied the strings of her scant bikini, then slipped on an oversized T-shirt. As she hurried to the street at the top of the beach, she shook the sand out of her blanket.

The doctor and her suitor stopped at the curbside while Kensington methodically removed the sand from everything in her giant striped canvas beach bag. The boyfriend appeared to be genuinely in lust with the tall goddess. He seemed mesmerized by her every move.

Trish sat on the hot rock wall while the twosome disappeared into a private dressing room complex. When they exited, they hardly looked like they'd just spent a day at the beach. Kensington wore a loose-fitting knit dress cinched with an artistic-looking belt, and her pal had on yet another pair of crisp linen shorts.

Trish hurried to catch up with them as they strode across the cobblestone square in the middle of town. Down a narrow street and then another. They definitely knew where they were going.

Not wanting to be noticed, Trish hung back as the crowd thinned. As they rounded a last corner, the man stopped and picked up a phone that was hidden inside a box next to a huge carved door. In a couple of seconds, a beanpole of a man with a completely shaved head greeted them. And judging from his reaction, the man was quite familiar with both Kensington and her beau.

As soon as they disappeared into the ornate little building, Trish sauntered over to read the bronze plaque next to the door.

Banca Carmelita.

Sounds like an offshore bank to me.

—

Camille stood on her couch and taped yet another expanse of butcher paper to her wall. She was convinced that if she could just get an overview of the information, she'd find the key to her case. Out of a feeling of guilt, she'd gone through her copies of the patient charts she'd taken from Kensington's office and blacked out the names. It really wasn't appropriate to have their identities broadcast all over her office. Besides, if she needed them, she still had the originals in her desk drawer.

After giving each chart an identification number, Camille labeled columns with those numbers, followed by a litany of statistics about each patient. Standing back with her orange magic marker in hand, she searched for any type of pattern to emerge. So far, nothing jumped out at her.

Dejected, she opened Helene Anderson's chart. If Helene had undergone artificial insemination, there would have to be some kind of entry in her medical record. And if that were the case, Anderson would at least fit Kensington's profile, strange as it was.

CHAPTER THIRTY-ONE

Bagley and Rhodes was one of Seattle's oldest and stuffiest medical malpractice defense firms. Not too expensive looking, but then again just nice enough to impress its gravity upon the unsuspecting doctors who graced the lobby on any given day. Camille wheeled her briefcase up to the bleached oak reception desk decorated with a cornucopia for the upcoming Thanksgiving holiday, and announced that she was there for Dr. Jessica Kensington's deposition.

"Have a seat." The middle-aged receptionist pointed at the tan couch.

Camille stood.

It was just like Bagley to make her wait a half an hour. The receptionist finally directed Camille down the inner stairway to the conference room on the floor below.

"Hi, Diane," Camille said to her court reporter as she unpacked her briefcase. As always, she went through the familiar ritual of stacking a pile of various colored "stickies" in front of her, along with her multicolored pens. The heavy unlabeled notebook containing the articles on gestational diabetes and the Zavanelli maneuver lay on the floor at her feet and the two lavender pads sat on the table in front of her. Camille stared anxiously at the door, waiting for Kensington to appear.

Medical statistics swirled around inside her head as she stood to look out the window at the mélange of high-rises spread out before her. Diane knew when to chat and when to be quiet. And this was definitely one of those quiet times. A good court reporter intuitively knew when a lot was riding on a dep.

Jessica Kensington walked into the room as if she owned it. In her high heels, she was over six feet tall, and her short black skirt made her legs appear all the longer. Her deep auburn hair curled easily over her shoulders, nicely framing her lightly tanned face. She nodded curtly and took her seat opposite Camille while her lawyer walked in behind his client, his chest thrust forward with an unassailable air of confidence.

This is it.

Camille turned to Diane. "Swear the witness, please." As always, she pushed aside the detailed outline she'd sweated blood over.

It was just the two of them now. Everything disappeared from Camille's line of vision except the woman who bore an uncanny resemblance to Camille's new pen pal from Maui.

"State your name for the record, please."

"Doctor Jessica Kensington." She emphasized the word "doctor."

"Doctor Kensington," Camille echoed Kensington's emphasis on the word "doctor." "Tell me what significance, if any, you drew from the fact that Helene Anderson suffered from gestational diabetes."

"Objection, lack of foundation."

Bagley, on the other hand, had every reason to drag this out as long as possible. It was going to be a long morning.

"Dr. Kensington, did Helene Anderson suffer from gestational diabetes?"

"Yes, she did."

"And what was the significance of Helene Anderson's diabetes?"

"Any pregnant patient with gestational diabetes is at risk for a unique set of complications."

"And what are those complications?"

Kensington paused. "The baby can be born with diabetes, it can be a large baby, there's a higher risk for unexpected stillbirths, there's a higher risk of neonatal respiratory distress in mildly premature babies of mothers with gestational diabetes, and the baby can suffer from hypoglycemia after it's born."

The doctor had clearly been well coached.

"And risks to a mother with gestational diabetes?"

"Mothers with gestational diabetes have a fifty percent risk of developing adult-onset diabetes later in life."

"What tests would you order for one of these patients?"

"Fasting blood sugar, glucose tolerance test, finger sticks, and follow a diabetic diet." Kensington stopped for a breath. "Weekly nonstress tests from thirty-two weeks and twice weekly nonstress tests from thirty-six weeks." The doctor had an educated look of concern on her face. The trial consultant sitting behind the large mirror at the end of the conference table would be pleased.

"Please explain why those tests would be necessary."

"In the mother, it's important to control the diabetes, since the better the control, the lower the risk of fetal macrosomia and intrauterine fetal demise."

The doctor had obviously memorized the same articles as Camille.

"Which if any of these tests did you perform on Helene Anderson?"

"All of them."

"Can you define cephalopelvic disproportion?"

"CPD means that there is a problem with the proportion between the baby's head and the mother's pelvis. Basically, it means the head won't fit through the birth canal."

Bagley beamed; his protégé had been a quick study.

"Is there any test that can be performed to determine whether a mother is likely to have CPD?"

"The best way to determine if the patient has CPD is to undertake a trial of labor and see if the head engages in the pelvis. If it fits, it fits." Kensington stopped and stared at Camille. "If it doesn't, you need to do a C-section."

"What is a shoulder dystocia?"

"It's when the baby's shoulder gets stuck under the mother's pubic bone, so it becomes difficult to get the baby out."

"Isn't it true that babies of diabetic mothers are more likely to experience shoulder dystocia?"

"They might be."

"Wouldn't you agree that an ultrasound at thirty-nine weeks would provide a doctor with additional information about the likelihood that the patient might suffer from CPD?"

"No, I would not agree with that statement." The doc seemed to honestly believe she was invincible.

"Isn't it true that a radiologist can provide an estimated fetal weight based on an ultrasound?"

"The operative word there is 'estimated.' In my opinion, the margin of error in a thirty-nine-week ultrasound is so great that those ultrasounds are largely meaningless." She waved her hand dismissively.

"What is the margin of error?"

"Plus or minus eighty percent chance they'll be twenty percent off and a ninety percent chance they'll be ten percent off."

Jesus, Kensington might as well just pick the articles up off the floor and read them into the record.

"So, based on those statistics, you elect not to perform a late ultrasound on your gestational diabetics?"

"Exactly."

Camille wasn't making much headway.

"But wouldn't it give you some kind of idea of whether the patient is a candidate for a trial of labor?"

"In my opinion, no."

Camille ignored Bagley's obnoxious smirk.

"Did you make any effort to determine the fetal weight of the Anderson baby?"

"Of course."

"How did you do that?"

Kensington looked at Camille as if she were the stupidest lawyer on earth. "I felt the size of the baby manually."

"Was your estimate accurate?"

"Obviously not."

"As Ms. Anderson neared the end of her labor, did it appear to you that the head was having difficulty engaging?"

"No."

"Where was the head when you applied the forceps?"

"Almost out," she said impatiently. "I was simply giving the baby a little extra guidance out of the birth canal since the heartbeat had dropped precipitously during the anesthesia."

"What is a difficult midforceps delivery?"

"It's where the doctor applies the forceps when the baby's head is still rather high in the birth canal."

"Any idea why the nurse in the Anderson case wrote difficult midforceps delivery?"

"Objection, calls for speculation!"

"Did the nurse chart difficult midforceps delivery?"

"Yes."

"Was it?"

"No."

"Do you recall where the nurse was standing?"

"No."

"In your experience, do nurses usually stand in a location from which they have a full view of the field where the doctor is working?"

"To tell you the truth, I don't pay that much attention to where the nurses are standing." She raised her voice indignantly. "I have more important things on my mind during the delivery of a baby."

"Do you have any reason to believe that Nurse O'Brien was not being truthful when she wrote midforceps delivery?"

"Of course not." Kensington sat up rigidly in her chair and leaned forward. "Look"—she hit the table with her index finger—"this was a very emotionally charged situation. It's devastating to everyone present when something goes terribly wrong during a delivery, and as you know, this was a tragedy." The doctor almost looked sincere. "I am absolutely positive that everyone in that room did the best they possibly could to save the Anderson baby. And to be honest, perfect charting is not at the top of anyone's list during a medical emergency." Kensington's voice became shrill. "It may be important to you lawyers, but it's the last thing on the mind of a good health care provider at a time like this."

Camille noticed Bagley move his chair closer to the doctor. It was lawyering 101 for a lawyer to sit close enough to their client to gently kick them under the table when things were veering off course. Camille thought briefly of looking under the table to confirm her suspicions, and then admonished herself to focus on the task at hand.

"Why then did the anesthesiologist chart midforceps delivery?"

Kensington calmed down. "Anesthesiologists typically get their clinical information from the delivery record, which is filled out by the nurses. In a situation like this, one mistaken entry tends to snowball."

"Dr. Kensington, did you personally perform the Pitocin induction?"

"Yes, I did."

"Isn't that something nurses typically do?"

"I suppose so, but it's certainly not mandatory."

"Can you tell me why you chose to perform Ms. Anderson's induction?"

Kensington shrugged. "The nurses were short-staffed that night, so I offered to help out."

"How often have you offered to Pit your own patients in the past?"

"Gee, I can't really say. I'm not one of those doctors who insists on being waited on by the nursing staff." She casually sipped her water. "I'm perfectly happy to pitch in and help when I'm needed." She smiled at Diane, who was clearly charmed by the articulate doctor.

It was a bad sign when your own court reporter was taken in by your opponent. Camille handed the fetal monitor strip to Kensington's newest fan and directed her to mark it as exhibit two to the deposition.

"Can you identify for the record the document I've had marked as exhibit two to your deposition?"

"It's the fetal monitor strip." Kensington sat back defiantly in her chair.

"Could you please review the section from two thirty to three?"

Bagley officiously unrolled the monitor strip and offered it to the princess.

Taking her time, Kensington slowly reviewed the strip, then looked up. "Yes?"

"How many contractions was Ms. Anderson having during any given ten-minute period?"

Kensington pointed at each contraction and counted aloud. "I'd say about seven or eight."

"What is the desired number of contractions one would want in any given ten-minute period when one is augmenting labor with Pitocin?"

Kensington sighed. "It depends entirely on the circumstances."

"Well, what do you teach the residents, or the nurses?"

"It depends."

Bagley stifled a smile.

"Wouldn't you agree with me that a patient undergoing an induction should have approximately five contractions in a ten-minute period?"

"That would be fine, but there's nothing written in stone about how many contractions one should have. Labor contractions vary considerably in intensity. So if the contractions aren't very strong, a patient can safely sustain more frequent contractions than if they're extremely strong. Lawyers think you can manage a labor according to some kind of cookbook, but in reality . . ."

Bagley put his hand on the doctor's arm. "Just answer the question."

Kensington pulled away as if Bagley had burned her with a lit cigarette. "All right."

"Can you quantify the intensity of Ms. Anderson's contractions?"

"By looking at the monitor strip?" Kensington asked in disbelief.

"Yep."

"No, I can't."

"Why not?"

"You know as well as I do that Ms. Anderson had external monitors."

Camille refused to get sucked into a verbal altercation, although it was certainly tempting to go head-to-head with the bitch. Instead, she calmly continued her questions. "And what is the significance of Ms. Anderson having external monitors?"

"External monitors aren't designed to provide an objective readout of the intensity of a patient's contractions," Kensington snapped. "They simply tell you how often they are having them."

The doctor appeared to be wearing down. This was generally when lawyers got their best testimony. "Well then, how did you know how strong the contractions were?"

"Clinical judgment. I felt the patient's uterus."

"Do you have a personal recollection of how strong Ms. Anderson's contractions were?"

"Yes." She almost whined.

"How strong were they?"

"Mild to moderate."

"And how do you happen to remember that?"

"This was the kind of case that any doctor carries with them for their entire career." Kensington's voice dropped to a whisper, causing Diane to lean forward in order to hear the testimony accurately. "I won't say I haven't relived this case over and over in my mind a thousand times. And as often as I go over this in the dark of night, I can't say that I would have done anything at all differently. The contractions just weren't that strong. If I had to do it over again, I wouldn't be all that concerned about their increasing frequency. In fact, I systematically decreased the dosage of Pitocin as the patient's natural oxytocin took over from the synthetic drug."

"Doctor! Just answer the questions she asks you," Bagley said curtly.

Camille ignored Bagley's obvious attempt at coaching the witness. "Then how do you explain the stacks of contractions, one after the other, if you were decreasing the dose?"

"Mother Nature."

Camille stared at the doctor.

"You know, there are some things about Mother Nature that we just can't change, try as we might," Kensington said emphatically. "And when that happens, we take as many steps as humanly possible in order to make things right. We make sacrifices we might otherwise not make, and we make decisions that under other circumstances we never imagined we'd make. And sometimes we know that there's a greater good that must be served, so we act on it. On these occasions, we answer to a higher order of being."

What greater good? This woman is weird.

Bagley stood abruptly. "Time for lunch." He grabbed his client's arm tightly and dragged her out of her seat and into the hall.

Camille looked at her watch as the entourage exited the conference room. It was only ten thirty. Lunch?

CHAPTER THIRTY-TWO

The remainder of the deposition had gone about as expected. Camille asked questions, and Kensington parroted back the medical literature. She smiled as she stepped over the piles of paperwork that she and Lucia had spread out across her office in preparation for trial. Motions in limine had been filed by both sides objecting to the other side's evidence in an attempt to hone down what would actually be presented to the jury.

Trish hopped up off the couch to greet Camille before she could collapse into her chair. "Welcome home," Camille said weakly. "I'm sure hoping that you haven't come up with another plan to spend more money chasing rainbows across the Caribbean."

"I am so sorry." Trish crossed her arms and hugged herself. "I really thought Kensington would lead us to some kind of smoking gun."

"Don't worry about it." Camille swiveled in her chair. "Your email said you figured out the one point two million went from her Seattle bank account to the Banca Carmelita. So I guess that's something."

"Yeah, then last night I revisited her account here. And guess what?"

Camille raised a tired eyebrow.

"That wasn't the only giant transfer of money."

The fog momentarily cleared from Camille's brain. "Go ahead."

Trish pulled out her phone and scrolled through her notes. "Almost a year earlier, three million flew through her account to the offshore account, then about a year before that another one million followed the same route."

"Any idea where it came from?"

"Not yet."

"Think you'll ever find out?"

"It isn't that easy to keep the source of five point two million dollars a secret. I'll figure it out."

"Well, it's an interesting query, but I'm not sure it has anything to do with our trial next week." Camille picked up one of the fat textbooks on her desk. "I need to focus on the medicine. And even if it mattered, there's no way I can get those bank records into evidence—how would I explain to the judge where they came from?"

Camille searched for a stray morsel of optimism, but after Kensington's stellar performance in her dep, there was none to be found.

"Why do you think she keeps lying about where she's going?" Trish asked.

Camille shook her head. "She's obviously trying to keep her boyfriend a secret from someone."

"Her father?"

Suddenly, Camille remembered the excuse Kip had given for wanting to talk with her at her mother's fundraiser. "You know, Kip mentioned that his daughter had been in a—how did he say it? I think it was something like a troublesome relationship with a man."

"Yeah, but wasn't that just a ruse to get you to have a latte with him?"

"Well, I thought so at the time, but maybe there was some truth to it."

Trish sat on the edge of the ottoman, her elbows on her knees. "What exactly did he say?"

"He said something about a guy causing her to make some kind of bad judgments."

"Like killing babies?"

"I don't know." Camille covered her face with her hands. "I don't know."

"Stay with me here," Trish said authoritatively. "Was he trying to give you a message?"

241

Camille looked at Trish between her fingers. "What do you mean?"

"Well, maybe he wanted to alert you that her judgment had been affected by this so-called troublesome relationship."

Camille covered her mouth with her hand, then dropped it. "You mean maybe he really believes she was so upset over some kind of romantic breakup that she lost touch with reality or something?"

"Maybe."

"It would certainly take our focus away from any kind of pattern of Kensington messing with other patients. Or," Camille surmised, "Kensington used the relationship to explain her behavior to her father."

"And then she promised to end it? Did I tell you that Kensington was reading your sister's book about how to get out of a relationship on the plane? Maybe she was planning to dump the guy."

They were on a roll.

Camille sat up straight. "I'm not sure Eve's book would be much help, but maybe she picked it up at the airport hoping for some insight." She glanced at her sister's book, sitting on the floor under a pile of paperwork. "Okay, here's the deal: Kensington explained the Anderson debacle by telling her father that she was involved in a relationship gone bad." The adrenaline began to surge. "And he got pissed and demanded she end it." She picked up a pen and shook it at Trish. "But she didn't."

"Or she couldn't," Trish added.

Camille continued, "So every time she goes to see the guy, she has to lie to her father, and therefore the hospital staff, about where she's going."

"And that explains why she seems so stiff when she's with the guy. She feels all conflicted about lying to her father."

"It's one theory." Camille slumped back down. "But it isn't going to make a damn bit of difference at trial. It's too late for me to explain why she did what she did. I simply need to show evidence that she violated the standard of care in her treatment of Helene."

"When's your expert flying in?"

"The morning he testifies."

"So, you've never seen the guy?"

"Nope, Bagley took his dep by phone."

"And he did okay?"

"He did fine."

"Hey, how'd Kensington's dep go?"

"Don't ask. I felt like I was deposing Gabbe himself."

"Who?"

"Steve Gabbe, from UW. He wrote one of the classic treatises on obstetrics." Camille slouched back into her chair. "Kensington had an explanation for every goddamn thing I asked her." She shook her head. "It looks like it'll boil down to a swearing contest between Kensington and her experts and my little doc from Wisconsin."

"Is there anything I can do to help you get ready for trial?"

"Not that I can think of right now." Camille pointed at a huge pile of poster boards. "I have to get to work on my trial exhibits. I can't afford to have them professionally done."

Camille picked up one of Gracie's royal-blue magic markers and began to outline a chronology of Helene's labor. The room filled with the smell of blueberries as Camille printed in block letters across the top of the poster while mentally reviewing the status of her case.

"We're going to trial next Monday, and we have no way to prove anything other than straight malpractice." She continued to print across the poster board. "There's no evidence that ties Helene to the other women who suffered miscarriages. There's no evidence of Kensington's mental condition, and even if there was, we can't connect it to Kensington's behavior the night of the delivery."

"Any good news?" Trish asked.

"Nothing that comes to mind."

"Well, I'll leave you with your art project." Trish pecked Camille on the cheek.

The next poster board smelled of raspberry magic marker and depicted the criteria that Kensington should have taken into account when deciding whether or not to perform a C-section on Helene sooner.

Camille stopped to admire her work, and was dismayed to discover that her exhibits looked like they'd been prepared by Gracie and her Brownie troop. An artist she was not.

Oh well, two down. Camille grabbed the corner of her desk and pulled herself up slowly in an effort not to put too much strain on her aching knees. God she felt old. A stinger shot across her lower back as she reached down to pick up a stray letter that had fluttered to the floor from her overflowing inbox.

What was this? Even without her glasses, she recognized Harvey Lowe's obnoxious scales-of-justice letterhead.

Great. According to Lowe, the letter was to serve as a "professional courtesy" that she was "officially on notice" of his intent to pursue his attorney's fee lien on the Anderson case. According to Lowe, he'd put in many, many hours on the case, and his fee agreement with the Andersons allowed him to receive payment for services rendered. Camille skipped to the bottom line. Fifty thousand dollars? What the hell had he done to entitle him to that kind of fee in a case that would typically bring a settlement in the neighborhood of seventy-five thousand dollars?

This was all she needed. Harvey Lowe suing her client for fees. And knowing Lowe, he wouldn't care whether or not Camille won the case at trial. She knew Lowe had it in for her, but why would he take it out on some innocent client?

As Camille worked into the night, her mind wandered to the list of women on the butcher paper surrounding her office. What was she thinking? Did she really think she could prove some kind of orchestrated wrongdoing?

—

The short couch didn't exactly lend itself to overnight comfort. Every time she tried to drift off, she imagined Kensington pulling Zachary's misshapen head from Helene's womb. There was no way a jury would condone that kind of care. Camille awoke at 4:30 a.m. with a wicked crick in her neck. She closed her eyes and this time dreamed of the tall, gorgeous redheaded doctor charming the socks off the jury as Camille fought to keep from literally drowning in stacks and stacks of motions. She got up in a cold sweat.

Getting her butt kicked was looking like a distinct possibility. Then, not only would the Andersons suffer the indignity of losing a trial that they should have won had their lawyer been able to afford a decent expert, but they might easily find themselves as much as fifty thousand dollars in debt to Harvey Lowe.

There was no point trying to sleep.

Bagley's underlings had filed another onslaught of motions that afternoon, and the responses were due the morning of trial. Reluctantly, Camille shuffled over and began drafting her answers under the bright halogen light on her desk.

Throughout the early-morning hours, her mind wandered to the butcher paper, looking for some kind of clue that would put an end to her nightmare.

CHAPTER THIRTY-THREE

"No, I don't want to read the fucking email now," Camille said firmly to her computer screen. She hated it when the email dialogue box kept popping up whenever she was deeply enmeshed in a project of some kind.

Three down. Six to go. She formatted another response to one of the ridiculous motions in limine. Jesus Christ.

By 9:00 a.m., she was ready for a break. She clicked on her email, for once hoping that someone had sent her a decent joke. A laugh would be a welcome distraction at this point.

She clicked through a couple of half-assed jokes and continued to scan the remainder of the list.

Oops. She inadvertently clicked on an unmarked message. Probably spam—she poised her finger over the delete icon.

What?

Document necessary to make "premium baby" argument in the Anderson case will be delivered by messenger today. Hang tight.

Camille froze, then reread the message. What did it mean?

—

Trish popped open her phone on the second ring as she ordered her latte from her new gay barista at the Coco Loco café. It was Camille on the phone, who else?

"Yo!"

"I just got one of those anonymous emails."

"What's it say?"

Camille read the short note.

"Got any idea what it means?"

"I can only hope."

"You gonna get Helene in and see why she's been bullshitting you all this time?"

"I don't have any proof that she has been. All I know is she gave Kip one of her wish boxes."

"Camille."

"It's entirely possible that Helene was an infertility patient but that this pregnancy was the real McCoy." She really didn't want to believe that the woman for whom she'd gone out on such skinny branches was just taking her for a ride.

"We'll see."

As Trish clicked the phone closed, she noticed Amy sitting at a table in the window of the small café. Predictably, Amy was consuming some kind of chocolate extravaganza.

No big shock, Amy hanging out at a place with a name like Coco Loco.

"Hey! What are you doing here?" Trish asked as she approached Camille's former gal Friday.

Amy jumped up, causing her briefcase to fall off the table and dump a pile of papers all over the floor. She hurriedly began to gather the mess as she looked up at Trish. "What a surprise!" Amy scanned the room. "You alone?"

Trish craned her neck to see around the cramped café. "Yep. I guess I am."

She must be embarrassed. God knew, she certainly left Camille in a lurch when she jumped ship for Harvey Lowe's.

Amy shoved the papers into her briefcase. "So . . . how's it going?"

This is awkward.

"Good." Trish nodded. "It's going good."

Amy clutched the briefcase to her chest. "Good."

"Things going okay at Lowe's office?"

"Pretty good." Amy nodded. "It's okay."

"Great."

"How's Camille doing?" Amy asked.

"Getting ready for trial."

"Oh my God, that's right. Anderson must be about to go out."

"Monday."

"Jeez, tell her good luck for me, okay?"

"I will."

Amy paused. "And can you tell her I'm still really sorry for what I did?"

"Sure. I'll tell her."

Amy turned and shut down the computer at her table. "Just checking my email," she said quickly. "Listen, it was really nice to see you."

"You too."

"I gotta get going. I . . . I don't want to be late for work."

"Okay, see ya." Trish watched Amy head out of the café, then turn the opposite way from Lowe's office. And amazingly, she'd left behind half a chocolate mousse. *Jeez, she must really be flustered.*

———

"Here you go." Lucia stood in the reception area dressed in her messenger gear. She handed Camille an envelope.

"What's this?"

"Beats me, I got a call to do a pickup right when I was on my way here. I gotta change. I'll be right back."

Camille ripped open the envelope. "Where'd you get this?"

"Some woman in the foyer of the downtown Barnes and Noble, where, by the way, your sister's book takes up the whole front display."

Everywhere she turned, Eve's success seemed to smack her in the face. She pushed the image of a cardboard cutout of Eve out of her mind. "What'd the woman at the bookstore drop-off look like?"

"To tell you the truth, I didn't really notice."

"But didn't you think it was weird to pick up something from a bookstore?" Camille pulled a single piece of paper out of the envelope.

Lucia shrugged. "Not especially. We get pickups from all over town. Last week I brought some guy a huge bag of lingerie from a fancy store." She smiled. "His secretary was quick to point out that it was his wife's birthday."

Camille was hardly listening. All her attention was focused on the transcription of Helene Anderson's artificial insemination procedure.

Maybe this case could be saved after all. Harvey Lowe didn't necessarily have an exclusive right to the so-called "premium baby" argument. If he could settle one of those cases for five million, she could get twice that at trial. Camille picked up the *Trial News* and imagined herself on the cover.

"Call Helene and get her in here."

———

Helene appeared in Camille's office carrying a plateful of freshly baked oatmeal cookies. "I figured you could use some energy to get you through the next few days before trial." She shot Camille a friendly smile.

"C'mon in and have a seat." Camille had a hard time trying to distinguish whether the edgy feeling underneath her skin was the normal adrenaline rush of getting ready for trial or the anger that had been brewing since she stumbled on Kip Davenport's wish box. She couldn't wait to find out why Helene had thought it necessary to lie about the origin of her pregnancy with little Zachary.

Without saying a word, Camille handed the large blond woman a copy of the transcription of her artificial insemination procedure.

"Where did you get this?" Helene demanded.

Camille ignored the client's angry outburst. "Do you know why this wasn't included in the records you brought me in September?"

"You have no right to get into my personal medical records." Helene ripped the paper in half, then in half again. She continued until the page had been reduced to confetti.

"Look, Helene. I can't effectively represent you if you're holding something back from me."

Helene unceremoniously sprinkled what had once been a medical report into Camille's overflowing recycle box. "This has nothing to do with this lawsuit."

"You need to let me decide what's relevant and what isn't."

Helene set her large jaw. "This is my lawsuit. I'll decide what's relevant."

"Let me give you an update on the progress of your case." Camille paced back and forth across the cluttered office, gesticulating. "I've been trying to come up with some kind of evidence to explain why Kensington treated you so cavalierly the night of your delivery." She stopped. "And I've come up with nothing that I can use at trial."

Helene stared back defiantly.

"So, on Monday morning, we will show up in court with one expert witness who thinks you should have gotten an ultrasound the week before you went into labor."

"Well, he's right. I should have." Helene might as well have been spitting icicles.

"Kensington, on the other hand, has three experts who are all highly regarded members of the University of Washington Medical Center staff. And they say an ultrasound wasn't necessary."

"So?"

"So, the only way to tip the jury in our favor is to garner their sympathy. We need to make them mad about what happened to you."

"And you don't think they'll be mad that that bitch pulled my baby's head out and pretty much killed him?"

"You know that Bagley's going to argue that while it's a tragedy baby Zachary died, you're young enough to have another baby."

"Might I remind you that that's exactly why I hired you. To make him look like the sleazebag that he is."

"I'd rather make the argument that this was your last chance to have a baby since it took you so long to conceive this pregnancy."

"Well, you can't."

"Yes. I can. I have a report that describes the insemination procedure."

"I will not authorize you to use that record. It's my private medical record." Her eyes narrowed. "And I expect you to keep it that way."

Camille couldn't believe what was happening. "Do you mind telling me why?"

"Tim doesn't know I had the procedure, and I'll do anything to prevent him from finding out. So just drop it!"

Helene slammed the door behind her as she left, leaving Camille staring blankly at the list of patients on her wall, feeling her career quickly slipping away.

CHAPTER THIRTY-FOUR

The bailiff and the clerk stared openly as Camille and her tiny blue-haired assistant schlepped boxes of notebooks and poster board exhibits across the linoleum of the aging courtroom. Little did the judge's staff know that the black skirt and the sweater that barely covered Lucia's midriff was the closest thing she owned to business wear—right down to the thick-soled black combat ankle boots.

Camille caught herself to keep from tripping on the thick TV cable that connected Bagley's state-of-the-art video equipment to the giant screen he'd set up directly in front of the jury.

"So, Marge, how'd your daughter do at the horse show last month?" Bagley asked the bailiff.

"She came in third."

"She riding that little filly again?"

She nodded as Bagley straightened his tie.

"Straight?" he asked the court clerk, who reached across her steno machine and pulled the lawyer's tie to the left.

"There you go." She patted the maroon-striped tie into place.

"Ah, thank you, ladies."

Who doesn't this guy know? Camille wondered as she cleared a place for her stuff on the bench behind the counsel table.

Bagley's minions scurried about numbering their thick, professionally produced blowups of excerpts from various medical textbooks, as well as several pages of Helene's medical record.

Camille hoped the blueberry smell had worn off enough that the jury wouldn't be able to smell her handmade exhibits. She propped the posters against the scuffed-up counsel table and bolted for the bathroom.

It wasn't all that unusual for an attorney to get nauseated before a trial, but it was usually due to the excitement of the upcoming opening statement, not because they knew they were about to get their ass kicked. She splashed her face with water and rinsed out her mouth, then buried her face in the brown paper towel in an effort to keep herself from hyperventilating.

Oh God.

On her way back from the bathroom, Camille ran into Helene and Tim, who looked awkward, to say the least, in their Sunday best. She wished she could just ignore them and get on with this nightmare.

"Ready?" She avoided eye contact with Helene.

"You bet." Tim smiled widely.

He reminded Camille of a big stupid cow being led to slaughter.

"I'll see you in there." Camille hurried off to review her opening for the thousandth time. She sat on the pew at the end of the faded marble hallway outside the courtroom and lost herself in the tragedy that had befallen the Anderson family. Regardless of her feelings for Helene, it didn't take much for Camille to lather herself up into a passionate argument about the devastation that a family feels after losing a baby.

Lucia stuck her head out of the courtroom door. "The judge is ready to hear motions in limine now."

Camille got up on shaky ankles.

———

Denied. Denied. Denied.

What a surprise. Even when it came to straightforward motions in limine, she was batting a big fat zero with Bagley's pal Judge McIntyre. Camille glared up at the judge and nearly collapsed at the counsel table, avoiding the self-satisfied grin on the face of the perky young female associate Bagley had selected to adorn him at trial. Obviously, he was trying to make it look like he wasn't going to out-testosterone his opponent. Camille wondered if the girl knew she was just window dressing.

Bagley strutted back to his seat after winning the lion's share of his motions. Another shocker. Out of the corner of her eye, Camille watched as Kensington and her father entered and sucked the air out of the courtroom.

"We're ready for the jurors, Michelle," announced the triple-chinned judge.

Camille sat up straight and plastered on her best look of confidence as a line of unhappy citizens filed in. Each person held a five-by-eight piece of cardboard with a big black number on it so that the lawyers could identify him or her and supposedly keep track of the responses to their carefully crafted voir dire.

Back in the beginning of her career, Camille had assumed that most people would be fighting for the opportunity to sit on a jury in a fascinating malpractice trial. But over time she'd discovered that she'd been flattering herself. Now she knew that few potential jurors relished the idea of having to take two weeks off work, with no pay, to perform their civic duty.

Nope, there wasn't a smile among them.

The judge smiled at the jurors—after all, it was an election year, and some of them might actually vote. "Ladies and gentlemen, kindly give your attention to the plaintiff's lawyer, Ms. Delaney."

Plaintiff's lawyer. Might as well just come right out and tell the jurors that the tall woman with the short dark hair might look like a fairly nice lady, but behind the deep brown eyes lurks the heart of one of the opportunists who is responsible for the downfall of the entire American economy. Camille expected the jurors to look over the ledge in front of them to see if she had on a pair of tassel-toed loafers.

Camille threw back her shoulders and picked her way over the wires and cables snaking their way across the floor. Best to take the bull by the horns.

"How many of you had a reaction to the words the judge just said?" She paused, then added, "Plaintiff's lawyer."

She surveyed the sea of confused faces on the potential jurors.

"Any of you ever heard that trial lawyers are behind the rising prices of insurance premiums?"

Most of the gallery raised their hands.

Camille nodded. "How 'bout trial lawyers being the reason for those lengthy warning labels on almost everything we buy anymore?"

Another roomful of hands.

It shouldn't come as a surprise that the collection of "average citizens" had bought hook, line, and sinker into the insurance industry propaganda. They'd been successfully brainwashing the public for the past decade.

"Anyone here fed up with reading about those outrageous verdicts?"

This time several of the hands waved wildly.

Camille smiled. "Which verdict did you find particularly bothersome?"

A gray-haired man with the classic raised shoulders of a chronic emphysema patient raised a card with the number fifteen.

"Sir?" Camille glanced to see that Lucia was taking notes on the various jurors and their responses to the questions.

Number fifteen crossed his thin arms. "McDonald's." He coughed as he chuckled and shook his head. "The lady who got millions for spilling hot coffee in her lap."

This guy wasn't a likely juror—might as well make an example of him. The challenge was to use his response to educate the other jurors without humiliating him. A lawyer never wanted the jurors to get mad at her for embarrassing a fellow citizen.

Here goes.

Camille walked over toward number fifteen, who sat in the middle of the second row. "Let me tell you some of the facts of the McDonald's case. I'm wondering, if you had more facts, if it'd make any difference to you."

He smiled smugly, clearly up for the challenge.

"First, can we agree that the jurors in that case were instructed, as you will be, should you be selected to serve on this jury, to listen to the facts and follow the instructions of the court?"

Lower lip thrust out and eyes narrowed, he nodded.

Talk about body language. *This guy probably hasn't changed his mind on anything since Kennedy was shot. Probably still waiting for the Mafia to confess.*

"I'd like you to assume that the restaurant in question had been cited a number of times for serving coffee that was thirty-five degrees over the temperature required by the health department."

Number fifteen crossed his arms and pulled his shoulders up in an effort to expand his obviously diseased lungs.

"Now, assume that the jury heard evidence that McDonald's knew full well that when they served coffee that hot, a certain number of patrons would burn themselves."

The smoker rolled his eyes, but several other jurors appeared to be following with more than a little interest. Camille made a mental note of those jurors' numbers.

"Now assume for me that the jury heard testimony and was presented with internal documents from McDonald's themselves that the company had determined that they had to have the coffee at a certain temperature in order for the aroma of the coffee to fill the restaurant. And that the coffee sales increased dramatically when they heated the coffee thirty-five degrees over the limit set by the health department."

Camille looked at the jury pool. "Have any of you heard this side of the story?"

Heads shook.

"McDonald's was faced with a dilemma: heat the coffee up to a dangerous temperature and deal with the fact that patrons will burn themselves, or lower the temperature of the coffee and suffer a decrease in sales."

The fidgeting and rustling in the room had ceased.

"What did they do?" She answered her own question. "First, they figured out how much they'd have to pay out in damages to the folks who they knew would burn themselves. Then they determined how much they'd suffer in lost sales if they lowered the temperature of the coffee." Camille spread her arms out. "What to do?" She paused. "They made a cost-benefit decision." She looked at the roomful of interested faces. "They decided that their profit was more important than the potential injuries they'd cause by keeping their coffee heated to an illegal, and highly dangerous, temperature."

Number fifteen went into a mild coughing attack.

Camille waited.

"But five million dollars?" It was a well-manicured woman with a slightly outdated hairdo. Camille guessed that she'd driven in this morning from the upscale eastside suburbs.

"The jury decided that as a punishment to McDonald's, they'd fine them one day's coffee profits."

A few eyebrows went up.

"Seem unreasonable?"

Number fifteen wasn't having any of this. He waved his hand at Camille in disgust.

"How many of you would sue if your mother got painful fourth-degree burns all over her genitals? And you discovered that a national restaurant chain had determined that it'd be cheaper to pay out a smattering of injury claims to people like your mother than to decrease the temperature of their coffee and sustain a lower profit on coffee sales?"

Lucia scribbled furiously as several jurors raised their cards.

"What if a member of your family died as a result of someone else's negligence? Is there anyone here who's given much thought to putting a value on a human life? And by that, I mean have you ever thought about the difficulty of determining how to compensate someone for losing someone important to them?"

In the back, a middle-aged woman raised her card: number twenty. It figured; the good jurors were always in the back. Not much chance of getting her into the jury box, but she'd be able to play her part by allowing Camille to get into a dialogue with her in order to educate the others.

"Ma'am? What do you think about putting a value on something that really has no logical way to be valued?"

"When I read about those horrible plane crashes, I wonder how much the families are gonna get."

Perfect answer. It was a great way to present the concept of compensating someone for a lost life. "And do you think they should get something for what they've lost?"

"If it was the airline's fault, they should. Like when they discover that the airlines were trying to save money by cutting corners on maintenance."

"Can anyone think of an example?"

Number nine shot up his card in the front row.

Ah, that's more like it. An answer from someone who will actually be in the box.

"That one company came down hard on mechanics who went too slowly, and punished the guy who blew the whistle."

"And then they lost a planeload of innocent victims, didn't they?" He nodded.

"So, how would you decide how much to award the families?"

A woman raised the number three high in the air. "A human life is priceless. There's no amount that'd be enough for me if I lost someone in an accident like that."

"Anyone else have any idea of how to put a value on the life of someone who died in a plane crash?"

A young man with a Metallica T-shirt raised his hand. "A lot." Camille smiled.

"Anyone else?"

A large woman in the front row scowled at Camille.

"Ma'am? How 'bout you? Would you award damages to the family of someone who was lost in a plane crash?"

She shrugged. "I guess."

"Why?"

"Seems like that's the American way. Give 'em a pile of money."

Camille looked around the room. "Any one of you think that people who file lawsuits are just looking for a free lunch?"

Heads nodded.

Camille pointed to a nicely dressed man in the second row. "How about you, sir. What would you do if you or someone in your family was seriously hurt or killed in an accident? Would you sue if you felt that someone else was responsible for what happened?"

"I don't know. I'd like to think I'd be able to put it behind me and go on with my life. But if someone was really at fault . . . I don't know."

Camille paused. "This case is about a family who lost a child." She turned and looked at her clients, whose faces bore the pain of remembering their devastating loss. "Helene and Tim have sued Dr. Kensington here because they believe she was responsible for the death of their newborn baby."

The room was quiet.

"Is there anyone here who disagrees with their right to bring suit?"

A couple of jurors shook their heads.

"Are any of you unwilling to consider the evidence presented here and then, if you believe that the doctor was responsible, award damages to the Andersons?"

Camille looked at the woman who'd proclaimed that human life was priceless. "Do you think there's any difference between the lives of those airline passengers and the life of an innocent newborn baby?"

Number three shook her head violently. "A life is a life. They all have value. No matter who they are."

"But what if Mr. Bagley over there tries to convince you that the Andersons can always have another baby to replace little Zachary?"

The woman pulled her chin back into her neck in disgust. "What?"

Where had this woman come from? There was no way Bagley'd let her on the jury, but again, she was certainly giving Camille the perfect opportunity to raise the appropriate issues in front of the other jurors.

"Anyone else have an opinion about whether the Andersons don't deserve to be compensated for the loss of baby Zachary simply because they can just replace him with another baby?"

Number five piped in. "I don't think that money is going to make up for the loss of a baby. I don't see how it could."

Thank God the woman had spoken up. Camille made a mental note to use her first preemptory challenge to get rid of her.

"Is there anyone who agrees with this woman?"

Five jurors raised their cards. Thankfully, four of them were far enough back in the panel that they shouldn't pose a problem.

Camille addressed number five. "Can you think of any way to make it right for the Andersons?"

The woman thought for a moment and slowly shook her head. "I really can't."

"Is there any other way in our society to compensate someone who's lost a loved one?"

A man with a beard, sitting by the door, raised his number. "Money is the only thing we have to give someone. It's all we can do. Maybe just having a little financial breathing room would give these folks a chance to grieve their loss and then get on with their lives. It's the least society can do for someone who's lost a child."

Wow. Put this guy on the jury.

The judge interrupted, "Thank you, ladies and gentlemen. Now it's Mr. Bagley's turn."

The next thirty minutes were filled with the predictable insurance company propaganda about the cost to the system of all the horrendous verdicts. At this point in any trial, Camille's anger began to rear its ugly head. She'd never been able to understand why jurors weren't allowed to know that the insurance company would be paying any verdict.

Bagley blathered on about the poor doctor who'd done everything in her power to save the baby. And to what end?

The smoker spoke up: to be sued by these ingrates.

Bagley asked the jurors if they could listen carefully to his hoity-toity experts. Evidently, there was no way that they could listen to the doctor's evidence and come back with a verdict for these money-grubbing self-proclaimed victims. The suburban housewife smiled every time Bagley made the point about how people like the Andersons were clearly just looking for a windfall.

She's outta here.

And as it turned out, accordingly to Bagley, the smoker was right. These lawsuits had gotten way out of hand. It was up to these fine citizens to do their civic duty and prevent another legal travesty.

Several of the potential jurors actually bought his shit. Camille looked at her jury chart and put big red *X*s through their names.

As soon as voir dire ended, the judge looked at Camille and requested that she provide him with her first preemptory challenge. The jerk. Any decent judge would at least let the lawyers take a recess to tally their notes. She quickly excused the smoker.

Bagley kicked off number three, the woman who had the audacity to believe in the system.

Camille got rid of number five, the woman who couldn't see her way to compensating anyone for this kind of loss. And Bagley responded by asking number nine, the guy who criticized the airline maintenance people for not doing their jobs, to step down.

Last one. Forced to choose between the lesser of two evils, Camille dismissed the suburban housewife and left on the old lady that had been making faces at her. Conventional jury selection wisdom said that elderly women don't usually have forceful enough personalities to turn around an entire jury, and Camille only had to convince ten of twelve. The lady from the eastside had arrogant troublemaker written all over her. Smug self-righteous people like her didn't have much patience for people who didn't belong to the right tennis club.

Bagley ended by bouncing off the guy with the beard, and they were done.

As the judge impaneled the jury by having them stand for their oath, Camille leaned over to Lucia and reminded her that it was time for her to go pick up their expert witness at the airport.

Camille looked the jury up and down. Oh well. One group of "concerned" citizens was probably as good as the next.

The judge looked over his Ben Franklin glasses. "Ms. Delaney, your opening statement?"

Jeez, what's his hurry?

Camille grabbed her flimsy poster board and climbed over Bagley's equipment, snagging a huge hole in her black tights.

It figured.

She took her place in front of the jury box and wiggled her toes. It was a trick she'd learned in one of the trial classes she'd taken long ago. Supposedly, if you wiggled your toes, it would relax your entire body.

She wiggled them again.

"Ladies and gentlemen of the jury." She tried to pace authoritatively in front of the box, but realized Bagley's fancy video equipment had completely hemmed her in. Besides, she now had to stand askew so that the jurors couldn't see the enormous hole in her brand-new tights.

"This case is about a tragedy that unfolded in the middle of the night in the Labor and Delivery Department of Puget Sound Hospital."

The courtroom door opened.

What the hell was Harvey Lowe doing here?

She abandoned the toe-wiggling routine and tried instead to breathe the tension out of her shoulders. *He's probably here to make sure I don't screw up his chance of getting his fees from the Andersons.*

"On the night of February 10, Helene and Tim Anderson came to the hospital anticipating a blessed event." She paused for effect.

Jesus. Wouldn't you know it? Lowe was salivating at the leggy doctor sitting at the counsel table next to Bagley and his girl-lawyer.

Camille turned so that Lowe was out of her line of vision. She had enough trouble as it was without him distracting her.

"Helene had been having labor contractions for the better part of the afternoon, and finally, she and Tim decided to head into the hospital." She smiled. "Excited is hardly the word to describe how they felt."

The door banged behind Trish, who slid into the pew at the far back of the courtroom. Finally, someone in the gallery for the home team.

A few of the jurors actually perked up as Camille walked them through the events that transpired the night baby Zachary came into the world. Veiled looks of concern came over some of their faces as Camille narrated in vivid detail what had happened in the delivery room. A couple of jurors looked questioningly at Kensington, who smiled confidently in return.

"Now, at the end of this trial, you'll be asked to place a value on the life of this precious baby." Camille stopped to look each of the jurors directly in the eye. "How can you do that, you might ask yourself." Camille shrugged. "I really don't know the answer to that. The only guidance I can give you is that the law is very clear that anyone can seek compensation for the overwhelming tragedy of losing a baby. We all know that babies are priceless gifts from God. And that the joy we feel when we look into the eyes of our beloved child can never be replaced by any amount of money. What's it worth?" She paused. "A million dollars? Two?" Another scan of the citizenry. "All of you will be asked to place a value on baby Zachary's life." Camille stepped aside so that the jury could see Helene and Tim. "The Andersons only ask that you listen to the testimony in this trial. Listen with your heart, and let it guide you to a just result." She stopped. "Thank you for your kind attention."

Bagley stood. "May it please the court. Ladies and gentlemen of the jury, we believe the evidence will show that this highly competent doctor did her absolute best when she cared for Ms. Anderson the night of baby Zachary's birth.

"In fact, you will be hearing from three stellar experts on the staff at the University of Washington, who will testify that Dr. Kensington not only complied with the standard of care in her treatment of Ms. Anderson, she actually exceeded those standards."

Bagley turned to the Andersons. "Now, every person in this courtroom can sympathize with the tragedy that these lovely people suffered. But it was nothing more and nothing less than an act of God. And no one is at fault."

The defense lawyer smiled. "Now, I understand that there's a teensy-weensy chance"—he held out his fingers as if he were demonstrating the tiniest of amounts—"that you might not agree with me." He winked. "Hard to believe, but there is a remote possibility that you may determine that you believe the evidence as set forth by my able opponent." The overweight woman in the front row of the jury returned Bagley's well-schooled smile. "That means you may come to believe that Dr. Kensington violated the standard of care in her treatment of Ms. Anderson. In that event, you will be asked to award the Andersons damages."

Bagley leaned on the front of the jury box and caught the eye of the same overweight woman. "Now, we all know that there's no way to put a price on a baby's life. But what we do know is that, through the grace of God, the Andersons are young and healthy enough to continue their family in the future. And I hope they do." He spread his hands widely. "I truly hope that the Andersons put this tragedy behind them and go on with their lives. I'm sure the best legacy that little Zachary could leave with the Andersons is that they live a life of love and joy with the children they will have together in the future. No amount of money can bring them the happiness that a warm and loving family can."

He paused. "I really don't have anything else to say. On behalf of Dr. Kensington, I thank you for your kind consideration of this matter. And I look forward to beginning trial first thing tomorrow."

As soon as the jury filed out, Lowe shot out of his seat and solicitously patted Camille on the back. "Taught her everything she knows." He laughed. "Nice job. Nice job."

What a phony asshole.

Camille pulled away and retired to the back of the courtroom where Trish sat, her mouth agape.

"Was I that bad?" Camille asked.

"No, no, you were great." Trish shook her head. "I was just wondering how you know Kensington's boyfriend."

The blood drained from Camille's face. "What are you talking about?"

"That guy." Trish cocked her head in Harvey Lowe's direction. "He was the guy Kensington spent the weekend with in the Caribbean."

Camille instantly felt light-headed. "Are you sure?" She grabbed the back of one of the spectator pews to steady herself.

"Positive." Trish rummaged around in her backpack, withdrew her phone, and handed it to Camille, opened to her album from the Caribbean.

There, plain as day, was a picture of Harvey Lowe and Jessica Kensington running hand in hand out of the turquoise water of the Caribbean.

"Oh my God."

CHAPTER THIRTY-FIVE

"Get me your notes on that money that went in and out of Kensington's bank account," Camille demanded as she and Trish whirled out into the hall. "I need to know the exact dates."

"What are you thinking?" Trish flipped her steno pad open to the list of deposits.

Camille had already memorized the dates of Harvey Lowe's big settlements against Kensington: the five-million-dollar settlement was November 9, 2017; the next brain damage case was settled on January 12, 2018; and the last one was February 29, 2020.

Camille held her breath as Trish read off the dates of the deposits into Kensington's bank account.

December 1, 2017, one million; January 29, 2018, three million; and March 21, 2020, one point two million dollars.

Camille did some quick mental calculations. Harvey Lowe's 40 percent fee on the five-million-dollar case would have been two million, and half of that would be one million, which was the exact amount that had jetted in and out of Kensington's bank account within a few weeks of Lowe's multimillion-dollar settlement.

Jesus Christ.

The January 2018 settlement had been twelve million, of which Lowe's fee would have been four point eight. In that one, according to the *Trial News* article, Kensington had implicated both the hospital and the anesthesiologist. Hence, the huge policy limits. At three mil,

Kensington had apparently gotten more than half of that one. Probably her bonus for dragging in every conceivable defendant.

Camille's mouth was so dry she could hardly swallow.

The last case had settled for six million. Forty percent of six million was two point four, and half of that was one point two million. Exactly the amount that hit Kensington's account shortly thereafter.

Camille looked at Trish in disbelief. "I think Kensington's fee-splitting with Lowe." She plopped down on the hard wooden pew.

"What do you mean fee-splitting?"

Camille grabbed Trish's steno pad and showed her the calculations. "It all makes sense." She shook her head. "Lowe soliciting Helene's case. He knew that he'd be able to make his famous 'premium baby' argument, and remember, Helene told me that Lowe'd just about guaranteed her that Kensington would roll over in her dep. Why wouldn't she if she's getting half his fee?" Camille's stomach hurled around inside her chest. "What the hell do I do now?"

"For starters, you march in there first thing in the morning and call the bitch to the stand and make her wish she'd never tangled with you."

"But you know as well as I do that I can't use these bank statements. I'd get disbarred for using these as evidence since we can't say how we got ahold of them." She looked knowingly at Trish.

"Just fake it—you lawyers do that all the time. Ask her how much money ran through her bank account. She won't be ready for that question, and she might provide some good testimony."

"Or it will backfire spectacularly." Camille stood. "And even if I did, there's no way Kensington's insurance company will pay a verdict. They don't cover doctors for murder."

Trish grabbed the handle of Camille's wheeled briefcase. "Let's get out of here." She turned and headed down the empty hallway.

—

Camille dropped her stuff in the reception area and hollered for Lucia. "What'd you do with the doctor?" She vaulted over to pull the *Trial News* articles down off the wall.

"He's at the wooden boat museum at the south end of the lake." Lucia held up a thick envelope. "Do you know a Serena Davenport?"

"What?" Camille bolted across the room. "Let me see that!" She grabbed it from the confused-looking Lucia.

"It came certified. And the Serena Davenport is in quotes for some reason—with a smiley face."

Trish's voice preceded her entry. "I got the entire printout of Kensington's bank account for the last ten years." She whisked into the room. "I thought we should see if there are any more weird financial patterns we should follow up on."

Camille looked up, the half-open envelope in her hand. "Look at this!" She held it up to Trish. "It's from Kensington's mother."

Trish dropped the extensive list of bank account data and hovered with Lucia as Camille tore open her prize. She hungrily pulled out a huge stack of legal pleadings entitled: "In Re: Marriage of Davenport." "It's Kip Davenport's divorce file," she announced curiously.

"Why'd she send you that?"

Camille shrugged. "Beats me." She leafed through the lengthy paperwork.

Trish reached across the desk and opened one of the two other envelopes that had fallen out of the pile. "What's this?" She held up an eight-by-ten photograph.

Camille grabbed the other envelope and pulled out a stack of bank records in the joint name of Moyna-Lou Davenport and Jessica Kensington.

Trish dropped the picture and ran over behind Camille to read over her shoulder.

Camille read from a big hot-pink sticky that was plastered on the top of the stack.

If my daughter is in trouble again, you might want to find out where she gets all her money, and why I'm locked up here. Can you rescue me?

Camille slowly laid the sticky on the desk. She and Trish locked eyes.

Camille was laser focused on the bank statements. "I can use these at trial. We got them from the actual account holder, so we can explain where they came from. They weren't obtained by an unnamed private investigator." She sighed with disbelief.

Lucia picked up the photo that Trish had just dropped. "Why did she send you a wedding picture?" Lucia asked.

"Looks like Kip and Moyna-Lou," Camille commented as she took it from Lucia's outstretched hand.

Trish was on full alert. Staring intently at Camille.

"Hang on . . ." Camille carefully perused the divorce pleadings. "Oh God."

She looked at Trish, her eyes wide with horror, and read aloud: "The petitioner, Moyna-Lou Davenport, is awarded lifetime maintenance since she has been rendered permanently brain damaged due to the repeated beatings she sustained at the hands of her husband, respondent, Dr. Kimbrough Davenport."

Trish and Lucia stood silently. This was big.

Camille continued, "The daughter, Jessica, and the son she conceived as the result of having been raped by her father, respondent, Dr. Kimbrough Davenport, should be immediately placed into foster care, since all living family members are either in prison or are otherwise unsuitable to serve as custodians of the children."

Camille stretched her imagination to encompass the possibility that Kip Davenport, politico extraordinaire, could have perpetrated these atrocities on his wife and daughter. "I can't believe this."

Trish was uncharacteristically quiet. Then she spoke. "'Rescue me'? Kensington is holding her mother hostage in a psych ward?"

Camille looked out the window, lost in thought. "The nurse in Hawaii told me that Kensington keeps her mother . . . what did she say . . . *one breath short of a coma.*"

"But what do we do with this information?" Trish queried as she tore open another envelope and discovered a batch of yellowed newspaper articles. She read the headlines. "Luther Davenport convicted of a string of rape/murders that stymied local officials in the Dallas–Fort Worth area for nearly a decade."

"What year was that?" Camille asked.

"It was 1980."

"Davenport's father?"

"Let's see . . . Davenport is probably around seventy, so he'd have been what? Around thirty in 1980? That would make his dad around fifty or sixty then. And this guy in the picture looks a lot like Davenport now." Trish looked at the man pictured in the article and compared it to the wedding photo. "Look at that head of red hair Davenport had when he got married."

"So, according to this, both Davenport and his father were supposedly sexual predators?"

Trish shrugged. "That's what it says." She skimmed another article in the pile. "And here's another Davenport, Luther's brother, Lionel, also in prison for"—Trish flipped the page—"murder." She looked up at Camille hesitantly.

"That's impossible." Camille put down the pleadings. "I've known Kip Davenport for years, and he's always been a perfect gentleman— when you're not suing his daughter," she hastened to add.

"I hate to break it to you, but that's what Ted Bundy's friends said about him."

Eyes closed, Camille lamented, "You think that's why both Kensington and her son have all those weird books on genetic predisposition to sexual deviancy?"

"Could be." Trish wrinkled her nose and paused. "But if Davenport really raped and beat his wife and daughter, why is he still free? Seems like he should be in prison."

"Probably because of the different legal standard between civil and criminal law. In a divorce the legal standard is more probable than not, which as you well know is a much lower burden of proof than the criminal standard of beyond a reasonable doubt. It's not at all uncommon for a family law judge to find that a party is guilty of domestic violence, and the prosecutor declines to press charges because they don't think the evidence meets the criminal burden of proof."

"I wonder what more they would need to have charged him?"

"Who knows? It may have been that the evidence of assault was likely to be easily attacked in a criminal trial. Remember, in family law, the issue is how to protect kids and make financial arrangements for a spouse. They are not depriving someone of their freedom. I expect this judge had enough of a feel for what happened just by the testimony presented—in a criminal trial they usually need more hard proof in order to bring charges and get a guilty verdict."

"Okay, then, we'll soon find out if that Texas prosecutor made a fatal mistake by not charging this asshole." Trish crossed her arms and set her jaw.

"No wonder Kensington's so whacked out." Camille's feelings for the murderous doctor transformed from utter disdain to deep sympathy within the space of a nanosecond. "If this is true, I can't imagine why she allows the guy anywhere near her."

"Call Laurabelle," Trish shouted. "She's an expert in this shit, isn't she?"

Camille lurched for the phone.

"Hi, Laurabelle, it's Camille. Can you get over to my office right away?" Camille crossed her fingers. "Great, see you soon."

"You want to look at the bank records while we wait?" Trish held out a stack of papers. "The only pattern I've been able to find, other than the money we already know about, is this withdrawal from Kensington's account every April first."

"Let me see that!" Camille grabbed a handful of papers and cross-referenced them to the pile that Moyna-Lou had just sent. "They're the same records." She nodded gratefully. She wasn't sure exactly how she could get these into evidence since Moyna-Lou wouldn't be able to authenticate them in court. But at least she had a copy that was admissible in court.

Trish pointed to her copies of the bank records, where she had highlighted the entries in question.

Camille read, "April first, 2012, sixty thousand dollars. April first, 2013, sixty thousand dollars." The withdrawals were echoed on an annual basis for the succeeding ten years.

"I wonder what the significance of April first is," Trish pondered aloud.

"It's the day Jessica Kensington delivered her baby when she was a teenager," Camille whispered.

Trish scanned one of the documents that lay on Camille's desk. "The pregnancy that supposedly resulted when her father raped her?"

Camille looked off into the distance. "I guess." *Where was this all going?*

"Then you're not going to believe where these checks were deposited."

Camille looked at Trish silently.

"Marblemount."

CHAPTER THIRTY-SIX

"So, it looks like the dude I tangled with out in the mountains last fall is Jessica Kensington's son," Camille announced to the transfixed psychology professor.

"Whom she conceived at the hands of her father when she was just a kid." Trish put the finishing touch on the sad saga of the Kensington/Davenport family as Laurabelle diligently took notes.

"So, does this make any sense at all?" Camille asked.

The professor removed her thick black glasses, stuck the earpiece in her mouth, and twirled them around.

"Actually, it's a classic example of Stockholm syndrome." She couldn't have sounded more professorial if she'd been behind a podium in front of a roomful of graduate students. "I'd love to have an opportunity to examine these people."

"I don't get it!" Trish slammed her open hand on Camille's desk. "Would someone please explain to me why the hell Kensington would stay by Daddy's side after what he did to her?"

Camille raised her eyebrows.

"Children of abusers are trapped in an enormously confusing love/hate relationship with their parent," Laurabelle explained.

"Mostly hate," Trish added.

"Not necessarily, dear. These kids love their parents."

"How can they?"

"Children have nothing to compare their childhood to. Whatever happens to them is quote 'normal' in their limited reality."

Camille nodded slightly.

"Odd as it sounds, these children don't consider it abnormal for Daddy to tuck them into bed, then rub their back, and eventually engage in some kind of sexual behavior with them. It's all they know."

Trish wrinkled her nose. "Gross."

"What happens when they get older?"

"The parent usually ensnares the child in some kind of highly dependent relationship. The parents actually love their kids and often think the inappropriate sexual relationship is simply their way of expressing their love."

"Don't the kids want to get away when they get older?"

"Sometimes. But these parents set the kids up to be completely dependent on them."

"How?"

"Well, it's not uncommon for these parents to encourage extreme financial dependence."

"Like paying the legal bills for her divorce?" Camille wondered aloud.

"Exactly." Laurabelle pointed at Camille as she might point at a student who had answered a question correctly in class.

"But there has to be more to it than money," Trish insisted.

"There is. It's some kind of twisted love. In fact, I'd hypothesize that there are times when Jessica seeks out her father to soothe and comfort her. She may long to be held and protected by her daddy."

"Sick!"

"Not really. Remember, she loves him. And she needs him." Laurabelle leaned forward. "And he needs her just as much."

"Jeez." Camille looked at her watch. "This is fascinating, but I have to get busy and prepare for my cross-examination of Kensington tomorrow. I think I have an inkling of an understanding of what went on between her and her father, but I'm not so sure how I can bring it together in a meaningful way."

Laurabelle stood. "Well, why don't you give me a call later on tonight if you need any help." She hoisted her gigantic purse over her shoulder. "You need to let this perc for a while. It's a lot to take in."

Camille smiled. "That's an understatement."

"Now, don't stay too late, dear," cautioned Laurabelle, as Camille and Trish moved toward the door.

"Don't worry."

The professor smirked at Camille. "I always told my students that one of the most important ways to prepare for a big test is to get enough sleep the night before."

"I hear you." Camille kissed the woman's dry, wrinkled cheek. "I promise I'll get out of here soon."

In a fog, Camille wandered over to the kitchenette and selected a sharply fragrant tea bag that promised increased mental acuity. "I'm holding you to this," she said to the colorful box.

Camille tiptoed over and lay on the couch so that her consciousness could wander across the data she'd set out on the giant flip-chart pages stuck to the walls of her office. Her mind reeled with information overload.

Suddenly, she shot up and riffled through her desk until she found her old litigation calendars. A potential pattern had emerged. All she had to do was compare the information on the charts to the dog-eared calendar.

That's it!

She crashed back onto the couch and gleefully kicked her feet in the air.

She couldn't dial Trish's number fast enough.

"I need for you to gather as many of the women who Kensington did the roto-rooter thing on as possible and have them in court tomorrow by noon."

"You have their names, I presume."

"I'm emailing them as we speak." Camille hit the send icon.

"What am I supposed to tell them?"

"Tell them anything you can think of, just get them there."

"Okay, okay, I'll try. You want to tell me why?"

"Tomorrow. We're both too busy right now. It's almost nine o'clock. Time's a-wastin'."

"Okay, I'm on it."

Camille grabbed the stack of library books on genetic predisposition to sexual deviancy and began to comb through them one at a time.

———

How the morning testimony played out would depend entirely on the desires of Helene and Tim Anderson.

She had told them to get to the courthouse early for an urgent meeting.

"Let's go," she said as soon as she saw Helene and Tim rounding the corner from the elevator lobby. She knew she sounded an awful lot like a lawyer. "There's a row of little cubicle-like rooms along the back wall of the library on the sixth floor. Go downstairs and I'll meet you in room five. It's important."

Helene held back as her husband hit the elevator button. "I trust this has nothing to do with that medical report we discussed recently."

Camille shook her head. "I promise. Now, please hurry." There was more to worry about now than whether Helene Anderson lied to her husband about being artificially inseminated. That'd have to be her problem.

Camille returned to Trish and held out her hand. "Give me your phone with that picture of Lowe and Kensington."

Her pulse pounded as she waited for the elevator. As the doors shushed open, she was relieved to see Lucia disembark along with a cadre of well-dressed men. Camille wondered which one was the doctor from Wisconsin who'd been so nice on the phone. She put down her briefcase to shake his hand. Her strategy had been to put her expert on first, but the recent discovery about Kensington and Lowe could be causing a rather dramatic change in plans. The expert might have to wait until tomorrow.

As the gentlemen dispersed, Lucia was left standing alone with an elderly man in an outdated polyester suit and a yellowish-gray ponytail that fell down to the base of his neck.

Oh no. This can't be my guy. Please no.

Lucia strode over and introduced Camille to Dr. Raskin of Whitefish Bay, Wisconsin.

As she shook hands with the doctor, Camille wondered how difficult it would be to get him a haircut before he took the stand. But nothing was going to get her down now. She sized him up. He was definitely too small to fit into one of Sam's suits. Oh well.

She made a quick apology for not being able to chat and sent Lucia and the doctor off to get coffee.

Tim and Helene were sitting at the metal government-issued-type table in one of the small attorney conference rooms in the law library. She skipped the hellos again.

"There was an auspicious change of events last night after trial."

Tim unwrapped his wife's breakfast muffin and handed it to her. "What happened?"

"Let me preface this by saying that what I'm about to tell you is quite possibly one of the most distressing things I've ever experienced in my entire career as a lawyer."

"What happened?" Helene asked softly.

"We don't have all that much time, so I'm afraid I'm going to be more blunt than I'd otherwise be in this kind of situation."

"It's okay, Camille," Helene coaxed. "It can't be any worse than what brought us here today."

Helene wasn't that bad a person. She was just trying to protect her husband by keeping his fertility troubles a secret.

Camille sat in a mismatched chair.

It didn't take long for the Andersons to grasp the enormity of Kensington's actions. Nor did they have any difficulty understanding the implications of disclosing the newfound evidence in court.

"This is criminal, right?" Helene demanded. "She killed our baby."

"It's technically a little more complicated from a legal perspective—Kensington could be charged with assault for each woman she caused to terminate their pregnancy." Camille explained. "But since she didn't actually cause the death of Zachary, there will likely be no criminal charge. But the fact that she and Lowe were defrauding the insurance companies would be the basis for another criminal charge."

"But you're saying that if the insurance company discovers that Kensington was responsible for the deaths of these babies, they won't have to pay on a verdict?"

"Exactly." Camille paused. "And as far as I've been able to determine, all of Kensington's personal money is in offshore bank accounts, so we'll never be able to reach any of her assets."

Helene looked at her husband, then back at Camille. "So, if we authorize you to put on evidence of Kensington's relationship with Harvey Lowe, we'll be throwing away any possible chance of compensation. Then again, if we ignore the evidence, Kensington is free to continue her hideous campaign against innocent women."

"It's up to you guys," Camille said. "I'll play it either way you tell me to." There was no choice; the rules of ethics demanded it. She held her breath, knowing that she was facing a crossroads. Either she was going to pursue the pot at the end of the rainbow, or she was going to have the satisfaction of putting a stop to this diabolical plan. She'd either be looking backward or forward. It was up to the woman who she'd come to resent more and more with each passing day. She thought of her mother, across the world making a difference one asylum case at a time. Each family's lives would be changed forever once they got their visas. It wasn't lost on Camille that the families she was about to put on the stand would never be the same either. Unless the Andersons refused to let her seek actual justice.

Suddenly, Camille realized that it wasn't up to Helene Anderson at all. If they said no, she'd withdraw from the case. After all, a lawyer could hardly be forced to continue in light of an ethical violation. It wouldn't be easy, but it would certainly be possible. Well, not just possible, but morally mandatory. As the couple huddled in the corner, Camille outlined her statement of withdrawal to the judge.

Helene licked her tissue and wiped the tears from her face. "Let her have it." Her voice dripped with disdain.

Tim nodded. "We have to put a stop to this madness."

Camille's pulse began to race. *Full steam ahead.*

"Thank you," she whispered as she took the large blond woman's cool hand. "Thank you so much." She blinked back the tears. *After today, Kensington won't be messing with any more pregnancies. Period.*

"What do we need to do?" Tim asked solemnly.

"You don't need to do anything. But if you don't mind, I need to get ready for court. I'm going to call Kensington to the stand."

Helene's frosty gray eyes softened as she paused to compose herself. "Tim and I need to talk. Can we use one of the other rooms back here?"

She was going to drop the bomb on him. She had to; it was going to come out in open court. "You bet, just take any one that's empty." Camille gave Helene a subtle nod of encouragement.

As soon as the couple closed the door behind them, Camille put her hands over her cheeks. "Bagley's gonna shit!" No plaintiff ever started their case by calling the defendant. But then, no plaintiff ever had a case like this.

———

Camille sat on the edge of the squeaky vinyl chair at the counsel table as the judge called in the jury. She fingered the picture of Kensington and Lowe that she'd shoved under the back of her legal pad. It was a plaintiff lawyer's dream come true.

"Ms. Delaney, you may call your first witness," the judge said sleepily.

Camille pushed her chair back so forcefully that it clattered to the floor. She ignored it and said in her clearest, most confident voice. "The plaintiff calls Dr. Jessica Kensington."

Bagley stopped drinking his Dixie cup of tepid water and slammed it to the table. "Objection!" He jumped to his feet.

Camille looked calmly at her adversary, then at the judge. She was in the zone. "Your Honor?" She raised an eyebrow.

The judge rolled his tongue around inside his cheek. "The basis of your objection counsel?"

Bagley smiled at the jury. "May we approach, Your Honor?"

"Certainly, Mr. Bagley." The judge beamed in return.

They were Oscar-winning performances—those two tripping over each other in a fairly successful effort to garner favor with the twelve slightly confused citizens in the jury box.

The judge leaned forward and covered the microphone in the center of the giant bench.

"What's up, Vern?"

Camille bit her tongue. That prick wasn't going to stop her from getting her claws into the soon-to-be-ex-doctor Jessica Kensington.

"The doctor has to be in surgery this morning—at 10:30," Bagley whispered through the grin he had cemented across his face for the jury's benefit. "I told her it was okay for her to come to court first thing for early motions and that you'd excuse her to go to work for the rest of the morning. I figured it'd be okay for her to schedule it since there was no way she'd be called on the first day of trial." He put his hand lightly on Camille's shoulder as if they were old trial buddies. Juries actually ate this shit up.

It was all Camille could do to keep from decking him. Instead, she said, "Please remove your hand."

The judge turned to Camille. "You got another witness, Ms. Delaney?"

Camille subtly pulled away from Bagley as she turned to survey the empty pews, thankful that Lucia and the hippie doc hadn't arrived back from coffee. "I'm sorry, Your Honor, I'd planned to put Dr. Kensington on first, so my expert isn't available yet."

The judge craned his neck to look out the window. "Any chance we can get a tee time this morning, counselor?" he whispered to Bagley. "We can get in nine holes over at Interbay if we hurry."

It was as bad as she'd expected, trying a case against Bagley in front of this yahoo.

Bagley turned his back to the jury and winked. "Can't think of any reason why not, Your Honor."

Why doesn't Bagley just get up on the bench and make the rulings himself?

The judge banged his gavel and smiled at the jury. "Ladies and gentlemen, you are dismissed until after lunch—see you at 1:30. Please remember not to discuss this case with anyone, including each other." Another solicitous smile. "Go out and have a nice walk in the sun." The judge stood.

"All rise."

Camille wandered back to the counsel table, dumbfounded. *So close, yet so far.* She couldn't stop herself from shaking as Bagley hustled his client out of the courtroom, leaving his entourage behind to close up shop.

———

Amy couldn't stand it anymore. She had to see how the Anderson trial was progressing. She looked at her watch. Court should be starting in a half an hour. She grabbed her brand-new gabardine coat and ran to catch the elevator.

"I'll be out this afternoon!" she shouted to the receptionist. Her heart was racing a million miles an hour. How would Camille react when she saw her?

On second thought, she knew how focused Camille got when she was in trial; she probably wouldn't even know Amy was there. *Just as well.*

—

The courtroom door whooshed closed behind Camille—she stood perfectly still and locked her prey in her sights.

Jessica Kensington gracefully crossed one leg over the other and laughed at another one of Bagley's insipid jokes as Harvey Lowe slipped into one of the pews at the front of the gallery to the right of the ever-dashing Kip Davenport. Camille shook off the intrusive vision of Kip manhandling his wife and daughter. There was no time to reflect on his insidious two-faced persona. There would be plenty of time to sort through her feelings later. Now she had to concentrate.

"Just protecting my fee." Lowe chuckled at Bagley, who nodded in return, oblivious to the leering grin Lowe shot at the utterly composed defendant.

Camille's peripheral vision fell away so all she could see was Dr. Jessica Kensington. She didn't take her eyes off the doctor as she marched directly over to her spot at the counsel table.

She owned the entire courtroom, and she knew it.

Camille smoothed the skirt of her charcoal-gray Armani suit and breathed easily through her diaphragm.

"All rise!"

The judge stood on his dais, obviously enjoying the power he exercised over his little kingdom. He sat, then waited a beat before granting permission for his subjects to sit. Slowly, he directed the bailiff to call in the jury.

As twelve of Jessica Kensington's alleged peers shuffled into their seats, the judge leaned forward and propped his chin in his hand. "Ms. Delaney? Your first witness?"

Camille looked at her clients sitting next to her, holding hands sweetly.

They nodded.

A feeling of utter calm enveloped Camille as she locked eyes with the defendant. "The plaintiff calls Dr. Jessica Kensington."

Kensington walked with the bearing of someone who'd had years of ballet training. Her lawyer held open the little gate that separated the witness from the rest of the courtroom.

Before the gate clicked closed, Camille headed to the stand. For some reason, even Bagley's array of high-tech equipment didn't faze her today.

She stood, unwavering, in front of the doctor and turned to the jury. "Dr. Kensington, can you tell the jury, in your own words, what happened the night Zachary Anderson was born?"

Kensington glanced at Bagley and then looked at Camille quizzically. There was no way she'd been prepared for a question like this. Cross-examinations were usually staccato-paced questions and answers: Isn't it true this? And isn't it true that? Defendants spent hours in front of jury consultants with whirring video cameras learning to dodge the heavily loaded questions.

Kensington leaned forward and spoke into the microphone, "You . . ." The microphone squawked as she began to speak.

"Lean back," directed the judge. "We can hear you fine, Doctor."

"You want me to just narrate?"

Camille could see Kensington's hands, with their long red nails, twisting in her lap.

She nodded. "Please."

"Well, I, uh, I first saw Ms. Anderson when she was dilated four centimeters. And I decided to augment her labor."

Bagley cautiously motioned for the doctor to direct her testimony toward the jury. He looked more than a little concerned as Kensington slowly explained her version of the Anderson fiasco.

As Kensington finished her monologue, Camille crossed her arms. "Dr. Kensington, have you ever been sued before?"

"Objection, Your Honor!"

"Sustained."

She didn't think it would be that easy, but it didn't hurt to try. "Are you aware of the name of the lawyer that originally filed this case?"

"I believe it was Harvey Lowe."

Camille nodded. "Very good. Now, what is the nature of your relationship with Harvey Lowe?"

Kensington flushed. "I . . . I beg your pardon?"

"Do you have a relationship with Mr. Lowe other than your having been a defendant in a lawsuit that he filed?"

"No. No, of course not."

Bagley twisted around just as his campaign cochair made a beeline for the door. Camille stifled a smile, enjoying the look of complete confusion on Bagley's face as Lowe bolted from the courtroom.

She paused a moment before pulling out the picture of Kensington and Lowe playing Beach Blanket Bingo and then, without going through the standard courtroom formality of asking Bagley if she could use his equipment, she threw the picture onto the overhead and searched for the "on" button.

"Objection!"

The judge leaned forward.

"This wasn't disclosed on the plaintiff's ER 904 exhibit list."

The judge looked at Camille. "Ms. Delaney?"

"Impeachment, Your Honor. The witness just testified that her only contact with Mr. Lowe is from the lawsuit he filed against her."

The judge shrugged. "I'll allow it."

"But she's using my equipment."

Camille grimaced jokingly at the jury. "Forgive me, Mr. Bagley. You don't mind if I use your overhead, do you?"

A couple of the jurors snickered.

Bagley strutted over to where he could view the picture that Camille was about to show the jury. The sleepy twelve perked up as the screen filled with a picture of Jessica Kensington and Harvey Lowe, hand in hand, running out of the crashing surf. Bagley stroked his chin thoughtfully, obviously trying to look way more collected than he could possibly feel.

"Who are the two people in this picture, Dr. Kensington?"

Kensington froze. She quickly scanned the courtroom, then turned back to Camille.

"Doctor?"

"It's me and Mr. Lowe." Kensington said it with the indignance of a woman caught in a tryst as she pulled the covers up around herself.

"And who is Mr. Lowe?"

"He's a lawyer here in Seattle."

"And he's the one who originally filed this case?"

Kensington nodded.

Camille paced back and forth in front of the jury. "Well, why don't you tell us what you and Mr. Lowe were doing together in this picture?"

"We had just finished swimming and were coming out of the water." Kensington's voice was barely a whisper.

"And where was this picture taken?"

Kensington took a moment to examine the picture. "I believe it was on Grand Cayman island."

Camille noticed for the first time that one of the local newspaper reporters who covered the judicial elections had just realized that she'd had the good fortune to pick exactly the right time to check out Judge McIntyre's style on the bench. Not wanting the reporter to miss the significance of the brewing story, Camille raised her voice. "Now, let me get this straight. You were vacationing with the lawyer who was suing you, correct?"

"He wasn't suing me at the time." It was a feeble response.

"But he's sued you before, hasn't he?"

"Objection!"

"Goes to motive, Your Honor."

The judge raised his hand to rule against her, then saw the reporter opening her notepad. "I'll allow it."

It was a political position, after all.

Kensington looked wide-eyed at the judge. "What do I do?"

"You answer the question," the judge directed the witness.

"Can you repeat it?" she asked Camille.

"Has Harvey Lowe sued you before?"

"Uh, yes, yes, he has."

"You remember any of the settlement amounts?"

Kensington shook her head. "I'm afraid not. You'd have to ask my attorneys."

"Let me refresh your recollection. The Smith case settled in November 2017 for five million dollars."

"In 2017? No wonder I couldn't remember it."

The jury didn't find the attempt at humor funny.

"Now, Dr. Kensington, I want you to assume that a plaintiff's lawyer's typical fee in a malpractice case is forty percent."

Kensington shot a panicked look at Bagley, who sat expressionless at the counsel table. It was what they always taught you to do when one of your witnesses was getting creamed.

"Can you tell me what forty percent of five million dollars is?"

"Uh, two million?"

Camille nodded. "Right. Now what is half of two million?"

"One million."

"Isn't it true that on December first, 2017, after your boyfriend settled the Smith case against you, you deposited one million dollars in your bank account?"

"I don't remember."

"Let me refresh your memory." Camille grabbed the printout of Kensington's bank deposits.

"Objection." It was half-hearted at best.

"Ms. Delaney?" the judge's voice was curt.

"Impeachment, Your Honor."

The judge sat back in his chair. "Go ahead, Ms. Delaney."

"Dr. Kensington, can you tell me what this is?"

"It looks like a bunch of bank statements."

"These are bank statements of an account you share with your mother, aren't they?" Camille held her breath. If Kensington said no, there would be no way to authenticate it. She stepped away from Bagley, hoping Kensington's eyes would follow her rather than looking at her lawyer, who should be jumping out of his skin to try to dissuade her from authenticating the bank record.

"They're mine," Kensington said before her lawyer was able to object. In a heartbeat, the sanguine doctor disappeared, and Camille recognized the ashamed expression of an abused little girl.

"Objection! We've never seen these before! Where on earth did you get my client's bank records?"

"Counsel?" the judge inquired.

"I'll lay a foundation, Your Honor." Without waiting for his response, Camille quickly turned to the witness. "Dr. Kensington, is this envelope from your mother at Kahana Care in Hawaii?"

"Yes." Kensington was deflated. "It is."

"Do you recognize her handwriting on this envelope?"

Kensington nodded.

"You need to answer verbally, Doctor," Camille instructed.

"Yes. It's my mother's handwriting." Kensington was beginning to look worried.

"And both her and your names appear as owners of the account?"

"Yes."

"I'd offer the bank statements as exhibit one, Your Honor."

Without waiting for a response from Bagley, the judge stated, "They've been authenticated, counsel, I'll admit them."

Camille recognized the pull between the judge's friendship with Bagley and his fear of being overturned on appeal during his election year.

Her attention turned back to Kensington. "Now, doesn't the statement indicate that there was a deposit in your account of one million dollars approximately three weeks after Mr. Lowe settled the Smith case?"

"Yes, it does."

"And then that same one million dollars was transferred to a bank account on Grand Cayman island, wasn't it?"

"Yes." The entire courtroom was leaning forward to hear the doctor's whispered testimony.

Camille repeated the exact line of questions regarding the other two cases until there could be no doubt that the doctor and her boyfriend were partners in a horrific crime.

Tears streaked down both Helene's and Kensington's faces as the doctor admitted to Camille's inferences, one after another.

Finally, Camille changed pace.

"How much does it cost to keep your mother in the psychiatric institute in Hawaii?"

"Objection, lack of foundation." Bagley held his hands out in frustration.

"Sustained."

"Dr. Kensington, is your mother a resident of an inpatient psychiatric facility in Hawaii?"

"Yes."

"Do you provide her support?"

"Yes, I do. I have to."

"'Have to'?"

"There's no one else."

"And the money you gained from this fee-splitting with Harvey Lowe has certainly helped you support your mother, hasn't it?"

"Objection. Misstates prior testimony. Dr. Kensington never admitted that she and Mr. Lowe were engaged in this so-called fee-splitting arrangement." Bagley had suddenly changed from a supercilious insurance defense lawyer to a highly alert advocate.

Good. Kensington needs someone to launch a zealous defense on her behalf. But Camille had never considered that Bagley had it in him. The guy actually looked scared shitless.

"Sustained."

"Okay, fair enough. Dr. Kensington, were you engaged in a fee-splitting arrangement with Mr. Lowe?"

Bagley bolted to his feet. "I'm advising my client to assert her Fifth Amendment privilege not to provide testimony that might incriminate her."

Camille stared at the doctor with a cross between pity and disgust. "I have nothing further." Camille returned to her seat.

Bagley approached the witness. "I have just a few questions at this time, Your Honor."

From the look on the judge's face, Camille figured that he'd be quickly replacing Lowe and Bagley as the illustrious cochairs of his judicial campaign. *Shitty luck.*

"Go ahead." The judge waved the back of his hand at his soon-to-be-former golfing partner.

"Dr. Kensington, you aren't trying to support your mother on your own, are you?"

"No, she gets maintenance from my father, and she got a substantial multimillion-dollar settlement in her divorce. My father owned several apartment buildings, and the court ordered them sold and Mother got a few million dollars."

"So there's no reason for you and Lowe to cook up some harebrained scheme to injure innocent babies and split the fees, is there?"

"Objection."

"Sustained."

Bagley turned around. His defense was thin, and he knew it. "Nothing further at this time."

CHAPTER THIRTY-SEVEN

Amy dried her hands and leaned into the mirror to examine her makeup in the ladies' room across the hall from the courtroom. She hadn't realized how nervous she'd be, seeing Camille for the first time after leaving her high and dry. And this was as good a place as any to hide. She pinched her cheeks and pushed her hair off her face. Poor Camille stuck with a blue-haired legal messenger as an assistant.

Amy rummaged around in her giant purse and extricated a makeup bag the size of a cantaloupe. Where was that frosted pink lipstick? She opened and immediately closed the Luscious Red, then the Summer Peach. There was no way she could wear either of those with her pink sweater set. Her hand shook as she lined her lips and began to fill them in with the tube of Very Berry. The shade was all wrong, but it'd have to do.

What would she say if Camille came in? She leaned over and pinched her cheeks again, trying to calm herself down.

Snap out of it, you're eventually going to have to face her.

Amy startled as Jessica Kensington hurried into one of the stalls, speaking rapidly on her cell phone.

Oh my God. Amy held her breath.

"I can make it. I'm leaving right now." Kensington snapped her phone closed.

Leaving? Where the hell does she think she's going? The afternoon break is only fifteen minutes long. Amy looked at her watch.

Kensington ran her hands under a thin stream of water and pushed open the door.

Might as well . . . Amy threw her array of makeup back into the bag and took off behind Kensington.

Out on Fourth Avenue, Amy hung back so as not to appear to be following the harried doctor. She looked up at the monolithic Columbia Tower, where her empty office floated seventy-four floors above the street. They'd fire her in a heartbeat if they knew she was out chasing a defendant in one of their competitor's cases. So what? Amy turned away and focused on Kensington, who was just about to get into her car at the garage down the block from the courthouse. It was the first time in months that Amy had actually felt useful.

A handful of bills fluttered to the ground as the parking attendant gave Kensington her change. He watched in confusion as Kensington hopped into her silver Jaguar and leaned on her horn to bring attention to the fact that there was a car blocking her in.

The guy shouted, "Be right there!" from his position on his hands and knees, where he was picking up the wayward denominations scattered in front of his booth.

A cab! Amy flailed her hands around in the air.

"Can you follow that Jaguar?" she asked when she got in.

The man in the white turban shrugged and nodded as he flipped on the meter.

Amy looked on as Kensington stood on the doorjamb of her car screaming at the flustered attendant. "Move that car!"

There wasn't too much traffic on southbound I-5 in the middle of the afternoon. The cab raced onto the freeway and pulled up behind the Jag.

"Not so close," Amy admonished the driver, who frowned at her as he rattled along in some foreign dialect on his phone.

—

Ten minutes until the afternoon recess was over. Camille rushed past the lackadaisical receptionist at the front desk of the King County Prosecuting Attorney Office on the fifth floor of the courthouse. She was prepared to explain that she needed to speak with her old law school buddy Senior Deputy Prosecutor Trent Conway. But there was no real need to convince the middle-aged woman, who was busily filing her nails.

Camille picked up her pace and rounded the corner and into her friend's cluttered office.

The tall, lanky prosecutor propped his feet on the windowsill and spoke loudly on his phone.

Camille bounced his chair from behind.

Conway waved gaily and continued to argue about the length of a sentence in a proposed plea bargain. He pointed at a chair covered with a two-foot stack of files and held up his hand, his index finger a half inch from his thumb to indicate he'd just be another minute.

Camille shook her head and pointed at her watch.

"Hang on, Saul." Conway put his hand over the receiver. "What's up?"

"I'm sorry to butt in, but can I have exactly one minute of your time? It's really important."

"Let me get back to you, Saul." Conway hung up. "What's going on? You look like you're going to pop a cork."

"I can't talk now; I'm trying a case in McIntyre's courtroom."

Conway grimaced. "Sorry to hear that."

"It's fine. But I've got a situation up there I'm positive you're going to want to take action on. Can you come up in about thirty minutes?" Camille moved toward the door.

"Jeez, Camille . . ."

Camille adopted a completely uncharacteristic aura of authority. "I'm not kidding. I need you up there." She held up her wrist and smacked her index finger on her watch. "Thirty minutes."

—

God bless Trish. The five women surrounding her in the elevator lobby outside the law library looked bewildered, to say the least. Introductions were short and sweet as Camille packed them all into the same austere cubicle where she'd had the "come to Jesus" meeting with Helene and Tim that morning.

Camille felt a brief stab of disappointment as she surveyed the women. As far as she could tell, there were absolutely no outward similarities. They were a true cross section of Americana; the kind of women you might see in the audience on *Ellen*.

"I really appreciate you coming here on such short notice," Camille began. "And I wish I had more time to explain exactly why you're here, but unfortunately I have to be back in court in"—she looked at her watch—"three minutes."

"Do we have to testify?" a short overweight woman with a cartoon-like voice asked.

"Yes, I'll be calling you each to the stand."

"And this is a case against Dr. Kensington?" asked a pretty Hispanic woman.

"It is."

The woman shook her head. "I always wondered about that doctor. You know, she caused me to miscarry the baby I'd tried for two years to conceive."

An elegant forty-something with curly salt-and-pepper hair gasped quietly. "You're kidding. Me too!"

The cadre of women slowly looked around at each other as the reason for their being there began to dawn on them.

From the back of the group, a wiry athletic woman came to the forefront and put her hands on her hips. "You mean to tell me that that quack did the same thing to each of us?" She was nothing if not direct.

Camille nodded. "And I really need your testimony in order to see to it that she doesn't do it to anyone else."

The overweight woman began to sob quietly. "Why did she do it?"

"I have a pretty good idea, but I need a bit more evidence to smoke her out." Camille held the door open. "So," she whispered as they walked single file through the library stacks, "I'd appreciate it if you'd each testify as I call you to the stand."

"Can we sue her too?" the wiry woman asked.

Camille felt the familiar butterflies in her stomach that she always got whenever she had a line on a potentially good case, then sighed silently. There wasn't likely to be any money from the insurance company at the end of this rainbow after today.

"We can certainly discuss it."

CHAPTER THIRTY-EIGHT

Thankfully, Camille recognized the newspaper reporter who'd happened into Judge McIntyre's courtroom at the most opportune of moments as the reporter who'd interviewed her in her capacity as chair of the Gender and Justice Task Force a few years back. She racked her mind for the woman's name. *Elaine!*

"Hi, Elaine." Camille shook the reporter's hand.

Elaine leaned toward Camille. "Any chance you want to tell me what the hell's going on in there?"

Camille smiled. "And deprive you of the excitement of watching tomorrow's front-page story unfold right before your eyes?"

"C'mon."

"Really. I can't." Camille shook her head. "You know as well as I do that there's no way of knowing for sure exactly how evidence'll play out in court." She turned toward the lineup of women on the ratty pew in the hallway. "But stay tuned."

The faces of the women reflected their differing reactions to having to relive the pain of their years-old miscarriages. A couple wiped away tears, a few seemed to be in shock, and the wiry woman looked like she'd jump up and strangle Kensington if she had the chance. Thankfully, they were at the far end of the hall, so Kensington wouldn't recognize them when she returned from the break.

"I'll be right back," Camille whispered to Trish and headed down the hall toward the courtroom.

—

Outside the courtroom, Vern Bagley spoke in a heated whisper to his harem of associates and his male junior partner. They glared at Camille as she strode past them and purposefully entered the courtroom.

The bailiff looked at the large institutional clock above the jury box. "Have you seen Mr. Bagley?"

"He's right outside," Camille answered as she riffled through the notes Trish had given her with each of the women's names and vital information.

A small commotion arose as Bagley et al. took their places behind the counsel table. He looked at the number-one associate. "Where's Dr. Kensington?"

The young woman's eyes darted around the room, and she jumped up out of her seat. "She must be in the ladies' room. I'll go get her."

Bagley glowered at the terrified young lawyer. "Get her in here now. Judges don't like to be kept waiting." He pointed at the clock and hissed loudly. "Don't you ever come back into this courtroom without the defendant."

Camille stifled a smile. *Serves her right for going to work for an asshole like Vern Bagley.*

A minute ticked by. Then another.

"Mr. Bagley?" asked the bailiff. "Is the defendant ready? The judge is a stickler for punctuality. He wants to get started."

Bagley shot up in a fit of petulance. "Of course. I'll go see what's keeping her." Kip Davenport beat him to the door and hurried out.

Camille approached the bench. "Actually, I have something to take up with His Honor. Maybe we can go over that while one of Mr. Bagley's entourage searches the courthouse for the defendant."

The bailiff smiled as one of the young generic female lawyers hustled out to the hall to summon her boss.

"Very well." The bailiff picked up her phone and called the judge back out of his chambers. "All rise!"

"Good afternoon. I understand you have something to take up with the court, Ms. Delaney?"

"Yes, Your Honor."

Bagley crashed through the double doors and took his place, front and center.

The judge looked past Camille at the serious reporter scribbling furiously in the front row of the gallery. "Mr. Bagley?"

Bagley hurried to the bench and threw down his yellow legal pad.

The judge looked down. "Ms. Delaney?"

Funny how his demeanor changed when Elaine Chambers showed up.

"I have a few new witnesses."

Bagley slammed his fist on the old oak counter in front of the bailiff. "I object! This is ridiculous! She can't add any witnesses at this late date!"

"Ms. Delaney?"

It was obviously killing McIntyre to have to treat her with even the tiniest bit of dignity, but in light of the upcoming election, he knew when he had to at least act like a fair-minded member of the judiciary. There was no way this guy wanted to go back to practicing real law. He was way too full of himself.

"They're foundation witnesses, Your Honor."

"What are they going to testify to?" The judge kept his voice low so that Elaine couldn't hear him.

Camille spoke up, "They're just going to give the background dates and a bit of additional foundation necessary for me to establish Kensington's motive for malpractice."

The judge shrugged. "I'll allow it, but only as to those limited areas of testimony." He surveyed the courtroom. "Have you found your client yet, Mr. Bagley?"

Bagley's face reddened as he turned to his team, who shook their heads in unison. "We'll find her, Your Honor," he seethed. "I'm sure she must have just stepped out for some fresh air." He pointed at his junior partner. "Get her in here!" He slapped the counsel table.

"Call the jury!" boomed the judge. "Ms. Delaney, your next witness?"

Camille grabbed the crumpled piece of paper Trish'd torn from her steno pad. "The plaintiff calls Samantha Stefonak."

Trish held the door for the overweight woman who shuffled into the courtroom, looking directly at her feet. While the judge swore the witness, Camille cobbled together her shaky easel in front of the jury. It was a distinct contrast to Bagley's plethora of technology. She clipped a huge pad to the top of the easel.

After being sworn in, the witness tugged at her short skirt and sat on the edge of her seat.

"Ms. Stefonak, were you a patient of Dr. Kip Davenport in 2018?"

"Yes."

"And did you undergo artificial insemination while under his care?"

"Objection! Beyond the scope of agreed testimony."

The judge looked at Camille.

"It's just foundation, Your Honor."

"Go ahead, counsel."

The woman looked quickly from Camille back to the judge.

"Answer the question, ma'am."

She froze.

Camille held her breath. It was every lawyer's nightmare, calling an unprepared witness at trial.

"Ma'am?"

"I, uh, I forgot the question."

The judge scratched his head. "Read it back."

The court reporter picked up the long strip of paper flowing out the back of her machine. "And did you undergo artificial insemination while under his care?"

"Yes. Yes, I did." She unconsciously picked at her cuticle as she spoke.

"Did Dr. Davenport himself perform the procedure?"

"Yes, of course. He's the best in town."

Camille uncapped a blue magic marker and ignored the aroma of blueberries. "Okay, now what day of the week did you undergo the insemination procedure itself?" She held the marker in front of the easel, prepared to transcribe the day of the week that the patient had been inseminated.

Another panicked pause.

Camille's heart began to race. "Ms. Stefonak, do you remember the day of the week that Dr. Davenport performed the insemination procedure on you?"

"I . . . I'm not sure."

Camille recapped the marker. "Well, was it on a weekend?"

"Objection! Leading the witness, Your Honor!"

"Sustained. Let's move along, Ms. Delaney."

"You have no idea the day of the week you underwent the procedure?" She unconsciously shook the marker at the witness, who looked like she'd rather be anywhere other than testifying in court.

"Objection, asked and answered."

Camille glanced nervously at Trish, who was hightailing it out into the hall.

"Okay, Ms. Stefonak, did you suffer a miscarriage after being inseminated?"

"Yes." Her voice fell to a quiet whisper.

"And can you please tell the jury the circumstances under which you suffered the miscarriage?"

"It was while Dr. Kensington was performing some kind of genetic-testing procedure. I don't remember what it was called."

"Well, can you just explain what happened?"

"Sure," she said tentatively. "Dr. Kensington was doing this test on me that required her to put some kind of instrument up into my cervix, and while she was doing it, I had a miscarriage." Samantha Stefonak wiped a tear from her cheek with the back of her hand.

The judge pulled a box of tissues out of his drawer and handed it to the witness, who smiled at him in return.

"Thank you, Ms. Stefonak. I have nothing further."

The judge looked at the seething insurance defense lawyer. "Mr. Bagley?"

Camille bit the inside of her cheek to keep from laughing. There was no way Bagley'd have any questions. He had no idea where all this was going.

Bagley looked at his watch. "I see no need for me to waste the jury's time by my questioning this witness." He waved his hand dismissively.

"You may step down, ma'am." The judge turned to Camille. "Next?"

She read the next name off Trish's list and looked at Trish, who winked and nodded in return.

"The plaintiff calls Brittany Kent."

The wiry ball of fire walked quickly up to the stand, swinging her arms wide at her side like a football player.

"Raise your right hand. Do you swear your testimony will be the whole truth and nothing but the truth?"

"I do."

Camille took over. "Your name?"

"Brittany Kent."

"Ms. Kent, were you a patient of Dr. Davenport in 2015?"

Brittany Kent leaned forward, one hand on each knee. "Yep."

"And did Dr. Davenport perform an artificial insemination on you?"

She nodded. "Yep."

Camille uncapped the lime-green marker and asked hopefully, "Do you recall what day of the week that was?"

"It was a Saturday."

She wrote *Brittany Kent—Saturday* in large block letters on her exhibit. "How do you happen to remember that?"

"Because I had to miss my rugby match that day, and we were in the semifinals. I got a real rash of shit from my team." She slapped her hand over her mouth. "Oh my God, I'm sorry."

Several members of the jury giggled.

"I didn't mean to swear here, in court and everything."

"It's okay." Camille smiled. "Can you tell the jury whether you carried that baby to term?"

"No, Kensington screwed up my CVS test and made me miscarry."

"Objection! This witness is hardly in a position to testify as to the medical causation for her having an alleged miscarriage."

"Sustained." The judge looked down and cautioned the witness. "Just answer the questions, ma'am."

Camille resumed. "Can you explain in your own words what happened when you underwent the CVS genetic testing?"

"I bled like a stuck pig, that's what happened. It was a giant mess. Blood everywhere. And that woman . . ."

"Objection!"

"Sustained. Just answer the question."

Brittany Kent shrugged and waited for the next question.

"Did you miscarry?"

"Yes, I did."

Camille wrote *miscarriage during CVS—performed by Kensington* next to the rest of the data on Brittany Kent.

"I have nothing further."

"Mr. Bagley?"

Another exasperated wave and a shake of the head.

The next witness took the stand and testified that she'd undergone insemination by Davenport on a Sunday. She remembered it because she and her husband had gone to church right after the procedure to pray for a healthy baby. As with the previous two witnesses, Mary Jensen had suffered a miscarriage during one of Kensington's genetic-testing procedures, although this time it was an amniocentesis.

Camille entered this data on her list with orange marker and called the next woman to the stand.

Another insemination on a Sunday. This time it was late afternoon, but it was a Sunday just the same. This witness also had a miscarriage immediately after a genetic CVS test that was performed by Kensington.

By the time the women were through testifying, Camille had a colorful list of four women who'd had artificial insemination on a Saturday or Sunday and had thereafter miscarried during a genetic-testing procedure performed by Kensington.

Bagley had his best courtroom poker face plastered on in an effort to hide his increasing confusion.

Camille approached the bench once again. "I have one more witness I was planning to call, but she's recently deceased, so I'd like to read her testimony into the record."

"Objection. This is going too far, Your Honor. Ms. Delaney has no dead witnesses on her witness list," Bagley hissed through his phony smile.

"I'd have called her along with the other women, but I can't. Her testimony will be very similar to that of the other women, Your Honor."

"Don't you think we have the idea already?" the judge asked.

"This one is different, Your Honor. It'll be quick, I promise."

The judge's face fell as he noticed that a photographer from the *Seattle Times* was whispering with the reporter in the front row of the gallery. Camille knew he couldn't afford to look prejudiced in any way.

"Go ahead, but be brief," he snapped.

Camille turned back to the jury and called Lucia to the stand to read from the deposition that she handed her. "For the record, this is the transcript of a deposition of Gina Cipriotti in the case of Cipriotti vs. Doe. It was a case involving a hit-and-run car accident. I'll read the questions and my assistant will read the answers."

Lucia tried, unsuccessfully, to pull her sweater over her midriff.

Camille cleared her throat. "Now, let's go over the circumstances of little Daniel's birth."

Lucia looked at Camille. "Now?"

Camille nodded.

Lucia read: "We tried for years to get pregnant, then through the miracle of modern technology, poof!" She paused for effect and looked at the jurors. "It happened."

Camille recognized Lucia's theatrical background shining through.

"Of course, not until we'd undergone a number of attempts at fertilization. I'll never forget the day we conceived our Danny." Lucia's voice cracked. "It was a Sunday, after church. See, he really was the answer to our prayers."

Camille smiled. "Hold on, Gina." She looked up at the jury. "I objected, then I said: 'Wait until there's a question posed.' Then the next question the lawyer asked her was: 'I'll need to order your medical records. Who provided your OB care?'"

Lucia took over. "Davenport Women's Health."

Camille stepped up and took the transcript from Lucia, then wrote *Gina Cipriotti* in large purple letters as she held the shaky easel, and after that she wrote *inseminated—Davenport—Sunday.*

CHAPTER THIRTY-NINE

Amy directed the unenthusiastic cab driver to follow Kensington's Jaguar into the parking lot at Sea-Tac Airport.

"I not pay for parking," he announced.

"It's okay." Amy thrust a twenty-dollar bill over the seat. "Here. This is more than enough."

"I not pay, lady."

"Just follow her!"

The driver shrugged.

"Hurry!"

The cab whipped around the spiral ramp up to the top floor of the parking garage, where Amy watched Kensington park and run toward the elevators.

"Take me back to the fourth floor!" She'd intercept Kensington on her way to the ticket counter.

As soon as the cab slowed in front of the elevator bank, Amy threw the driver two twenty-dollar bills, then flew across the glass-enclosed sky bridge. She surveyed the crowd and quickly located the fugitive doctor ascending the escalator to the main terminal. Amy was able to get close enough to Kensington on the escalator that she could smell Kensington's perfume: Obsession. Amy grabbed the handrail, panting from her sprint through the parking lot.

Kensington marched up to the first-class check-in and quickly purchased a ticket. Trying to look nonchalant, Amy studied the TV monitor that transmitted the arrivals and departures and quickly bought a ticket to Portland, saying a quick prayer of thanks for her fancy new salary.

Okay, let's go! Amy hurried to get in line behind Kensington at the TSA checkpoint and followed her prey as she headed for the gate.

The doors of the subway train to the South Satellite Terminal closed behind the two women. Amy grabbed a pole with her sweaty hand to keep her balance. As the train lurched forward, she stumbled into Kensington.

"Excuse me," Amy gushed.

Kensington shot Amy a sideways glance and focused on the long dark tunnel as the train sped down the track. She looked at her watch.

Upon arriving at the terminal, Kensington jogged down the concourse to the international departure area. The reader board at gate fifteen said the next departure would be American Airlines flight 12324 for Rio de Janeiro leaving at 4:45.

Oh God. Rio?

Amy looked up and down the concourse. She had fifty minutes to come up with a plan. After that the doc would be winging her way out of the country and, more importantly, away from the long arm of the law.

What was she going to do? There was no way she could stop the doctor by herself. She could try Camille, but she knew that judges always required the attorneys to keep their cell phones off in the courtroom. Frantic, Amy pulled out her cell phone and dialed Missy Barron at Lowe's office.

"It's Amy. I really need a favor."

"Hey, can I call you back? I'm in the middle of indexing a dep."

"No! I need you now!"

"Are you okay? Is something wrong?"

"I'm fine. I just really need you to do something for me."

"It'll have to wait about twenty minutes. Harvey's out for blood. I need to get this to him pronto. Gotta go."

"No! No, don't hang up. I can't wait. I need you to run over to the courthouse and get a message to Camille for me. It's really, really important."

"Camille?"

"Yeah, I don't have time to explain right now. You've got to do this for me."

"I can't. Harvey'll shit if I don't have this to him by five thirty."

Amy watched as the agents readied the gate for boarding. She hopped from one foot to the other.

"Please. You gotta help me. Camille is in trial in Judge McIntyre's courtroom and her defendant is getting ready to board a plane for Rio."

"What?"

"Can you please go over to the courthouse and tell her? Please."

"Even if I could, I wouldn't know where to go. I've never even been in the courthouse."

God, the woman works for the self-proclaimed premier lawyer in Seattle and she's never been in the courthouse? This office sucks. "It's Jessica Kensington. If you don't help me, she's going to get away, and she'll never get what's coming to her. You told me yourself that she needs to be put in her place. Please, it's our only chance to stop her."

"Can't you find anyone else?"

"Look, Missy, we might make a bunch of money up at Lowe's office, but when was the last time you had a chance to do something meaningful? You'll have to live with yourself if this doctor gets away."

Amy could hear Missy shuffling her paperwork. After a long pause, Missy said, "Okay, what do you want me to tell her?"

"Jessica Kensington is waiting to board flight 12324 for Rio de Janeiro. The flight leaves at four forty-five. Hurry!" Amy was nearly shouting into her phone. She dropped her voice. "Camille's on the seventh floor of the courthouse, Judge McIntyre's courtroom. There's an information board in the lobby if you get lost. Just remember: Judge McIntyre. You'll find it."

"I'm on my way." Missy sounded tentative.

Amy closed her phone and paced back and forth in front of the Jetway.

———

The judge looked at the clock and then at Camille. "We have time for one more witness."

"The plaintiff calls Dr. Kip Davenport." She turned and scanned the courtroom, catching the eye of her prosecutor friend, who looked more than a little bewildered. She nodded and held up a finger to him. "Is Dr. Davenport here?"

Trish jumped up and said loudly, "He's out in the hall, on his cell."

"Very well." The judge motioned the bailiff to bring him in.

Camille took the pad off the easel as Kip Davenport strutted up to the stand.

She stopped to gather all her confidence as her former friend was sworn in. Before he could get completely settled, she pulled out the ominous Davenport divorce file. It would take everything she had to make it through the next several minutes.

Elaine Chambers looked on attentively from the front row of the gallery as Davenport easily adjusted the microphone.

Camille looked at the Andersons. Helene scooted up and winked at Camille, then nodded and pointed to the witness stand.

Davenport smiled condescendingly as Camille slowly reclipped the pad to the easel. It fell to the floor.

"Bear with me." Camille smiled at the jury. "I'm afraid I can't afford all the fancy video equipment that my colleague Mr. Bagley has at his beck and call." She tried, unsuccessfully, to clip the huge pad on again. "Never mind." She leaned the pad up against the high-tech overhead projector.

A slight look of concern briefly shadowed Davenport's face as Camille pointed to the list of patients who'd just testified.

"Dr. Davenport, while you were in the hall, several of your former patients testified that they'd undergone artificial insemination procedures by you at your clinic on various weekend days."

Davenport stroked his chin. "Yes?"

"And thereafter, all of them suffered miscarriages during genetic-testing procedures performed by your daughter, Dr. Jessica Kensington."

The jurors perked up upon discovering that the debonair doctor testifying was, in fact, Dr. Kensington's father.

Camille crossed her arms and planted herself in front of the witness box. "Tell me, Dr. Davenport, who all is present in your office on weekends when you perform these procedures?"

Davenport chuckled. "I frequently come in on weekends to perform inseminations. My patients have no control over when they ovulate." He beamed at the jury. "You can't control Mother Nature, you know."

"Move to strike the doctor's answer as nonresponsive. Would you please answer my question?"

"Which was?"

"Who's present in your clinic besides yourself on the weekends?" An image of her watching Davenport alone in his lab drawing up his patient's husband's—or someone's—semen drifted across Camille's mind.

"Well, no one, of course. My staff works very hard five days a week. There's no reason for them to come in on weekends. I am fully capable of handling a simple insemination procedure myself."

Camille took a deep breath and tried not to let the jury sense that her heart was about to burst out of her chest. "Dr. Davenport, whose sperm did you inject into Ms. Kent?"

"I'm sorry, I'm afraid I can't tell you without looking at my medical record."

"Whose sperm did you inject into Ms. Jensen?"

"I don't recall."

"Whose sperm did you inject into these other women?"

"I don't recall." His voice was firm.

Camille climbed over the fat wires laid across the floor and grabbed the *Newsweek* from a file in front of Helene. "Do you recognize this boy?" She slapped the picture of Danny Cipriotti on the cover.

"I'm afraid not."

"I'll represent to you that this is the son of Gina Cipriotti, a former patient of yours."

"Okay."

"Now, you performed an insemination procedure on Ms. Cipriotti on a Sunday, didn't you?"

"I don't recall."

"Do you recall whose sperm you injected into Ms. Cipriotti?"

"I said I didn't know if I even performed an insemination procedure on her." Davenport leaned forward and said, "I'm at a bit of a disadvantage here. You're asking me about patients from years ago and expecting me to testify under oath without the benefit of the medical records."

Camille ignored the doctor and pulled out the pictures of two children, both in wheelchairs with all the bells and whistles needed for severely disabled children. "Do you know who these two children are?"

"No." His voice was icy cold.

"I will represent to you that these two children were delivered by your daughter, Jessica Kensington, and were represented by Harvey Lowe in malpractice cases."

Davenport shrugged.

"Did you know that both of these children passed away as toddlers?"

Davenport shook his head. "I don't know why I would have occasion to know that."

"Do you know if either of these children were conceived as a result of your having performed artificial insemination on their mothers?"

"No, I don't."

Camille read from the pleadings she'd copied from the Smith trial brief. "The baby was especially important to this lovely couple since he was conceived as a result of an artificial insemination procedure performed by the defendant, Dr. Kensington's partner, Dr. Kip Davenport."

Davenport sat, stone-faced.

"Does that aid in your recollection?"

He shook his head very slowly. "I'm afraid not."

She turned to the Weston trial brief. "This particular pregnancy was even more precious than most, since the plaintiff's mother had undergone several insemination procedures by the defendant's partner." She looked up at Davenport. "Jog your memory, Doctor?"

His face was expressionless. "Sorry."

Camille looked at the lopsided easel. There was no way she'd jeopardize this moment by having the thing collapse again. She turned to Lucia. "Can you please come and hold these pictures up for the jury to see?"

Lucia stood and showed the jury the two pictures of Lowe's clients and the *Newsweek* cover with Danny Cipriotti's toothless grin on the front.

"Dr. Davenport, do you notice any similarities between these pictures?"

"I'm not sure what you mean."

"Well, do you notice that they all have red hair?"

"Now that you mention it, I do."

Camille took out the Davenport wedding picture and put it on the overhead. "Who is this?" She pointed at the young Davenport.

"It's me."

Camille nodded. "When did that head of red hair turn gray?" She smiled knowingly at the jury.

"I don't remember." He wasn't amused.

"You know, to my eye, there's a striking resemblance between young Kip Davenport and all three of these children. What do you think?"

Davenport shrugged.

"Would it surprise you to discover that the reason this cute little redheaded boy is on the cover of this magazine is that he killed his parents in cold blood while they slept?"

"Objection. This is ridiculous! We are not here to discuss an unrelated murder."

The judge looked at Camille.

"I really need some latitude here, Your Honor. I promise I'll tie it all together."

McIntyre actually looked curious himself. "Go ahead."

"Did you know Danny Cipriotti killed his parents?"

"I don't know who Danny Cipriotti is."

"He's the little redhead on the cover of this *Newsweek*."

Camille picked up one of the books on the genetic predisposition to psychopathic behavior. "Dr. Davenport, are you aware that there are certain types of antisocial behavior that some scientists believe are genetically coded and therefore impossible to overcome?"

Davenport shook his head. "No, I am not aware of that."

Camille stopped and made eye contact with each of the jurors separately. "Dr. Davenport, I want you to assume for me that my hypothesis is true. Or at least that you believe it to be true."

"That what is true?"

"That there is a genetic predisposition to psychopathic behavior."

"Okay, I'll assume that."

"Thank you. Now, please assume that you were the daughter of someone who you believed to be a psychopath; and you believed that your grandfather and great-uncle had also been psychopaths. And then assume that you yourself had been sexually victimized by your psychopathic father." Camille stopped and looked at the jurors. "Wouldn't you go to great lengths to see to it that society was protected from anyone who also carried these genes?"

Davenport scowled formidably at Camille. "I don't know."

"You might even kill to prevent those genes from causing havoc on society, wouldn't you?" Without waiting for an answer, Camille turned to the divorce file. "Isn't it true that the judge in your divorce found that you had impregnated your daughter, Jessica, when she was only fourteen?"

The jurors were riveted. Camille could swear she felt them holding their collective breath.

"My divorce was many years ago."

Camille thrust the file in front of Davenport. "Can you please identify this?"

He glanced at the front page of the thick document. "It's my divorce file."

"And doesn't the highlighted portion say that you impregnated your daughter when she was fourteen?"

"It does."

"Do you know where Jessica's son, Eric, is living now?"

"I believe he's in the mountains somewhere around here."

"Marblemount?"

"Perhaps."

"Okay, can you please read from page five of the judge's findings in your divorce?"

Davenport shuffled the pages. "The petitioner, Moyna-Lou Davenport, is awarded lifetime maintenance since she has been rendered permanently brain damaged due to the repeated beatings she sustained at the hands of her husband, respondent, Dr. Kimbrough Davenport."

He looked up, fuming.

"Continue."

"The daughter, Jessica, and the son she conceived as the result of having been raped by her father, respondent, Dr. Kimbrough Davenport, should be immediately placed into foster care, since all living family members are either in prison, or are otherwise unsuitable to serve as custodians of the children."

"Which of your family members is in prison, Dr. Davenport?"

No response.

Camille held up the stack of yellowed newspaper articles Moyna-Lou had sent her and read one of the headlines. "Luther Davenport convicted of a string of rape/murders that stymied local officials in the Dallas–Fort Worth area for nearly a decade." She stopped and stared at Davenport. "Luther Davenport was your father, wasn't he?"

"He was."

Next article. "Lionel Davenport executed for raping and killing as many as nine women in the North Dallas area." She paused. "Your uncle?"

He crossed his arms.

"Okay, Dr. Davenport. Let's get right down to it. You abused both your wife and your daughter, didn't you?"

"No, I did not."

"Now, on those fateful weekend days, you impregnated these women with your own sperm, didn't you?"

"Of course not."

"Well, who would know if you exchanged the donor sperm for your own when you were alone in your lab preparing the specimens?"

"This is absurd." He turned to the judge. "Can she ask me this?"

The judge nodded. "You bet she can. Now answer the question."

"I take the Fifth."

Camille whirled around. "I'll bet that your daughter wasn't very happy when she discovered what you were up to, was she?"

"The Fifth."

"I'll bet she decided that she had to do whatever she could to ensure that none of these children could ever cause the kind of mayhem that you and your family had caused to those innocent women they victimized."

The eyes of every single person in the courtroom followed Trent Conway as he approached the bench.

"Your Honor, I'm Trent Conway and I represent the People of the State of Washington. The state is hereby taking over jurisdiction of this matter." He turned to Vern Bagley, whose blood had completely drained from his face. "Mr. Bagley, I am hereby issuing a warrant for your client's arrest." He looked at the bailiff. "Marge, please call an officer to the courtroom." He turned to Bagley. "Where's your client, counsel?"

Bagley shrugged his shoulders.

Conway addressed Davenport. "Sir, you have the right to remain silent, if you give up the right to remain silent, anything you say can be used against you in a court of law."

The judge banged his gavel and ordered the jury from the room as Bagley slumped down in his chair and held his hands up as if to surrender.

"I have absolutely no idea where Dr. Kensington is." Bagley perfunctorily glanced around the courtroom. "The doctor never returned from the afternoon recess."

Conway walked over and stood in front of Bagley. "If you had anything to do with your client's disappearance, I will have you charged as an accessory."

A uniformed officer walked in to confer with the prosecutor. She and Trent clearly knew each other—they had the familiar back and forth between cops and prosecutors. Camille strained to hear their whispered conversation.

Conway turned to Camille. "Any idea where she could have taken off to?"

"I don't know."

Conway took a handful of paperwork from the bailiff. "I'm charging Jessica Kensington and Kip Davenport with felony assault."

Out of the corner of her eye, Camille noticed a thin woman with a high-fashion haircut and an armful of impressive bracelets standing in the courtroom doorway surveying the pandemonium in front of the judge. *Must be another reporter. Word travels fast in this building.*

The woman tentatively stepped forward.

"Are you Camille Delaney?"

"Yes. If you'll wait just a second, I'll give you a statement."

"I'm Missy Barron, a friend of Amy Hutchins?"

Great. The woman probably wanted to catch her up on Amy's whereabouts. "I'm a bit busy here. This will have to wait."

Lucia strode over and whispered into the woman's ear.

"But I know where Dr. Kensington is," the woman answered loudly.

The officer bolted over to the woman. "Who are you, ma'am?"

Missy stepped back and wrapped her arms around herself. "Missy Barron. I work with Amy Hutchins."

Conway interrupted. "Who is Amy Hutchins?"

"My former paralegal," Camille answered quickly.

"Will someone please listen to me?" Missy whined. "Jessica Kensington's at the airport about to board a plane to Rio. Amy followed Kensington to the gate. If you don't hurry, she's going to be on her way to Peru, or wherever Rio is."

CHAPTER FORTY

Camille grabbed Conway by the arm as he hurried toward the door.

"Hang on, there's more."

Conway looked questioningly at Camille. "What do you mean more? More what?"

Camille perched on the edge of the counsel table right in front of Bagley and his bevy of groupies, who were frantically barking directions at each other, the pecking order rearing its ugly head. The once arrogant young woman at Bagley's right elbow throughout the trial firmly clenched her jaw, obviously trying not to burst into tears.

Camille didn't release her grip on Conway's forearm. "I have evidence that Kensington and Harvey Lowe were involved in a fee-splitting arrangement in cases where he represented plaintiffs in malpractice against her."

Conway raised his eyebrows and followed Camille over to her side of the long table, where she handed him various documents and explained the unholy alliance between Kensington and Lowe.

"And why do you think she agreed to cause brain damage to innocent babies?" Conway asked.

"She wanted to get rid of all the biological progeny of her evil father."

"And she hooked up with Lowe so she could financially profit from her insanity?"

Camille nodded silently.

"Un-fucking-believable."

"And there's one more potential victim."

"Who's that?"

"That little redhead on the cover of *Newsweek*."

Conway looked askance. "What?"

"I represented him in a hit-and-run."

Conway cocked his head questioningly.

"It was a phantom vehicle. A silver Jaguar."

"And?"

"Kensington drives a silver Jag, and the kid was hit in a crosswalk in front of his school, where Kensington just happens to have been an after-school tutor."

"She tried to kill the kid?"

"I believe so."

"Jesus Christ. I guess I may have to add attempted murder to the charges." Conway looked around the rapidly emptying courtroom. "Looks like I'd better get busy and dispatch an officer to go pick up Harvey Lowe. We'll talk soon."

As Conway stepped away, Elaine Chambers hurried up and stood directly in front of him. "May I have a statement from each of you?"

Camille turned around and found herself face to face with a newspaper photographer, who immediately flashed his camera in her eyes.

Elaine leaned over and whispered to Camille, "The TV stations are on their way. You may want to go freshen up. You can use my lipstick if you'd like." Elaine reminded Camille of Amy as she held up a silver tube.

—

Amy leaned her head against the cold airport window as the 747 taxied away from the gate. As a last-ditch effort, she looked around desperately for an airport cop. For whatever good that'd do.

Despondent, she watched through the drizzle as an all-too-familiar Learjet with an ostentatious scales-of-justice logo on the side cruised out toward the tarmac.

Oh my God. Lowe's right behind her.

She jumped up just as a band of sheriff's deputies hustled to the gate from which Kensington had just departed. They dodged passengers with wheeled baggage and screaming children. As Amy ran through the observation area parallel with Lowe's Lear, she saw the 747 reconnecting to the Jetway.

Amy tried to get the attention of the tall Asian cop with the tight butt as he strong-armed his way up to the gate. Ever on the prowl for the perfect guy, Amy fluffed her hair.

"Excuse me!" she hollered.

"Back up, miss."

"Excuse me, I have information . . ."

"I'm sorry, miss, you'll have to move aside; this is a potentially dangerous stakeout. We're clearing the entire area."

The officer smiled at her as he unwrapped a roll of yellow tape and urged the angry passengers to back away from the waiting area.

"But . . ."

Another officer grabbed her firmly by the upper arm and forcibly shoved her behind the tape. "Please, miss, you need to wait over here." He raised his voice and spoke to the gathering crowd. "The planes are being held. There's no cause to worry about missing your flights! We'll be finished here shortly!"

Amy sat down hard and tried to catch the eye of the blue-eyed officer.

She had no choice but to call Camille. Presumably, court would no longer be in session and she'd have her phone on.

"Hello? Camille Delaney."

Amy's heart skipped a beat. "I'm at Sea-Tac watching Harvey Lowe's Learjet taxi out onto the tarmac."

"What in the world?" Camille paused.

"You don't have time to chat; this place is crawling with cops. You gotta get them to stop Lowe."

"I'm not sure what to say."

Amy watched proudly as the police led Kensington, in full handcuffs, down the concourse. "They got Kensington! Now go."

"Okay, I will. I can't thank you enough." Another pause. "Can you stop by the office later this week?"

"Sure. Now get off the phone and do something!" Amy clicked off and headed slowly back to the main terminal. Maybe if she walked slowly enough, she'd get on the same train with the cute cop.

The pastry case in the Starbucks at the top of the escalator beckoned Amy from across the huge walkway. She got in line behind a group of Japanese tourists. As it came closer to her turn, the strangest feeling came over her. The magnetic pull of the huge chocolate croissants in the front row of the case seemed to be diminishing. She hardly recognized her own voice as she assertively ordered a double tall nonfat latte.

Nonfat? Huh. For some inexplicable reason her overwhelming need for chocolate had disappeared. It wasn't every day you got to stop a fugitive from fleeing the country. *Maybe this is what they call a "natural high."* Whatever it was, Amy decided she could definitely get used to it.

She took a sip of the latte. Not too bad. She dialed Missy as she walked along the crowded concourse back toward the terminal.

"I'm giving my notice."

"What?"

"I can't do it anymore. Life isn't just about money for me. I need to work somewhere where I feel I'm making a difference."

Missy was silent for a moment. "Are you going to go back to Camille's?"

Amy watched the obedient passengers going through the metal detectors. "If she'll have me."

"Do . . . you . . . uh . . . do you think she needs any more help? Cuz I could . . . I, maybe . . . I could help out over there. If you think she needs any help, that is."

"I'll ask. But I'm not even sure she has room for me anymore."

"Good luck, Amy."

"Thanks, Miss. I gotta go."

CHAPTER FORTY-ONE

Seattle rarely enjoys a sunny day in November. Camille sat back on the dock in front of her office and soaked up the welcome sunshine reflecting off the water. It had been a hell of a ride these last several months. It was pretty neat to have been interviewed both by the newspaper and on TV, but the real satisfaction had come from stopping Kensington and her wicked father.

She drank in the feeling of success and was immediately overwhelmed; success wasn't going to pay her bills. Last night the family had splurged and gone to dinner at the Pink Door with Trish and Lucia. Camille had decided to wait a week or so before confessing to Sam about the reality of their financial situation.

She was nearly fifty thousand in the hole and had no workable plan for getting out. Although she'd promised the Andersons she'd do her best to pursue Kensington's offshore accounts, she didn't hold out too much hope. They didn't seem to mind. They were just thrilled that they'd been able to play their part in stopping the madness. And Helene had organized a support group of women who'd been victimized by the heinous father-daughter team of Davenport and Kensington, and she seemed to be getting closure in that regard.

Now what? It was easy to say that it wasn't about the money, but reality was rapidly catching up with her. She shut her eyes tightly and tried, unsuccessfully, to stop the tears.

"Want some company?"

It was Amy.

Camille turned her face up and smiled through the tears. "I can't thank you enough."

Amy sat next to her former boss. "Don't worry about it. I felt more fulfilled yesterday afternoon in four hours than in over a month at Lowe's office." Amy took out the afternoon edition of the *Seattle Times* with Camille's picture in the center, above the fold. "You're famous."

Camille dried her eyes with the back of her hand.

"I saw you on the eleven o'clock news too." Amy took a tissue out of her purse and maternally wiped the mascara from Camille's cheeks. "And when did you start wearing bright pink lipstick?"

"Pink lipstick?"

"On TV. You had this shocking pink lipstick on. It really isn't your color, you know."

"I borrowed it from a reporter. Did it look that bad?"

"Nah, only to a sophisticated eye." Amy puffed with pride. "Actually, you gave a great interview."

"So, how'd you find out that my Ojai doc was in trouble with the disciplinary board?"

"Lowe set him up."

Camille stared at Amy. "Come again?"

"I found an invoice in the Anderson file over at Lowe's office. The asshole actually paid a couple of female private investigators twenty grand to make the accusations against Fitzharris."

Camille shook her head. "He's one sick cookie."

"Oops, I almost forgot, the cute gal with the blue hair gave me this." Amy held out a message slip and read: "Northwest Women's Law Center wants to know if you can take a pro bono custody case for some woman in prison."

"Like I can afford to work on another case for free."

"Maybe you should tell them some other time." Amy paused. "You might want to find some paying clients so you can rehire a really good, and really humble paralegal."

"You're kidding."

"There's more to life than a giant paycheck, you know."

"At this point, I'd take any paycheck, big or small."

"It can't be that bad."

"It's worse than that bad." Camille picked at a chunk of wood from the dock and threw it in the water. "I think I may have to go back downtown myself. If you want to reconsider your options, I'd be happy to drag you along."

"Kensington's criminal lawyer is on the phone!" Lucia yelled as she sprinted down the dock, phone in hand. "She says it's urgent."

Camille grabbed the phone and sniffed to shake off the tears. "Camille Delaney."

"Hi, this is Shoba Desai. I'm Jessica Kensington's defense lawyer."

"Yes?" Camille looked at Amy and Lucia, pointed at the phone, and shrugged.

"Dr. Kensington would like you to attend her arraignment and then meet privately with her afterward."

"Do you mind telling me why she thinks I would even consider meeting with her?"

"According to Dr. Kensington, she wants to provide your client with the closure she's been seeking."

What did she have to lose? "Okay, where and when?"

This ought to be good.

"Today. At eleven thirty in Judge Benson's courtroom."

Camille looked at her watch. "I'll be there."

CHAPTER FORTY-TWO

Jessica Kensington looked more like someone on the shore of an isolated beach than someone swimming in the sea of humanity that made up the arraignment calendar in King County Superior Court. She appeared completely unfettered by the handcuffs and the shocking orange jumpsuit.

One of the reporters recognized Camille as she slipped into the back pew behind the assemblage of print and TV journalists.

The microphone reminded Camille of a huge licorice ice cream cone as the reporter shoved it in her face. "Ms. Delaney, how does it feel to see this defendant being brought to justice after all the lives she ruined?" whispered the reporter.

Justice? Was this justice?

"I'm very pleased to see that Dr. Kensington is being charged for her crimes, and I have full confidence that justice will be served," Camille answered quietly.

"Ms. Delaney!" a voice shouted from the back of the sea of reporters. "When did you notify the authorities of your suspicions about what Kensington and her father were up to?"

So much for courtroom decorum.

"I notified the authorities as soon as I felt I had sufficient evidence."

"Any chance your clients will ever see any money as a result of their lawsuit?"

"My clients are satisfied just knowing that Jessica Kensington and Kip Davenport will no longer be manipulating others' lives to serve their own twisted needs." Camille intentionally declined to use the title "doctor" when referring to the vile twosome. It wouldn't be long before they were stripped of the appellation, and she wanted to be among the first to emphasize the point.

"All rise!"

Judge Catherine Benson, the newest appointee to the King County bench, looked like a young Whitney Houston. Rumor had it that she was a legal dynamo that didn't take any guff from anyone.

The crowd hushed as the bailiff read the charges and the judge put on a pair of thick black glasses to review the file. After a moment, she looked up and asked, "How do you plead?"

Oddly, Kensington remained completely composed.

"Dr. Kensington pleads not guilty by reason of insanity," Shoba Desai announced loudly.

Kensington leaned over and whispered emphatically into her lawyer's ear.

Shoba gently put her arm around Kensington. It reminded Camille of her criminal law class in law school. They taught criminal lawyers to have physical contact with their clients as if to show the judge and jury that they weren't afraid of them and society shouldn't be either.

Kensington abruptly pulled away. "I'm guilty, Your Honor."

Cameras flashed as the gallery erupted in a huge murmur.

The judge removed her glasses and looked seriously at the defense counsel. "Ms. Desai?"

"May we have a moment, Your Honor?"

The judge leaned over the bench and spoke authoritatively. "Dr. Kensington, this is an extremely serious charge."

Shoba interrupted the judge. "The doctor understands the gravity of her situation, Your Honor." She glanced at her client. "I think we need some time to discuss the doctor's plea."

"Very well, the court will continue this arraignment until two o'clock this afternoon."

"That's not necessary, Your Honor." Kensington was obviously not about to change her mind.

Shoba Desai's face portrayed a steely determination. The grip she had on Kensington's arm was more forceful than the friendly attorney-client contact of a few moments ago.

"Dr. Kensington, the court will hear your plea on the afternoon calendar." The judge quieted the escalating disruption in the crowded room with a swift crack of her gavel. "Next case." The judge empathetically looked down from her bench at a disheveled-looking young woman as the bailiff read off a litany of drug charges. Camille couldn't hear what the judge said to the defendant, but her tone was refreshingly warm and calming. She turned to follow Kensington and her team out of the courtroom.

Camille trailed behind the still regal-looking Kensington and her entourage as they wound their way through the frenzied paparazzi. All the while, Kensington held her head high and looked directly into the popping flashes as her attorney shouted "No comment!" to every question hurled at either her or her client.

By the time they reached the elevator, the throng had entirely surrounded Seattle's newest celebrity defendant. Suddenly, the chaos turned silent. Camille's face flushed and her heart skipped a beat as a guard nudged Harvey Lowe out of the elevator.

Without warning, Kensington pulled away from her escort and made her way over to the once arrogant attorney. Curiously, the only sound in the marble lobby was that of cameras clicking. Lowe looked around in bewilderment. He was a caged animal. There was no way out. He tried in vain to hide his face from the inquisitive press corps.

The contrast between Jessica Kensington and Harvey Lowe in their matching orange jumpsuits was more than striking. Kensington proud and Lowe abjectly humiliated.

Although they stood face to face, Lowe refused to make eye contact. Everyone leaned forward to hear what words would pass between the lovers.

Kensington's eyes narrowed as she looked the portly man up and down. Slowly, she shook her head and said loudly, "You scum."

Lowe's legs buckled slightly and the guards steadied him as they shouted at the crowd, "Move aside! Move aside!"

With that, Kensington's guard whisked her into the elevator. The press stood in stunned silence as the doors slid closed.

Camille startled at the gentle pat on her shoulder. "Follow me." She took one last look at her former nemesis shuffling down the hall. For once, the press coverage would be entirely out of his control. Camille felt numb. It was too much to take in. Shoba tugged her sleeve, and Camille allowed herself to be led by the savvy defense attorney up a couple of flights of stairs to the holding area of the jail.

Having been a civil lawyer her entire career, Camille was completely unfamiliar with this part of the courthouse. The small lobby was teeming with jail guards in brown uniforms who joined each other in razzing Shoba about her infamous client's confused plea. Camille tried for a moment to imagine His Highness, Harvey Lowe, spending the next several years in a place like this, with his every move being displayed on the screens of the video monitors lining the wall.

"Over here," Shoba motioned.

Camille followed Shoba's lead and held her arms out to the side as the metal detectors beeped across her torso, her attention still glued to the lost-looking characters whose images were portrayed in grainy black and white across the imposing console. *Lowe wouldn't last a week in here.*

"You need to leave your purse with me, ma'am."

The guy who'd led the good-natured teasing of Shoba Desai shot Camille a friendly smile and held out his hand for her purse. How could the guy be so jovial in these surroundings? The cherub-faced guard exchanged a locker key for her soft black purse. Camille tried to look chill. Actually, if you thought about it, where would anything be safer?

The impressive doors clanged closed behind the two women, and the guard led them down a hall to a room that looked exactly like the rooms Camille had seen a thousand times on TV.

In a moment, Kensington shuffled in, hands cuffed behind her back and ankles in chains.

"It's okay." Shoba nodded to the female guard, who gently unlocked Kensington's handcuffs and pointed at the window facing the hallway.

"We're right outside if you need anything, Shoba."

Shoba smiled. "Thanks."

With no makeup, Kensington looked hauntingly like her mother: a true natural beauty. And for some inexplicable reason, she continued to be immersed in an aura of tranquility. It gave Camille the creeps.

She glanced sideways to assure herself that the friendly guard really was within eyesight.

"Thanks for coming, Camille." Kensington stared levelly at her adversary. "You don't mind if I call you Camille, do you?"

What was she going to say? No, it's Ms. Delaney to you? "It's fine."

"Someone had to stop my father. It had to be me." Her voice was crystal clear. "There really was no one else." Kensington shook her head of shiny auburn hair. "No one else could have known what he was up to and how evil he really is."

Camille was speechless. The doctor wanted to explain herself.

"I knew it was just a matter of time before I got caught. But I had to bring him down one way or the other. He deserved to be publicly humiliated."

Shoba patted her client's hand.

Camille's curiosity got the best of her. "Why the fee-splitting deal with Lowe?"

"Money. I'm the sole support of my mother and my son. I knew I'd be caught eventually, and I wanted to be sure that they'd be set for life." Her face softened when she spoke of her family.

"I thought you said your mother got a huge settlement in her divorce."

"You have any idea how much it costs to keep my mom at Kahana? And it's not cheap to keep my son up there in the mountains so he doesn't hurt someone. By the way, I'm sorry about the difficulties you had with Eric. I have his cabin surrounded with an underground wire now, and he wears an ankle bracelet that shocks him if he attempts to leave. He's really quite compliant, as long as he stays on his meds, which is obviously difficult to monitor."

Camille's face flushed, remembering her run-in with the wild man in the isolated mountain cabin.

Kensington continued, "You shouldn't have gone up there. I've tried to figure out a way to keep people from tangling with him, but it isn't usually a problem. No one ever ventures that far up that mountain road. But I'm putting in an electric fence just to be sure." She paused. "I tried to put him in a facility like the one where my mom is, but no decent facility would keep a patient who becomes so violent when he falls off his meds, which is unfortunately quite often—even in an institutional setting. I hope he didn't hurt you."

Camille felt decidedly like she was in *The Twilight Zone.* "I'm fine."

She had so many questions for this enigmatic woman, and this was likely her only chance to get some answers. "Can I ask you, why the affair with Lowe? You obviously have nothing but disdain for him."

"I was a mess the first time that asshole sued me, and he approached me about a fee split if I'd roll over in my dep. To be honest, it seemed too easy."

Camille was caught off guard. As much as she despised Harvey Lowe, it was difficult to believe that he'd stoop so low as to offer a fee split with a defendant in a lawsuit. She paused to let that sink in, then slowly said, "Okay, that explains the money issue, but why on earth would you sleep with that jackass?"

Jessica looked at Shoba and held up her hand. "I'm going to plead guilty. I lost my children in my divorce, I've now lost my practice, and so at this point, I have nothing else to lose." She turned to Camille. "As you can imagine, I had a terrifying upbringing, especially in my early teen years right before my parents divorced. My mom was pretty much incapacitated, and my dad was a psychopath. So, I turned to street drugs."

An image of the scored white pills in the unmarked brown bottle in Kensington's penthouse flashed across Camille's memory.

Kensington continued quietly as though no one was in the room. "It was the only way I knew to numb the psychological pain." She looked directly into Camille's eyes. "It's what girls do when they don't have access to any kind of treatment. I see it in my volunteer work at the public health clinic all the time. A young woman is the victim of an assault, and her only recourse is to turn to street drugs because she's often afraid to tell her parents. It's the only way for them to deal with their untreated trauma. Without insurance or mental health care, they can't get a prescription like one of your kids could."

Camille was familiar with the ongoing issues around opioid addiction among people from all walks of life but hadn't considered the fact that it was often used to numb the pain of sexual trauma. "I'm so sorry," she said as she instinctively reached out and patted Kensington's hand.

"As you probably know, Harvey Lowe leaves no stone unturned when he investigates a case, and so he had me followed." Kensington's eyes narrowed in a flash of anger. "His investigator followed me right up to the front gate of the rehab facility where I've gone more times than I can count to try and shake my addiction." She stopped and picked at her long red fingernail. Without looking up, she continued, "Then he blackmailed me. Either I sleep with him, or he turns me in to the disciplinary board and ruins my reputation. I tried a few times to break it off—the last time I met up with him, I even bought a book in the airport bookstore about how to end a traumatic relationship—it was called *Extricate*."

"My sister wrote that book," Camille said before she could reconsider.

Kensington cocked her head slightly and looked Camille straight in the eye. "Your sister can't hold a candle to you. That book was a bunch of drivel—you are the real deal."

Camille was taken aback by the doctor's honesty. She tried to find some words, but nothing came out.

"You have single-handedly taken down a dangerous psychopathic doctor, and saved more families than you will ever know." Jessica paused for a beat. "Actually, you've taken down two—Harvey Lowe is a disgusting excuse for a lawyer. Your sister makes money by promising help, but not delivering. I bet you compare yourself to her and covet her success. But don't. You just made the world safer by taking down two predators—my father and Harvey Lowe. Don't you dare minimize that."

Camille felt a brief wave of dizziness come over her. A few hours ago, Kensington was her nemesis. And suddenly she seemed like an old friend who knew all too well about her feelings of inadequacy around her sister. "Thanks for saying that." She cradled her chin in her hands. "You're right, it's a lot to have a sister like Eve."

"I can imagine." Kensington smiled. "And I know you used to be partners with Lowe. So, I expect you know as well as I do what he's really like. You did a good thing—he'll be disbarred and hopefully criminally charged. You did that."

"Harvey Lowe is a pig!" Camille said more loudly than she had intended.

"He absolutely is, but I'm responsible for the part I played in this sick drama. And I'm ready to face the consequences." Jessica looked squarely at Shoba. "I know you advise against it, but I am going to plead guilty and deal with what's next for me." She took a deep breath. "Maybe detoxing in prison will set me on a new path."

"It's going to be awful for you in there," Camille said softly.

"Honestly, I'm ready to put this behind me. And to move forward in my life, the next step for me is to explain to Helene and the other women why I did what I did."

Camille looked quizzically at the doctor as she pushed her hair back from her face and held it in a ponytail for a moment before letting it fall around her shoulders. "As you've learned, the Davenport family is sicker than you could have imagined." She leaned forward. "Most everyone on my father's side of the family is either dead as a result of some heinous crime or in prison. Violence is bred deep within our genes. I've researched it for years and am convinced that there are some people who are just incapable of morally and socially acceptable behavior." Kensington looked down. "Including me, which explains, but doesn't excuse, my addiction."

It was increasingly obvious to Camille that she and Jessica Kensington were in this conversation alone. Her lawyer had absolutely no idea of what had transpired in her client's life that had brought her to this place.

"I promise you on my mother's life that none of those women would have wanted a child who'd be carrying the Davenport family legacy. Believe me, they're better off grieving their losses and getting on with their lives than being saddled with a little Davenport." She stared deeply into Camille's eyes. "Look at what happened to the Cipriottis. I did everything I could think of to stop that kid."

For the first time since Camille had been dealing with Jessica Kensington, the doctor teared up.

"I'll have those peoples' blood on my hands for the rest of my life."

Shoba's eyes darted furiously back and forth between Kensington and Camille. Intuitively, she seemed to know that it was best to be silent.

"At any rate," Kensington sighed, "I asked Shoba to bring something in for me to give you."

Camille tensed and tried to subtly check and see that the guards were close by, as promised.

Kensington held out her hand and waited for Shoba to place a legal-sized envelope in it.

Probably some kind of apology.

"Please, open it." Kensington smiled slightly as Camille gently tore open the thin envelope. How could this woman be so at peace with herself when she was facing certain prison time?

Camille blew in the end of the envelope to free up the paper inside, then pulled out a blank sheet of bond paper folded around a stack of personal checks. She drew a sharp breath. The top one was made out to Helene Anderson in the amount of two million dollars.

She looked at Kensington in disbelief and then shuffled through the next several checks: one hundred thousand dollars for Brittany Kent; one hundred thousand dollars for Samantha Stefonak.

"There's a hundred-thousand-dollar settlement check for each of the women who miscarried those evil fetuses and two million to settle Helene and Tim's case with you. I assume you will have them sign releases."

Camille was completely unable to distinguish her feelings for the woman sitting across the metal table: Pity? Sympathy? Anger? Confusion? Certainly confusion.

"Shoba has a note from me to each of the women, as well as the ones that Harvey represented. I don't expect anyone to forgive me, but I know in my heart that I did what I had to do. And I'd do it again if I had to."

"I don't know what to say," Camille murmured, fingering the checks drawn on the Banca Carmelita logo.

"You should be very proud of yourself. It's not often that a lawyer actually gets to save people from a dire fate. You've played a major part in stopping my father from his wicked plot to sire as many children as he could—hopefully boys. It's all he ever wanted. To have more sons to carry on his heritage." Kensington looked at her hands. "He's really a very, very sick man." She looked back up. "He'll plead not guilty." Kensington stood and knocked on the window to get the guard's attention. "Promise me you'll do whatever you can to have him put away forever."

Camille stood. Before she could stop herself, she reached out to take Kensington's hands in hers. "I'm sorry."

Kensington smiled. "I know you are."

This poor woman. Camille felt tears beginning to well up. "You know, you have to plead insanity."

Kensington shrugged. "No one understands what I've been through. They'd never let me off. I've seen women go to prison for assaulting or killing their abusers. If those women end up in prison for what was clearly self-defense, my case will garner absolutely no sympathy."

A sudden surge of energy shot through Camille. "You can convince a jury. All you need is the right expert." She grabbed a sheet of Shoba's legal paper. "Here, call Laurabelle Flores. She's a dear friend and an international expert in Stockholm syndrome. She knows all about your case, I'm sure she'll help you."

The loud click of the electronic lock interrupted the meeting. "You ladies ready?" the guard asked quietly, as if she sensed what was going on inside.

"Don't give up." Camille grabbed Kensington by the shoulders. "You can beat this."

Camille held eye contact with Kensington as the guard reattached the handcuffs. As soon as the door closed behind the doctor, Camille turned her tear-stained face to the utterly confused defense lawyer and said, "Get me out of here."

CHAPTER FORTY-THREE

What were the chances of two sunny days back-to-back the last week of November in Seattle?

Camille turned on the classic rock full blast and headed out of the financial district. Maybe Kensington was right, maybe she should quit comparing herself to Eve. She had, after all, toppled a cold-blooded duo whose days of victimizing families were over for good. And, with her share of the Anderson check from Kensington, she'd be able to stay in Fremont after all. She could send a chunk of money to her mother's asylum program on Lesvos. And then she'd replenish the girls' college funds . . .

The phone interrupted her as she was mentally preparing her Thanksgiving shopping list as she sped north on Westlake toward her office. Finally, some time with Sam and the girls. "Camille Delaney!" she shouted a bit too loudly into the car's speaker.

Life was good.

It was Harry Goldman, CEO of Kensington's malpractice insurance company.

"The executive committee just adjourned from an emergency meeting we called to determine what the company is going to do about the settlements we paid out to Lowe and his clients on behalf of Jessica Kensington."

So why were they calling her?

"Yes?" she responded.

This ought to be good.

"We'd like to retain you to sue Harvey Lowe on our behalf to recover the money we paid out to him. You know the case better than anyone, and we certainly know how you feel about Harvey Lowe."

Sue Harvey Lowe? It was almost too good to be true.

"We'd offer you forty percent of anything you're able to recover."

She did the mental math as she pictured herself hand delivering a subpoena to Banca Carmelita. *Forty percent of how many millions?*

"We'd like to set up a meeting at your earliest convenience, say Monday morning?"

"Let me get this straight. You want me to represent Doctor's Inc.?"

"That's right. We know it's a bit out of the ordinary, but we feel you're the best lawyer for the job."

No way. There was no way she'd even consider going over to the "dark side." Why should she help the assholes who prided themselves on chewing up and spitting out innocent plaintiffs? The big bad insurance company would have to find someone else to clean up their mess.

"Sorry. I'm afraid you'll have to find someone else."

"But . . ."

Camille laughed as she hung up and sped up to beat the flashing lights of the familiar drawbridge. She barely made it under the yellow-and-black-striped arm as it stopped the string of traffic directly behind her.

No fucking way.

She picked up the phone to call Amy and tell her to make an appointment for her to run down to the women's prison in Gig Harbor so she could meet with the pro bono custody client. It was time to do something just because it was the right thing to do.

ABOUT THE AUTHOR

Amanda DuBois started her career as a registered nurse before becoming a lawyer. She has practiced in the areas of medical malpractice and family law. She is the founder and managing partner of the DuBois Levias Law Group in Seattle, Washington, where she is actively engaged in litigation. She also founded Civil Survival Project, an organization that teaches advocacy skills to formerly incarcerated individuals. Amanda serves on several boards that support social justice and women's issues. Her most recent passion is funding her Full Circle Scholarship, which provides tuition assistance at her alma mater, Seattle University School of Law. This scholarship is specifically granted to students whose lives have been impacted by the criminal legal system. All of the author's profits from your book purchase will be donated to the Full Circle Scholarship and social justice organizations. Amanda's goal as an author is twofold: to introduce readers to her lead character, Camille Delaney, and Camille's quest for justice, while at the same time inviting readers to take an interest in how we define justice in our legal system.

Amanda and her husband split their time between the San Juan Islands in Washington State and Todos Santos, Mexico. They have two adult daughters and two beautiful grandchildren. This is the second novel in the Camille Delaney Mystery series.

DON'T MISS *THE COMPLICATION,*
THE FIRST BOOK IN THE CAMILLE DELANEY MYSTERY SERIES

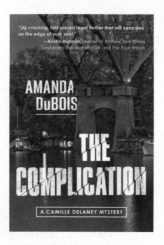

"[A] cracking, fast-paced legal thriller that will keep you on the edge of your seat."

—Kristin Hannah, author of the #1 *New York Times* bestsellers *The Nightingale* and *The Four Winds*

The first in the Camille Delaney Mystery series, *The Complication* is a fast-paced legal and medical mystery filled with greed, murder, and intrigue.

After her friend Dallas Jackson suffers a fatal complication during routine surgery, Seattle attorney Camille Delaney is determined to find out why. Dallas was like a father to Camille, and she feels she owes it to him and his family to get answers. Knowing she could lose her partnership at her high-profile law firm for undertaking such an investigation, Camille takes a huge risk and starts her own firm, determined to bring Dallas's killer to justice. She turns for help to her friend Trish Seaholm, a quick-witted chameleonlike private investigator with an uncanny knack for blending into any situation.

As the two dive headfirst into a dangerous investigation, they discover disturbing evidence that Dallas's case is not an isolated incident. A shocking number of patients are dying during run-of-the-mill surgeries at small-town hospitals—at the hands of the same two surgeons. Can Camille uncover the reason for these unexplained deaths before more patients fall victim? Or will her search for answers land her in the crosshairs of a killer?

Hardcover 978-1-954854-34-5, Ebook 978-1-954854-35-2

CPSIA information can be obtained
at www.ICGtesting.com
Printed in the USA
JSHW011447050223
37298JS00003B/8